The name of J. I. M. Ste...  several decades, been ass... the City of Oxford. No... his career as a novelist, barked on a series of five linked novels; and his richly varied characters are all associated, in one way or another, with Surrey, a college of that University. *A Staircase in Surrey* (the general title of the pentalogy) is the perfect setting for displaying his delightful gifts: his literary expertise, his urbane wit, his joy in eccentric characters, his mastery of intricate plotting. This first volume opens of course in Oxford, on the night of a Gaudy—one of those grand annual dinners which a college lays on for some of its old members. The Chancellor of the University attends (currently he is a former Prime Minister), there are very distinguished guests, and indeed many of the alumni have become distinguished too—as Duncan Pattullo discovers when, in his forties now, he attends his first Gaudy, and meets old friends and enemies of his undergraduate days.

There's Tony Mumford, now Lord Marchpayne and a member of the Cabinet; Ranald McKechnie, his rival even in prep school days, and now a don; Gavin Mogridge, who shot to fame with a best-selling account of his extraordinary adventure in a Brazilian jungle; and many more. As they all foregather, there are cautious overtures, wry reminiscences, startling revelations: an occasion like this is both nostalgic and disconcerting. And as the even-

THE GAUDY

J. I. M. Stewart

THE GAUDY

A Novel

LONDON
VICTOR GOLLANCZ LTD
1974

I.S.BN. 0 575 01881 x

Printed in Great Britain by
The Camelot Press Ltd, Southampton

A Staircase in Surrey

*

THE GAUDY

I

THE STAIRCASE HAD changed in the twenty years and more elapsed since my last view of it. The meniscus curve of the dull grey stone treads was deeper. The walls were in a new colour scheme. I remembered everything to which paint was appliable as tinted and textured to an effect resembling chocolate when it has been disastrously hoarded through a long sea voyage. Now the pervasive note was pastel pinks and blues, and these had naturally grown grubby quickly. Muddy track suits, sweaty jerseys, wet towels had brushed or lounged against the lower surfaces; quite high up the walls were flecked and spotted in a manner perplexing until one thought of violently shaken-out mackintoshes and umbrellas. This, as much as the hollowed stone, was a matter of honest wear and tear. I noticed that the effect was nowhere enhanced by scribbles. It appeared that *graffiti* were judged improper at least within one's own preserves. They were for the enlivening of the outer walls of other people's colleges. I had seen many of these minor portents of change as I was driven from the railway station. We'd never have dreamed—I told myself—of prowling the streets of Oxford with coloured chalks.

The only thing legible here was on a perched-up square of cardboard. Plainly the work of a harassed scout, it said *Please wipe your feet*. The last word had been struck out by another hand, and nothing substituted. It was this abstention, I believe, that brought home to me how much I was on familiar ground.

For two years the staircase had been my own. The rooms I was briefly to occupy had been my own rooms. I wondered whether this was chance, or whether the domestic bursar, a retired admiral with time on his hands, had amused himself by looking up office records and adding a sentimental grace note to the entertainment to be offered to old members that night. However this may have been, sentiment had its moment now, so much so that I set down my suitcase and stepped back into the quad to take a long breath before the larger scene.

I was making no exhibition of myself. The big lidless Palladian box within which I stood, honey-coloured and sparely ribbed with reticent Ionic pilasters, was deserted. The undergraduates, I supposed, had departed; like migrating birds (but in confidently thumbed cars and *camions*) had departed for southern climes. If a few lingered it would be in forlorn immurement, on this hot June afternoon, within the Examination Schools. And it looked as if I was the first arrived of the Gaudy guests. I shared Surrey, the second of the larger quadrangles, with the eroded statue of Provost Harbage and a sleeping black cat. It must have been a college cat. The porters would no more admit a strange cat within the walls than they would admit a hawker of oriental rugs or a babe in a perambulator. (At the gate of the college garden a large notice, ancient but preserved in a state of full legibility, recorded the duty of these servitors to exclude persons of improper character or in dirty clothes or—more mysteriously —'carrying large burthens'.)

There is nothing mediaeval about Surrey except its name, which had belonged to one among a congeries of halls and inns on the site, humble cradles of Oxford learning long ago. Through centuries these had been conjoined, disparted, extinguished or revived, until all were bulldozed out of existence in the interest of the Augustan decorum on view today. One is sometimes told by those concerned with lauding the ancient universities that their material fabric constitutes in itself an education alike of the senses and the spirit; that fine architecture elevates and refines the nascent mind in much the manner claimed by Wordsworth for the permanent and beautiful forms of nature. I dare say there is something in it. By almost anybody planted amid such surroundings a sense of certain graces and amenities must be at least a little sopped up.

Glancing about me now, I knew it had been my own case. A bleak and murky Doric had frowned upon me both at

8

school and dispersedly elsewhere in my native town, so that I must have found in the façades of Surrey quite as much of clean-cut elegance as they in fact possess; at the same time I had picked up at home—although it was never urged upon me —a certain alertness before the deliverance of art. Had I first arrived at Oxford in the twenties and not the forties, I would have been thinking of myself as an aesthete within a week. I was, I suppose, a lively and receptive but quite unintellectual boy, and I had been whisked into a new social situation. Among the resources I rapidly mobilized was that of being something of an authority on matters artistic and architectural. I was even entirely willing to instruct my father in them—and this although I firmly believed him to be (as in fact he was) the best landscape painter in Scotland. How disastrous—I remember telling him—to the great free-standing library which closes Surrey on the south had been certain tinkerings with the design while the building was going up. All because of a clutter of pictures, I said, given to the college by some distinguished *curioso* at just that time. Space had to be found in which to display them. So the notion of an open lower storey or piazza, such as Wren had created at Cambridge for Trinity College, was abandoned. The result was the massive structure, dominating Surrey like a liner dwarfing a harbour mouth, before which I was inviting my father to adopt a critical stance.

My father didn't comply, perhaps seeing more of Michelangelo in the building than I saw, or affected to see, of Baalbek. He would in any case have considered adverse comment discourteous, since, if only in a formal sense, the library was in part the property of his son—lately become a scholar on the foundation of the college largely through, as will later appear, a somewhat eccentric action on his, my father's, own part. Now he simply remarked that he looked forward to viewing these fatal canvases, wherever they chanced in these days to hang.

The door of the library opened, and my solitude was ended. The man who had emerged struck me for a moment as merely

9

roughed in upon the scene, and also as too small to be true; he might have been one of those subtly diminished strollers or standers-by that architects insert in the foreground of a sketch in order to render an enhanced impression of the consequence of a projected building. But here the building had consequence already. The door, that it might appear in some sort of scale with the march of gigantic Corinthian pillars on either hand, was in its mere valvular part ten feet high, so that a Hobbit-like semblance was necessarily taken on by anybody passing in or out. But this was no Hobbit. It was Albert Talbert. The realization came to me as quite a shock. Perhaps I had carelessly supposed him dead.

Although we were separated by the entire length of Surrey it was apparent that, just as I had recognized Talbert, so had Talbert recognized me. His was the more remarkable feat. Talbert had been my tutor, and of one's tutor one is likely to preserve an image adequate for the purpose of identification many years on. I, on the other hand, had simply been Talbert's pupil—and of pupils half a dozen to a dozen fresh specimens come within a college tutor's purview every year. Talbert seemed to be considering what to do. He wasn't a man to shout, and as his arms were full of books it would have been impracticable for him to wave. Or would it? Always of a sedentary habit, Talbert now seemed to reveal himself as owning the corpulence of a man who isn't wearing well. I told myself that the resulting paunch, dropped so as to suggest a woman immediately before childbirth, presented an almost shelf-like structure upon which the pile of books might have been let balance of themselves during a moment of at least cautious gesticulation. Talbert, however, remained immobile, and I therefore advanced upon him myself with a show of alacrity which wasn't altogether a matter of civil pretence. I was curious about him. Indeed, but for discovering in myself some revived curiosity as to the college and its present inhabitants in general, I should not, it was to be supposed, have accepted the invitation to the forthcoming feast.

My cordial haste took me straight across the grass of Surrey, and I found myself wondering whether this might not be a breach of etiquette. Wasn't it only the dons who were let walk on the grass, and must I not consider myself present more in the character of a perpetual undergraduate than of any sort of authentic senior member? On the other hand the turf was warm and dry underfoot; I wasn't going to injure it, nor it to incommode me; the taking, in these conditions, of a circuitous route to the waiting Talbert would have been absurd, and might even have suggested a discourteously leisured disposition on my part.

Later on, I was to recollect this dubiety to have been meaningless, reflecting merely one of those confusions which steal upon us with the passage of time. Only in the Great Quadrangle is the grass a preserve of the elderly; that in Surrey and elsewhere had in my own day, as now, been freely scamperable upon by the most junior among us. I might have remembered this at once rather than tardily had not another occasion of perplexity presented itself. *Was* the waiting man Talbert?

From eighty yards off there hadn't been a doubt of it; identification had been immediate and, as I have said, apparently mutual. Now—the distance between us having been halved—the state of the case was different. The appearance I had distinguished in front of the library door had said 'Talbert' to me at once, and must therefore have corresponded to a picture of my former tutor that I carried about for intermittent consultation in my head. But, as I approached, the visual phenomenon before me drew away from this. Its coincidence with the Talbert image had become disturbingly blurred, rather in the manner of two figures within an imperfectly manipulated stereoscopic toy. I found myself believing that I had fallen into some embarrassing mistake.

Of course Talbert now would be much older than Talbert then; but I somehow knew that it wasn't a factor of this sort that could account for my perplexity. The perplexity increased when I got nearer still, since I now seemed to discern in it a state of mind which I shared with the person who must in another moment become my interlocutor. Was he too confronting embarrassment and the need for apology? It did look as if each of us had misidentified the other.

But this supposition survived (at least as to its reciprocal nature) only for a moment. I then saw Talbert as incontrovertibly in front of me and my confusion as something of common enough occurrence. As with scraps of verse, or natural scenes, or episodes of personal drama, the features of people once familiarly known seldom return to the memory untransformed. Each time we call them up imagination asserts its claim to retouch the picture—perhaps radically almost from the start, perhaps gradually and as with a stealthy artistic intention. Hence our frequent surprise that a person (like, it may be, a coast or city or painting revisited) is not at all as we remember him. Yet the first and veridical image seems to survive beneath its later variants in some limbo of the mind. On this occasion it had stirred at my first glimpse of the man across the quad, so that Talbert's name had come to me instantly. Then some more recent, and delusive, Talbert-image had fought back, to a resultant moment of confusion. Finally here I was—my mind having come full-circle—acknowledging myself in the presence of the authentic Talbert after all, the Ur-Talbert upon whom through a long period of years my unconscious fancy had been plastically at play.

It was now that I noticed, too, how I had been under a further deception: one which might have interested my father more than it did me. Contrary to my impression of moments before, Talbert had by no means notably deteriorated as to the physical man. His possessing a paunch had been an illusion created by some play of light and shade, perhaps even some quiver of the warm air, within those massive Corinthian shafts—as in a Mannerist painting, I reflected, the Madonna, although with her Child already in her arms, may appear gravid still only because we fail to read correctly some freak of *chiaroscuro* which has pleased the artist's fancy. As for Talbert's books, they were few in number, and lightly carried under his left arm; his right hand was free and now confidently extended to me. Yet he was not himself wholly confident. The doubt which I had detected in him had not, as had my own, dissipated itself.

'Ah—Dalrymple!' Talbert said. 'We are very pleased that you have been able to come to our dinner.' His voice held all its old unbelievable degree of huskiness—and its old effect, too, of a *gravitas* quite beyond the reach of a common scholar's capacity. He might have been announcing something of the deepest import arrived at that morning in an arcane divan, a *hortus conclusus* dedicated to the just privacy of the councils of princes, and now by him responsibly divulged to some person of desert and discretion among the outer profane. 'Our trifling foolish banquet,' Talbert added. Amazingly, but in a manner instantly approved by memory, silent yet powerful laughter was convulsing his frame. His eyes lit up with a remote elfin glee wholly unexpected in one so evidently of the sober sort. He brought his hands together—this at hazard of letting his little cache of learning tumble to the ground—and rubbed them joyously each on each. 'Our trifling foolish banquet,' he repeated as if relishing a rare stroke of wit. 'Eh, Dalrymple?'

'Thank you very much.' I knew I ought now to come out with something from Shakespeare myself—capping, as it were, old Capulet. But (as frequently, long ago) my resources failed me. 'Only,' I said, 'I'm not Dalrymple. My name is Duncan Pattullo, and I was a pupil of yours—a sadly unrewarding one, I fear—rather a long time ago.'

'Pattullo?' Talbert frowned. No learned man cares to be indicted of inaccuracy, and in particular of a misattribution. I could see that he was tempted to dispute with me the legitimacy of my claim. Instead of which, however, he asked, 'Do you still write plays?'

It was said by Dr Johnson (who had reason to know) that the manners of men of learning are commonly unpolished, and I believe it to have been by the learned that this particular question has most frequently been fired at me. To a refined sensibility it might occur that, if a man *does* happen still to write plays, he will fondly suppose the fact to be known to all cultivated persons. In the present instance, since a comedy of mine was then running in a London theatre, it might have been my reasonable hope that Talbert, the college's English don, would own some semi-professional awareness of it. Not that I was offended by my old tutor's ignorance. It was true to his form, as was his surprising instant memory that I had ever written plays at all.

'Yes, indeed,' I said. 'I still write them. In fact, I've at last come to make some sort of living that way. So nowadays I do nothing else.'

'There's money in them?' Talbert had returned to gravity—but to gravity, this time, of fresh implication. It was now a man-of-the-world to man-of-the-world kind of gravity. 'How right I was to dissuade you from that mad thought of a fellowship! I've been a laborious scholar for forty years, my dear Duncan, and I haven't a penny. Not a penny!' Further to fortify this sudden passionate cry, Talbert slapped his right-hand trouser-pocket—as being the area, no doubt, in which the scholar's proverbially empty purse might be imagined lightly to repose. It was a gesture of unfortunate effect. The books under his other arm went to the ground, after all. The next few seconds were devoted to our both scrambling for them.

I found myself touched that Talbert had addressed me by my Christian name. In a moment—and with a brilliance quite akin to that succeeding upon Marcel's tasting the made-leine—there flooded in upon me a whole treasury of memories. These didn't run, it is true, to any conjuring up of the mad thought of a fellowship: that reference had conceivably marked a fleeting return to the Dalrymple-theory of my identity. But I did recall how in my last year, when I had frequently gone to tea with the Talberts in the wilds of Headington (there to play with their children instructive games of a lexicographical character) first Mrs Talbert (also a deep scholar) and then occasionally Talbert himself had taken to addressing me in this more familiar fashion. Nowadays Oxford dons, like young people at a party, know both each other and their pupils by their Christian names alone, so that upon formal occasions they are at a loss as to who is being designated Smith or Brown. Talbert's habits had been formed in an earlier era. For several terms he had invariably addressed me as *Mr* Pattullo, much as if this were his only sure means of continuing to distinguish me, in his unfathomably brooding and often alarmingly absent mind, from one or another of the young women from Somerville or St Hugh's whom the *res angusta domi* (as he would have phrased it) constrained him to be perpetually tutoring on the side.

The Talberts' house in Old Road (so conveniently disposed, Talbert would explain from amid one of his baffling seizures of subterranean mirth, in relation to the Warneford hospital for nervous cases) was a red brick villa with the proportions and virtually the dimensions of a doll's house. That I felt at home in it from the first was not because of its architecture. In that regard, as it happened, I was more familiarly placed in Surrey, since I had been brought up amid similar although more austere echoes of the Palladian idea in Edinburgh's new town. In Old Road it was the *res angusta* that I recognized: and that here in a new form was the kind of activity known to me as producing such a state of affairs.

The senior Talberts—rather as if resourcefully improvising in the course of domestic charades the roles of necromancers, or ancient philosophers, or professors of the exegesis of holy scripture—were apt to be discovered severally poring over leather-bound tomes of jumbo size. Of these they owned a score or more, which were kept in a locked bookcase of answering magnitude and served a little to mitigate what was in general a somewhat culturally disfurnished effect in the rest of their surroundings. The children, it is true, possessed (or held in trust) a number of cardboard boxes containing Lotto, Word Making and Word Taking, Scrabble, and similar diversions. I also recall a gramophone with a horn—not a hypertrophied horn such as was modish at that period, but a small horn of the old-fashioned sort before which one felt there ought to be perching an attentive dog. I never heard music from this instrument. The only record I recall (as I well may, having sat on it with disastrous results during the excitement of a session at Lexicon) was one holding out a promise of elementary instruction in the field of articulatory phonetics. It was a subject about which I felt no urge to knowledge, although I did detect myself wondering whether phonetics of a non-articulatory order was an alternative option which the curious student might embrace.

The elder Talberts both held their big books in requisition (it would be inapposite to say 'read' their big books) two at a time and side by side. They were perpetually engaged, in fact, in collating texts. At week-ends (which was when I went to tea) they carried out this task with the help simply of their own select resources; at other times they kept long hours in the Bodleian Library. The motions of collation recall those of watching fast tennis. Since two columns of print are to be compared with each other not merely word by word but letter by letter, the eyes (and also, perceptibly, the head) must be flicked from side to side with metronomic regularity. Watching the Talberts thus engaged, I thought at first of a species of toy, at that time readily to be acquired from street traders, in which a clergyman or duckling or hippopotamus or oriental sage has been so constructed with its head balanced and pivoting within a socket that the flick of a finger will keep it becking and bobbing for some time. But this didn't really fit the Talberts, whose muscular efforts had to be on a horizontal plane. I then remembered, in a Christmas fair held in a subterraneous market-building in Edinburgh, certain mannikin figures, derived from vulgar American comic strips or cinematographic cartoons, which unrestingly jerked their hydrocephalic heads from side to side above the entrance to some shooting-gallery or raree-show. This was a comparison mechanical in every sense, and to be deprecated as even having crossed my mind, since nothing could be less vulgar than the spectacle of the Talberts pursuing their priestlike and lustratory operations upon the text of Chapman or Dekker or

Middleton or whoever the object of this strange devotion may have been. For strange it undeniably was; material consequence seldom attaches to a comma here or semi-colon there; to devote one's life to a single long-drawn-out activity of systematic and conservative scholarship has certainly something heroic about it but also something a shade absurd. And if in the Talberts' efforts I didn't descry the absurdity alone, this can scarcely have been because I wasn't callow enough so to do. It was rather because (as I have hinted above) I was conscious of a surprising affinity between the Talberts and the Pattullos. A sort of *discordia concors* bound them.

It is sometimes said that there is a sharp antithesis, even a strong potential antagonism, between the intellectual habit and the imaginative; and that, as one instance of this, dons and artists don't often get on. I scarcely know whether Albert Talbert and my father would have got on, but at least neither would have found anything puzzling or antipathetic in the other's wave-length. Each was the head of a household in which everything—and particularly any prudent degree of regard for the material means of comfortable living—went down before a large impersonal purpose unrelentingly and indeed obsessively pursued. My father was as singly concerned to return from Islay or Coll with, as he would express it, 'the spindrift on the canvas' as was Talbert to banish from the text of his chosen playwright the corrupt readings of foolish and insufficient Victorian editors. Yet neither man was a fanatic, in whose presence one might feel pushed around by violence or self-will. They both took singleness of purpose for granted in a gentle and matter-of-fact way. But all this does not mean that I think of them as particularly like each other. I suppose, for example, that I see Talbert as essentially a comic character, whereas I am unable to view my father in that way, although I am conscious of his having had a comic side: indeed, something of this must soon transpire.

Again, the Talberts, like my parents, were an incongruous pair; and with the Talberts this began at the level of physical appearance. Talbert was a man of unnoticeably medium stature and possessed no features to speak of, so that what one chiefly marked were the superficialities of a large white moustache, a complexion to be described as baby-pink, and gold-rimmed spectacles of somewhat old-fashioned suggestion. Mrs Talbert was very tall, angular, almost scraggy in a distinguished and fine-boned way, and with a commanding arched nose which took off from her face with the boldness of a skier on some Olympic run. The voices of the pair chimed well with these visual contrasts. Talbert's was—but for that deep huskiness which distinguished him from all living men, and suggested, indeed, the ghost of Hamlet's father as he might have appeared in Mr Wopsel's production—an accent standard in the sense of being unremarkable; I supposed his to be the English of a provincial boy who had moved from a small grammar school to a Cambridge college, and there approximated his speech to that of those around him without ever having been particularly aware of the fact or in the least concerned with its social implications. His wife's voice was wholly different. It swooped up and down just as did her features; it drew out some syllables to almost sentence-length, totally suppressed others, and owned skill in articulating a few—and with the greatest precision—upon an enormous indrawn breath. The effect, which ought to have suggested the ill-judged attempts at enchantment sometimes ventured upon by cacophonous exotic birds, had on the contrary a claim to be called musical. And nobody versed in phonetics, whether articulatory or not, could be unaware that its creatrix had tumbled into Old Road, Headington, from some perch well up the English social ladder.

Mrs Talbert, again, was a good deal younger than her husband. She was supposed to have first come to him from Somerville in a tutorial way, although another theory declared her to be a Balliol man and a noted pioneer of academical transvestism. At least there seemed to be a probability that educational processes, rather than any more general polite intercourse, had been the occasion of their first meeting. Mrs Talbert addressed Talbert as 'Geoffrey', and research in works of reference revealed that this must be a pet name, not an alternative stacked up at the baptismal font for possible future use. Since 'Albert Talbert' is lacking in euphony and even a shade ludicrous, Mrs Talbert's rejection of it—whether upon marriage or from the earliest phase of courtship—may well have been prompted by aesthetic feeling. But *The Oxford Dictionary of Christian Names* (which is among a writer's most useful works of reference) records that, on the marriage of Queen Victoria, the name Albert 'soon became very popular, especially among the poorer classes with whom it is still common', and I suppose this to be an observation relevant to the case. Be all this as it may, the Talberts were a devoted couple.

It is certain, too, that they were devoted parents after a fashion, although with neither the temperament nor the habits which would have made possible a discriminating sense of their children's varying needs. Charles and Mary (the very names suggest only a relaxed attention to identificatory exigencies) were well-mannered young people, and docile at least to the extent of being resigned to Scrabble as a species of Philology without Tears. But they were distinguishably in Topsy's plight, entitled to suspect that they had just 'grow'd'. It was this that made me approximate them to the former condition of Ninian and myself. My brother and I, indeed, had been more extreme instances of the state of affairs I describe, since (with two perfectly loving parents alive) we had been children detectably unwashed, hideously clothed or misclothed, and of a defective complexion suggesting a random, unpunctual, and ingeniously innutritious diet. At times we suffered fiendishly from the humiliating consequences of thus coming from what, in Edinburgh, was inevitably thought of as a disreputable Bohemian home; and it is possible that the young Talberts suffered similarly, if in lesser degree, from their upbringing in a household where quartos and folios were regarded as the only objects given by God to man for any purpose of serious contemplation. But on balance they were lucky, as Ninian and I had been, to have had their upbringing in a household in which scant attention was given to other than disinterested purposes and activities.

'A white tie,' Talbert said—abruptly and on a note of admonition. For a moment I was at a loss. Then I remembered how it had been his custom—little appreciated by some—to assume in all his pupils indifferently regarded an abysmal ignorance of social forms. It used to be said that he had once instructed some young heir to a peerage on the direction in which it is prescriptive to pass the decanters at dessert. He had certainly explained to me that I was not to begin a letter to him with the words 'Respected Sir' nor end it with 'Yours faithfully' or any similarly inadmissible locution. Now he was letting me know in what attire I must turn up that evening. And this, incidentally, told me that our present colloquy beneath the library portal was at an end.

I took leave and retraced my steps across Surrey in the direction of the staircase and my abandoned bag. It occurred to me that I had failed to inquire about Mrs Talbert's health. Although already in middle life, I was still at an age inclined to believe that even the no more than moderately elderly are quite likely to be dead, so it had been the fear of a possible *faux pas* that had held me up. But it is an obvious hazard in any encounter after a long period of years, and had Talbert been skilled in minor social occasions he would have taken the initiative by himself making some reference to his wife. As it was, I should have to ask elsewhere whether the lady was still alive, and hope to have some further brief exchange with Talbert in the course of the evening, when the proper civil expressions could be produced.

I found myself wondering about Dalrymple, and slightly vexed that Talbert should have hailed me under that delusive name. This was unreasonable—for had I not myself been uncertain about Talbert's own identity? As a young man I had dined out on the Talberts often enough; they were among the earliest of my adult acquaintance to have been transformed into imaginary beings by passing through my typewriter.

But I must have set more store than I had known by my admission to that Headington villa, and had thus been a little aggrieved that 'Duncan' had come back to Talbert only under pressure. As for Dalrymple, the name rang no bell. Its owner must have gone down before, or come up after, my own time. It would be nice to think that the character with whom Talbert had confounded me had been a reasonably agreeable man.

II

NOTHING STAYS PUT. The Heracleitan commonplace, which the venture upon which I had launched myself would in any case have been bound sooner or later to bring to mind, had got off to a brisk start with Albert Talbert's turning up on me. Now, once more alone in Surrey, I found the mere architectural spectacle to be performing another of the tricks of time.

Scenes never revisited since childhood are said to be found smaller than memory has held them to be, and the effect perhaps holds true over other long terms of years. But Surrey had not merely thus contracted; it had proportionately sprung into air. I have called it a lidless Palladian box. The box was now much deeper than I remembered it: an oddity the explanation of which I was to stumble upon only some months later. Among my books was one on architecture in Great Britain since the sixteenth century, and it contained a number of photographs of the college. No doubt I had paused on them with decent affection from time to time. And it so happens that, confronting Surrey, the camera has misbehaved, thrusting one angle of the building far into distance, and producing in general a sprawling and stunted impression, as of hutments or hen-houses round a paddock, totally at variance with any that a living spectator could receive. There is nothing surprising about this; before subjects in which values of perspective are prominent the term 'photographic accuracy' has little meaning, as anyone watching a cricket-match on television is aware. What interests me is the fact that this bad photograph, perhaps half a dozen times surveyed, should have superseded in my mind my own first-hand impression of a building in which I had lived for two years, so that for some seconds I was actually indignant with Surrey for being as well-proportioned as Surrey really is. As in my doubts over the identity of Talbert, the true culprit was my own mental constitution.

At the time, and lacking the clue of the photograph, I concluded that I was merely experiencing some side-effect of one marked and veritable change in the scene. Formerly the whole place had seemed to be tumbling to bits. The library had literally been tumbling; sizable chunks of it used to fall off from a great height, particularly in frosty weather. Unwary dons had even been getting killed from time to time, or so we affected to believe. It had been a state of affairs occasioned by the march of progress. The builders of mediaeval Oxford brought their stone from a distance, and where not subsequently knocked down by expanders and improvers their work remains intact to the present day. Later on, local quarries were opened up—not far from the subsequent site of the brick abode of the Talberts. The enterprise was popular, since it conduced to cut-price jobs. Unfortunately the local stone proved to dislike being dug from its bed; the climate of the Thames valley was ungrateful to it (as to a good many humans); eventually it declared its mortality by turning black and beginning to flake away. From the leprous fabric that remained we had been able to detach with a finger-nail great scales of rotten stone.

The effect of this secular decay was often rather splendid. Of the library in particular the Baalbek aspect was enhanced: or as one surveyed it one could think of Piranesi, wringing from the ruins of Rome scenes which—as Horace Walpole said—would startle geometry. The entire university, moreover, was in like case; the Roman city of Bath must have owned a similar appearance when so abraded as to suggest to our Saxon forefathers only the ancient work of giants. There was thus presented a problem on a challenging scale. It must already have been so in the period of Thomas Hardy's Jude Fawley, who is recorded as grounding his hope of employment in the city upon his observation of its dilapidated state. But a further half-century had to pass before a great deal was done.

Then—and largely, no doubt, beneath the wand of trans-atlantic munificence—a transformation-scene reminiscent of one's childhood's pantomimes was achieved, and all Oxford sheathed and carapaced anew.

I looked now at the refurbished façades and found they gave me no particular pleasure. The library, unflawed and glittering in stone which faithfully reproduced its pristine alternations of milk and cream, had gained in sheer mass from its renovation, and appeared more than ever a large-limbed Gargantua in the refined cradle of Surrey. Along the strong horizontals of Surrey itself the eye, no longer impeded by the old jumble of pied and peeled masonry, ran with a facility emphasizing the slight jolt with which, in each of the building's two angles, it was suddenly held up. This is an odd phenomenon, which I have heard attributed to the amateur inspiration of the design. It is as if no advance warning has been given that each of the three sides is not to be of indefinite extension.

But now the staircase was before me. I grabbed my suitcase, and climbed.

By this time other guests were arriving; and among them numerous men, eminent as I was not, were similarly humping bags up wearisome treads. For the Lord Chief Justice of England himself, I supposed, the laying on of a porter would not have been the thing. Grandees, scribblers, assistant masters ageing in obscure private schools: we were all old members and nothing more. Such pious conventions induce an 'in' feeling irritating to those without, but surely harmless as manifestations of the gregarious instincts go. Not that the very top grandees were yet around; it was the university's day of high festival as well as the college's; august preliminary junketings elsewhere probably still detained those of the most superior regard. These dignitaries, festooned with medals and orders like so many Christmas trees, would appear at the Gaudy dinner later on.

Undergraduates are exhorted to remove their private property from college rooms during the long vacation—

chiefly because the college, like every other college in the university, moves into the hotel business at that season of the year. Officials of the National Coal Board, oecumenically minded prelates, Byzantinists, associations of learned women, the liberated spawn of American colleges and high schools: all indifferently throng these guarded courts for the time. A useful revenue is thus raked in. But no young man is prepared to believe that his rooms can really be thus stolen from him, and few do much clearing out. I was not surprised to find my old quarters, as I entered them, present very much a lived-in appearance. Somebody—probably not the owner—had done a superficial tidying up. Nevertheless a firm individual proprietorship everywhere declared itself, and the sharpness of its accent had the effect, for some moments, of calling up for me more vividly than might otherwise have been the case, the appearance of the room during my own occupancy. Over the mantelpiece hung a reproduction of that most popular of Japanese actor prints, Sharaku's Mitsugorō II as the ferocious Ishii Genzō drawing his sword. It is a kind of ultimate in bug-eyed monsters, and was in the place once occupied by a preliminary water-colour sketch for my father's celebrated if historically dubious painting, *Young Picts watching the arrival of Saint Columba*. (The young Picts had been Ninian and myself; we had been required to crouch uncomfortably for hours in the middle of a clump of prickly whins.) In one corner of the room, in which I had kept an elegant but totally unfunctioning Dutch bracket clock bought in Edinburgh's Grassmarket for eight shillings, lay a tennis-racket, a hockey-stick and a guitar, tumbled together in a manner suggesting an early composition by Braque; and on the walls this *motif* might be said to be caught up in a number of large but inexpensive reproductions of works of art which had been affixed to the panelling with scraps of sellotape. From these last the eye, upward travelling, came upon a less sophisticated exhibition. The whole room was dominated by bottles which had been ranged side by side, dozens and dozens of them, on a substantial cornice near the ceiling as if convenient to the hand of a barman nine-foot high. They were empty bottles: exhausted wells of champagne, beer, gin, claret, cider, hock, ouzo, tokay and chianti all juxtaposed in a spirit of the finest egalitarianism. It was an innocent ostentation, and attractive to me; in fact I received from it a first hint of how fascinating I might find—moving through those middle years as I was— a closer view of the mysterious business of growing up.

So once I had unpacked and washed in the little bedroom I settled down comfortably enough amid the possessions of an unknown young man. There were a couple of shelves of books—paperbacks for the most part, but interspersed with three or four bound volumes which turned out to be prizes bearing the inscription:

Nicolas Junkin
History Sixth
Cokeville G.S.

This was one discovery; another was that Mr Junkin posses-sed two of my early plays. The circumstance naturally predis-posed me in his favour, and I even entertained the thought of purloining an empty brandy-bottle from the forthcoming festivity and leaving it on his writing-table as a species of rent. Meantime, I looked at my watch, and decided that it would have been agreeable if, for early arrivals, there had somewhere been a cup of tea. I filled a pipe instead, found myself without matches, and searched the room for a box in vain. Deciding to seek further, I left Nicolas Junkin's set and went out to the landing. But I don't smoke heavily, and had no urgent need of the matches. What drew me from the room was the staircase itself.

Except in colleges of modern foundation, the corridor is not an Oxford institution. One lives on a staircase: commonly one set of rooms on either hand, storey by storey, from ground floor to attics. A hospitable man will give a party for the whole staircase. It is to that extent an entity. Indeed, there is a kind of mystique of the staircase; it has, in any one year, its tone —this however diverse the temperaments, interests, backgrounds of the persons who pound up and down it, bang its doors, exploit its resonances in the interest of nocturnal disturbance.

Or so it had formerly been. For all I knew, it might be different now. The bond of simple contiguity used to knit together even men who in some instances scarcely acknowledged one another's existence as their shoulders brushed. Perhaps this no longer obtained.

Yet staircases, significantly, are still being built—although to dispose young men laterally would be the rational procedure today. Rooms on a corridor can be tidied and swept through by arthritic old women wheeling vacuum cleaners, whereas staircases require the services of a virtually vanished race of menservants, able and prepared to trudge up and down round the clock. Nevertheless I had been told that, when some extension of undergraduate accommodation is proposed in the form of a new quadrangle, it has to be on a staircase plan—this lest the sentiment of old members (whose pockets must be touched if the project is to succeed) should be alienated by a more rational design. 'We were on the same staircase in '25,' elderly gentlemen report of one another. It is in the spirit of such reminiscence that the cheque-book is brought out.

At the moment, the staircase feeling certainly commanded me. For example, Tony Mumford had lived in the rooms immediately opposite mine. I wondered what had recently happened to Tony, with whom I hadn't at all kept up. Hadn't he been moving ahead in politics? I didn't really know. But the memory of his rooms came back to me as vividly as that of my own. I wondered what they looked like now.

At least they, too, were being occupied by a Gaudy guest: a fact apparent because (as in my own case) a hand-written card had been attached to the oak by the staircase's scout. I crossed the landing and looked at this. It read *Lord Marchpayne*. The name obscurely touched my mind, but to no particular illumination. I wondered whether Lord Marchpayne had yet arrived. Still telling myself that my foray was a matter of matches, I banged on the door with a lack of ceremony which testified to the extent of my having recovered the spirit of the place, and walked boldly in.

There was nobody around. A first glance told me that here was the term-time abode of an undergraduate distinguishable from the one over the way. There was nothing to correspond to the bottles. There seemed to be no books at all. A few aquatints, illustrative of sporting occasions and probably of some value, ornamented the walls; so, with marked aesthetic regardlessness, did a peculiarly hideous Cecil Aldin colour-print in which an aggressive clerical thruster, with the hounds almost beneath the hoofs of his mount, was deservedly taking a toss into a ditch. That the proprietor of these objects owned a practical as well as an artistic interest in field-sports was attested by the presence in a corner of the room of a saddle and a pair of hunting boots with shiny tops. The entire spectacle was one to which nothing very out-of-the-way attached. It was my second glance that momentarily astonished me.

Over the mantelpiece hung a large oil painting in a strikingly erotic Late Victorian taste: it might have been by some libidinous follower of Sir Laurence Alma-Tadema. Adequately clothed but suggestively posed on couches and amid marbles evocative of the last decadence of Rome, several languorous ladies awaited appointments the nature of which, in what was so evidently an antique *maison de tolérance*, it wasn't hard to guess. Tony Mumford had set great store by his heirloom, of comparatively recent accession in the family though it must have been. I could recall numerous jokes, not of the most refined, which had turned upon his supposed recurrent emotional dependence on this private lupanar. It seemed odd that Tony should simply have abandoned the picture to the college on going down a quarter of a century ago.

I was still puzzling over this when a sound made itself heard on the staircase—a sound so familiar that I at once turned to the open door behind me in the simplest expectation of what was going to appear. And I was not mistaken. A man of about my own age was framed in the doorway, carrying a tray from which the small rattle of crockery had come.

'Good afternoon, my lord. I thought you might have a fancy for a cup of tea. Plot is the name, my lord. I haven't been on the staircase all that long. But I remember you, if I may say so, very well. Very well indeed, my lord.' Plot (and I remembered, on my part, his not unmemorable name, but not the man himself) advanced towards a table in the centre of this room the just occupancy of which I had so rudely usurped. It was a situation requiring immediate clearing up.

'That's very kind,' I said. 'But I'm not Lord Marchpayne. My name is Pattullo, and I've been put in the rooms opposite. I was only looking for matches.'

'On the bedside table, sir.' Plot touched a reproachful note. 'We keep having those power-cuts. Strikes, go-slows, refusing an honest bit of overtime: quite shocking, it seems to me. As bad as them in the motor-works, who come out if they have to walk through a small puddle to their job. So the matches, you see, are sometimes a convenience to the gentlemen in the night.'

'Yes, of course. It was stupid of me not to look in the bed-room.' The neutrality of Plot's 'the gentlemen' had caught my ear. It would not have been possible to say whether this traditional manner of designating the young men on his staircase existed in a comfortable and uncoloured way in his mind or was there conditioned by ironic reservations. Certainly he was not the man indiscriminately to abnegate the distinc-tions of class. There would be lads in the college kitchens whom he would address as from a just remove. Correspond-ingly, although his manner had turned a shade less deferential upon his discovery that I was not a peer of the realm, it still held quite enough deference for any reasonable commoner to be going on with. I concluded that there had been Plots around the college for generations, and that with this one it would be possible to establish excellent relations.

'I'll just take the tea into your own rooms.' Plot made to

pick up the tray he had set down. 'As you see, I thought I'd make a little anchovy-toast, and it oughtn't to be let grow cold. I think I'm right in saying the gentlemen were partial to it in your time.'

'That's perfectly true.' The anchovy-toast was something I had already become aware of, its aroma being the more striking since some time happened to have elapsed since this particular delicacy had been offered to me. 'But what about Lord March-payne? He may turn up at any moment.'

'Plenty more, sir, where this came from.'

'I'm delighted to hear it,' somebody said from the doorway. 'Another cup and saucer will be just the thing.'

The newcomer was certainly Lord Marchpayne: he had a suitcase by his side. And Lord Marchpayne was certainly Tony Mumford. The voice was a little changed, having become distinguishably a public voice. The figure and even the features had changed too; both were heading towards the massive. But I hadn't the slightest doubt about Tony. Nor had he about me.

'Well I'm blessed—Duncan! And Plot, isn't it?' Tony had turned instantly to this ministrant character and shaken hands with him. It was something it hadn't occurred to me to do, and I tried to remember whether it had been our habit with our scouts at the beginning and end of term. Plot appeared not overwhelmed.

'Quite correct, my lord. And pleased to be looking after you. I was telling Mr Pattullo that I hadn't been on this staircase long. I take it you'll hardly object to using this young gentleman's crockery?' Plot, who was opening a cupboard door, asked this with some humorous intention which I was dull enough to fail to elucidate. 'Promotion comes rather slowly, you might say, in my department of college life. All the better when it does, of course.'

'Capital!' Tony had tossed a bowler hat on the table, and I found myself questioning this slightly archaic object as if it might tell me something about its owner. What was eluding me was whether as an undergraduate Tony had been in some sort of succession to a barony or the like, or whether he was now Lord Marchpayne as a consequence of services rendered to the nation. It was not a point of which he would expect a former intimate to be ignorant. 'Capital!' Tony was now repeating. 'Bicycle-boy, wasn't it? Any of them around today?'

'No, my lord—and not all that many bicycles, either. Nothing but motor-cars. Why, a freshman is let run a motor-car, if only he can produce a scrap of an excuse for it. Go down to where the piggeries were, and you'll find—in term-time, that is—a whole car-park of them.'

'Ah, changed days.' Having briskly established relations with Plot, Tony as briskly switched off. And at this Plot, having satisfied himself that our hot-water jug was adequate to the replenishing of our teapot, and impressed upon us the circumstance that he would be within call, retired to his pantry. Tony and I were left regarding each other with the ghost of constraint.

'This is quite splendid!' Tony said—and added (having paused to pick up a finger of toast), 'I rather thought you never came to these affairs, Duncan? For our generation they happen every three or four years, you know. You must get the invitations?'

'Yes, I do. But I'm afraid I've never been to a Gaudy in my life. I've been living abroad a good deal.'

'Dodging the tax-gatherer—eh, Duncan? But hang abroad! Cut out of it, my boy. Live at home and look about you. Your plays will improve no end.'

'That's an amateur fallacy,' I pronounced firmly—but wondering whether what Tony had said was true. And even although there was something factitious about his bold reaching out towards our juvenile candour, I rather admired the prompt force with which he had gone after it.

'You're losing your command of modern English idiom, for one thing,' Tony pursued with bland authority. 'Your people—even the young ones—talk exactly as we talked in this room God knows how many years ago. And we went in for something rather archaic then, for that matter. It was an affectation of yours, Duncan.'

I felt that this brutality was something at which I, too, must play.

'Were you always going to be Lord Marchpayne?' I demanded. 'It must have been on the strength of being somebody's grandson or nephew, if you were—since you were plain Tony Mumford, without a doubt. Or is it a hastily improvised disguise?'

'Oh, quite the latter.' Tony was amused. 'I've been pushing around—perhaps not in departments of activity you keep an eye on. Nothing dramatic, let alone theatrical, about being a reliable junior Minister with the right contacts in the City.' Tony smiled charmingly. 'That's me. Unfulfilled renown, and all that.'

'I write about obscurely private life, you know, and keep my eye on *that*. My characters are all virtually idiots—in the original sense of the word.'

'You always had a smack of the don in you, Duncan.' Tony's thus greeting my inconsequent piece of pedantry was fair enough. But his renewed smile told me he wasn't too pleased at my ignorance of his career. If we were to horse around innocently as in days of yore we should have to watch our steps, at least in the initial stages.

'I suppose,' I asked, 'that these are your son's rooms?' Plot's question about the crockery and my own familiarity with the picture over the mantelpiece had belatedly come together in my mind, and the inference to be drawn was clear. 'When he came up, you arranged for him to have your old rooms here in Surrey?'

'More or less. Ivo—that's my boy—liked the idea. You see, they were my father's rooms too—although I mayn't ever have mentioned the fact. Do you know? Not long ago I met a very nice chap who'd written a book. Blameless bit of literary history of some sort. And he'd talked about undergraduates who might turn over letters written by their great-grandfathers when *they* were undergraduates. Idea was to show how totally incomprehensible one generation's interests may be to another. Husky lads solemnly concerned over Dr Pusey's latest sermon, or the Eastward Position, or whether it is edifying to visit the good poor. And this chap was rebuked in some public print by an egg-head professor from heaven knows where for being snobbish or, as they say, divisive. Comical, wouldn't you say? After all, everybody has great-grandfathers—I suppose with the sole exception of Jesus Christ.' Tony paused, and I felt he had thrown in this as an appeal to what he thought of as the pervasively sceptical spirit of modern literature as embodied in my person. 'Still, one has to mind one's p's and q's, no doubt. Pointless to get thought of as snooty in such matters. Make your standing clear and then be gracefully modest about it. Think of that convention at Cambridge. I wonder if it still goes on.'

'I don't know any convention at Cambridge.'

'Ah.' Tony paused to finish a cup of tea and pick up a further finger of toast. 'It may only have been at one or two colleges. When boys with handles to their names were due to come into residence, their full style was put up over their door: Visc. This, or just the Hon. That. But when they arrived, it was regarded as the thing for them to direct that the title of honour be painted out. A bit wasteful of somebody's time—but a graceful gesture, if you care to regard it that way.'

'I can't say that I do. It sounds thoroughly foolish.' I secured the last sliver of toast. 'They've put me in my old rooms opposite, quite without my asking them. Did you ask to be shoved in here?'

'Oh, no—although it seems Gaudy guests do make such nostalgic demands. I had a word with the head porter as I came in. He told me that last year, when they had the most senior lot, there was a nonagenarian clergyman who asked for his old rooms four floors up in Howard. And stipulated for a pot.'

'Fair enough.'

'But I certainly didn't suggest being put in here.' Tony

glanced casually round the room. 'It's one thing for a lad to apply for what were his father's rooms a generation ago, and quite another to quarter a man in his son's present rooms like this. That's a shade obtuse, if you ask me.'

'Oh, do you think so?' I paused on this—and, indeed, knew I oughtn't to take it further. 'Do you mean it gives you a feeling of being a spy?'

'That's a crude way to put it, Duncan. But something of the sort, yes.'

'Ivo may have skeletons in his cupboards?' I was now on my feet and prowling myself. There was, as it happened, a cupboard before my nose: it corresponded, on one side of the fireplace, to that on the other side from which Plot had produced the auxiliary cup and saucer. 'Shall we have a look?' I said, and pulled open the door.

It was a graceless small performance, as I knew at the time, and I can only suppose that its occasion was the effort both Tony and I were making to be something like undergraduates together once more. And the cupboard didn't, of course, reveal anything horrific. It did, however, show that the man over the way wasn't alone on the staircase in having a taste for bottles. Only Ivo Mumford's bottles weren't empty, but full. There were a couple of dozen of champagne, as many of brandy, an array of glasses, and a large bowl containing lump sugar.

'That's what they drink at the moment,' Tony said. He had, I believe, been startled, but now showed every appearance of ease. 'Most damnably expensive, I'm bound to say. But wholesome, as alc goes.'

'I see. When do they drink which?'

'Which? They drink the two mixed fifty-fifty, and on a couple of lumps of sugar.'

'As a midnight carouse?'

'As elevenses, I believe. Carries them on till lunch.'

Our reunion had gone faintly awkward, and I wondered whether Ivo Mumford was not merely extravagant but in some

34

danger of turning into a drunk as well. There was nothing for it but to try to talk about something else. It was with the thought of contriving this that I strolled to one of the windows.

'It's from up here,' I said, 'that the library looks best. Has it ever struck you as extraordinary that a lot of these buildings were designed by the dons themselves?'

'Were they? I'm afraid I know nothing about it.' Tony didn't sound interested. In fact, he was betraying a tendency to brood.

'Lord, yes. Surrey is the work of Provost Harbage. He simply drew the plans, and called in a master-mason to get on with the job. And he was something of a pioneer into the bargain. He'd got going on this style of thing a dozen years before William Kent returned from Italy with Palladio in his pocket.'

'Had he, indeed.'

'And his was the general idea for the library, as well. The design was modified later, but by another amateur of the same sort—a fellow, I think, of All Souls.'

'Interesting. Feeble of me never to have read it up.' Tony was silent for a moment. 'If you ask me,' he said abruptly, 'dons are a great bore.'

If this sudden judgement on our hosts disconcerted me, it may have been partly because Tony was barely concealing a persuasion that I was becoming a bore myself. I determined to import a livelier note into our exchanges.

'Tony,' I said, 'come here. Do you remember how in this window of yours we could have the sensation of being in a kind of stage box?'

'Gaping down at the quad?'

'Not that at all. Diagonally into the corresponding room on the staircase round the corner. It must be just the same in the quad's other corner. You remember how people didn't much draw their curtains——'

'Unless they were on the ground floor.' Tony had joined me now, and appeared vaguely interested. 'A species of tabu, like not shutting the doors in those awful underground baths. So when the lights were switched on——'

'That was at night. But on summer late afternoons, you got the same effect as now. Look.'

We both looked, just as we had occasionally done, in luxurious idleness, a long time previously. Sunshine was striking through the two tall windows slantwise presented to us, and in the middle of the room thus revealed a portly and bearded man was holding up some sort of dress-coat on its hanger and disapprovingly shaking his head. Presumably he was deciding that the garment had been badly packed and become unsuitably creased in consequence. He walked out of sight with it. A minute later he appeared again, sat down on a big sofa, put up his feet, and almost instantly gave every sign of having fallen asleep.

'The sofa reminds me,' Tony said. 'Do you remember the term when we had a vintage time as young *voyeurs*? Can you recall the name of the chap who had those rooms then?'

'I don't think I can.'

'Ah, I can tell you why. It's because he was a disreputable countryman of yours, Duncan, and with a name as grotesque as your own. Killiecrankie—P. P. Killiecrankie. Wasn't that it? I don't believe either of us ever spoke to him.'

'He was a revolting womanizer.'

'Of course he was—but troubled by your Scottish Calvinist sense of sin.'

'I doubt it's being that. Indeed, I can remember maintaining it was just a morbid delicacy. He couldn't bring himself to do anything so crude as to invite a girl into his bedroom. So it all had to happen on that sofa.'

'And, by God, it did!' Turning away from the window, Tony shouted with laughter. '*Viva* Killiecrankie! We learnt something from him, didn't we? I'd no notion it could be so vigorous an exercise.'

'But all the same—and again as a matter of delicacy—an affair of not much more than disordered dress, as in old-fashioned erotic French engravings.'

'Yes—but then, and as you may say *post hoc*, he'd get up, strip starkers, and solemnly take a turn up and down the room. Helped him to the second bang.'

'Ornithology. We called it that. Bird-watching, of course. Exquisite undergraduate joke.'

We were both laughing now; indeed, we had sunk into chairs in what was in part a pretence of helpless mirth. Then we caught one another's eye and were abashed. We were, after all, no longer bawdy and joyous young cronies, with minds completely open to each other except on a few guarded family matters. We were respectable citizens in our forties, and we hadn't run across one another in a donkey's years. Perhaps Tony felt more strongly than I did that we had succumbed to unbecoming behaviour, since junior Ministers of the Crown probably keep more steadily decorous company than writers do. At any rate we now, as by common agreement, sobered up. It was in the resulting calm that I noticed Tony's glance going to the picture over the mantelpiece. He seemed not too pleased with it. Perhaps he was wondering whether Ivo was any chaster than Killiecrankie had been. But then having the mildly lascivious painting there had been no whim of Ivo's own. It was seemingly prescriptive with the Mumfords. I determined to inquire into this.

'Tony, you say your father had these rooms once. Did he bring up those abandoned wenches with him—just as you did, and Ivo seems to have done?'

'Certainly he did—and my grandfather before him. And that, I believe, was in the very year my great-grandfather bought the thing at the Royal Academy's annual show.'

'So it goes to and fro.' I cast round for some harmlessly humorous remark. 'I suppose your great-grandfather had these rooms too?'

'Nothing of the kind. He was a self-made man from the Midlands. But four generations of us have.'

'I'm sure you kept very close about that—although Ivo, come to think of it, was still in the womb of time. But even as many as three generations makes quite a claim.'

37

'A claim?' Rather strangely, Tony shot the word back at me. 'I'm entirely of your opinion there.'

'The staircase ought really to be named after your family, or at least after your broad acres. Where's Marchpayne, Tony?'

This mockery failed to catch Tony's attention. He had again jumped up, and was pacing out the length of the room. He walked over to the cupboard with the brandy and champagne, and closed the door on it gently.

'The staircase?' he echoed. 'Well, yes—in a way.' He turned back to face me. 'I declare that this stair,' he said, 'is my ancestral stair. So perhaps you've hit the nail on its bloody head.'

There was a silence, since I didn't know what to make of these words. They came from some poem by Yeats—whom I'd scarcely have supposed to be much resorted to by up-and-coming politicians.

'If you turn up when it says on the card,' Tony said, 'you stand around in the quad for half an hour, drinking not the best of sherries. That's O.K., if you want an absolute orgy of the old chums.'

'Then I'll make it a little later.' I had stood up, because I felt that this abrupt change of subject indicated that Tony would be quite glad to be rid of me. I was an interloper, after all, in these ancestral Mumford rooms. 'But I suppose that sort of orgy is more or less what one accepts the invitation for.'

'Oh, there are speeches, you know, by selected big-wigs. Plus one or two sycophantic ones by the more prominent ushers.'

This once more pulled me up. If Tony really had it in for a harmless lot of dons in this way it was hard to see why he'd presented himself for the annual spree now ahead of us. And I think my expression must have betrayed this perplexity, since he now added something on what appeared to be a sudden impulse.

'As a matter of fact, Duncan, I've come up to case the joint. Something has happened that makes me want to see how the land lies. You wouldn't expect—would you?—that this college would change much. But I'm not at all certain that it ticks quite as of old. And I want to find out.'

'I see.' I waited a moment for Tony to explain himself further, but this he did not do. 'Have you decided to send another son to follow in Ivo's footsteps?'

'I haven't got another son. But I do have two daughters. They're still at school.' Tony had made this transition rapidly, and for a further minute he talked about the girls, while I stood with my hand on the door knob. I realized that he had embarked on some confidence and then thought better of it, at least for the time. Having no wish to give the appearance of hanging around for more, I made a vague remark about the mysteries of female education, and then went back to my own rooms.

III

The invitation from the Provost and Fellows said:

Full Evening Dress with Decorations
Gowns are worn; Doctors in Scarlet

I had at least brought the white tie urged upon my recollection
by Talbert, but the necessity to wrestle with it was still some
time off, and I decided to sit down and read. Nicolas Junkin
would hardly resent my taking a book from his shelves, so I had
another look at what was on offer. Junkin took an interest in
drama—although my own two plays struck me as sufficiently
isolated in kind to suggest their having been left behind by a
previous tenant of different tastes from his. Beckett led the field,
backed by Ionesco, Adamov, and other absurdists. There were
Unity Theatre things of one sort and another, including—what
must be a prized possession—a cyclostyled text of *Harold
Muggins is a Martyr*. John Arden, in fact, was a favourite, as was
anything hitching on to CAST. (At that time those letters
stood for Cartoon Archetypical Slogan Theatre, but they
may stand for something quite different now—perhaps with
Anarcho-Syndicalist in the middle.) There was also a pile of
little reviews and fugitive magazines concerned with theatrical
affairs. One was produced by university students, and it was
this I picked up. I found myself reading an article called *The
Insignificance of Bernard Shaw*.

Shaw's insignificance was argued on the basis of a Marxist
theory of drama. It was highly relevant that he had begun as
a novelist, and he must be regarded as a displaced person, a
refugee fleeing to the theatre from the disintegrating territory
of realistic prose fiction. He had carried with him all the
privatization of experience that characterizes bourgeois life,
and as a consequence was impotent before the central problem

of dramatic writing, which is that of exhibiting socially significant types in collision, of giving to personal motivation more than a merely individual significance by displaying it as the concrete embodiment of a universal factor in the dynamic of a given class of men of whom the dramatic hero is the exemplar.

The article ran to twenty pages. But if the writer found Shaw's plays interesting, there was no sign that he found them entertaining. 'Comedy' and 'comic' were terms making no appearance. 'Significant', 'relevant', and 'objective' were the key words throughout. In Shaw's time, I read, 'the objective conditions of social life imposed a highly compartmentalized subjective existence upon its individuals'.

There was nothing novel about these ideas. That I finished the essay without impatience was, in an odd way, a function of my interest in Nicolas Junkin of Cokeville Grammar School. It was necessarily a guessing kind of interest, and of a sort familiar to me. An inhabited room, temporarily without its occupier, sets conjecture stirring, and in a quite involuntary way evidences of personality urge themselves into some sort of pattern in my fancy. Junkin had been establishing himself there as a representative young man of a kind that now regularly gains a place at a university. His gown, hanging from a peg in the bedroom, was a commoner's, not a scholar's; this suggested, although not at all securely, that he was no cleverer than most of his fellows. The hockey stick (by no means heroically battered), the tennis racket and guitar (each with a broken string), the Japanese print, the op posters and conscientiously paraded bottles: these, and the run of books I had glanced at on the shelves, seemed to speak of a youth having a go now at this and now at that in a wholly unremarkable way.

The emphasis on drama remained; it had led me to read the article on Shaw, and to wonder whether Junkin approved of it. (There was no Shaw on his shelves.) But a lively interest in theatrical matters by no means took him out of the unassuming main stream in which I was imagining him. In addition to the OUDS, I knew, every college now had its dramatic society, liable at any moment to come up with anything from *The*

Representative to *Toad of Toad Hall*. Were Toad's adventures given a Marxist slant, or perhaps subsumed within the Theatre of Cruelty? (Either treatment would be feasible.) Was a distinguishably aesthetic approach to drama at a discount? Somebody had lately assured me that, music aside, the only authentic artistic interest of the young today is in the cinema, but that it is unfortunately much more difficult and expensive to make films than to produce plays: hence *Mother Courage* and *Ubu Roi* all over the place. Why, I wondered, were these mimetic arts so vulnerable to engulfment in ideological abstraction—Marxism, Existentialism, or whatever it might be? Was it an accidental consequence of the cropping up, over two or three generations, of a small number of powerful and seminal intelligences: Toller, Brecht, Sartre, and so on?

Sitting in this nostalgic and, as it were, transitional room (since—as during my own occupancy—it was neither a boy's nor quite one with which a grown up would furnish himself) I considered a number of questions of this sort. Since they were professional questions, more or less, I was inclined to provide prescriptive answers of my own as I went along. It was a profitless activity, or was so until it hinted to me one salient fact. My knowledge of a present student generation was all at second hand, which meant that for sympathy, interest, speculation it was an area of contemporary life substantially closed to me. My own age group—Tony Mumford, now Lord Marchpayne, for instance—was beginning to have sons and daughters at the universities. It was probable that Talbert had some former pupil's son among his current pupils now, and that in vacations parent and child would swop anecdotes about tea parties in Headington.

For a few minutes this train of thought landed me in fantasy. I was at a breakfast table and occupied with a coffee-percolator—from which it might be inferred that I was unprovided with a wife. I did, however, have two sons. Slim, long-limbed, long-haired creatures of perhaps sixteen and nineteen, they had sauntered in, lazily but even at this early hour prepared to gossip. Their Scottish ancestry was not apparent; they were entirely English and very public-school. In fact these agreeable phantoms were miraging up in this spuriously filial relation from my very first weeks in Surrey long ago—before, even, I had made Tony Mumford's acquaintance, and when I was still merely an observer of young men marvellously known to each other, idly talking, parting and disparting, shouting from windows, banging doors: a society of liberated schoolboys, wholly and astonishingly owning all that antiquity of blackened and flaking stone. How deeply I must have been sold on the place! No wonder I had scarcely ever ventured to come back.

The fantasy flickered shamelessly on. Learned in the ways of women, I was seeing to it unobtrusively that my boys should here be armed. 'Believe me,' I was saying to the elder now, 'Virgil's *varium et mutabile semper femina* gets it dead wrong. It doesn't square with the implacable female will. Having made up her mind about you—and it happens in the first moment you enter the room—a woman will never alter it. Circumstances may make her swear on the book that she has. But it won't be true.'

This shallow aphorism, sounding on my inward ear, broke up the reverie. Instead, and as I stared absently at Ishii Genzō over the grate, I reflected that my surroundings of the moment afforded me rational ground to feel the disadvantage to a writer, in particular, of losing contact with younger people. One ought not, clearly, to haunt or badger one's juniors: the leisure they have for one is limited and often created out of courtesy. Yet they represent the grass roots of mature generations to come, and perhaps one ought to claim among them such grazing-rights as one may. I had returned to the college, I told myself, at the wrong time and for what would probably be a boring occasion. It would have been much more fun to be coming up, say, to talk to a college dramatic society—one doubtless involved, if not with *Ubu Roi*, then with *Ubu Cocu* or *Ubu Enchaîné*.

I was interrupted by the reappearance of Plot. Not that

43

'interrupted' is quite right. This time, Plot entered the room in the character of an Invisible Man, and as an Invisible Man made his way to the bedroom opening off it. I recalled that college scouts put on this turn when their job called them into a don's room in which a tutorial was going on. I had not myself owned sufficient sophistication to be unperturbed by this; it had appeared to me that when somebody thus presented himself there should be at least a momentary passing of the time of day. Even at this moment I was not quite at ease. Observing, that is, that I was going to be respectfully ignored by Plot, I affected, before the journal still open in front of me, an absorbed regard such as might lend some colour to this lack of communication between us. Plot disappeared soundlessly, shutting the bedroom door behind him. I found myself straining to catch what he was up to.

He was, of course, laying out my evening clothes. Whether he regularly performed equivalent valeting services for the set's more permanent proprietor, I didn't know. I wondered whether he had to do a great deal of simple tidying round. Did youths from unassuming homes, accustomed to fold things more or less neatly or risk a row with Mum, quickly adopt the habits (if they still were the habits) of their more privileged contemporaries, persuading themselves that the right place for a discarded garment was any corner of the floor from which a servant—thus wholesomely redeemed from idleness—could be expected to pick it up? Perhaps this lingering convention (among my astonishments long ago) had passed wholly into desuetude. It is, after all, only in detective stories and in romances of the neo-silver-fork school that nursery-maids, housemaids, footmen and the like abound any longer. (But here and there, of course, there are still fags. I used to believe that some of my companions spent the whole of their freshman year in perplexity over the absence from their new environment of personal assistants of that sort.)

Plot now returned from the bedroom, announced all to be in order there in the matter of cuff-links and socks, and moved to one of the windows. It was still hours too early, on this mid-June evening, to draw the curtains, so he contented himself with a motion apparently designed to shake them (somewhat meagre and indeed scruffy as they were) into more graceful folds. I took this lingering to be an invitation, or at least permission, to converse.

'Is there anybody else from my time on the staircase again tonight, Plot?'

'A Mr Mogridge in the rooms below these, sir. His old rooms, too, it seems. I can't say he comes back to me. But he would be the same year as his lordship and yourself, all right. Mr Killiecrankie's year.'

'Ah, yes.' Identificatory phrases such as 'my year', 'your year', 'our year' were familiar to me as turning up in encounters with old members of the college. But here was something new. It was quite reasonable, no doubt, that college servants, living out their lives in contact with so many ephemeral generations of youth, should evolve a calendar of the kind thus hinted—one of Oriental suggestion, as one should say 'the Year of the Monkey' or 'the Year of the Dog'. I should myself have thought of P. P. Killiecrankie's heyday as to be associated with the Goat. 'Do you know whether Mr Killiecrankie is coming to this Gaudy?' I asked.

'I think I've heard he is, sir. Always interesting to meet, Mr Killiecrankie is. Done very nicely for himself, too, I'd say.'

'I'm delighted to hear it. Not that I ever got to know him, so far as I can remember.'

'Is that so, sir?' Much more distinguishably than when I had turned out not to be Lord Marchpayne, I had declined in Plot's estimation. 'I'd have thought everybody knew Mr Killiecrankie. Quite a name with *us,* he was.' Plot paused on this—fleetingly, but long enough to sweep into the picture, as it were, a cloud of below stairs witnesses. 'I was never his scout, mark you, since you'll remember it was before I got a staircase. But I used to take a message for him, from time to time. A bicycle-boy could go anywhere in those days. Without, as you might say, being noticed.'

A longer pause on Plot's part had preceded this last fragment of communication. I was compelled, and slightly alarmed, by a momentary equivocal glint in his eye. He was a most respectable-looking man, and I didn't doubt that to this there corresponded a most respectable manner of life. Like myself, he had passed the ambush of young days. He might well, unlike myself, possess grown up children: even a daughter at Somerville or a son lately become a Fellow by Examination of All Souls—such story book social inversions I knew to be of real occurrence in contemporary Oxford. I much doubted whether, with the nineteen-year-old boys whose shoes he polished, he would permit himself a word or a wink suggestive of any complicity in moral misdemeanour. But with a man of his own age (and especially one who wrote stage plays) it might be different. And for a moment, indeed, Plot's conversation did continue in a promising vein.

'No older than myself, Mr Killiecrankie was. And, of course, a public school man, as more of the gentlemen were at that time. Not places, from what I've heard of them, where a lad has much scope for learning his way about. You know where, that is.'

'But Mr Killiecrankie knew his way about?' This question I believe I asked quite unblushingly, although it happened to be one which Tony and I had been in a position, long ago, to answer in the most literal sense.

'I won't deny that I learnt something from him,' Plot said —all unconscious that he was echoing Lord Marchpayne's words. 'Still there's been a bucket or two of water under Folly Bridge since then—and taking our own follies with it, we must trust, sir.'

This pious hope was plainly designed as a close down upon P. P. Killiecrankie for the moment. Discretion had returned to Plot, and I wasn't going to learn whether my deplorable contemporary had actually set up as a tutor in licence to the youth who ran or pedalled on his dubious errands. To avoid the appearance of, as it were, fishing the murky waters under Folly Bridge, I brought up a change of subject, and asked about Mr Junkin, the present tenant of these rooms.

'A very pleasant gentleman, and settling down nicely. Inclined to be a little familiar at first—you'll understand me, sir—but got his bearings in the end.'

I supposed I did understand Plot. Junkin, whether out of natural decency or ideological persuasion, had tried to get himself treated by Plot as the social equal (and, at the same time, much younger person) he in fact was. He had persisted in addressing Plot as 'Mr Plot' and had said things like 'My friends call me Nick and I think you should too.' Had Plot replied: 'It doesn't work, sir. I can't call you Nick if I don't call Mr Mumford Ivo'? Probably Plot, although a perfectly sensible man, had for some reason of caste refrained from any such lucid statement and merely been inflexible. Whereupon Junkin had been hurt in his feelings, and was now inclined to be slightly bloody minded about college servants.

I wondered whether I had got this wrong. If I had, it was again because I didn't know an entire age group. I felt a wish to meet Nicolas Junkin. Ivo Mumford would be not without interest, but Junkin was the real attraction. At the same time, there was an obvious question I could ask about the two together.

'Have these two young men on either side of this landing much in common, Plot?'

'Well now, you may say any two young men will have in common with each other what those like ourselves won't have with either of them.'

'That's very true.' I found encouragement in Plot's thus asserting the existence of a bond between us. 'But I dare say you remember more about being that sort of age than I do. You're in contact with it all the time.'

'And a funny old life I sometimes feel it to be.' Plot had produced a duster out of air—it was a facility I recalled scouts as having—and was flicking it over the mantelpiece and the frame of Sharaku's print. The time of day seemed inappropriate to such an operation, and I realized that Plot

47

was automatically justifying to himself or to me this lingering over an agreeable gossip. '"Nanny Plot" is what Mr Mumford—Mr Ivo Mumford, that is—sometimes calls me. Very pleasant, of course, since he's entirely the gentleman. But I know what he means.'

'He's making fun of you for trying to get some order and decency into his entire gentleman's ways?'

'I dare say it might be put like that.' Plot had received with momentary suspicion, but at the same time with the faint gleam of an understanding eye, this subversively slanted question. 'As for him and Mr Junkin, I'd say they don't much get along. They're both the party giving sort, though—and I sometimes wonder how it will be when they both hold a party —"throw a party", it's still called—on the same night.' Plot paused darkly for a moment on this. 'Different types, of course. Very confident, Mr Mumford is. And gay, you might say, when he hasn't been crossed in something. It has all come his way easily, I don't doubt.'

'Mr Junkin isn't confident?'

'Desperation, he's sometimes in. He's said to me that if he didn't do all that play acting, and pretending he's not Junkin but Winston Churchill or the Pope of Rome, he'd be clean potty and in the Warneford by this time.'

'I see.' This modified my sense of the owner of the bottles. It also made me warm towards him. Although I was aware of much substance in the conventional view that one's student days are the most 'carefree' and therefore the happiest of one's life, I had a very clear memory of the nevertheless unfathomable intermittent melancholy of the undergraduate condition. 'Do you feel more drawn to one sort of lad than the other, Plot?'

'Well, now.' Plot hesitated for a moment before so unprofessional a question. 'I'd say Mr Mumford's sort is easier to get on with. You know where you are with them, even if you mayn't always like it. With Mr Junkin's sort it's more chancy. Very awkward and unexpected, they can be. Very much so, indeed.'

'But perhaps that makes them more interesting?'

'Yes, that may be. There's not much variety, you might say, in those from Eton and such places.'

'But Eton is supposed to encourage individualism, Plot, and even to tolerate a good deal of eccentricity. It's the smaller public schools that are said to iron boys out.'

'I wouldn't know as to that, I'm sure. But I couldn't say there's much variety among such gentlemen—not even generation by generation, there isn't. Take Mr Ivo and Mr Mumford, and you couldn't have two more alike.'

'The lad is just a repeat of his father?'

'Well, that too, perhaps. But I don't mean his lordship as now is. Old Mr Mumford himself, I'm thinking of—Mr Ivo's grandfather. Before my time or yours, of course, he is; and that by a long way. But he came up for last year's Gaudy.'

'And he was lodged in his old rooms over the way?'

'Oh, certainly, sir. The big picture over the chimney took his fancy a great deal. It had just been moved in with other of his grandson's things. The old gentleman would stand chuckling before it for minutes on end.'

'Would he, indeed?' I found myself trying to visualize Tony's father—a Tony thirty years on—thus experiencing a trick of the old rage. 'What is old Mr Mumford like?'

'Very pleasant, indeed. Commanding, of course, as is only natural. Mr Ivo as he'll be one day, you might say. Anybody could see it's some time since the first Mumfords bought boots. They're aristocratic. Not like the old gentry, though. You can always tell *them*.'

'Ah.' I was impressed by the invoking of this mysterious and superior social group—the ability to distinguish which must have been inherited by Plot from a grandfather of his own, who had trudged up and down such a staircase as this with coal-scuttles and hot water cans long ago.

'Mr Sandys, now—that spelt his name with a *y* and had this very set three years back. Aloof, in a way—and yet as natural as your own brother. What was due and proper passing between you. But never a word less polite than a prince's from Michaelmas to Trinity. Not like Mr Ivo, that isn't. You could tell Mr Sandys as old gentry, all right.'

'I'd like to have known him.' I saw that if Plot himself were to be categorized, it would have to be as a romantic, and I almost asked whether any real princes, abounding in *politesse*, had come his way. But he was now preparing to go about the staircase's business, and I found myself turning back to something else. 'I'm sorry Mr Junkin gets so desperate,' I said. 'It spoils my pleasure in being in his rooms. Have you any notion what his trouble is?' I had no sooner asked this question than I felt it to transgress the bounds of legitimate curiosity—even a writer's legitimate curiosity—where a total stranger was involved. So I substituted a more general query. 'What sort of troubles do the young men mostly have?'

'Well, sir, there they *are* much like you and me. It's money, as often as not. Particularly with them that are here on government grants. They're none too generous, the grants, it seems to me. Especially for a raw lad coming up against his betters and their goings-on in a place like this.'

'Like the present Mr Mumford and his brandy and champagne, for example?'

'But then, again, it may be a matter of a lady.' Plot's ignoring of my question was a very proper rebuke, and I had no doubt that he practised the same technique with the young men. 'Demand and supply, sir; that's where the hitch is. Not nearly enough ladies to go round. Unless, that is, they *did* go round as quick as among fornicating savages beside a camp fire.'

'And they don't do that?' I was struck by the picturesqueness of the image offered me. 'No brisk promiscuity?'

'Well, now, Mr Pattullo—you and I know what sex has become, if we're to believe them in the newspapers and on the wireless. Just plain in-out, in-out, and then look round again.' Plot appeared unperturbed at having produced this yet more robust expression. 'But I can't say I see much of that with our young men. It isn't just cunt, begging your pardon, they're after, if you ask me. They may chew their sheets half through the night, thinking it is. Yet sensualists—if that's the word—is just what they are not. Wouldn't you say?'

'With reservations, Plot. Deplorable exceptions certainly occur.' (Fleetingly I thought of the early erotic life of P. P. Killiecrankie.) 'But I'd go with you in a general way.'

'Young Casanovas is how they may see themselves—and they may be raging, fair enough, just to get a finger there. But it isn't as much their thing as they fancy it. They want a lot going on in the old fashioned heart as well, if you ask me. And that takes time and decency, you'll agree. It doesn't go with what you might call a quick turnover. Add the supply problem to that—— But you probably see my point, sir.'

'I think I do. You make it seem surprising the whole lot aren't right round the bend.'

'But Mr Junkin, now, isn't in that trouble—or not that I know of. And not that bad in the money one either. He has an old aunt, he says, who comes down handsome at need. She gives out she has nothing but a sweet shop, but really owns a whole street of houses as well. He had a Honda from her the day he was seventeen.'

'Ah, I never had an aunt like that.' I saw that Plot was in an admirable relationship with Nicolas Junkin. 'And I don't expect you had, either.'

'That I had not. And it's his studies he's worried about. Very worrying in a general way, the studies seem to be nowa days. Examinations here, and examinations there—and going on long after they ought to be over, if you ask me. Why, there are gentlemen still up now, on one such score or another. More work for the servants, and more vexation for themselves.'

'But that doesn't apply to Mr Junkin at the moment?'

'No, it doesn't. But he has a bad time coming, he says, later on.'

'Perhaps he spends too much time being Winston Churchill or the Pope of Rome.'

'That's what the masters tell plenty of them.' ('Masters', I remembered, was the college servants' word for fellows, tutors, and senior members generally; they used it precisely as it is used in a boys' school.) 'But what they tell Mr Junkin, it seems, is that his headpiece isn't right.'

'You mean his tutors tell him he's a bit insane?' Not unnaturally, I was disconcerted by the notion of such brusque candour.

'Oh, no. What Mr Junkin says is that they think he can't think. Can't get the second thing he says or writes hitched on to the first—or the third to the second. And yet I've seen Mr Junkin in print. It doesn't make sense.'

'What Mr Junkin has had in print doesn't make sense?'

'Well, I don't know that it does to *me*.' Plot had hesitated, as if feeling we were at cross purposes. 'But there he is—in *Isis* and the like. Poetry, some of it is—which is harder than anything else, by all accounts. And yet the masters say that of him. You can't blame him for being worried, having his way to make as Mr Ivo and his like have not. I'm sure I'd be, if it wasn't just the old brush and Hoover that was my end of the boat.'

'He oughtn't to make too heavy weather of it.' I uttered this with conviction, having known a certain number of talented people (as well as numerous worthy ones) quite notably deficient in the elusive art of concatenating ideas logically together. 'He has time and the great world ahead of him.'

'That's what I tell the lad.' It was increasingly evident that Junkin (after his shaky start) had come to enjoy a certain warmth of regard on his scout's part. '"Wait until you get out in the world," I say to him. "You'll be heading the lot of them when it comes to going after the jobs." I tell Mr Junkin that.'

'We must hope it will turn out that way.' I couldn't tell whether there was a secure objective basis for Plot's prediction, but approved his instinct to play down the significance of examinations. 'Is Junkin facing some affair in the Schools soon?'

'Ah, there he's in the same boat as Mr Ivo Mumford, all

right. Both failed the same exam twice, they have—with less than a canvas between them, it seems, so far as the marks went.' Like most scouts, Plot was fond of a metaphor drawn from the river. 'So they have to sit it again, at the end of next term. A last chance, Mr Junkin thinks it will be.'

'And Mr Mumford?'

'Well, it isn't book-learning of any sort that Mr Mumford's mind dwells on, by a long chalk. He takes a very high line about such things. Quite in the old college style that you and I remember, his lordship's son is. As it should be, no doubt— him having a title coming to him now. But I see you'd better be getting changed, sir.'

I realized that this was true, and said good-night to Plot, who departed with the assurance that he would bring me a cup of tea at eight o'clock next morning, or earlier if I cared to open the door and give a shout. He must be wrong, I knew, about Ivo Mumford's having a title ahead of him, since Tony's elevation had certainly been to a life peerage. It seemed to have come his way at a comparatively early stage in his career, and his having accepted it must imply that he was not ambitious of the highest political office. I got out of my day clothes, and did honour to the coming occasion by a careful evening shave.

Screwing small pearl headed studs into small gold sockets, I thought about careers. They were going to be all around me in an hour's time. Careers, so to speak, in mid career. *Nel mezzo del cammin di nostra vita*: I had gathered that this Gaudy was to be so structured that Dante's celebrated line would fit it perfectly. It wasn't for the senators and patriarchs of the college. Old Mr Mumford's Gaudy of the previous year had been that. It wasn't for those comparative youngsters who had gone down from five to fifteen years ago; it would be in the following year that these would get their invitation. This Gaudy was for the intermediate group. Tony and myself, P. P. Killiecrankie (if he had indeed come up) and Gavin Mogridge (at this moment, according to Plot, in his old rooms downstairs): these would constitute one of its more junior echelons.

With leisure to recall Mogridge now, I was conscious of a genuine start of curiosity which exposed as a shade factitious the incipient interest I had been parading to myself (and Plot) in unknown boys barely out of school. Mogridge's career—and he had decidedly enjoyed one—abundantly invited to philosophical speculation on the role of Crass Casualty and the like in individual human destinies.

I remembered him clearly: a large vague youth, fair and gangling, never viewed except wearing perfectly circular steel rimmed spectacles. About these I had used to suppose that there must be something ophthalmically defective, since they by no means obviated the necessity of their owner's surveying the world perpetually slant-wise—rather in the manner of some bust of Alexander the Great faithfully portraying the torticollis afflicting that emperor. Nobody would have supposed it likely that Mogridge would ever himself be reduced to seeking desperately round for fresh worlds to conquer. Yet something of the kind had happened to him.

His only ambition—and we understood it to be a consuming one—was to play the 'cello at a virtuoso's level. He saw himself as the Casals of his generation. Unfortunately his command of the instrument never rose to playing it quite certainly in tune. As a consequence, towards the close of his undergraduate days his family was under the necessity of viewing him primarily as a vocational problem. But his father had prudently kindled in him some small spark of interest in archaeology; and being a professor of some sort at Cambridge had succeeded in attaching his son, although wholly unqualified scientifically, to an expedition proposing extensive excavations in a remote region of the South American continent.

In just what capacity—although doubtless humble—Mogridge was programmed to perform never, as it happened, appeared. The plane carrying the entire personnel of the venture, together with various other people to a total of some fifty souls, having risen punctually from the airfield at Lima and vanished at its predicted point over the horizon, was never seen again. Aerial reconnaissance turned up no trace of it, and when days had passed into weeks all hope of the existence of survivors was abandoned. The catastrophe was one of the dozen or so more sensational horrors of its year.

Yet no immediate fatality had occurred. The plane, while through some technical fault out of radio contact, had cracked up, lost all power, and then simply floated down to a belly-flop in what was fortunately a cushioning but not instantly engulfing swamp. As the last man scrambled out (only the last man, as Mogridge's narrative makes clear, was a woman), the plane burst into flame, and was presently wholly consumed. The final thing to vanish (Mogridge chronicles) was a golden phoenix emblazoned on the fuselage, the emblem of the air-line which had imposed this signal degree of inconvenience upon its clients. From the ashes of the bird nothing arose. The stranded passengers can scarcely have regarded the symbol as felicitously chosen.

I had more than once called up the curious scene before my inward eye, and I did so again now. Many writers have exploited a situation of the kind: notably Shaw (of whom I had lately been thinking) in the third act of *Man and Superman*. But the suddenly transformed condition of Mogridge and his companions (who, minutes before, had been reading scientific journals and drinking martinis) proved far more disconcerting than that of Jack Tanner and his talkative friends, who confronted merely 'one of the mountain amphitheatres of the Sierra Nevada'—although that, indeed, proved to be 'a strange country for dreams'. The swamp, into which the metallic remains of the perished plane were sinking with a sinister ease even as they gazed, appeared initially to extend in illimitable vastness on every side. Curiously enough, it was the purblind Mogridge himself who first discerned (through spectacles which happily had remained unharmed on his nose) certain dim serrations at one point on the horizon. By some this was taken to be a city—but only because a city was what they very much wanted to see. Others declared confidently that, even if mere vegetation, here was an infallible sign of a comfortably navigable river. Mogridge said it was more probably a jungle into the middle of which this whole swamp could be dropped with the effect of a penny tumbled on a billiard table. Mogridge was to prove to be right.

It was, as it happened, his twenty-second birthday; with the exception of a junior cabin steward, he was the youngest person on the plane. He had passed, all decent mediocrity and with that single inept musical ambition, through an unnoticing school and college. One would have conjectured that, if rescued, he would for certain months conscientiously measure and record the dimensions of such chunks of temple masonry and the like as were indicated to him for the purpose, and then return home to equally honourable obscurity in a shipping office or a bank. Instead of which he was to produce *Mochica*.

That Mogridge was able to do this—not, I mean, that he so mysteriously had it in him, but that it was physically, mechanically possible—confronts us with one of those artistries of Chance. His digestion was upset, and it so happened that, when the emergency declared itself, he was privately ensconced in a small compartment at the tail of the plane. To his hand was something from which it was clear to him that he must not, in his uncomfortable condition, be separated. It thus came about that, when he presently found himself knee-deep in mud, his sole possession was a roll of lavatory-paper. From various fellow passengers he was able to requisition pencils. As the grand virtue of *Mochica* consists in its being so unchallengeably (in television parlance) 'live', and in catching, moment by moment through terrible weeks, the fleeting minutiae of an extraordinary situation, it is evident that Mogridge's career might be described with almost literal accuracy as based on bumf.

For some time, indeed, in the literary circles into which he had been rocketed, Mogridge was known as 'Bumfy' Mogridge. But the joke, or jeer, didn't stick. *Mochica* itself, after all, was emphatically not bumf; it was one of those rare books which, while enjoying riproarious popular success, at the same time owns sufficient intrinsic merit to achieve among the critical a kind of classic status straight away. Mogridge himself had become a celebrity, and one with a large sum of money in the bank, before his father and uncles and other concerned persons had ceased wondering where and how to find him £12 a week.

Mogridge's moment had been born out of sudden and unpredictable hazard; and in the sequel something like that confronted him all over again. Even the money might be as swamping as that Peruvian mud, if he failed warily to consider the interest the Inland Revenue was going to take in it a twelvemonth after its arrival. What did, in fact, happen to him thereafter was sufficiently enigmatical to make me regret that I had never once run across him since we both went down. I was going on now to reflect on what hearsay had brought me when there came an interruption in the shape of a knock on Junkin's outer door.

I emerged from the bedroom and gave a shout to come in— not at all deterred by the fact that my movement was of the shambling character enforced upon a man who is only half into his trousers. I thought this might well be Gavin Mogridge himself; it would be a reasonable thing that, having heard from Plot of my presence, he should come upstairs to renew our acquaintance. It was certainly not in my head that I was in other than an exclusively male society. So I was casually buttoning my flies with one hand and feeling for my braces with the other when the door opened at my call and a young woman walked in.

IV

'DUNCAN, I VERY much want you to meet Mabel.' The
words came to me—but only just, since the voice was not a
strong one—from somewhere behind the lady in the doorway.
It was not immediately apparent that the lady, on her part,
wanted to meet me. Her demeanour was shamefast—an
archaic word to be excused as carrying a useful ambiguity. It
was only modest in the girl—thus suddenly confronting a
man fumbling with his buttons—to cast her gaze fixedly upon
the shabby college carpet, but her bearing also hinted a
shyness in excess of this situation—one approaching the
awkward or even mildly pathological. Awkwardness, however,
might be something merely reflected upon her by her escort,
who had made such gauche haste to introduce her without
for a moment pausing to identify himself. But he did now
advance, edging clumsily round his bashful companion to
reveal a slight, almost *chétif* figure of about my own age. He was
dressed in tails which failed to fit him very well, and over
which he already wore his M.A. gown. 'Cyril Bedworth,'
this person went on, seeing me at a loss. 'Duncan, congratu-
lations on a splendid new play!'

Bedworth was somebody else I hadn't seen for many
years, but there was nevertheless something peculiarly unfortunate about my moment's blankness before him. He
carried around with him the effect of being a forgettable sort
of man, and was to be presumed sensitively aware of the fact.
And here he was, saying a generous thing with obvious
sincerity—whereas he might perfectly well have produced that
familiar 'Do you still write plays?'

But if I was embarrassed it was only partly because I hadn't
been quick enough. Cyril Bedworth's tone had recalled to my
memory a salient feature of his character long ago. This had

been, quite simply, his artless admiration for myself, for Tony Mumford, and for what an old fashioned writer might call our set. It couldn't have been a rational admiration, since we were singularly without qualities meriting solid regard. He had simply been in love with us collectively—rather as Helen Schlegel had been in love with the Wilcoxes. But at least no ill consequence, such as Forster's novel records, had resulted in Bedworth's case. And now, as if all loyalty to that fallacious estimate of my worth, he was eager to reveal the wonderful achievement of having acquired a wife.

So I paid my respects to Mrs Bedworth in form, and invited her to sit down on the less broken-springed of Junkin's two arm-chairs. She did so still without venturing to raise her eyes, and also with what seemed unnecessary care in the matter of disposing her skirt round her ankles. I reflected that I myself was still in my shirt-sleeves. Then it struck me that Mabel Bedworth, whose note was so decidedly quiet, was nevertheless almost as much as her husband dressed for a formal evening occasion. Why, I asked myself in sudden panic, was she here at all—only some minutes before the Gaudy guests would be beginning to assemble? Had Bedworth, whose early circumstances had not permitted the acquiring of much social expertness, fallen into a stark misconception, in some bizarre fashion persuading himself that wives, too, were bidden to the college board? It would be an error too monstrous for contemplation. Ought I to contrive an oblique remark that would alert them to the truth, and enable them to withdraw without confusion and rearrange their evening? Fortunately this imagination of chaos at once proved unfounded.

'Mabel has to fly,' Bedworth said. 'But she did so very much want to meet you. She has heard a great deal about you, Duncan, from time to time. And she does greatly admire your plays.'

Mrs Bedworth corroborated none of these statements. She just sat perfectly still. There was nothing hostile about her, nor any suggestion of being bored. Indeed, I had a sense that she felt something more electrical to be in the air than was objectively there at all. I might have solved this small enigma at once if it hadn't become necessary for me to put up some conversation myself.

'I wonder how many of us have been lodged in our old rooms.' I said. 'Here am I. And Tony—you remember Tony Mumford, Cyril?—is over the way.'

'Yes, Tony—of course.' Bedworth had jerked oddly in his chair, so that a spring twanged alarmingly. It was almost as if, unaccountably, he was troubled by this unremarkable information 'I mustn't miss having a word with him. It would be a mistake.'

'He'll be looking forward to it.' Bedworth's last remark had puzzled me. 'And it seems that Gavin Mogridge is down there on the ground floor. The celebrity among us, he must be called. But it's only Tony that the scout on the staircase pretends to remember. When you and I become lords, Cyril, he'll pretend to remember us too. Are you in that very attractive attic?'

'No, no—in Howard.' Bedworth produced this with an enhanced and almost startled lack of ease which made me suppose I had been tactlessly patronising about the attractiveness of the attic. Already in my time, although there were plenty of wealthy men in the college, there can have been few who were exceptionally poor—whose poverty, that is, was much deeper than that of a substantial number of their companions. One would have had to go back to between the wars—to the generation, that would be, of Ivo Mumford's grandfather—to find poor scholars who were struggling at Oxford on pretty well nothing at all. But Cyril Bedworth through some unknown special circumstance *was* notably poor, and it seemed reasonable to suppose that he felt touchy about it, and about the unimpressive character of his accommodation beneath the leads. His poverty in itself would have limited the freedom of his association with many of us; in addition to which I am afraid we were sometimes inclined to mix up being poor with being poor-spirited. Not that we lacked delicacy (something of which young men have a surprising command) in any direct dealings with narrow budgets. If Bedworth became covertly a figure of fun with us it was on no such account. Physically he had been notably unattractive. He was, for example, still in serious adolescent trouble with his complexion. So in one nonsense-saga of our contriving he became the reigning college catamite of his year, and we affected to feel the blood hammering in our temples when we passed him in the quad. It is possible, I suppose, that his mere name provoked whimsy of this sort.

I saw now that his spots had cleared up, and also that something, not immediately definable, had happened to his features which must be connected with processes going on behind them. But he was still what we had called a grey man. Ivo's grandfather, I believe, would have said a sub man, and Ivo's contemporaries no doubt had a term of their own. (Vocabularies change; intolerance does not.) As for his capacity for admiring others—a trait not unamiable in itself—it seemed only too likely that worldly experience had attenuated any disposition of the sort. Perhaps he had transferred the balance of it to his wife, of whom he was obviously immensely proud, and to the children who might be conjectured to have blessed their union.

'Do you think Oxford has changed much?' I asked Bedworth. It seemed a banal question in the uttering, and in fact I had substituted it for another that had been forming on my tongue. What did Cyril Bedworth do? It is reasonable to ask a former acquaintance, after an interval of many years, about his walk in life. But Bedworth knew that I wrote plays, and had handsomely referred to the fact, so there seemed something uncivil in an inquiry which *ipso facto* relegated him to the anonymous crowd. The question upon which I had fallen back seemed to afford him difficulty, and at the same time to strike him as of substantial import.

'I find it hard to decide,' he said seriously. 'I should like to hear what you think yourself. Yours ought to be the sharper impression, really.'

I didn't know quite how to take this. It appeared to be a recrudescence of the admiration theme, a tribute to the superior acuity of mind which a writer must necessarily bear over persons in some such unassuming employment as Bedworth's own. (By this time I had decided, I believe, that he was respectably ensconced with an old-established firm of chartered accountants.) Before I could take the matter further an extraordinary thing had happened.

Up to this moment Mabel Bedworth had preserved, immobile, her dim downcast presence in Junkin's best chair, and only the picking up of her handbag indicated that it would indeed be necessary for her presently to 'fly'. This doesn't mean that she was a negligible presence. Two or three discreet glances had persuaded me that I found her a good deal more interesting than her husband. She was by a number of years the younger of the two; and, of course, it wouldn't have been difficult for her to be much the better looking. She was, in fact, beautiful in a soft, slightly obliterated way—not colourful but monochromatic: a composition in sepias, and with features which seemed in a perpetual quiver, as if being viewed through a veil of all but imperceptibly stirring gauze. Such was Mrs Bedworth, and by this time I believed I had the shamefastness diagnosed. Either the blood rather easily hammered in Mrs Bedworth's own temples, or she was the sort of woman who is fated, through no particular volition of her own and upon principles inviolably arcane, herself to set it hammering in a high proportion of any male temples coming her way. She carried round with her, whether she liked it or not, the mysterious power to generate acute sexual awareness.

This was an interesting discovery, but the extraordinary happening was something other. Hard upon the abortive exchange of views between her husband and myself on the perennial problem of a changing Oxford, Mrs Bedworth had looked up for the first time. It was for the purpose of giving me a momentary glance of intense amusement. And then she was on her feet.

'The little women,' she said to me—and her voice, low and husky, has to be recorded as doing something to my spine—'must be off to their poached eggs.'

She kissed her husband on the cheek and walked out of the room.

I was again reduced to rash hypothesis. The Bedworths, I told myself, had for the occasion of the Gaudy joined up with perhaps two or three other old-boy couples (if the expression is admissible), and the women were going to dine together in a restaurant while, in hall, the august and masculine feasting went on. I would have asked Bedworth if this were so, had I not noticed that he was upset. He appeared to judge that his wife's conduct had been lacking in decorum. I felt no patience with this, and I believe I almost said to myself, as I should certainly have done twenty odd years before: 'Lord, what a silly little man!' That I didn't actually do so was to the credit of a lurking intuition beginning to build up in me about this nervous person's quality. There was more to him, somehow, than memory suggested.

'Mabel is very fond of Virginia Woolf,' Bedworth said suddenly.

This was a piece of knock-out bewilderment. For a moment I even thought that Cyril Bedworth had been drinking; that he was now in a fuddled way confounding me with a more celebrated dramatist; and was announcing that my *chef-d'œuvre* was one of his wife's favourite plays. To such wild misconception there was no reply, and into my confounded silence Bedworth spoke again.

'I must really have a civil word with Lord Marchpayne,' he said. 'With Tony,' he emended quickly. He jumped up and made for the door. 'I do hope, Duncan, we'll meet again later in the evening.' He moved as hastily as he had spoken, so that in a moment he was gone. But his tone, although wholly un-assertive, had mysteriously put me in possession of a discon-certing truth. Cyril Bedworth was a fellow of the college—and thus one of my hosts, not another guest. It was my large and confident unawareness of this that had amused his wife. So much was entirely clear. But something in the way he had spoken of Tony was as baffling as had been the remark about Virginia Woolf.

When I went downstairs a few minutes later I ran into Gavin Mogridge. The hero (for he had been that too) and historian of the ill-fated Mochica Expedition stood surveying Surrey through the doorway much as if the quadrangle were a trackless waste for guidance across which the white man must patiently await the arrival of some trustworthy native. This appearance was enhanced rather than diminished by the circumstance of Mogridge's being in evening dress; one felt that—this night as every night—the garments had been extricated from a tin trunk and composedly donned by the light of a hurricane lantern round which there flapped unspeakable insects and an occasional vampire bat. Bleached, stringy, dehydrated, Mogridge might have been described as the typical all-weather model of the late-nineteenth century wandering Englishman. Were he to walk across the Sahara, one felt, it would be without troubling to unfurl the sunshade nonchalantly slung on his arm; if he unexpectedly met an old acquaintance in the vicinity of Kampa Dzong or the Rongbuk Glacier he would infallibly join the stroll to the summit of Mount Everest.

What I tried to recall now was the extent to which these potentialities had already been written upon the 'cello-walloping Mogridge of my distant recollection. At least here was the mature man, and I had an instant sense that he hadn't changed a bit. His vagueness, his absence of mind were gigantic; at this moment he was eyeing me so unregardingly that I wondered whether he commonly distinguished between a man and a newel-post.

'Oh, Duncan,' Mogridge said, 'do you gather they're anywhere running to a drink?'

He had spoken—thus in the instant of glimpsing me for the first time in twenty years—precisely as if we had been in a room together five minutes before. I felt it incumbent upon me to make equally little fuss about this picking up of threads.

'Drinks are in the Great Quad, I believe.'

'The Great Quad?' Repeating the words on a note of interrogation, Mogridge peered now in one direction and now in another across Surrey, so that I almost persuaded myself I should actually have to take on the role of that faithful black and proceed to hack a path for him through the jungle. 'Ah, the Great Quad!' He turned a little, and pointed to the notice concerning itself with the wiping of feet—Plot's handiwork, as I now understood it to be. For a moment I took it that Mogridge's myopia was such that he was mistaking this for a ground-plan of the college, courteously provided by the Provost and fellows for the convenience of tourists. 'I think it's a joke,' Mogridge said. 'Don't you?'

'It has crossed my mind.'

'Just striking out *feet*, I mean.'

'I know you do.'

'One of the men on this staircase, I expect.'

'A good guess, almost certainly.' I had forgotten the pace at which the unkindled Mogridge's mind moved. 'We could ask Plot.'

'Plot? Oh, the scout. Yes. Whether there's a left-handed man.'

'Left-handed?'

'Yes.' Mogridge was now according Plot's request all the attention which (had things fallen out as planned) he would once have been able to direct upon some fragment of Mochica masonry. 'The stroke cancelling that word runs from ten o'clock to four. That's left-handed. A right-handed person would make his from two o'clock to eight. Don't you agree?'

I saw no reason not to. Mogridge hadn't in the least been showing off a mental affinity with such fictional characters as Hercule Poirot and Lord Peter Wimsey. He must simply own some habit of precise observation which didn't (as so much of him was celebrated for doing) slumber for years at a time. At the moment, I seized upon the reference to eight o'clock as suggesting that our aperitif must be secured now or not at all. Several other guests were hurrying across Surrey, converging upon the lofty archway that led into the Great Quadrangle. We set out in pursuit of these.

'Do you remember Cyril Bedworth,' I asked, 'who used to be on our staircase? He seems to have become a don.'

'Oh, yes—of course. I've met him several times at these dinners. Haven't you?'

'This is the first I've been to.'

'Ah, then you wouldn't have met him.'

'No.' I realized how, with Mogridge, every stage of a discussion had to reach a full close. 'But he looked in on me a few minutes ago. He brought his wife.'

'Bedworth is married?'

'That would seem to be the inference.'

'It's perfectly natural.' Mogridge said this a shade severely, as if I must be indicted of attempting some pointless levity. 'And you would have met him again if you'd come to *any* of these Gaudies over the past twenty years. He has been here pretty well all the time. He stayed up, I think, and took a second degree.' Mogridge paused; he obviously felt this had been quite something. 'It was probably a B.Litt. That's a Bachelor of Letters.'

'So I've heard. But I've always supposed things of that sort were pursued by a pretty dim crowd. Of course Cyril didn't exactly sparkle.'

'I suppose not.' This time, Mogridge's pause was a brooding one. 'Do you still write novels, Duncan?'

'Plays. Yes, I do.'

'Of course I remember that you were thinking of taking up literature right from the start. You will probably find that you and Bedworth have a good deal to talk about. Bedworth is literature also. I believe he is your old tutor's Number Two. Talboys, isn't it?'

'Talbert.' I was astonished by the information about my

66

late caller. 'Do you know what sort of thing Bedworth goes in for?'

'He has published at least one critical study.' The author of *Mochica*—that unchallengeable masterpiece in its kind—communicated this further intelligence in a tone of deep respect. 'I am sure you will have heard of it, Duncan. It is called *Proust and Powell*. Or perhaps it is *Powell and Proust*. Two novelists. One English and one French. So I suppose Bedworth must be said to go in for Comparative Literature. It is probably a particularly difficult field.'

I found myself glancing at Gavin Mogridge askance—which was, of course, the manner in which his own curious trick of vision made him appear to be regarding me. As we passed under the archway (its multitudinous bosses are a blaze of heraldry, with the carved stone brilliantly painted and gilded in the fashionable manner) we must therefore have presented the appearance of a couple of white-chested china dogs, eyeing each other across a fireplace. I tried to remember what kind of a sense of humour Mogridge owned in an earlier time. Nothing came to me, and I had to conclude he had owned none at all. So he hadn't in any way been pulling my leg. Nor was there anything much odder in his telling me that Proust was a French novelist and Powell an English one than there was (when I came to think of it) in Bedworth's having taken up these two particular writers for the purpose of critical disquisition.

Had I been asked in recent years (as I certainly had not) about Cyril Bedworth's undergraduate studies, I should probably have believed myself able to recall them as concerned with the extreme antiquities of English literature. But this would only have been a consequence of a generally held persuasion that the more reclusive personalities around the college tended to occupy themselves in that field. In fact, Bedworth must have begun by reading Modern Languages, and it was I myself who, inspired by an elderly don called Timbermill, had for a time absorbed myself in the pursuit of mere-dragons, marsh-steppers, eldritch wives, whales, loathly worms, and argumentative nightingales and owls. Yet even if Bedworth had been bred among monsters, the preparation would not have been inapposite to encounter with Charlus and Widmerpool, both of whom own that dimension of the grotesque without which, as Proust himself remarks, major art cannot be.

This rumination took me into the Great Quadrangle, and simultaneously out of the company of Mogridge, who drifted away with as little stir as he had drifted up. His goal, one felt, might have been indifferently a glass of sherry or whatever today is the equivalent of the sources of the Nile. It was part of the mystery of his career that, ever since *Mochica,* he had doggedly if intermittently projected himself as a traveller and natural-born travel-writer without ever attaining striking success again. He seemed not a man who came alive before a mere itinerary, even if it was of a tolerably taxing sort. Mogridge needed—all too plainly, he needed—an occasion, an hour, a crisis of the most absolute order. If he had a second time found such, it had hitherto passed unrecorded. The published episodes of his later wandering life were, if the truth be told, a little dull. I thought—it appeared the idlest of thoughts—that it would be fun to be present when, or if, his moment came again.

I had a few minutes to look round. It was an animated scene: animated in compressing within the view some three hundred living souls, and literally a scene to the extent that their setting held its hint of the theatrical. The Great Quadrangle was like a child's fort as such things were when my father was a boy: this chiefly because battlemented within as well as without, as if in a less urbane age rival factions of the learned, although all quartered within the curtilage of the college, had been accustomed to direct cross-bows at one another from behind these lurking places. The inward-facing crenellations had replaced a balustrade during some phase of Gothicizing exuberance in the early nineteenth century. Equally suggestive of the nursery was the large flag—exactly square, like the Great Quadrangle itself—which at moments blew so stiffly out on its staff above the leads that it might have been made not of fabric but of tin, like those which astronauts round about that time had taken to planting on the surface of the moon. This one displayed in an improbable-seeming blazon the personal standard of the most magnificent of England's kings.

Sunshine slanted into the quadrangle still. It caught the jets flung up by the central fountain. In the surrounding lily pool it glittered on the scales of the great chub and its attendant goldfish, ide, and orfe, so that these became a watery analogue of the land monsters now assembling around them. It fell, too, on the long linen-covered tables (where the drinks were) along the terrace to the east. On one hand it already showed the college's lovely tower in gentle semi-silhouette; and on the other continued to bathe in a full summer warmth the hidden chapel's ancient spire.

If all this made up the toy castle, the guests were the toy soldiers. The majority, whose black tails were for the most part concealed beneath equally black M.A. gowns like my own, presented a predominantly sombre show. But the gleam of their shirts and waistcoats and the glitter of their decorations (for it was remarkable how many of these middle-aged men had picked up something of the kind) provided enough relief to suggest at least those splendidly dark-uniformed but braided and beribboned hussars who formed the aristocracy of the toy-box. One missed, it was true, the horses—to say nothing of the field-guns. But the more learned, or at least senior, academics outshone in splendour the redcoats, the Highland regiments, the whole Household Division. 'Scarlet' was no more than a code-word for the doctoral finery; one could rehearse the whole spectrum or palette without exhausting the gorgeousness of their array.

Quite suddenly, I understood about Mrs Bedworth and Virginia Woolf. Like that spirited feminist, the serious Cyril's wife found masculine hierarchy, pomp, circumstance and adornment exquisitely absurd. *Three Guineas* (which contains a

69

satirically presented photograph called 'A University Procession') was one of her sacred books—and no doubt *A Room of One's Own* was another. Whenever, but it can't have been often, she raised her eyes to the Oxford spectacle, she found in it perhaps a prompting to indignation, but certainly an enormous joke. She must at this moment be settling down, with other dons' formally attired wives, to what she had called the little women's poached egg. I made a note of Mabel Bedworth in my mind as one new acquaintance I wanted to meet again.

A servant bore down upon me with a tray laden with glasses of sherry; the stuff came in two steeply contrasting shades, so that there should be no mistaking sweet for dry. Another servant, seemingly of greater consequence, handed me a sheet of folded pasteboard which proved to provide a menu, information about a number of wines, a toast list, and a seating plan for the entire company. I was about to consult this *vade mecum* in order to discover on whom I should presently be dependent for my more immediate entertainment when I found that Albert Talbert was once more confronting me.

'Ah,' Talbert said at his huskiest, 'Dalrymple again!' But upon this his distant seismic mirth immediately followed, and I realized that what was being registered was the absurdity of his ever having mistaken me for so unlikely a personage. I might, I knew, be Dalrymple to him once more in an hour's time, but it was nice to be securely Pattullo for the moment. 'I believe the Provost is bound to have much to discuss with you,' Talbert went on—mysteriously and with an instant switch to his inexpressible gravity. 'But there is tomorrow. It would give my wife great pleasure if you could come to tea in Old Road.'

This was *verbatim* a formula from twenty years back, and disconcerting for that reason. But it was disconcerting, too, because I had no thought of lingering in Oxford more than an hour beyond breakfast next morning, nor any belief that the college would in the least want to put up with me (or anybody else) for longer than that. But I saw that I must either plead another engagement or return a genuine acceptance at once. It was likely, indeed, that the proposal would vanish from Talbert's recollection almost on the instant. I couldn't risk a mere diplomatic murmur, all the same; in addition to which I found even the polite fiction that Mrs Talbert would like to see me unexpectedly pleasing.

'Thank you,' I said, and just stopped myself from adding a respectful 'Sir'. 'I shall look forward to it very much.' This, too, was formulaic, but more sincerely uttered than sometimes in the past. 'I think it's four o'clock? I'll walk up.' Talbert had always liked to hear of his pupils as engaging in pedestrianism, which he regarded as the most wholesome employment of periods of leisure.

'Four o'clock.' Talbert nodded weightily, almost as if some sombre astrological significance attended this hour, and prepared to move away. But he paused for a moment longer, and I saw he was making sure I had put on my white tie. His own tie was white, but so yellowed at the edges that it had the appearance of a rare species of butterfly. I noticed that his shoes, correspondingly, although now decently black, showed signs of having begun life as brown, and I remembered that Dekker and Massinger hadn't brought him a penny. I was still feeling decently ashamed that half a dozen over-sprightly comedies had put me within reach of a modest competence when he turned and toddled off. 'Toddled' is the necessary word. I recalled a stage direction in which, somewhat extravagantly, I had required the actor playing some Talbert-figure of my imagination to progress in the manner of that sort of street toy (for I love such things) constructed thus to move down a gentle inclined plane. It wasn't a motion that seemed to cohere with Talbert's rather spare figure; one would think of it as right for a tubby man with short legs. The explanation lay in Boanerges, the Talberts' dog. Boanerges was an ill-trained dog—having suffered, I suppose, like the Talberts' children in some respects, through that excessive household addiction to folios and quartos. For years Boanerges, straining (doggedly, one may say) on his lead, had hauled Albert Talbert at a precarious bodily incline all over Oxford and its countryside. I had frequently been privileged to accompany them. Boanerges must long since have passed away. But the inclination remained, and produced the forward-slanted toddle.

There was now much noise in the Great Quadrangle, and I got the impression that an unnatural proportion of the guests —a proportion, that is, in excess of the moiety that balanced conversation would posit—must be talking simultaneously. Hunger, nervousness, exuberance, and perhaps a persuasion that in such a hubbub it is easier to utter than to hear, contributed to this conduct. People were also doing much charging at each other, laughing loudly in one another's faces, and vigorously shaking hands. As group behaviour this perhaps represented a syndrome of middle-age. Old Mr Mumford's lot would show more restraint, and the younger generation due to turn up to the Gaudy following this one would not quite have forgotten the casual grace that attends undergraduate social intercourse. I decided that I hated this *nel mezzo cammin* business and being myself like all these men so inescapably entered upon what another poet has called the stupidity of one's middle years. Although already aware of a number of people whom it would be mannerless not presently to greet, I elected for the moment a watching role. Some others were doing the same thing. There were men who combined an odd-man-out stance with a composure in which nothing factitious appeared; wine glass in hand, these simply contemplated the scene as one might contemplate a waterfall or the monkey-house in a zoo. Others were uneasy and irresolute—doubtful here of a welcome, and suspecting there the hint of an amused regard. A few behaved in a manner I have observed among practiced party-going women awkwardly circumstanced amid strangers or uncongenial persons— moving rapidly here and there, now with a parting glance or gesture over a shoulder, and now with the air of edging their way towards some suddenly glimpsed boon companion in a farther corner of the quad. I was wondering how this particular vagary of self-consciousness could be made lucid on the stage when I became aware that the evening's activities were entering a new phase.

So far, I hadn't remarked what, in another context, would be termed the top brass. The Provost, the Chancellor of the University, the Vice-Chancellor, the personages of high distinction—whether academic, political, or even artistic—who had elsewhere been receiving sundry honours earlier that day: these and others of consequence had not been provided with their sherry, as had the majority, *en plein air*. They had been hob-nobbing together in the senior common room, appropriated for the occasion to the uses of a VIP lounge. Now a door of this *arcanum* giving on the Great Quadrangle had been thrown open, and these important people were emerging in a kind of half-hearted formal procession, and with a diffident dignity at once comical and impressive. The Provost walked beside the Chancellor, a former Prime Minister. The Pro-Provost guided the tottering steps of a Swedish physicist, even more eminent than aged. Similar notabilities followed, and then came a few of the more senior fellows, together with a handful of old members who were to be presumed marginally more distinguished than the main body of their contemporaries—whether in Church or State, Learning, the Law, or the armed forces of the Crown. I was edified to see that Tony—Lord Marchpayne, as I ought now to think of him—had made the top grade. He was far from looking out of place in it.

The appearance of this company—in multi-coloured shambling state, like a file of richly caparisoned camels emerging from a caravanserai—caused some abatement, although not anything so absurd as an awed silence, in the larger concourse dispersed as with an appropriate symbolism at a slightly lower level around it. The drop in volume was the occasion, as it happened, of a curious effect of orchestration. As when the trumpets and the tubas, breathless, cease to blare, and are succeeded by the melody of the wood-winds calling from a different world, so now there percolated into the Great

Quadrangle from some adjacent corner of the college the clear voices and brief laughter of young men enjoying themselves. They may have been outrageously skylarking, or they may have been playing croquet—but they were certainly undergraduates, and probably in one way or another expelling the stale air of the Examination Schools from their lungs. The sound ceased. It was as if it had floated through glades and ridings to touch the ear of a bustling rout or hunting party—this only for a moment, since the alien folk producing it were departing under the hill.

I was probably alone in thinking of the fairies. General salivation was taking place at the promising signs that dinner was going to happen at last. The procession moved on towards the broad staircase leading up to the hall. Only one incident interrupted its progress, and Tony was responsible for this. He had observed some elderly acquaintance down below: a retired fellow of the college, perhaps, who had modestly taken his station amid the herd. Tony's gesture was to break ranks, run down two or three steps, shake hands with this person, compress into seconds what had the appearance of a leisurely exchange of talk, and skip back into his place just as the Provost's party began its climb. It would have been easy—crudely put—to make a muck of this turn; a breath of the over-affable, the slightest forcing of the cordial note, and any observer of the kind congregated here would have judged that the chap thought too much of himself. I saw at once, however, that Tony owned skill in such small performances.

'A pleasant fellow, Marchpayne.' A clergyman—vaguely known to me, and with whom I had already exchanged a nod—murmured this as we fell into step together. 'I'm delighted by his signal promotion.'

'I haven't heard about it.'

'Marchpayne has gained a seat in the Cabinet. The reshuffle came over on the six o'clock news.'

I said that I was delighted too, and it struck me that Tony must have known about his elevation while we were consuming

Plot's tea and anchovy toast together. But he had kept it under his hat—the bowler hat that had lain on the table between us—and spoken of himself casually as a reliable junior Minister. Perhaps it would have been awkward in him to say anything else—particularly since I had so culpably known hardly a thing about him. He was evidently hard-working, and didn't readily take time off. That handshake had seemed to me entirely political—as much a reflex action as the patting or kissing of babies. Yet I already possessed evidence that it was not in the interest of his career or his party that Tony, on the present occasion, was pertinaciously engaged.

I might have got further with this had I not, on the very threshold of hall, at last consulted my *vade mecum*, and discovered to my surprise that Ranald McKechnie would be seated on my right.

V

RETROSPECTION MAY be among the pleasures of advancing age, but it can prove an unnerving indulgence as well. Memory trundles us at will back to any point on the lengthening corridor—and there waiting for us is not a dead but an unfinished self. We join him on his journey and walk with him for as long as we please, yet our companionship is on unequal terms, since as revenants we command a forward vision which he lacks. The corridor turns, darkens, deceives with whispering ambitions. We, because we have walked this way before, cannot be surprised or disillusioned like our doppelgänger, but of the two it is we who are the more aware of the constant play of the contingent upon the small unfolding history. Were we philosophers surveying the macrocosm, we might view unperturbed what tiny accidents, unidentifiable by the most pertinacious historian, have controlled humanity's dance through recorded time. But as seen in the microcosm of our personal fortunes the unslumbering, pouncing inconsequence alarms.

This is a portentous way of introducing McKechnie—in whose company I was about to eat (as the *vade mecum* told me) a number of uncomplicated dishes beginning with smoked trout and ending with strawberry meringue. But the point is that he and I had been at school together, and that his coming to Oxford had been the sole occasion of my coming too. I was to be sitting beside a man who had brought Chance into my life very prominently indeed.

Our school, a mixed affair of day-boys and boarders after a fashion infrequent in the English scheme of things, had been founded as a device of the *haute bourgeoisie* of Edinburgh for segregating their sons from less privileged boys and thereby gaining them a firmer grip on the professional hierarchies of the city. That had been when the Modern Athens was enjoying its Indian Summer. Bleak and Doric (as I have said), brutal (until shortly before my generation), Philistine (still): the school was 'classical' in the severest way, treating drill in the ancient languages as the sole purpose of education. It dominated the Scottish bench and bar, the university, the consulting-rooms and, to a lesser extent, the established presbyterian Kirk. It was a highly successful monopoly affair, erected on a strong regional basis, and I don't know why, by my time, it had taken to slanting itself southward as it had. Its Rector was a diminutive Etonian; its masters were nearly all large, expatriate, and slightly bewildered Englishmen, dismayed by the absence of county cricket, murmuring to us of Balliol and New College, Emmanuel and King's. On Sundays we went—the day-boys—in kilts to St Giles' or St Cuthbert's, and along with our parents and aunts hearkened to persons of quasi-Calvinistic persuasion wrestling with the Lord in conceived prayer. But on weekdays the whole school temperately hinted to the same deity that he should fulfil the desires and petitions of his servants as might be most expedient for them, or direct and prosper the High Court of Parliament, under our most religious and gracious King at that time assembled. (These extraordinary Anglican prayers, given a final polish by a flock of divines at the command of a defected Scottish monarch, were among my first glimpses of the urbanity of the English tongue.) Nearly all the alert and clever boys had a notion of going to Oxford. With some of us the pull appeared to be romantic and poetic rather than intellectual. The Scholar Gipsy fled our gaze amid the contours of the Pentland hills. The Last Enchantments blew around us as we played our barbarous games with wooden bats (employed, too, as instruments of correction by prefects) and napless tennis-balls in the pebbly playgrounds we called the 'yards'.

My father professed to be an Anglophobe. Next after the French, whom he regarded as our nearest civilized neighbours, he liked the Irish—this even although they had never produced a great painter. He liked seeing Shaw's plays. He would sometimes pore over *Ulysses*, although he was a man who didn't often read a book. Had I, at seventeen, gone to him and announced that the time had come for me to take up residence in Dublin, or even better in Paris, I believe he would at once have consulted his bank manager about what could be done. But the idea of Oxford he didn't care for at all. If I wanted to write, he said, I had better keep clear of a country that had produced H. G. Wells and John Galsworthy. Such talk on my father's part was mere random prejudice. But he was an obstinate man.

Then he received a commission to paint Professor McKechnie. At that time he still undertook occasional oil portraits, as well as more numerous portrait-sketches in crayon or pastel: these last for what he called dentist's money, although I imagine the proceeds were quite enough to pay my brother's school fees and my own. He would almost certainly have become a distinguished portrait painter had he not so firmly settled his allegiance elsewhere.

> *Nature and Nature's laws lay hid in night*:
> *God said*, Let Monet be! *and all was light*.

I remember his delight when I thus perverted for him Pope's couplet.

The occasions with Professor McKechnie were not a success; nor, I imagined, was the portrait, although I had never set eyes on it. There were both social and temperamental incompatabilities. My father was a man of the people, and an artist; in my mother he had married, by what was virtually a *mésalliance*, the daughter of a Highland laird. The McKechnies had been scholars and allied to scholars for generations; the present one was a philosopher, a belated representative of a branch of the species known, I believe, as the Scottish Hegelians. He was very shy, but very chilly as well; he must have hated having his likeness taken by an ill-dressed limner smelling of whisky; no spark could be struck out of him—nor the acceptance of anything except a cup of tea and a minimum of polite conversation.

Even so, the odds would have been on my father's merely laughing at Professor McKechnie, and perhaps making ludicrous sketches of him for the amusement of fellow artists in congenial hostelries. For some reason, however, he took an active dislike to his sitter, and thereafter referred to him as the Dreich, a Scots word so inherently expressive as to require no gloss. The Dreich appeared to have been a little less than dreich only on one topic, that of his son Ranald, whose accomplishments—my father took it into his head—he exhibited with a tedious particularity as being comprehensively superior to my own. There was certainly plenty of scope for such a comparison. Ranald McKechnie, although nearly a year younger than myself, was already what we called Dux of the school; he had graduated from Virgil and Horace and Herodotus and Euripides to more mysterious writers such as Lucretius and Pindar; he had been the recipient of sundry medals, prizes, and bursaries; and he had lately gained an Open Scholarship to Oxford. Moreover, it appeared that Ranald was a promising performer on the violin. (To this last brag it pleased my father to assert that he had responded with the information—which was totally untrue—that I had lately switched from the bagpipes to the big drum in the JTC band.)

This episode in my father's professional life, which I had no difficulty in accepting as gospel at the time, has come with the years to bear a character altogether implausible in my mind. It is impossible that Professor McKechnie should have delivered the sustained comparative discourse attributed to him. My father must have made up at least the greater part of the encounter, a recital of which would keep him happily employed for half an hour on end. But as virtually his own brain-child he was all the fonder of it, so that he rapidly came to believe in its substantial reality. At the same time, there must have been a kernel of truth in the little saga of the boastful Hegelian; otherwise my father would not so dramatically have proceeded from words to action.

I have recorded that he was in many ways a negligent and even scandalous parent. It would not normally have occurred to him that my progress at school ought to be the subject of encouragement, admonishment, or any sort of notice at all, any more than it would have occurred to him that I needed a bath or a new pair of shoes. He was aware that I had taken to scribbling, but would have supposed this in a normal order of things even had I persisted in the activity twelve hours a day. He occasionally read what I had written, and commented on it not as to the schoolboy I in fact was but as if I were a contemporary of his own. This could be disconcerting, but I was to come to regard five minutes of it as having been a good deal more useful than five hours of Talbert's tutorials. It was these tutorials that now lay unexpectedly ahead of me.

Because of his indignation against the Dreich, it occurred to my father to rummage through some drawer of my mother's until he found a stack of my school reports. I doubt whether he had so much as glanced at them when, twice a term, they arrived by post. Now he read them through, and his main discovery was that over a period of ten years (for it was a school at which one was expected to spend a quite dauntingly high proportion of one's total life-span) I had been wholly undistinguished in the studies principally approved by the place. But I had always come first in the subject vaguely known as English, and within the previous twelve months had collected in this field prizes open to competition by the entire school. On the basis of these facts my father conjectured— correctly, although he might well have been quite wrong—that I had twice triumphed over Ranald McKechnie (whom he now referred to as Wee Dreichie) as a juvenile authority on *Old Mortality, Idylls of the King* and, I seem to remember, *The Advantages and Disadvantages of Civilization*. What then came to my father was the thought that I could repeat this performance on other territory.

My father packed a bag, called a taxi, and went off to the Waverley station. We supposed his destination to be London, since he had a number of friends there, for the most part senior to himself. (Sickert and Steer, his early masters, had both died at a great age a few years before, but he kept in touch with some minor men who had remained faithful to the ideas of the Camden Town Group.) He was in fact on his way to Oxford.

He put up at the Mitre and walked around. Tony Mumford would have said that he was casing the joint. I have an idea that it shook him much as Carcassonne or Albi had once done. He walked up to Boars Hill, and from that modest altitude surveyed the city in late-afternoon sunshine. He was sufficiently impressed to make the same expedition five hours later—thereby coming to identify, I don't doubt, the line of festal light in Christ-Church hall. On the next day he took a fuller view of the several colleges. He was later to admit having expended almost an hour in studying Magdalen Tower from several viewpoints. Why he decided against that particular place of education I don't know. Conceivably he had once dipped into Gibbon's *Autobiographies*, and derived the impression that matters were rather slackly conducted there. He eventually plumped for the Radcliffe Observatory, for he had once seen the real Temple of the Winds and judged that here was a pretty good English imitation: he was distressed upon discovering this particular architectural landmark to be unprovided with residential accommodation. But a further prowl brought him within what was to become known to me as the Great Quadrangle. He traversed it, turned, and was looking at another tower—one under which he had passed on entering. It was only one look, since he owned a practiced eye. He walked back to the gate, and asked to be directed to the office of the Principal.

I have failed, I see, to mention that my father was an impressive person. I should be giving a misleading sketch if I were to let the whisky and the unpromising attire suggest that he was any sort of Gully Jimson. Within a few minutes he was in the presence of the Provost, and informing him that he proposed to commit his younger son Duncan to his charge.

It was to be a moot point on the staircase whether the Provost, in his early prime, was more handsome than urbane or more urbane than handsome, but there was agreement that a certain masked and even august indecisiveness attended his character. Certainly he didn't know how to cope effectively with my father. It was a date at which a couple of generations must have passed since even a Duke of Buccleuch could reasonably have walked into the place and announced such a simple disposition of things. The Provost professed an extreme of interest. Told that my particular line lay with *Old Mortality* and *The Advantages and Disadvantages of Civilization,* he may have thought that he saw a gleam of light. The college, he explained, offered a single Open Scholarship for young men proposing to study English Language and Literature, and nothing could be more agreeable to him than that Mr Pattullo's son should offer himself for the examination—the more so as all other places were unfortunately booked up. My father brought out a pocket diary, and begged to know the date upon which I should present myself for the competition.

The Provost, as was proper in one in his position, was a respecter of persons. He was also a judge of them, and he was presumably beginning to like his visitor. He amiably suggested that it might assist my candidature were I to be provided with some printed particulars of the test, and on this pretext he got himself out of his library. Perhaps he employed his short absence in consulting the current issue of *Who's Who* in his secretary's room—a volume in which it happened to be recorded that my father was President-Elect of the Royal Scottish Academy. (This was a circumstance which was to produce a dramatic change in the Pattullo domestic economy.) When he returned it was with an invitation to stay to luncheon. It appears that the meal produced some conversation about Albrecht Dürer. My father was thereafter to judge the Provost, as a scholar, a decided improvement on the Dreich.

Chance had not closed its innings with me. The examination, when I presented myself for it a few weeks later, had every appearance of a shambles, so that I understood the whimsical but kindly regard which my headmaster had cast upon me when I told him it was going to happen. English literature turned out to occupy rather less of the show than I had expected, and the questions about it posited a kind of teaching and sophistication—although not, perhaps, an extent of reading—of which I was innocent. The ordeal ended with an essay paper. 'Intolerance,' I read, 'is twin-brother of conviction. Only those who believe in nothing can tolerate absolutely anything. Do you agree?' Whether or not I agreed was something, I felt sure, about which I could arrive at no decision in two hours flat. So could I 'discuss' as a 'proposition': 'No theatre is worth supporting that cannot support itself'? My subsequent fortunes suggest that I ought to have had a go at that one. But what arrested me was the last of the lot. It asked simply: 'Why do painters paint?'

I can see now that this was a stupid question, fudged up by a tired examiner. It asked eighteen-year-old boys to produce some sort of coherent thought in the field of aesthetic theory, which is absurd. But I saw it at the time as a very pertinent question indeed; one I was staggered to find had never entered my head, and which I somehow owed it to my father to get clear now. I unscrewed my pen and waded in.

I was sometimes to wonder, later on, under whose examining eye this last-ditch and fateful effort came. Could it conceivably have been Albert Talbert's own, reluctantly diverted to the chore from the more responsible task of determining whether *Keep the Widow Waking* can indeed be a lost play by Dekker, while Charles and Mary played Scrabble on the well-worn carpet at his feet? Whoever read it must have had a good deal of rational opposition to crush among those who had acquainted themselves with the rest of what I had written. But it was as a transformed personage styled John Ruskin Scholar that, in the following October, I again walked into the Great Quadrangle, and then on into Surrey, like a man entering his own house.

I seem to have been recounting these incidents as exemplifying the reach of the fortuitous in life. Had that portrait commission not come my father's way, and had his sitter not irritated him by dwelling on a son's precocious scholastic attainments, my career would have been shaped for me by quite other impulsions, probably as arbitrary as these. And at the time, excited and elated though I was, I certainly owned an occasional alarmed sense of being freakishly shoved around.

But were my father's motives quite as he represented them? He was a highly intelligent man, as most good artists are, although like many artists of his time he felt that this was something artists were wise to keep to themselves, since it wasn't intelligence that clients and patrons felt they were coming forward to buy. Again, inattentive to his children as he commonly appeared, it is probable that he took a hard look at us from time to time, and he may have thought to discern in me some slender talent which would be the better of removal for a time from its home ground. His own training had taken him far afield; at an age when I was still messing around with my bad Greek and worse Latin his eye had been already fixed on Rome. He had a feeling for the larger traditions and the major centres. If I were to write, he may have reflected, it would be in English—and better that, *pace* Wells and Galsworthy, than in some cranky synthetic Scots, comprehensible to nobody north of Perth or south of the Tweed. And he may have thought, finally, that if I could bring off something rather surprising it might do me a lot of good, and that if I failed I should only be learning what most of life is like. All these rational considerations may have been behind his descent on the Provost, and may have prompted him to sink his—itself rational—distrust of the hideous materialism of mid-twentieth century England. At the same time I don't doubt that my father genuinely pleased himself with the idea that Wee Dreichie and I were to continue in competition on the larger stage of the University of Oxford. This was sheer fantasy. Ranald McKechnie and I were going up to different colleges, to read different subjects, and there was no conceivable manner in which we could ever be thought of as rivals again.

I didn't suppose that we should become intimates. He had been regularly ahead of me, and we were arriving in Oxford simultaneously only because the John Ruskin business had erupted on me after an improperly brief period in the Classical Sixth. Moreover, Ranald McKechnie was an unobtrusive boy, much taken up with his books. Still, I did now assume we should acknowledge each other, and I was startled when, in my first Oxford week, he scurried straight past me in the street. More than that, he adopted a ducking posture which was unnerving; he was a pallid youth with a tip-tilted nose which he was now directing at the pavement of the Corn-market much like a maniac deep in some fantasy of being a plough or a bulldozer. I ought to have told myself that the man was extravagantly shy—as I had *my* father's word for it that *his* father was. There was no other reasonable interpre-tation of the incident. I had never been in a position to insult or bully him, even had I wanted to; indeed, I believe there must have been at least a brief period in which he would have been entitled to thrash me with one of the wooden bats had he been inclined that way. No doubt I had regarded him with the easy contempt that an impatient, facile, and versatile boy feels for anybody he regards as a swot. But then he must have been fairly widely acquainted with the similar opprobrium, rather more vicious in its incidence, visited upon learned children like himself by the merely stupid and oafish always in generous supply in any school.

What I did upon the occasion of this abortive encounter feel was that the sight of me in Oxford's Cornmarket dis-concerted McKechnie in a way that the similar sight of me in Edinburgh's Princes Street would not have done. Oxford was his place; it was territorially his by a sort of hereditary right—rather as it was to be Ivo Mumford's after a different fashion. I belonged to an alien order. Since the Dreich had probably thought of my father like that, here was a pattern repeating itself in a younger generation. Subsequent experience was to suggest to me that I had not been wholly astray in admitting this persuasion. Scholars and artists often feel a strong mutual attraction, and the history of literature or of painting, as of philosophy, displays processes of cross-fertilization constantly at work. But antipathies exist as well. Talbert was one day to confide to me that he regarded poets as unreliable and disagreeable people, to whom he would always accord a wide berth; yet Talbert's life was wholly devoted to the minutiae of their accomplishment.

This is almost the whole story of my relationship with Ranald McKechnie during our undergraduate years. No circumstance existed to bring us into contact in default of some specific move by one or other of us. Our schoolfellows at Oxford were sufficiently numerous to hold an occasional dinner or to field an eleven or a fifteen, but McKechnie was not a man for affairs of that sort. As for myself, I was in a phase of regarding my native town as a provincial, snobbish, Philistine place, which my own cleverness had triumphantly thrust behind me. I managed to feel this even although I was in love with an Edinburgh girl, so I must have been more or less drunk not only on Oxford itself, but also on England and the English at large. Today I am inclined to view as a simple ethnographical or topographical truth the proposition that persons and things become steadily more chewed up and rubbishing as one moves down Great Britain from north to south. But this may also be a judgement on the sweeping side.

And now here I was, standing behind my chair beside Ranald McKechnie while grace was being sung. It was an elaborate affair. The college organist (in the most gorgeous of all Oxford's robes) conducted a whole squad of choristers and singing men, and between bursts of song the Provost and chaplain antiphonally chanted. Thus edified, we sat down. McKechnie had taken the initiative in murmuring a good evening with a courtesy that told me one thing at once: he was, of course, another of my hosts. By one of those mysteries of the Oxford scene, he had been accorded the sort of promotion, presumably to a Chair, which involved being shunted from one college to another for the purposes of such social life as he cared to enjoy.

It wasn't, I felt at once, an enjoyment that came to him easily, and I myself took a glance of misgiving round the immediate set-up. So far, I have in the main been recording contacts with academic persons, or with Lord Marchpayne (who had that day joined the Cabinet), or with Gavin Mogridge (the celebrated writer and traveller)—with this or with glimpses of men yet more distinguished. But the character of the gathering at large was quite different. Here were simply several hundred former members of the college, fairly close to each other not only as an age group but also in social stratification. Most of them had been putting in the last twenty years or so pushing ahead in the financial or industrial or professional life of the community. Their success-quotient was high. They interlocked through marriage relationships and sundry fields of common activity, and they shared a large stock of common assumptions. Individually they weren't all that remarkable, but collectively they suggested—and not least to themselves— a formidable reservoir of power. Collectively again, one wouldn't much have identified them with the life of the mind.

I took a quick glance at McKechnie's other neighbour. He was a brick-faced man, and wore a monocle; he would certainly be, among other things, a rider to fox-hounds. Beyond him was another brick-faced man, wearing what his friends would call the right sort of gongs, meaning the DSO and MC. On my own other hand sat a bearded person in clerical dress. The dining-list named him, not too informatively, as the Prebendary of Tullytumble. I recognized him as the man glimpsed by Tony and myself in P. P. Killiecrankie's old rooms, holding up a jacket and then composing himself for a pre-party snooze. Beyond him was another cleric, in attire running to much purple and lace.

It wasn't, I told myself, too good a look-out. Whoever had arranged the *placement* for this small corner of the feast had thought in terms of two ecclesiastics chumming up, two brick-faced men doing the same, and between them McKechnie and myself as a couple of happy schoolfellows. And like that it would have to be. I mightn't for my own part have all that difficulty when turning to the Hibernian clergyman. But I doubted whether Ranald McKechnie had any future worth speaking of with the fox-hunting man.

'I hope that your play is enjoying considerable success?'

McKechnie asked this as we settled down, and I am afraid I received the inquiry without pleasure. It was even more depressing, somehow, than 'Do you still write plays?' Since an eternity of fame—I took it to imply—was unlikely to attend my effort, or even the approbation of the judicious either, it was reasonable to hope that I was getting out of it the modest monetary reward with which it was alone apposite to associate such a concoction.

'It's doing well enough,' I replied, not the less shortly because I was perfectly aware that my reaction was absurd. 'One writes these things, and rather yearns that they may make somebody a moment merry. I hope this Gaudy is going to make you just that.'

'Oh!' McKechnie looked at me in a startled way, as he well might upon such a graceless performance. 'Well, as a matter of fact, I know hardly anybody here. I expect you know nearly everybody. I've only recently become attached to the college, and begun to get the hang of common room. I try to dine three or four times a term.' McKechnie spoke as if of facing up to the dentist or some other species of possibly painful therapy.

'Yes, of course. And, Ranald, it's a great pleasure to congratulate you, even belatedly, on your appointment. I've forgotten whether it's what is called a Regius Chair?'

'Yes—yes, it is.' 'Ranald' had made McKechnie blink, as it well might. He had waived any words of self-introduction, but not otherwise acknowledged our previous association; and certainly we had never been on Christian-name terms in youth. I saw him take a quick glance at his list of diners: it did record the fact that I was Mr Duncan Pattullo. 'And thank you very much, Duncan.' He paused. 'I suppose we never knew each other very well. Although I think we might find we actually came up to Oxford in the same year.'

'I think so, too.' I judged this presumably genuine vagueness impressive. 'Of course, I went down immediately after taking Schools. And I haven't always lived in England, which is something which curtails one's acquaintance a good deal.'

'Yes.' McKechnie appeared to weigh the sufficiency of this reply. 'Obviously so,' he amplified, rather as Mogridge might have done.

'Do you have to do a lot of lecturing?' I inquired. My tone must have been that in which one asks an elderly gentlewoman to whom one has been introduced at some rural occasion whether there is a good vicar in the parish.

'A certain amount. And, of course, there is examining every few years. But none of it is sufficiently burdensome to interfere with one's work.'

A quick vision of Talbert absorbed in his folios enabled me to understand this remark, which a stranger to the place might have found perplexing enough. I wondered whether McKechnie and I could be said to be doing well. It wasn't difficult to feel a terminus to our small-talk as looming uncomfortably close ahead. And more than an hour must elapse before the important people ranged at high table began delivering themselves of their speeches, so that we could sit back and listen. It was clear that my schoolfellow and I must either open up some joint area of boyhood reminiscence, or find a topic of current interest as a basis for conversation. What I tried was, roughly, in the first of these categories.

'Do you still keep up your violin?' I asked.

It seemed a harmless question, although its phrasing was perhaps unfortunate. It echoed, after all, a form of words I didn't judge too happy when addressed to myself, and moreover it faintly invoked an image of McKechnie with the instrument tucked under his chin. But this was no reason for McKechnie to greet it, as he did, with a surprised and even offended glance. I realized that at school we had probably known nothing about his violin-playing; that it had been—

as it now possibly remained—an activity cherished in privacy; and that I owed my knowledge of it to an occasion between our fathers which I couldn't with any discretion refer to.

But McKechnie's discomposure, although momentary, told me something beyond this. As I moved up the school, and gained a certain confidence militating against the clinging sense of inferiority suffered by Ninian and myself as a consequence of our permanently scruffy *tenue*, I had come to exercise myself a good deal in the character of a wit. It hadn't, of course, *been* wit, but merely juvenile mockery, prompted by a quite wholesome sense of fun and an awakening eye for the absurd. And at this moment, as a result, Ranald McKechnie was recalling me as one whose proper image was that of thorns crackling under a pot.

So, at least, I now thought. Perhaps I was confused by the two-tier time-shift or double regress in which I was involved. Almost everybody round about me, everybody I had encountered since Tony had turned up in his son's room, belonged to my undergraduate years. And now here in the person of Ranald McKechnie were my schooldays as well.

But at this moment there came an interruption to the imperfect communion between McKechnie and myself. In hall the behaviour of the college servants had always been less that of professionally qualified waiters than of under-keepers in a zoo, concerned to get through feeding time as expeditiously as possible and in consequence putting a good deal of raw vigour into thrusting the gobbets through the bars. This code of conduct had now brought a shoulder sharply between us, its owner having been prompted to grab an empty plate from the other side of the long table. So I had a second or two in which to recollect myself. Could I retreat from McKechnie's violin by way of a brief ludicrous account of the difficulties of the young Gavin Mogridge with his 'cello? This idea, not too felicitous in itself, came to nothing. The nearer of the brick-faced men had taken advantage of McKechnie's disengaged state to bark a question at him. And in the succeeding moment I was addressed by the bearded ecclesiastical dignitary on my left.

'The Bishop and I,' he said with grave courtesy, 'are discussing current standards of conduct among the undergraduates. Disturbing rumours reach one.'

I felt this to be unpromising. The topic would certainly produce no gaiety. Presently the permissive society would be mentioned; I should advance the vain contention that we live in the most multifariously repressive society yet achieved by man; mutual irritation would be the result. Meanwhile, it was only a question of whether sex or drugs would be the first evil to raise its ugly head. It turned out to be sex.

'In the rooms I am occupying for the night,' the Bishop said across his colleague's stomach, 'I have found, I am grieved to say, an erotic manual and a package'—he hesitated, as if seeking some approximation to decency—'and a package of sexual engines.'

'It sounds,' I said, 'as if the owner switches his interests during vacations.'

'As he well may do, if there is anything in the saying that variety is the spice of life.' It was the Prebendary who produced this, the Bishop having regarded my remark as meriting no direct response. But any liveliness of mind it might have suggested evaporated at once, and the Prebendary turned solemn. 'It is hard not to feel that a great mistake has been made.' He had a glass raised to his nose as he spoke, and became conscious of a possibility of misunderstanding. 'An excellent madeira,' he said. 'A grave mistake by the dons.'

'A grave mistake, indeed.' The Bishop had taken another look at me. 'Heaven forbid that I should be so muddle-headed as to treat fornication as among the gravest sins——'

'Yet it is scarcely a venial one,' the Prebendary said— rather to the effect of one ecclesiastical court cautiously correcting the judgement of another.

'It is at least a cheapening activity.' The Bishop, finishing his own madeira almost synchronously with his last spoonful of soup, again glanced at me across the Prebendary (who, as a physical barrier, was already in an expanding phase). 'It is what I say, simply and frankly, in any confirmation address I give at a public school—at a boys' public school, I need hardly add. I tell them that they are free to consider me an old square, but that a bishop, like any other chap, has to do his thing.' The Bishop paused, perhaps to admire his command of expressions supposed to be popular with the young at that time. 'The lads take it very well. I see them murmuring comments to each other.'

'Isn't it possible,' I asked, 'that they are laying wagers on how long you will continue to talk? I can remember doing just that.' I felt instantly that this sally was rude rather than funny, and wasn't too pleased to hear it draw from the Prebendary—who struck me as rather a coarse-fibred man—a quickly repressed guffaw. 'As for a grave mistake,' I went on—for I felt I could best redeem my error by speaking seriously—'I don't know that it's quite fair to charge university authorities with that. Not if what you are talking about is, as I suppose, changing sexual behaviour in a place like this. If it *is* changing——'

'Of course it's changing,' the Bishop interrupted briskly. And he added, a shade elliptically, 'You'd have to be an ostrich to deny it.'

'All right, it's changing—but to an extent which I suspect is much blown-up in newspapers. Of course if it's really true that these young men put in an inordinate amount of time chasing young women hugger-mugger into bed, then I agree with you that it debases honest sexual currency. But the main point must be what the dons—supposing them to subscribe to traditional Christian views on the matter—can effectively do about it. I suspect them of having such scant room for manœuvre that very little in the way of making grave mistakes is open to them. It's as with the politicians. They're much given to denouncing each other as making colossal mistakes. But the whole thing is no more than delusions of grandeur. You can only make quite small mistakes when you are simply being bumped around by forces over which you have no control.'

'I rather agree with you—although the analogy is perhaps an imperfect one.' The Bishop seemed a practised conversationalist. 'For undergraduates, after all, are not intractable economic forces. They are young people *in statu pupillari*.'

'Fair enough. But there's a limit to declaring a college, or any similar place, a closed society, to be unaffected by whatever is going on outside. And I'm not sure that a shift in sexual *mores* begins typically with the young. They take a great deal of their colour from their seniors. So perhaps we ought to begin by shaking our heads and wagging our fingers at our own generation.'

'A sobering thought,' the Prebendary said.

'The effective argument has to be from function and purpose.' Hearing myself say this might have pulled me up, since I am not insensible that the dinner-table is an inappropriate setting for harangue. But I was too well launched on my theme. 'Young people come to a university to study—most of them to study quite hard. I don't assert that their motives are altogether of the scholar's disinterested sort. They want to do well in their examinations, and so gain merit with the powerful, and so get themselves decent jobs. But it follows that they don't want to be all-that distracted by boy-and-girl stuff. From which it follows again—at least to some extent—that the problem is a statistical one.'

'I have gone with you so far,' the Bishop said. 'But your last point eludes me.'

'Admit a hundred young women on easy terms to something rather more than the fringes of an adolescent male society like this, and a considerable amount of distraction must result. But nothing like the amount you will get if the young women number only fifty. The spectacle of the males in possession—and they will be the most confident and personable ones, on the whole—will drive a fair proportion of the others mildly dotty.' I did pause on this, conscious that it owed a good deal to my recent conversation with Plot. 'So if you are constrained to have girls all over the place,' I concluded rather abruptly, 'it's up to you to see they're in adequate supply.'

'On one view of the matter,' the Bishop said judiciously, 'your argument is perfectly sound.'

'But it is essentially a pragmatic and utilitarian view,' the Prebendary pronounced. 'I should associate it with what is now so loosely called humanism. And we must have other thoughts in mind. Notably——'

'A remarkable gathering, this.' The Bishop, although vainly, attempted a diversion. Bating a legitimate dash of episcopal pomposity, he was a sensible man.

'Notably,' the Prebendary said with firmness, 'the absolute value of pre-marital chastity.'

Not altogether surprisingly, this brought us to a halt. The Bishop turned discreetly to his other hand, and between the Prebendary and myself there was an uncertain pause. Then he appeared to remind himself of something unsaid, and turned again with some formality to address me.

'I ought to have introduced myself,' he announced. 'We were up together, but scarcely acquainted, and I don't think you remember me. My name is Killiecrankie.'

'As I'm Pattullo, and the man on my other side is called McKechnie, we must sound rather a Hyperborean trio.' This was the best I could manage by way of covering a moment of considerable astonishment. Prebendary Killiecrankie's beard (to say nothing of his opinions) had served to obscure any memory of him. But here he was, established for the night in his old rooms. And in the enjoyment, it could be added, of his old sofa.

For some moments I couldn't think how to continue conversing with P. P. Killiecrankie. He was presumably unaware of the scandalous and indecent use to which Tony Mumford and I had occasionally put our vantage-point in Tony's window. (This, incidentally, recurring to me again now, suggested that I had been talking a certain amount of nonsense only minutes before; for upon Tony and myself, at least, the spectacle of the Killiecrankian conquests had been wholly without dire nervous impact.) But Killiecrankie must be conscious that a considerable number of his contemporaries present at the Gaudy could recall at least the report of his amorous courses, and this struck me as an odd piece of awareness for so obviously respectable a member of the higher clergy to carry around. His past did not, of course, impugn his present in the least, since the rolls of sanctity are alive with reformed rakes. But there was the breath of comedy in it, all the same. I wondered whether I might a little tease Killiecrankie, perhaps calling upon him to remember Plot, that useful bicycle-boy. For the moment, at least, I turned this frivolous idea down. Instead, we discussed the curious fact that, in an oecumenical age, certain professors of theology in the university were still required to be in Anglican orders. This was a most blameless subject, even if not to my mind a momentous one. Killiecrankie talked about it with a gravity which could scarcely have been exceeded by Albert Talbert himself.

It was a failure in gravity, however, that now occasioned a reassortment of interlocutors in our corner of the feast. The brick-faced men, who had again become absorbed in their own conversation while leaving McKechnie to his own thoughts, must have hit upon something highly entertaining, since they had simultaneously emitted a roar of raucous merriment. Locally, at least, the effect was startling, since the dinner, although becoming animated, was plainly not of the sort that turns rowdy. McKechnie, being the main recipient of the full acoustic effect, was more startled than most, and when he turned to me I had the absurd thought that he was going to beg me to change places with him. I must have been accustomed to think of wee Dreichie as what we called a rabbit, meaning a timid boy wholly without aptitude either for games or for ragging around.

'Nothing so illiberal and so ill-bred,' McKechnie murmured in my ear, 'as audible laughter.'

There is a popular persuasion that the learned classes go in for quotation-dropping rather as the snobbish go in for name-dropping. But I have never observed this to be particularly true, and I felt that in thus invoking Lord Chesterfield McKechnie had boldly stretched a point in order to make me a sign—approximately of the order in which Freemasons communicate some sort of token of solidarity by way of a peculiar handshake—in face of the mere Boeotia represented by the brick-faced men. And now he took a step bolder still.

'I always remember,' he said with firmness, 'those tall stories you used to tell us. And many boys didn't *know* they were stories. It was something quite remarkable, Duncan—and, of course, it pointed to your future career. I've never had such an experience since.'

I glanced at McKechnie, and again caught his eye. He was trying hard. Indeed, it was almost as if he were prepared to like me, which was an attitude to which I felt absolutely no entitlement at all. But there was still something alarmed in him as well.

And I remembered, quite suddenly and for the first time in years, that I had been a pathological liar.

I must have started in Miss Miller's form rather older than most—seven and a few days, say, over against six and a few months. It had occurred to nobody to send me to any sort of toddlers' school before that, or to have somebody come in and teach me my ABC. In Miss Miller's there was a boy called Douglas James, who could stand up and confidently communicate to us from a printed page such striking circumstances as that the Cat sat on the Mat. I was quite, quite certain that never in life (which I had an obscure intuition of as going on for a long time) could I beat Douglas James. By the end of the year, however, I had done this. In reading and writing, in sums and in looking after tadpoles, in mixing up the three primary colours in my paint-box until they turned to mud: in these and other lores and skills I had Douglas James where I quite ardently wanted him. In Miss Fuller's in the following year it was just the same. I defeated even Bobbie

Dalgetty, who was judged to have developed cheating to so fine an art as to be virtually impregnable.

But after this they pushed me into Miss Frazer's. This meant skipping Miss Clarke's—something I was glad of, since Miss Clarke beat phrenetically on a piano and screamed like a cockatoo. The idea was that I ought to be among older, not younger, boys as I moved up, form by form, through the school. This didn't work, since it reckoned on my being an academic rather than a merely lively little boy. Latin appeared to have been happening briskly in Miss Clarke's, and I didn't in the least enjoy the privilege of now learning its rudiments on the side and on my own. Instead of being 'top' I was now regularly fourth, fifth, or sixth—a shame emphasized by the fact that we spent most of the day actually changing, minute by minute, the seats on which we sat. Whenever you successfully answered an oral question you moved up above all those who had failed in turn to do so. The move up was easy: you simply collected your books and walked. But if you moved up twelve boys had to shuffle down one. Sir Walter Scott describes the system in the Edinburgh High School when he was a boy there, and we may well have adopted it from that ancient institution. I don't know whether such archaic educational techniques anywhere survive today. It was vastly time-consuming. It was also undeniably rather fun, just as Snakes and Ladders can be. (I was sometimes to wish that I could substitute Snakes and Ladders for Scrabble in Old Road, Headington.) I can still feel as a physical sensation the heady business of occasionally reaching top again (or, in English, of recklessly rather than doggedly defending that position day after day and week after week).

In Miss Frazer's I entirely cracked up, all the same. I suppose I wasn't willing to do the work; was temperamentally incapable of undergoing the discipline. So I ought to have accepted the small spectacle of boys with what I knew to be very much my own quantum of intelligence sitting confidently above me. But I didn't manage it. And this was how my short but rather splendid career as school liar began.

My reading at that period was exclusively in what my mother anachronistically called penny dreadfuls—supplies of juvenile pulp fiction being already unobtainable at less than fourpence a time. What happened was that I simply enlisted myself in the universe of these publications. As soon as I left the school gates I became Duncan the Secret Service Boy or something equally glamorous. The fantasies must have been extremely fluent, and I conjecture that I myself was in a state in which I more or less believed them to be true. I doubt—odd as the paradox is—whether it crossed my mind that anybody else would believe them to be so. But this was to reckon without a certain hypnotic effect which a precocious verbal facility must have been capable of generating for the time; and also without the difficulty inexperienced children must encounter in distinguishing between what is credible and what is not. It is certain that a number of my companions half-believed in the prodigy they were entertaining in their midst. In fact it required a nascent intellect out of the ordinary—McKechnie's, indeed—not to be taken in. Probably McKechnie was a little shaken himself. I was providing him with a first glimpse of the irresponsible character of what he would later learn to call the imagination. This was why, as we sat side by side as grown men, I was still capable of engendering in him a vague irrational alarm.

One person who could not be deceived was my brother. Ninian, a year my senior and both harder-headed and physically stronger, eventually took it upon himself to expel the aberration—which he regarded as a deepening of our general family disgrace—by means of corporal persuasion. The process took him a couple of terms, since it seldom went beyond a vigorous knuckle-scrubbing of my imprisoned scalp. But it was entirely successful. My skald-like powers and proclivities eventually vanished as abruptly as they had appeared.

McKechnie and I were now talking, and we kept it up for some time. It wasn't, however, with any real sense of increasing intimacy. There was a substantial, if grotesque, reason for my feeling discomfort in neighbouring the regenerate P. P.

Killiecrankie, since with him I was rather in the position of a revived Actaeon required to sit demurely beside an elderly Artemis, or of Ham at a family party subsequent to the drunkenness of Noah. Actually, with Killiecrankie I felt no awkwardness at all. But between McKechnie and myself there was a cause of embarrassment which, lying just as far back in time, retained some vitality because it was mutual. Faintly but perceptibly, we were encumbered as we conversed by the memory of having spent three years pointlessly avoiding each other here in Oxford.

I did most of the talking, being for some reason anxious to contravert McKechnie's simplistic view of my juvenile taradiddles as pointing the way to my eventual career as a writer. I was now totally, I explained, without the faculty of improvisation; I couldn't even 'tell stories' to my brother's children; my case was that of a total surcease of one habit of mind before the close of childhood, and the emergence of a radically different one in adolescence. McKechnie must have judged me to be on decidedly uncertain as well as boring ground, and he no doubt reflected on the egocentricity of the artistic character. But if I was talking about myself in this way it was at least partly because I quite failed to coax him into anything of the sort himself. I suppose he would have answered direct questions—whether or not he was married, for example—but he carried about with him an indefinable air that somehow discouraged challenge. It wasn't reticence; one didn't feel him to be, for example, the sort of man who regularly leaves something painful at home and doesn't want his mind drawn back to it. It was almost as if, apart possibly from that violin, he had no private or personal life to be reticent about. It hadn't occurred to him to stock up with anything of the kind. He had been, after all, just the sort of boy who develops into an obsessional scholar.

Having come to this conclusion about Ranald McKechnie, and decided that our dim decent impulse to reach out or back to one another wouldn't come to much, I was relieved to notice him beginning to show signs of interest in a man sitting opposite. The nearer of the brick-faced men being the next thing to a brick wall so far as my schoolfellow was concerned, here was a propitious development. The tables in hall, indeed, although so long that they appear very narrow, are in fact as broad as a marriage-bed (the comparison had been Tony Mumford's), and I remembered that conversation across them, and against a background of noisy dining, had never been easy. But McKechnie was addressing himself with surprising vigour to overcoming the difficulty, and I caught enough of the exchange to grasp the reason. He had discovered from his dinner-list that the man opposite was qualified to discuss with him some third man's edition of Martial. *Each knows the man his neighbour knows*, the poet says disparagingly of scholars. But here at least, on just that basis, was McKechnie comfortably fixed up until speech-time.

My own attention was drawn across the table by this shift of balance. For a moment I looked blankly at the man facing me. Then I noticed that he was amused, and realized that it was my blankness which was the cause of this.

'Come, come, Duncan!' this man said. 'Wake up. Acknowledge the obscure companion of your youth.'

'Robert—well I'm blessed!' It was odd not to have recognized Robert Damian. The boyish complexion had turned florid, or at least ruddy, and he had put on a little weight. He seemed otherwise unchanged. I told him this at once.

'Duncan, *you* are changed—changed utterly. A terrible beauty is born. Spruced up, groomed, metropolitanized, admirably smoothed all over. And wearing almost alarmingly well. I give it as my professional opinion that you will live to be a hundred, and end up indistinguishable from Graham Sutherland's Somerset Maugham. Or will it be his Beaverbrook? I'm not quite sure.'

'Thank you very much, my dear Robert. Have they put you back on the staircase for the night, as they have me?' Damian had succeeded a man called Kettle directly above my head—above what would now be Nick Junkin's head.

'Not needed. My humble home's in Oxford.'

'Oh, Lord! Then I've done it again.'

'It?'

'Getting people wrong. Cyril Bedworth, for a start. He came into my room this evening, and I asked him in a kindly way if they'd put him back in his little attic for the Gaudy. And it turned out he was a fellow of the college—a status it's seemly that all old members should revere. And now you too. Fellow and Tutor in Physiology, I suppose. Or is it Regius Professor of Medicine?'

'Nothing of the sort. I'm a simple GP in a respectable North Oxford practice—pretty well a professional embalmer, really, since most of my patients are nonagenarians. But I'm college doctor as well, and attend to the young gentlemen's injuries—whether sustained on the rugger field or in bed. It makes a nice change.'

'In bed? Do you mean a chap can——?' Much to Damian's amusement, I hesitated to complete this juvenile inquiry.

'Lord, yes. I put it down to the *Kama Sutra*, and Japanese pillow-books, and so forth. Occidental joints and sinews just don't seem to be up to it. A pity—but there it is.'

'I see.' I'd have supposed Damian to be talking outrageous nonsense if I hadn't remembered, absurdly enough, the manual my near neighbour the Bishop had been distressed to find in his room. 'Do you attend to the dons too?' I asked.

'No—it doesn't seem to be in the contract. But they give me the freedom of the feast. There's a tacit understanding, as a matter of fact, that I turn up every year as a sort of casualty service. Last year, when it was the dotards, we had to carry out a couple of them on stretchers. Mild CVA's as the port went round the second time.'

'I hope they made a good recovery.' It seemed unnecessary to ask Damian to decode his jargon. 'Have you run into Tony yet?'

'I've had a gracious wave and a cheerful smile. Quite up with the nobs, isn't he?'

'Cabinet rank. Today's headline news.'

'Well, well!'

'He's in his old rooms opposite mine. Full of *l'esprit de l'escalier*. He says it's his ancestral stair. But there's something odd about our Tony. He hasn't come up just for the claret.'

'Tony has a son.'

'Yes, I know—Ivo. It seems he believes in taking sugar with his brandy and champagne. He hasn't been injuring himself on the rugger field?'

'Wrong time of year, old boy—and most improbable at any season. Still, there's a spot of trouble in that direction, it seems. I'll tell you later.' Damian paused on this spark of discretion—an impulse which didn't, however, survive his now taking a glance at P. P. Killiecrankie, who was again absorbed in grave conversation with the Bishop. 'Natty ecclesiastical outfitter, P. P. must have.' Damian had leant forward, and was speaking in a kind of loud murmur. 'He must have forgotten his old persuasion that there's more enterprise in walking naked.'

I remembered suddenly—and there had already been several occasions upon which it might have come back to me—that Yeats had been for a time something between a cult and a joke on the staircase. I also realized that Robert Damian must have been among the privileged few to whom either Tony Mumford or I had confessed our culpable spectatorship of Killiecrankie's pleasures.

VI

THE HALL BUTLER had rapped on high table, and the Provost was on his feet. The uninstructed majority, which included myself, grabbed their glasses as they stood up, loyally prepared to drink the health of the Queen.

'*Benedicto benedicatur.*'

We shoved our glasses furtively aside, and assumed expressions of solemnity. The Provost's manner of delivering this decorous supplication was notable. Into the Latin words there had been fed the most cultivated modulations of the English tongue, and the pause between each syllable, fractionally longer than might have been expected, seemed to declare a just repose within unchallengeable authority.

I thought again of those extraordinary prayers at school—prayers in which, as at some Council of State, inordinate demands are preferred in tones suggesting the moderate and level private exchanges of gentlemen. I thought again of my own favourite: *that all things may be so ordered and settled by their endeavours, upon the best and surest foundations, that peace and happiness, truth and justice, religion and piety, may be established among us for all generations. These and all other necessaries, for them, for us, and thy whole Church....*

It seemed odd that the Provost's modest request should recall this omnibus prayer to my mind. What united them, perhaps, was an underlying social assumption. God is the most powerful of our connections, and we are entitled to his patronage and regard—provided we hit off with him, as head of the family, the right note of respect without servility.

Differently phrased, these thoughts might not be incompatible with orthodoxy, and that they came to me satirically slanted told me how much a Scottish presbyterian I remained in bone. I wondered about Ranald McKechnie's sense of this matter, and might have startled him with an inquiry if the Provost hadn't now been on his feet again. It really was the Queen this time. A kind of unbuttoning succeeded, and soon the first cigar smoke began to drift about the hall. I sat back and made a more comprehensive survey than I had yet done.

The hall if stripped to its sombre panelling and dusky raftered roof would still be impressive; as it is, it is dominated by the portraits that stretch in an unbroken line round its walls. As freshmen we had ticked them off as one witness to our having arrived within an ambience of gratifying grandeur. After that we had more or less forgotten about them, and certainly didn't study them very much. Between ourselves and these notabilities so confidently filling out their frames there had been a gulf alike of years and of circumstances and expectations which worked against any sense of relationship.

But tonight, as not when it was simply rows of hungry undergraduates at the tables, there was a connection of sorts between the living and the dead. These diners were in process of closing the gap. Two or three of them would be hanging on the wall when the twenty-first century came round; already many were taking on the weight, the lineaments, the assumption of knowledgeableness and authority, the obligation to be unaffected because eminent, which Reynolds and Gainsborough, Hudson and Knapton and Devis, had recorded of the judges and bishops, the soldiers and scholars and statesmen looking down on a festivity familiar to them in their time. If there was a marked contrast, it was perhaps in flesh tones or complexion. The men sitting around me were ruddy; those on the walls were pale. This was partly because the hour was drawing on and the wine good; partly, too, it was a matter of certain conventions of portraiture long ago, when to be pallid, ashen, or faintly green had been the distinguished thing. Only Raeburn—my father had once remarked—acknowledges that men live on beef and ale.

At right-angles to the dais, three long tables ran in parallel down the hall. At a smaller table immediately behind me I discovered that there were seated the young men who had formed part of the choir. These undergraduates, who must have remained in residence to grace their seniors' festive occasion by singing for their supper, were presumably surveying an unfamiliar scene. I wondered what they made of such outmoded if innocent ostentation: the florid satisfied faces, the confident commanding voices, the varying degrees of fancy dress, tables unfamiliar beneath their load of silver and silver-gilt—everywhere cups and bowls and goblets of a size suggesting the potations of giants. To this question, as it happened, I was later to receive an answer.

My glance went back to the portraits, and I decided that most of these silent witnesses, at least, approved what they saw. Only here and there a poet, a lean and tormented philosopher, an old religious man, cast on us what was perhaps an alienated regard: these might have been sniffing in the cigar smoke, in the vinous miasma, in the considered after-dinner eloquence now getting under way, an odour and a resonance foreign and profane. And it was indeed arguable that, as the old members with the decorations glinting under their white ties pursued their nostalgic and sentimental exercise, the deeper life of the place, which was the life of teachers and taught, was in abeyance.

I looked round for the teachers. Apart from those whom seniority, or an appointed part in the proceedings, placed at high table, the dons were scattered thinly over the hall. Ranald McKechnie apart, the nearest to me was Talbert, and he was a dozen yards away. He was putting a good deal of vigour into smoking a cigar, so that his large white moustache had the appearance of vaporizing at its tips and floating away in air. His gaze was into the rafters, and I wondered whether he was listening to what was being said; it was exactly the speculation which had frequently beset me when I was reading him my weekly essay. I used to believe that he had developed some power of total recall over his texts of the moment, and was in a position to collate one with another as a pure act of memory.

The first speech of the evening was well advanced. A junior fellow of the college had the task of proposing the health of the guests, and the job consisted in the main of taking felicitous notice of each of the principal visitors in turn. He had begun nervously, and a lank lock of black hair falling over his forehead gave the impression of some stiff physical labour being performed. But brief applause was punctuating his speech, since it was the business of the company at large to express admiration tinged with affection for a number of people about whom most of us probably knew very little. The young man gained confidence from this, and as he finally raised his glass he was relaxed and secretly radiant—knowing that he had brought it off and gained some sort of decent alpha mark from his colleagues. His colleagues were on their feet: both those at high table beside him and the scattering of thirty or so around the hall. A further small round of applause followed the toast, mixed with a little coughing; men who had been too diffident to strike matches during the speech did so now; servants moved in to plant replenished decanters in the place of empty ones. It was one more phase of the ritual accomplished.

'A very good speech,' McKechnie murmured to me—whether conventionally or sincerely, it was impossible to say. 'Are you fond of this sort of thing, Duncan?'

'It wouldn't be too civil to turn up and then declare the affair a bore.' McKechnie's question had surprised me. 'And it all doesn't lack its interest. About a third of these people ring a bell with me—either faintly or middling loud. And that's quite fun. But I've been thinking I'd rather be seeing the college in working clothes, and with the young men around. Do you know, Ranald, I think I'd like to become a don? For a couple of years, say. I believe I could hold my own, after a fashion, for just about that long.'

'And write a play about us?' McKechnie had given me a glance of a sharpness which seemed unmerited by my wholly fanciful remark. 'There was a man who did something of the kind at Cambridge. His name escapes me, but he wrote two or three novels about the place. Rather good as stories, holding the interest well.' McKechnie paused on this; he seemed to have a flair for temperate praise. 'But not quite getting his academics in their habit as they live.'

'I think I'd myself produce a merely rambling sort of record. No hold on the interest at all. Mere expatiation.'

'I doubt that very much. Are you not a thoroughly Aristotelian man? What I notice about your plays is that you are careful to give them middles as well as beginnings and ends.'

I was more surprised still at this serious scholar's being prompted to make fun of me. But it was, of course, agreeable to be called an Aristotelian man. I replied that middles are the great difficulty, and that it is in the middles that the muddles come.

'Have you had any talk with the Provost yet?'

'I haven't so much as made a bow to him. And he wouldn't remember me from Adam.' I was about to add: 'Or if he *did* remember me, it would be as my father's son; they once discussed Dürer together.' But I refrained from this—I suppose because of the reminiscence it carried in my own mind of the Dreich and Wee Dreichie. The inconsequence of McKechnie's question had struck me—this and the fact of its somehow echoing a remark of Talbert's shortly before we entered hall. I might have put some answering question to McKechnie now had the butler not banged on a table again. The aged Swedish physicist was going to reply for the guests.

This turned out to be a long speech, delivered in fluent although at times erratic English. The savant's voice was more powerful than his appearance of advanced decrepitude would have led one to expect; every now and then, whether by accident or rhetorical design, he would simultaneously raise its pitch, increase its volume, and thrust his mouth hard up against the microphone standing on the table before him. The effect was of an intermittent divagation into Tamil, Telugu, or Chinese emitted through a loud-hailer. These exercises, moreover, could be judged to perform a cadenza-like function. Acoustically brilliant in themselves, they appeared to serve as bridge-passages between one theme and another in the course of a singularly wide-ranging oration. Into the punctuating uproar would vanish thoughts on molecular physics or the whaling industry; out of it would emerge reflections on contemporary architecture or on Oxford as a perennial battle-ground between science and religion. This bizarre eloquence was variously received. Talbert, I felt certain, wasn't listening to a word; he had passed into brooding reverie on the incompetence of the Rev. A. B. Grosart or the ignorance of Sir Edmund Gosse. The Provost, courteously inclined towards the speaker and thus presenting a noble profile to the body of the hall, remained grave except when some relaxation into the mirthful became mandatory. McKechnie was taking in what was intelligible, and would have his appraising word to murmur at the end of the speech. But, broadly, I felt him to fall within the same bracket as Talbert; he would have preferred to be continuing that conversation about the edition of Martial. As for Bedworth, who turned out to be sitting in a position of semi-distinction looking straight up one of the long tables, I wondered whether I was not suddenly glimpsing in him some curious current of hostility to the whole affair. Among the mass of us there were numerous men whose walk of life took them to a dozen functions of the sort every month; these sat impassive and relaxed—with perhaps one occasionally catching the eye of another across the hall. But the great majority of the guests were unaffectedly enjoying themselves. Some were in a state of delighted admiration as they contemplated in the versatile orator standing before them one whose actual dwelling lay presumably amid the farther mysteries of the cosmos.

The eminent Swede reached his peroration at last. Oxford, and this the most prominent of its colleges, were, most properly, well to the fore. So were Roger Bacon, Robert Boyle, Newman, Shelley, and Matthew Arnold. The distinguished physicist had been doing his home-work well. 'Beautiful city!' he bellowed, and seized the microphone with both hands. I found myself wondering how he was going to cope with the overtone of irony which Arnold's celebrated apostrophe carries. 'Home of lost grouses,' he suddenly shouted, 'and unpopular games, and impossible royalties!' He sat down.

Had I, as I listened, invented this incursion into the world of *Finnegans Wake*? Perhaps I had, since nobody seemed startled and nothing except the regulation applause succeeded. Nevertheless, it had been a speech not easy to follow in the batting order. The elderly statesman who next stood up must have been aware of this, and may even have noticed that the decanters were all but empty down the long tables. Practised, apt and witty, he moved rapidly to the business of proposing the toast of the college. Here the formula for success is adequately to modulate from the light and amusing into a final warmth of sentiment in the expression of which words like loyalty, affection, and love are honestly spoken out. They were very well received now. For brief moments the evening touched the sacramental. And then brandy or a liqueur was being served. The more resolute even had opportunity to possess themselves of a second cigar.

The Provost came last, and struck me as having the most difficult assignment. His wasn't the role of a raconteur, or of one fondly recalling golden generations long ago. What was prescriptively expected of him was an account of how, in the past two or three years, the college had been getting along. And this was something in which, curiously enough, the loyal old members showed little more interest than did the miscellaneous distinguished guests who knew nothing about the place. The news was news about dons: how one had died, another had been promoted or translated, and a third had retired. Such matters, and all those problems of university politics and administration which are as life and death to the governing bodies of colleges, were clearly felt as of small significance by men who had for long been breathing the larger air of the world of affairs. Only when the Provost began to talk about the present generation of undergraduates did interest momentarily quicken. But his remarks here were of the considered rather than the informative sort. The college had its problems with the young men—but then when had it not? Present intellectual standards gave perhaps some cause for concern; in the Examination Schools, at least, recent performance could not be called outstanding. But we need not be too downcast. The junior members today were quite as kind to their tutors, quite as active, versatile, well-mannered and charming as their predecessors had been a quarter of a century before.

The Provost moved smoothly on to other thoughts. He was profoundly sensible of the support which the college received from all its members, present or past. He was deeply grateful to his colleagues for the loyalty he unfailingly received from them. The Senior Tutor, the Dean, the Chaplain, the Bursar: all were paragons. Last, but not least, there were the servants, to whom our debt was so incalculable. We mourned the death of Lickfold, which had taken place shortly after his completing forty years of devoted labour as scout on Howard Six. Gelly, the Head Porter, had retired that day; at a small presentation made to him there had been a very large turn-out. Freeguard, although no longer able to work in the buttery . . .

Freeguard, I conjectured, had succumbed to the professional risk of operating amid kegs of ale. The Provost's corresponding risk was a Ciceronian *copia*. But now he was preparing to wind up the formal part of the feast. The night—he urged upon us—was still young, and the college's resources in the way of modest entertainment were by no means exhausted. In the common rooms—and in the garden, too, so mild was the air—further refreshment awaited us should we care to partake of it.

We got to our feet. The Provost bowed ceremoniously to the Swede and to the Chancellor, and made a gesture indicative of his intention to escort them from the hall. The other men at high table, taking their tone from this, began also to move out as a body and in a formal fashion. Tony was an exception; he had slipped rapidly along the table, detained in his place the junior fellow who had made the first speech, and had now sat down beside him and begun to talk. It was obvious—as with everything Tony did—that this was quite in order. In the body of the hall most of the guests were strolling out but some lingered—either continuing to gossip with their neighbours or reassorting themselves in casually seated groups. I supposed that Tony was making promptly sure of having an opportunity to congratulate this low-ranking youth on his performance. Lord Marchpayne, I realized again, had trained himself never to miss a trick. It was an art in which he had taken his first distinguishable steps as an undergraduate.

I spent some time wandering round the hall, talking to people not all of whom I very clearly remembered, or who at all clearly remembered me. Yet another man asked me if I still wrote plays; the implication seemed to be that, like basket-ball or hurdling, it was an activity scarcely to be pursued with any dignity into middle life. If one is to attend reunions at all, I told myself, one ought to attend them regularly. This feeling made disagreeable for the moment the thought of now plunging into some crowded and noisy common room. The garden might be more attractive for the next half hour.

As I thus made my way, unaccompanied, out of hall, my progress was impeded by a small group of the choral scholars (as I remembered them to be called) who had dined with us after singing grace. They were blocking the wide doorway with a casual regardlessness which, although wholly unaggressive, failed quite to square with the Provost's assurance about the continued good manners of the young. One of them, a handsome lad who was for some reason wearing a large nosegay by way of buttonhole, was haranguing his fellows excitedly as I edged past.

'I've never heard such a load of self-exaggerating crap in all my life!'

These were the first distinguishable words I had caught from an undergraduate that day. They may have been intended as applicable to the evening's eloquence as a whole, but I rather suspected that the Provost's speech was being specifically alluded to. In which case one saw the point. It had been a good speech, but one certainly delivered under the persuasion that it is the business of a Provost to project a praeposital persona. I wondered whether the young man would denounce with equal vehemence a contemporary of his own similarly sustaining an elected role in a discothèque. And I felt momentarily—for it was in a moment that this entire encounter was over—an elderly indignation. I wanted to murmur to the speaker as I went by that even all his life hadn't been all that long as yet, and perhaps that one doesn't denounce one's host with a *brio* borrowed from his wine. But I also felt, and in the same instant, something quite different: that it would be entertaining to enter into casual talk with these youths, drift away with them to some hospitable haunt of their own, and hear everything subversive or otherwise instructive that they had to say. Unfortunately the second of these impulses would be as inadmissible as the first. I went on out of the hall—aiming for the garden but taking a circuitous route through Rattenbury.

Rattenbury is a mid-Victorian exercise in Venetian Gothic, and supposed to be very ugly. Perhaps because of this, and despite the comfort of its large solid rooms and a provision of baths and privies dating from the first great age of such amenities in England, it had been regarded in my time, if not as a dump or slum, at least as a species of academic Stellenbosch to which young men of unimpressive personality or inferior social consideration were apt to find themselves, through the operation of some wholly mysterious mechanism, relegated in a second or third year. I had always felt a pleasing quaintness as attending the pile. It is enormous, like an only slightly stunted St Pancras Station, but runs to a variety of decorative features and excrescences executed in the spirit, and on the scale, of a Pugin parsonage. Thus in front of each staircase there protrudes a hutch-like porch entered through a pointed archway so symbolically low that anybody of normal height has to behave like a double-decker bus approaching an arched bridge—carefully centring himself, that is to say, in order to pass through without bumping his shoulder or even his forehead. It was as I passed one of these orifices that I heard, yet again, the voices of young men. They were—as was customary—expertly shouting above the clatter of their own shoes as they came tumbling down a stone staircase. A moment later they had shot through the archway into open air in a huddle so compacted that it was incomprehensible that they hadn't tripped over one another's flying feet. There was a lantern above us, and I had an instant's impression of tossing hair, of alarmed and flashing glances all around me, of a kind of graceful mock-panic and the swift scattering of long-limbed bodies in all directions. A crackling of under-growth; fawns breaking clear of a dark wood, momentarily at gaze with an alien creature, darting away, startled, vanishing: this, once more, was the effect I fleetingly received. Then the young men had turned a corner, and there came back from them a sudden burst of laughter. They were not laughing at any spectacle I had casually afforded them; however wild their spirits, that wouldn't come into their heads. Their laughter belonged to an inviolable world of their own, un-touched by the irruption among them of tail-coated elders toddling round behind cigars. These were not singers. They must be among the undergraduates who, according to Plot, had been obliged to take a plunge into examinations in this midsummer week. It didn't at all appear that the irksome circumstance had got any of them down.

VII

THE DAY HAD been unremarkable for June, but the night
was of that Mediterranean sort which, straying beneath English
skies, troubles like a portent. There was no moon, and the
stars hung in an electric brilliance suggesting frost—but frost
powerless to chill the skin of air through which the earth's
warmth breathed. In the great dimly blottesque garden it was
an air heavy from the scented limes; and heavy here and there,
too, with tobacco-smoke where in twos and threes guests
like placid penguins perambulated. Some, still wearing their
doctoral robes, were like flower-beds gone adrift in the dark.
One large area was garish with coloured lights left over from
the Commemoration Ball which I knew the undergraduates
to have held, no doubt with prescriptive lavishness, a couple
of nights before. Elsewhere it was by starlight that one moved.
At a middle distance the cigars and cigarettes danced like
fireflies, or glowed and faded like lighthouse signals very far
away.

I looked round for fresh company. One had to get close up to
people before it was possible to identify them. But most of the
men taking this after-dinner breather had wandered into the
garden in groups, and any of these was likely to contain one or
two fellow-guests known to me at least as well as those with
whom I had been talking in hall. I was about to move over
to the first such gathering I saw when a hand was laid on my
shoulder from behind. I turned round and saw Tony, with
Gavin Mogridge beside him. Tony seemed not quite sober.

'Oh, Duncan,' Mogridge said at once, 'I'm so sorry.' He
spoke on a note of serious self-reproach. 'I quite forgot. Many
happy returns of the day.'

It was certainly my birthday. But Tony was the man I'd
have thought of as able to recall the fact. He had given me a

complete Anatole France on my twenty-firster, and by that time we had exchanged such presents on a smaller scale on a couple of occasions. This memory reinforced my sense of what intimates we had been. It would never have crossed our minds that years might later pass without so much as a meeting. At the present reunion there were probably a number of people being visited by similar reflections.

'Thank you very much,' I said. Mogridge had not been so close a friend. But his prime characteristic was tenacity, and this extended to a memory surprising in one so much given to absence of mind. 'I suppose we're known to our hosts as the middle-aged lot.'

'Tempus fugit,' Tony said. 'Tempus fucking fugit.' He radiated, for the moment, a mild alcoholic gloom.

'At least it brings in its revenges. Do you know who I was sitting next to? Killiecrankie! He's made the higher clergy as something called a Prebendary. In Ireland, I think.'

'A kind of Venerable?' My information cheered Tony up to the extent of making him shout with laughter, but then his mood changed again instantly. 'The Rat Race Dinner,' he said. 'That's what this affair should be called. Hundreds of chaps getting on ever so nicely. Look at the labels round their necks. Some P. M. ought to have found you a K., Duncan. What's known in literary circles, I'm told, as the poor man's C. H.'

'I don't think I've ever heard it called that.' Mogridge said this at his flattest and most serious, and it wasn't clear to me whether or not he was intending to rebuke Tony's gibe. 'They call some car or other the poor man's Rolls-Royce. And that reminds me of something rather odd I saw as I arrived.' Mogridge sat down on a garden chair after inspecting it carefully; he might have been suspecting it of harbouring a tarantula or a lethal tropical snake. 'Somebody I didn't know drove up in a Rolls. It was an old Rolls—but you may have noticed how, the older they are, the bigger and grander they come. Of course there were half a dozen Rollses, but this was certainly the largest one.' Mogridge paused, as if feeling that he had been going too fast for us. 'You may have noticed, too, that Rollses have a little statuette-thing on the radiator. You'd perhaps suppose it was a Winged Victory. But it isn't. It has a head, you see, and for some reason Winged Victories have all lost their heads. It's probably conceived as the Spirit of Speed, or something of that sort.'

'Well?' Tony said humorously. He seemed again amiably disposed.

'The first thing this chap did when he got out of his car was to unscrew this figure and lock it up inside. Then he brought a perfectly plain radiator-cap out of his pocket. It's probably called a radiator-cap. Anyway, it's what screws on radiators.'

'And he screwed it on instead?' Tony asked.

'Yes—just that. And bang in the middle of our own private car park. It was curious behaviour. Do you know what I think?'

'One seldom does,' Tony said.

'I think it's possible that people sometimes souvenir such things, and that Rolls owners regularly take that precaution. Only I've never noticed it happen before. I must keep a look out.'

A spell of silence succeeded upon this not very striking anecdote. We were now all three seated within what, in sunlight, would have been the impenetrable shade of a cedar of Lebanon, the grandest tree in a garden not lacking in impressiveness. Above our heads it blotted out half the pierced and powdered sky. Only conspirators, it occurred to me, would seek out so inspissated a gloom. Perhaps we really were going to conspire. The effect was mitigated, however, by a glimmer from those coloured lights which had been left undisturbed after the undergraduates' Ball. It would have made a good stage set.

I remembered that I hadn't yet congratulated Tony on his elevation to the Cabinet, and I did so now. His reply was adequate, and yet there was something edgy about it. Did this promotion only emphasize that his career had got itself out of shape? Why—so early in it as such things go—had he been railroaded into that disabling Upper Chamber? Was he perhaps not, of his sort, quite first class? Was he liable to muff things? He was in college now, I had no longer a doubt, in the pursuance of some design. In such circumstances it couldn't, surely, be a good idea to get slightly tight? Or could it? There wasn't the least impropriety, during a feast like the present, in letting liquor temperately show. It was an open question whether there wasn't an unslumbering cunning in Tony. The situation deserved sounding.

'You're both dead sober,' Tony said, much as if he had been reading my thoughts. 'And so can I be—you'll be relieved, Duncan, to hear—at the drop of a hat. So what about a drink? There's a buffet in a marquee at the other end of the garden—another left-over from the youngsters' Ball, I'd suppose.'

'Not yet,' I said. 'Queues for drinks and queues for loos. And all top people. I'm tired of ribbons and gongs.'

'That gong-tormented pee.'

Tony could scarcely have produced a less witty or more nonsensical remark. But it was the Yeats joke again, and both Mogridge and I responded to it. I wondered how I could have been at sea (or pee) when Tony had declared earlier that day that the staircase was his ancestral stair. And now I saw an opportunity of gaining some information.

'I never went to a Commem Ball,' I said. 'I wasn't able to dance anything except foursome and eightsome reels. Did Ivo go to this one?'

'No need to fish for information about the boy, Duncan.' Tony put out a hand and touched my arm, apparently to make quick amends for this unreasonable rebuke. 'It's all coming out in the next five minutes. Indeed, you've guessed the trouble already.'

'They don't feel he's making any very good use of his time here?'

'Just that—except that "they" needs defining. They're not quite all of them dreary pedants, mumbling about their betas and gammas.'

'But some feel he'd do best to go down?'

'Some feel he ought to be sent down, which isn't quite the same thing.'

'Is Ivo not all that keen on his books?' In the gloom I could just distinguish the glint of Mogridge's spectacles directed slantwise upon Tony as he asked this. He spoke as if here were a doubtful point which ought to be determined at once.

'Ivo's no scholar, if that's what you mean. But I suppose he may get something out of the life of the place without that.'

'Yes, of course. But one has to understand a college's point of view.' Mogridge, if slow, was firm. 'About education being the main thing.' He was now looking up into the darkness of the cedar, as if searching for some practical approach to the problem in hand. 'Do you think he might be interested in travelling?'

'It's what he'll come to in no time, if they have their way with him.' Tony's good humour was restored by this odd suggestion from the Mogridge world. 'Of the commercial variety. Peddling encyclopaedias from doorstep to doorstep on the strength of his nice Oxford accent and delusive appearance of being prepared to offer gallantry if the lady invites him inside. Seriously, it's simply taking a young man's prospects of a livelihood away from him to treat him in such a fashion.'

'I don't buy that one, Tony.' It struck me as wholesome to do a little being firm myself. 'Staying up and collecting what will probably be a mediocre degree isn't going to enhance your son's prospects in the least. Take him away now and shove him into whatever you'd be shoving him into in two years' time. Banking or broking or insurance or whatever. Nobody in your sort of set-up is going to give a damn for the boy's having fallen foul of the dons. Think of your blessed Cabinet. Full of thoroughly able chaps who either asked for their cards after a year here, or were chucked out because of the excessively contumelious character of their drinking or wenching, or who did remain on the strength and ended up with a Fourth Class in the sole company of the Crown Prince of Waga-Waga.'

'Absolute balls, Duncan. The sort of rubbish one hears talked in outmoded plays.'

'It's not rubbish. It's only picturesque exaggeration, for which I apologize. Junkin's father might advance the argument about livelihood with some colour of truth. But not you. You're just creating, my boy, as a matter of family pride. I declare this stair to be my grandpapa's sacred stamping-ground.'

'And who the hell is Junkin?' Tony was taking my challenge, or its tone, very well.

'You haven't heard of Junkin? Hasn't Ivo brought him home for a week-end or a square meal? He's Ivo's nearest neighbour on the staircase.'

'And at school with him? How very odd—I haven't heard of him.'

'He was at Cokeville Grammar School, and the pride of its History Sixth. And he's in precisely the same boat as Ivo— except that I don't think his father is likely to be at this Gaudy, sizing up the current race of dons.'

'What do you mean—in precisely the same boat as Ivo?' Tony's pounce on this had a speed the significance of which didn't at the moment come to me.

'I mean that if Plot is reliable—and scouts always know these things—your boy and this lad Junkin have failed the same examination second time round—and that at the second go there was nothing between them so far as the marks went. Just nothing at all.'

'Which means that Junkin must be in danger of being sent down too.' Mogridge produced this as if it were a piece of advanced logic—and then went on, rather unexpectedly, to a further inference. 'And therefore, Tony, if you feel that you must make representations to the college about your son's case, it will probably be right to include a plea for his friend as well.'

'But Junkin isn't his friend—and he isn't my son, either.' Tony had spoken impatiently, but now checked himself. 'But, of course, *not* to—supposing it known that I know about

Junkin——' He broke off. 'Interesting,' he said. 'Interesting and tricky. As Duncan points out, this absurd Junkin's father isn't likely to come around about the thing.'

'And is not a Cabinet Minister,' I said inexorably.

'Yes, yes—one has to face all that. It might become a matter of how one works it. It would be totally out of turn for me to breathe the august name of Junkin when discussing the matter at present. But there's no absolute hurry about the situation. I might contact Junkin *père*, and fix it that we move in on the affair together. Two parents, differing widely in their circumstances, come together out of a common concern. It's not a tactic to rush at. But it deserves thought.'

'No.' The monosyllable came from Mogridge, but with a new quality which made both Tony and myself glance round as for another speaker. 'And you don't want, either, Tony, to give the appearance of going round all these people as if you were thinking of forming a caucus. Some of them, at least, must be aware that you have your son's position much in mind. They'd think it very proper that you should be concerned; in fact you probably have a patch of common ground with them in overestimating the importance of the matter. For I rather agree with Duncan, you see. It won't in the least be a tragedy if Ivo has to call it a day. If a chap is no good at a thing, it may be a blessing in disguise if he's booted into something else. I myself had an experience like that long ago, as a matter of fact. But what I was saying was that dons think highly of what they have on offer, and are most of them very conscientious on the whole, and would tend to go along with a troubled parent just as far as they felt they could. But I think they'd very quickly come to resent the application to them of what you might call the techniques of persuasion. You ought just to speak to the Provost, Tony. That's the proper thing.'

This produced silence—in myself because I was, quite irrationally, astonished that Gavin Mogridge should be capable of such massive common sense. As for Tony, I believe he was a little shaken in his estimate of his own sufficient guile.

'The Provost,' Mogridge resumed, 'is the head of the college.' He paused as if to mark this recovery of his common form. 'And it's always best to go to the head man. That's what a head man's there for—to be gone to. I think you should have a talk with the Provost.'

'I'm not having a talk with anybody tonight,' Tony said with recovered ease. 'It wouldn't be the thing. And, as I said, there's plenty of time.'

'For a preliminary softening up?' I asked.

'You can put it that way. As for the Provost, I'm not sure that I like the man. Professionals tend not much to care for amateurs.'

'You mean he's a politician?'

'Of course he is. And there's another thing. I'm not sure of his stuffing. The art of manipulating a corporate body the way you want it is to nose out the true power nexus behind the formal one. Take the Governing Body of this college. It's now, I'm told, between forty and fifty strong. That's including, of course, chaps who are only hangers-on: professorial fellows and so forth, like that dim creature McKechnie. Pretty large, by Oxford standards. Well, some must carry a lot more weight than others, and it's not too difficult to discover what's roughly their pecking order. But there are dark horses as well—and niggers in the woodpile, for that matter.' Tony paused to register amusement before this jumble of expressions. 'Hidden hands. Even a top hidden hand. And that's the question for the jack-pot. Gavin, who would be your bet as the college's lurking strong man?'

'I don't know them all that well. One doesn't get to know people very well if one meets them only once in so many years. You would get a more reliable answer, Tony, from somebody who knew them all intimately.' Thus excelling himself, Mogridge paused. 'Perhaps it would be Cyril?' he said.

'In God's name who is Cyril?' Tony demanded.

'Cyril Bedworth, of course.'

'Most amusing.' Tony was contemptuous of this absurdity. 'With old Halberd, I suppose, as *proxime accessit*.'

'Talbert,' I said—and remembered how Tony's affecting

121

never to be able to get my tutor's name right had irritated me long ago. 'And now,' I added baldly, 'I'm going to talk to some other chaps.' And I got up and wandered away.

But in fact I avoided chaps again, although not for very long. I think I felt displeased by, and wanted to reflect on, the way in which I had reacted to this not very important Ivo Mumford affair. Here was Tony Mumford, forging ahead in the High Court of Parliament under our most religious and gracious Queen at that time assembled, but showing every sign of an injudicious obsession with a purely domestic matter. I had thought to detect some sort of pride or arrogance underlying his attitude: an assumption that at least a measure of special treatment was his due and therefore Ivo's due. And I had reacted too crudely as the old and candid friend. For who was I to judge how strongly a man should feel about the fortunes of his son?

As I walked obliquely across the garden now I tried to project one of those dream children of my own into Ivo's situation, and to estimate how I'd comport myself in relation to it. But dream children—however long-haired and long-limbed and charming—are much too insubstantial to base such an exercise upon, and I had to reaffirm to myself that I was on territory destined to remain largely unknown to me. I was, indeed, convinced that Tony would do wrong to insert other than the gentlest of oars into his son's academic affairs. Instead of planning a campaign among our present hosts, he ought to be tackling the boy himself. He ought to be saying something like: 'Look, you'd better decide either to have a damned good shot at any further chance your tutors give you, or to cut out and work hard at something more to your fancy—and I've a perfectly open mind as to what.'

But how easy to be wise—quite genuinely wise—on behalf of other people! Distance the Mumfords, father and son, only a very little, and it was crystalline that Ivo, whatever his character and temperament, was likely to take less mischief from having a university career cut short than from a father who patently felt that strings must and could be pulled for him. This was what I ought to have said to Tony—and not, perhaps, even in the presence of the loyal and sagacious Mogridge. I ought to have kept if for later and for a wholly private occasion—perhaps for the final half-hour which Tony and I were likely to spend together, whether in his son's rooms or in Nick Junkin's, before we went to bed. I had bungled my possible part in the affair. It was a discovery making me feel that I wanted to hear no more of it.

I found that I had strayed out of the garden into Howard. The great square space was dimly lit from the ancient iron lanterns hanging above the staircase entrances. The Commem Ball, although it had probably, in one way or another, submerged the entire college, appeared to have been centred here. The main marquee must have occupied the whole quad, and its evidences were not yet all cleared away. A dance floor, naked to the sky and seeming faintly to reflect the stars, still covered nearly half the grass. The rest was littered with huge masts, spars, coils of rope, great rolls of canvas. I might have been surveying in the dim light the stage of some enormous German opera-house, with an impropable *Tristan* or *Der fliegende Holländer* cooking up—or perhaps the Lyceum or His Majesty's with Irving's or Tree's carpenters labouring at a sensational *décor* for the opening of *The Tempest*. And it was a stage not wholly untenanted. In a corner remote from that by which I had entered I could distinguish a number of dark figures, seemingly closely huddled together. This effect at least was melodramatic. It was as if I had blundered upon a nest of assassins or *banditti*.

They were, of course, nothing but a group of diners who had not discarded their gowns. Quite probably they were all unknown to me, and this made bearing down on them slightly awkward. On the other hand I had a sense that my advent had been remarked, so that to retreat would be graceless. I compromised by drifting in the general direction of the group with an air of thoughtful leisure. And then, as I passed under one of the lanterns, I was recognized.

'Oh, Duncan,' Cyril Bedworth's voice said, 'how very nice! Do come and join us.'

There were introductions, from which I gathered that all three of the men with Bedworth were his colleagues. But I picked up only two of the names: James Gender and Charles Atlas. Gender I had a faint memory of as a young man who had turned up in college in my final year as a junior lecturer in law. Atlas seemed just such a young man now. And I could see that the third man was much the oldest of the group.

I supposed that these people had turned into Howard by way of taking a few minutes off the job of acting as conscientious hosts. But this was a little odd, and after the introductions came a pause which put a different idea in my head. It was that Bedworth, in hailing me, had acted with the social infelicity intermittently to be remarked in him. He had noticed me; he did feel for me a certain warmth of regard which didn't the less please me for being a survival from times long past; as a consequence he had given that cordial hail. It was talk of a confidential sort, however, that had been going on, and the pause was a result of a need to change the subject.

'We've been indulging thoughts,' the man called Gender said, pleasantly if not veraciously, 'prompted by these ruins of revelry. They're all over the place. The coal-yard, for instance, is a vast dump of fading flowers and palm-trees in pots. I suppose dances have always required such embellishments. But nowadays, it seems, the young people also demand four distinct bands, a cabaret show, and a complete amusement park in Long Field for people who don't want to be bothered with dancing at all.'

'Which is why a double ticket costs fifteen guineas.' This came—I fancied with an edge to it—from the unidentified elderly man, who was smoking a pipe. 'And you don't cut much of a figure if you can't pay for extra champagne.'

'Oh, rubbish, Arnold,' Gender said. 'The whole affair is a harmless once-in-three-years fling. And you'd find far more emphasis on conspicuous expenditure in a working men's club in the Midlands.'

'I'm afraid I can't feel the fling to have been entirely harmless on the present occasion.' This time, the man with the pipe spoke with an exaggerated gentleness the effect of which was scarcely friendly. 'It doesn't upset me that the place is turned into a brothel——'

'Really, Arnold, that goes a bit far.'

'So it does. I apologize. It doesn't upset me, or in the least astonish me, that some of the young people find themselves—probably to their own mild surprise—involved in episodes of successful fornication. On such an occasion the whole set-up of an Oxford college invites quite comically to simple indoor games. And the consequences are not likely to be other than trivial. Now and then, perhaps, a shot-gun marriage? Yes—but there is little evidence, I imagine, that such marriages are more frequently calamitous than are maturely considered ventures of the same sort. But the casualty we have just heard of is another matter. It startles me, I confess.'

'Do you know what Howard at this moment suggests to me?' This came from the young man, Charles Atlas, and was plainly intended as a diversion. Atlas, indeed, had to pause for a moment to discover what Howard *might* suggest. 'The Duchess of Richmond's ballroom in Brussels. On the morning after, that is. And with the guns of Waterloo in the distance —if there's a thunder-storm coming up, as I think there is.'

'That would seem to make a Waterloo of this Gaudy,' I said, rather at random. It was increasingly evident to me that, here at the moment, something was on the carpet which was no business of mine. But I had at least to offer a remark or two before repairing Bedworth's error by making myself scarce. 'I've been seeing Howard myself,' I added in pursuance of this need, 'as a backdrop for something like *Peter Grimes* or *Billy Budd*.'

'Ah, yes—or the destruction of the Spanish Armada.' The man called Arnold, who was thus merely giving a civil indication that he had taken my point, paused to put a match to his pipe. For a second the spurt of light brought me inexplicably contradictory impressions: I had certainly never seen him before, yet about his features there was a certain haunting familiarity as from a long time back. 'But the Gaudy is no Waterloo,' he went on. 'It's more like a Field of the Cloth of Gold. And in the present instance—if we're to pursue the figure—Waterloo is simply one of the public examinations of the university. That's where the casualty has occurred.'

'But at least it's not a tragedy,' Atlas said, and then turned to address me directly. 'Something we've had to have a word about,' he said. 'You'd have found it entirely boring.'

Neither the air of apology with which the words were spoken nor the tenses of the verbs employed inclined me to receive this very well. I was without the slightest wish to barge in on whatever academic storm in a teacup was brewing itself up at this unlikely hour, and if these people were so unseasonably involved in confidential talk it had been their business to shelve it for a few minutes more effectively than they had done. So I was about to walk away with a minimum of ado when I was prevented by Bedworth.

'No point in making a stranger of Pattullo,' he said. 'I seem to recall that we happen all to be among those agreed on that.'

'Indeed, yes.' James Gender, who appeared to go in for courteous diffidence, made a kind of murmur of acquiescence out of these perplexing words, and the elderly man gave me a glance which seemed to signal amiable complicity which I didn't in the least understand.

'My name's Lempriere,' the elderly man murmured to me casually. He paused, as if waiting for some recognition that didn't come to me. 'Of course we'll be glad to hear what you think of this business. We're rather close up to it ourselves.'

I believe I felt for a moment an unaccountable alarm. It didn't prevent my being conscious that the junior man, Atlas, still didn't want me in on this confabulation. There seemed nothing personal about this, and I had to put him down as a stickler for the forms. You don't chuck shop—and still less rifts in the lute—at a dinner-guest.

'As you'll have gathered,' Bedworth said, 'it's this business of the Commem Ball clashing with examinations. It's undoubtedly an awkward thing.' Bedworth was very serious. I had a glimmering sense of him as a dedicated man.

'But didn't it always?' I asked. 'I seem to remember something of the sort happening bang in the middle of when I was taking Schools.'

'Perfectly true.' Lempriere had struck in with an effect of abruptly grim incisiveness. 'But that's different: Finals are for seasoned third or fourth year men—most of them living out of college. Nowadays we have another whole rash of Classified Honours affairs—all that damned rubbish of Firsts and Seconds and Thirds—confronting infants with no more than twenty-four weeks of university life behind them. And all brought up in their admirable grammar schools——'

'Forty-six per cent,' Bedworth interrupted sharply.

'And half of them brought up to regard all examinations as life or death affairs. So what do we do? Arrange that on the eve of this spurious but alarming ordeal they have to sleep through—or skulk around the fringes of—an uncouth imitation of the polished ungodliness of the metropolis. In fact, a Commem Ball.'

'We try,' Bedworth said, 'to move them into the quieter parts of the college.'

'And that is our supreme wisdom, indeed,' Lempriere said. 'Do you know that when an Australian aborigine stole a chicken he used to be trucked half across the continent to what was regarded as the appropriate court for dealing with him? And the mere journey meant an exposure to unspeakable terrors, with alien spirits and a foreign magic all around him. It's just the same with our little brutes. They've grown accustomed to the security of their own familiar rooms. And suddenly you tell them to grab their pyjamas and tooth-brush, and you huddle them into Rattenbury. Hitler did much the same thing with——'

'Come, come, Arnold.' Atlas spoke quite amiably. 'Don't run away with yourself, my dear chap.'

'Very well. But then there's this notion of Cyril's that they're asked to move in order to have a chance of a quieter night. Complete poppycock. Of course there's no quiet to be had anywhere in college on such an occasion. They're herded over to Rattenbury—and they're still there, you know, at this moment—because it makes it easier to prevent them gate-crashing that opulent and ostentatious revel. Cyril, that's not to be denied, is it?'

'It was one consideration involved, I agree.' Bedworth spoke slowly. 'It's best not to put temptation to plain dishonesty in people's way.'

'I don't think I'd like to call it that,' Gender said judiciously. 'Gate-crashing is only a lark—at least when it's an affair at another college. But attending one's own dance without a ticket isn't perhaps quite the thing.'

'Well, it's what this unfortunate boy Lusby decided to do.' Lempriere had turned to me as if minded to enter upon a narrative. 'We know that he actually made it the subject of a wager. He'd borrow a dinner-jacket—for you can attend these things in dinner-jackets nowadays—and go right through the ball undetected.'

'Didn't he own a dinner-jacket?' Atlas asked.

'Apparently not—and why should he? He's a very simple lad—which I see as part of the mischief. Anyway, the hopeful young Lusby succeeded in his design, so that dawn found him still among the revellers. Cyril, that's right?'

'Quite right.'

'Among them, but not of them. That, I imagine, is the nub of the matter. There was nobody he could dance with, and he felt in constant danger of being detected and chucked out. For a more privileged lad that would just have been part of the fun, and a matter of losing his bet. But Lusby would view it as a humiliation. He had misjudged the thing, he was strained and miserable, and he never got to bed. He simply changed his clothes, walked to the Examination Schools, sat down at his place, and fell fast asleep. He'd probably been working into the small hours, remember, over the week-end. He'd treat an examination that way.'

'I suppose somebody woke him up?' I asked. As I was plainly to be told Lusby's whole story it seemed polite to show some interest in it.

'Nobody did. No doubt it's a point the college could make itself unpleasant about, and it reflects small credit on whichever of the examiners were doing the invigilating. I imagine any of them who took a glance at the boy supposed him to have closed his eyes for a few moments in the interest of more powerful cerebration. However that may be, he woke up—or more or less woke up—at the end of three hours, and found that he had only a blank manuscript-book to hand in. He did so, and staggered out of the Schools.'

'We don't know that he staggered,' Bedworth said. 'There was still really nothing to alert anybody to the fact that trouble was brewing. If only Lusby had been sitting near any of the other men from the college, they'd probably have tumbled to the situation and yanked him along to his tutor. Or got on to his tutor themselves. Undergraduates are extremely reliable in such situations.'

'Perfectly true,' Lempriere said. 'The young pests can be trusted to rally round in an astonishing way. It's one of the few traits that sharply distinguishes theirs from other criminal societies. If one must get in a scrape, an Oxford college isn't a bad place to choose for it.'

'Yes,' Atlas said. 'They need any alphas they can pick up, the Lord knows. And they do generally raise one on the primitive loyalty paper.'

And James Gender produced his acquiescent murmur again.

It had never occurred to me, when an undergraduate, that our tutors could take any sort of pride in us—except, conceivably, on account of some exceptional agility displayed in jumping through the paper hoops of the Examination Schools. But here were these four men, oddly disturbed about poor

Lusby and betraying certain signs of being not quite at one on the matter, making each other this passing token of accord. They had the good luck to be in a decent regiment. It was something like that: the assertion, almost in a secret code, of those convictions about the college which, earlier that evening, it had been the Provost's business to express in terms of public eloquence. And the effect of this perception on me was to make me feel a genuine if necessarily tenuous concern for the unknown Lusby myself.

'This examination,' I asked, 'is a full-scale, day-after-day affair?'

'Pretty well,' Lempriere said, and glanced at Gender. 'Jimmy, would it be nine papers?'

'Six, which is almost as bad. Two on Tuesday, the day after the Ball. Two today, Wednesday, and two tomorrow, Thursday.' Gender glanced at his watch. 'And tomorrow will be with us in no time at all, which shows what a successful Gaudy this is turning out to be.'

'Gaudies last till midnight-plus, but Commem Balls carry on into late breakfasts round the town?' I asked.

'One sees you remember the drill,' Lempriere said. 'And now we return to Mr Lusby. He needs help. He has emerged from that non-paper, and is wandering around. Does he get any luncheon? We don't know, but we conjecture not. He will be shy of going into hall and facing all that cheerful gabble about what the paper was like.'

'Bad,' I said. It was evident that the sardonic Lempriere possessed imagination.

'Half-past two arrives, and Lusby is back in the Schools. What he chiefly feels now is that he must not turn in another wholly blank paper. So, every twenty minutes or so, he manages to write down a disconnected sentence. This at least takes him right out of any category of persons whom invigilators need concern themselves about, but it isn't going to help him to pass his Moderations, whether with credit or otherwise. He is realizing now that he ought to have gone straight to Jimmy Gender after the morning's fiasco. Jimmy

Gender is his tutor. He quite likes Jimmy. Jimmy, a competent performer, has afforded Mr Lusby certain cautious tokens that he, Jimmy, quite likes him. Jimmy, the situation might be more or less that?'

'We needn't romanticize it,' Gender said. 'When this kind of thing happens, one simply has to acknowledge having fallen down on the job. Of course my pupils knew I'd be on the bridge. It's only simple sense to make that clear to them. But Lusby didn't come along.'

There was a silence in which I made the further discovery that the fact or fantasy of a close personal relationship with the near-children who were their pupils was important to all four of these variously assorted men. I tried to relate this to my memories of Albert Talbert, who would sometimes take me for one of his undergraduates (which I was) and sometimes for a tenuously identifiable research student from another college (to say nothing of being Dalrymple every now and then). And I saw, with a kind of sudden awe, that there had been nothing in those bizarre intermittencies of memory to prevent Talbert's having been rather fond of me.

'To continue,' Lempriere said. 'The mischief in these affairs is that the point of no return comes so quickly. If those damned examiners had spotted their young Rip Van Winkle straight away, and got on the telephone, all might have been well. Lusby would have had his luncheon—sherry, chocolate Bath Olivers, and black coffee, I rather imagine—in Jimmy's rooms, and enough of the right chat from Jimmy to take him through some sort of show in the afternoon. By that time we'd have had in Robert Damian, who'd sign on the dotted line—and honestly enough—that Lusby had been under strain, and so forth. We'd have had a very good chance of selling that successfully to the proctors, who wouldn't be too keen on having negligent invigilation in the examination-room publicized. So Lusby, if he'd performed with any shadow of competence in the rest of the papers, would have been sure of an aegrotat, and might even have got a class. As it is, it's no go.'

'And not all that important,' Atlas said, 'except in Lusby's head'.

'Just so.' Lempriere's voice had returned to its sardonic mode. 'But the state of Lusby's head is what we wonder about.'

'Where is Lusby now?' I asked.

'Where, indeed? But let me return to an orderly exposition. At the end of his disastrous day, Lusby slept in college. But, remember, as a displaced person in Rattenbury. The scout on the staircase didn't know him from Adam, or pay any attention to him. Which was a pity. It's well known that a boy's best friend is his scout. And Lusby didn't want to talk to any of his acquaintances—those, that is, who were taking the same examination, and remaining in residence during this first week of the vacation for that purpose. They would all just be wondering whether they had done rather better, or rather worse, than they had hoped. Lusby couldn't bear the thought of revealing himself as in a position so remote from that. He was right back with the sort of loneliness of his very first days in college. Only, he'd had his hopes and ambitions to help him then. He didn't have them now.'

'Arnold,' Atlas said, 'stop so obligingly making things vivid for us.'

'Very well, Charles. But we do want to arrive at the young man's state of mind.'

'We want to arrive at his whereabouts, for a start.'

'Then let me tell Pattullo what we know about that. This morning, Lusby didn't turn up at the Schools at all. And that, of course, at last started something. When he hadn't appeared in his place within the prescribed twenty minutes of the first hour the examiners contacted our Senior Tutor. Or rather— since he is away ill at the moment—our acting Senior Tutor, who is Cyril here. And Cyril set inquiries going. We're still waiting for an answer to them.'

'The scout on that staircase in Rattenbury has a notion Lusby said something about going home.' Bedworth, anxiously precise, had taken up the story. 'Unfortunately he's not at all an intelligent man—and moreover, as Arnold has hinted, he hadn't much interest in Lusby. So that piece of evidence is rather unreliable. Lusby has certainly vanished, but he doesn't appear to have taken any of his possessions with him. And perhaps you see, Duncan, that I've had rather a difficult decision to make. The problem does crop up from time to time, but I think it can be dealt with only on an *ad hoc* basis. In terms, I mean, of one's sense of the particular situation and the particular man.'

'I can imagine that.'

'You know how chary the police are of classifying anybody as a missing person. If your husband, or your grown-up daughter, doesn't choose to come home, or walks out of the front door and fails to turn up for tea, it's no good expecting a hunt to be set instantly on foot. Roughly speaking, people are entitled to take themselves off where they please. And that goes for an undergraduate member of a college. He has come of age, and is free to choose between one lawful course of conduct and another. So you see what I mean. If Lusby has run away, we can only try to catch up with him in some unspectacular way, and reason with him. If it is really home to his parents that he has bolted, that would seem to be simple. But then there's the question of confidence. The theory that college authorities stand *in loco parentis* with these young adults has worn pretty thin by now. Suppose Lusby has got himself a job on a building site, and is going to receive a pay-packet for the first time in his life. Surprising his parents with that in a week or a fortnight's time may be his notion of rehabilitating himself in his own regard. So am I right in going clucking to them now—and it may be alarming them very much?'

'I see the problems,' I said. It struck me that Bedworth, although now an authority on two writers distinguished for a subtle movement of mind, retained a certain laboured explicitness of his own characteristic note.

'But my dear Cyril,' Lempriere said, 'the art of administration consists largely in ignoring the problems, or at least in not being diverted by them. Lusby's hypothetical pay-packet simply has no business in your mind. What are you going to *do*?'

'Drive to Bethnal Green in the morning.'

'Bethnal Green?' Atlas repeated blankly.

'Certainly.' Bedworth now spoke briskly; his rise to challenge had been immediate. 'It's where the lad's parents live. If there's no news by morning, I'll go and see them. Until I've seen how things lie, they need have no notion such a call is anything out of the way. They're not university people.'

'That's the right thing,' Gender said quietly. 'Only, Cyril, it ought to be me. I'm the boy's tutor. I should have thought of it.'

'I know you'd do it more skilfully than I shall, Jimmy. But you'd better remain, I think, on that bridge.' Quite simply, I realized, Bedworth was giving an order. 'Much the likeliest thing is that Lusby will turn up in college again—rather battered and needing his hand held.'

'Very well. And if he does, I'll try to do a bit better than those chocolate Bath Olivers.'

This lengthy discussion, so oddly located and timed, had been increasingly surprising. I felt it to be based on some premise not revealed to me, but about which I might now without intrusiveness inquire.

'What sort of a young man is Lusby?' I asked.

'Erratic,' Gender said. 'But I suppose that's self-evident. His allowing himself to be lured into that silly wager shows it. A serious man, working hard for an examination that means a great deal to him. And suddenly this! It's dotty.'

'Or it's what Damian,' Atlas said, 'would call an aberrant episode during an identity-crisis of adolescence.'

'Rubbishing jargon, Charles. I'd only say that Lusby is withdrawn and not easy to know—in addition to which he's probably very able indeed. He ought to be performing outstandingly in this examination, and he knows it. I suppose that will make the muck-up all the more bitter to him. Perhaps a hostile observer would say he had more brains than guts.

But that would be shallow and unfair.' Gender hesitated. 'As a matter of fact, and as Cyril knows, Lusby has a little come Damian's way already. He has a depressive tendency to contend with.'

'That has scarcely been concealed from any of us,' Lempriere said drily. 'It's plainly the occasion of this tizzy.'

'Very well. But it's my experience that such chaps often have an underlying toughness—a sort of stoicism—which keeps them in the race. I just hope Paul Lusby has. I've been rather looking forward to getting something really going with him over the next three years. I'm very distressed about this.'

'But you don't mind,' Lempriere said, 'requiring your Paul Lusbys to fight their way into the Examination Schools through harmless once-in-three-year flings. And if one only gives the matter a little thought, one realizes that conspicuous expenditure is more prevalent in Bethnal Green than Mayfair.'

The sudden ferocity of this, expressed between men who clearly respected one another, disconcerted me. Perhaps it was something merely verbal, like a nervous tic. Perhaps it belonged with that order of ritualized combat under which one barrister briefly flashes out at another in the simple interest of keeping things lively. But certainly it reflected some condition of strain. These four men hadn't slipped away to confer merely because a young man had failed to sit through an examination. They had other fears about him. And Gender had touched on the ground for these.

So far, we had been talking undisturbed. Not a soul had strayed into Howard. The quad wasn't being used, presumably, to accommodate Gaudy guests; otherwise some of them would by this time be making their way through it to bed. It was past midnight, and every now and then I had been conscious of the starting up of an engine in the distant college car-park as somebody of the less leisured sort prepared to drive, or be driven, away. I was conscious, too, that the character of the warm still night was changing. To the west the stars had vanished behind an inky wash, and the air in the shadowy stone trough we stood in felt ominous and electrical.

'Yes, there *will* be a storm,' Atlas murmured to me, as if his observations had matched mine. 'We'll be driven under hatches.' His glance had been over the nautical-seeming litter on the grass, but now it travelled further, and my own followed. A figure was advancing on us from a far corner of the quad. He was in evening dress, but wore a bowler hat. For a moment I thought, absurdly, that it was Tony, who had at least arrived in Oxford in a bowler. Then I saw that here was a college servant—perhaps the common-room butler—dressed in the main for the formal evening occasion, but wearing in addition this token of day-time consequence. It certainly wasn't required against the night air, but did prove to have a function. He walked up to the acting Senior Tutor, and took it off in style.

'Mr Bedworth,' he said. 'A telephone call, sir.' He paused for a moment, and looked round the rest of us. 'A gentleman on a newspaper.'

'At this time of night! Haven't you told him——'

'I told him about the Gaudy, sir. He at once asked questions about it. And then about the Ball.'

'What did he want to know about that?' It was Lempriere who snapped out this question.

'What might be called its scope, sir. Whether most of the gentlemen attended, and the price of a ticket. I need hardly say I have given him no satisfaction. We are told always to be careful about the press.' The man glanced at me briefly, as if suspecting that I had a notebook in my pocket. 'I think we may presently have another call from elsewhere. But it might be wise for Mr Bedworth to have a word with this person now.'

Bedworth turned away without speaking, and the two men disappeared into the gloom together. The four of us remaining fell to walking slowly up and down the quad. Nobody said anything like 'I hope it's not a disaster' or 'This sounds bad'. We were perfectly silent. I was surprised to find myself confident that I ought not to slip sway. Again a car started up in the distance, and then there was a brief straggling chiming of those of Oxford's bells that concern themselves with the quarter-hours. Gender produced a cigarette-case, thought better of the action, and shoved it away. And then Bedworth was walking slowly back to join us.

'That second call did come through,' he said. 'A police station.'

'Ah!' Atlas said softly. 'Where, Cyril?'

'Bethnal Green. Lusby did go home. There was only his mother in the house. He told her everything was fine, and persuaded her to go round the shops and collect him a nice supper. As soon as she went out he turned on the gas. He's dead.'

VIII

I RETURNED TO Junkin's rooms. For me the Gaudy was over. For the men I had just been talking to it was going to continue for a time. They had come together out of an uneasy sense that Paul Lusby's foolish exploit ought to have been spotted; that it had constituted, in his particular case and together with his subsequent disappearance, a danger-signal plain to read; that a course of action must be decided upon. But action had been overtaken by event. And however they felt about the matter, they weren't dispensed from now returning to entertain their guests through the tail-end of this annual jollification. There would be old members rather short of company, who yet lacked the gumption to go to bed or drive away. There might be others who had drunk rather too much, and needed unobtrusive managing. When it was all over, and the guests were more or less tucked up, the hosts—apart from the few who were bachelors and lived in college—would return to their North Oxford or Headington homes, and to wives either asleep or grimly awake in bed reading *The Decline and Fall of the Roman Empire*. Even Mrs Bedworth and whatever other college ladies had gallantly dined together in style could not possibly have supported each other's company for nearly five hours at a stretch. They would be home by now, and laying the family breakfast table.

These fancies went through my head without amusing me. I was troubled by the death of the unknown young man. Looking around the miscellaneous possessions of Nicolas Junkin now, I even experienced a fleeting confusion of mind in which I believed that it was Junkin—equally unknown to me—who had died. I may just have been tired—or perhaps the college's wine was at work. But such mental vagaries are not uncommon in sober states. Writers may be peculiarly vulnerable to them, since they have the habit of fragmenting and reassorting authentic experience in the interest of concocting fictions.

The muddle could last only for a moment, but its vanishing produced the sensation of relief we feel when, awakening from a bad dream, we realize it isn't true. I suppose because his rooms had once been mine, my imagination had adopted Nicolas Junkin. I'd even been taking sides with him against his neighbour, Ivo Mumford, although Ivo was the son of my first close Oxford friend, whereas Junkin's Cokeville background was a blank, and the boy himself I was unlikely ever to set eyes on.

There had been in my mind some notion that Tony and I might finish the evening *tête à tête*. I now felt disinclined for this. Lusby's fate was so much with me that I should probably be impelled to come out with an account of it, and if Tony was uninterested the effect would be cheerless and awkward. He might even react to it as he had reacted to my casual mention of Junkin's examination result—seizing, with his swift political instinct, upon this miserable fatality in Bethnal Green as a useful exemplification of the fact that the college today was clumsy in its dealings with its young men. This would be unfair. Arguing about it with Tony didn't appeal to me.

So I ought to have gone to bed. Instead, I behaved in a manner which, although I scarcely realized it, reflected the fact that Junkin's room was my room too. I had often returned to it late at night, whether from a party or from some rambling discussion of abstract topics with serious men, and paced the carpet into the small hours in an effort to sort out not such issues as had been debated but the character or quiddity first of one of my acquaintances and then of another. I picked up on this habit now—so that presently I found myself walking up and down, trying to feel my way, at least to the extent of a few initial inches, into the personalities of the men I had lately been involved with.

As a professional category I scarcely felt any special interest in them. Fellows of colleges existed for me merely as a species of part-time schoolmasters, some of them possessed of scholarly or scientific inclinations. This reductive view didn't conduce to lively curiosity—and yet as soon as individual specimens detached themselves from the notional class of instructing and investigating persons they began to demand attention. Three of the four men encountered in Howard I had never seen before—nor, indeed, had I seen them as much more than obscure nocturnal presences then. I had glimpsed Arnold Lempriere by match-light, and I now realized he had fleetingly reminded me of somebody else. He was a short stout man, grey-haired and grey-complexioned, with a closely-trimmed moustache over a firm mouth. He was much older than his companions, and they had treated him with an un-emphatic but perceptible indulgence which might merely reflect this fact, but which could have another occasion as well. Alone of the group, Lempriere had suggested to me the possession of a stage sense. He had talked effectively, once or twice even pungently, from a pronounced stand-point: that of a man sharply critical of the disposition of things around him. The competitive examination system—Firsts, Seconds and Thirds—was damned nonsense, and a hard-boiled attitude was required before it. Even so, the nonsense, if subscribed to, ought not to be telescoped with turning the college into a ballroom; nor, in the interest of such revels, ought bewildered or bewilderable youths like Lusby to be picked up and dumped in Rattenbury.

In his talk Lempriere had seemed to prize an old-fashioned flair for the vivid and picturesque; in his brief description and analysis of Lusby's plight he had enjoyed deploying a certain rhetorical resource. But his colleagues had not struck me as all that impressed. If one of these were to be seriously convinced of the identical propositions Lempriere had been putting forward he might still, I obscurely perceived, not estimate highly the worth or reliability of Lempriere as an ally. For what I have called stage sense (a dramatist's possession, but one with which he must endow his characters) is a very unacademic thing. It is an alert waiting for a role, for an effective turn that can be put on. In a closely knit body of scholarly men such an impulse—which is a kind of misplaced creativeness—must always appear as irresponsibility. Perhaps something of the sort was imputed to Lempriere.

At this point I didn't exactly surprise myself by a yawn. I made to glance at the clock—at my own clock, since this had become again my own room. My glance didn't go, however, to the corner in which there ought to have stood the Dutch bracket affair, but to the mantelpiece where, beneath *Young Picts watching the arrival of Saint Columba,* I had kept a small electric clock owning the pleasing ability to tick or not to tick according as one set a switch. There was no clock now, but only the demonic Ishii Genzō. He looked more furious than ever, and I thought idly that this was because somebody had casually perched an envelope against his frame. I hadn't noticed this earlier. Before the Gaudy, certainly, there had been nothing there. A closer look revealed that it was a letter addressed to me, and I realized that it had been thus deposited according to the custom of some college messenger on an unhurried evening round.

I picked up the envelope and opened it—and to a curiously melodramatic accompaniment. During the past half-hour thunder had been grumbling in the distance; prowling the Chilterns, the Berkshire Downs; enfilading, circling the city of Oxford. Now there was a single brilliant flash of lightning, the effect of which was seemingly to bring the massive façade of the library hurtling across Surrey and hard up against Junkin's windows. It was instantaneously followed by a loud peal of thunder directly overhead. And torrential rain was falling when I was still unfolding the Provost's letter.

Dear Pattullo,

   May I send you, without being too boring, a line of welcome to the Gaudy? I have, as you will find in a moment, an ulterior motive! But your turning-up really is a particular satisfaction to many of the older-established among us. The college, illustrious (as we shall hear proclaimed tonight) in so many fields, has always been a little lagging in the possession of members who have attained, like yourself, to the highest distinction in the arts. And it is certainly many years since you and I met. It would not be easy for me to forget the pleasure of a conversation with you. I hope we shall manage one this evening. But I shall, of course, have to be assiduous in all those proper attentions to Establishment figures, so the point is a little at hazard.

I wonder whether I may venture to beg you, if it can possibly be fitted in with your plans, to linger in Oxford tomorrow for at least as long as will permit you to lunch with us in the Lodging? My wife is particularly hopeful of a favourable response!

The fact is that we have on our hands—the college corporately and the university, I mean—a problem upon which I should be most deeply grateful for your advice. It has been decided to establish, and with all convenient speed, a University Readership in Modern European Drama, and the appointment will carry with it a Professional Fellowship at this college. As a consequence—and you probably know about this—my colleagues and myself have a substantial (although, in formal terms, not preponderant) voice in choosing the Reader. We have already had a certain amount of debate: lively but not, I *think*, to the extent of being characterizable as dispute or controversy. There have been some 'away out' suggestions and some uncommonly dull ones. The wiser sort (among whom, with the passing of the years, I am beginning to presume to see myself) are quietly maturing their own plan. I do hope that, by one means or another, you can spare a little time to talk it all over. Our luncheon hour is one o'clock.

Yours sincerely,

EDWARD POCOCKE

P.S. I heard with great pleasure of the brilliant success of your Harvard lectures.   E. P.

Although a lightning flash and thunder clap had been an excessive prelude to the reading of Dr Pococke's letter, I concluded them, after only a moment's thought, all to come together appropriately enough. What dumbfounded me was not simply the perception of what 'the wiser sort' were deviously being depicted as after; it was also the character of my own response. I had, it was true, much enjoyed that American trip. My interest in drama has always been broader than my own tenuous achievement in the theatre might suggest. I can talk, or even lecture, about it at least with satisfaction to myself. But in the United States I had seen my role merely as that of temporary playwright on campus after the hospitable habit of that part of the world. And hadn't I, this very evening, been thinking of academic characters and courses in a mildly derogatory, perhaps even a disagreeably superior way? Yet here I was, suddenly suspecting that I wanted to be something called a Reader in Modern European Drama. Or was that really quite the point? I led—it couldn't be denied I led—a rootless and unattached sort of life. A small villa in Ravello and a smaller *pied-à-terre* in London: these were the limits of what I tangibly possessed, and among the intangibles had chiefly to be reckoned the mere shift and drift of acquaintanceships and associations held loosely and impermanently together by theatrical projects and literary interests. Were I to stop writing, to stop circulating in that amorphous and faithless world, I should within a year or two be as isolated as Robinson Crusoe. What lured me now was the idea of life within a society: a stable and closely-knit society—changing, indeed, decade by decade or lustre by lustre as old men went and young men came, but preserving a constant sense of permanent and impersonal purposes.

I was here romanticizing, it can't be doubted, the life of an Oxford college. But at least I now reread the Provost's letter with as rational a regard as I could muster. The scrutiny didn't in the least alter my view of what he was in effect saying, although I was more aware of how much of it was being said by implication only. Apart from that evening's glimpses, I possessed and had preserved no more than what had been a juvenile sense of Edward Pococke's character. But what one lacks of experience at nineteen or twenty one may more than make up for in sharpness of observation and the alert intuitive judgements of a young and vulnerable animal. And in fact I found this letter to be wholly by the man I had been aware of twenty years before.

This led me to a sobering reflection. The references to lively debate, to 'away out' suggestions and dull ones, to the quiet maturing of a plan: these had not been idly penned. I was being, in some degree, softened up for the eventual discovery that I had come into the picture late and as a safe man, a compromise candidate whom nobody with any 'liveliness' exactly wanted to go to the stake for. There was diplomacy ahead—so decidedly so that it would be injudicious overtly to cast me at the moment other than as somebody whose advice would be gratefully received.

But was that right? Or was I imagining things? The letter rendered intelligible a number of fleeting remarks that had been made to me that day; when I totted these up it looked much as if a considerable number of people were already taking it for granted that I was going to be 'in'—and, for that matter, that I was going to consent to be 'in'. Some of these people had even seemed to suppose that the proposal must already, in some form, have come to me. I felt that I recognized in this the hush-hush technique frequently adopted in such affairs.

I suddenly much wanted to put this letter in front of Tony; to have a reading of it by one who was no less than a Cabinet Minister. I must have been conscious of the naïvety of the impulse, but this didn't seem to mute its appeal. Poor Lusby, moreover, had been entirely banished from my head; if Tony was still around and to be talked to, it wasn't with that wretched business that I should burden him.

I took another turn round Nick Junkin's room. I walked to the window and stared into the darkness of Surrey. The night sky was still overcast. It seemed incredible that, only an hour before, it had been brilliant with stars. I could hear water trickling in the gutters. A damp smell came up warm from the grass.

It was probable that everybody had gone to bed. Nevertheless I went to the door and opened it. The light on the little landing was extinguished, but Ivo Mumford's oak had not been sported, and there was a pencil line of light under and to the side of the familiarly ill-fitting inner door. I walked over to it and—again all-familiarly—opened it and surveyed the ancestral Mumford room. Tony's had been the only door in college on which I had ended up by never thinking to knock.

Tony was standing in front of the empty fireplace, beneath the ancestral Mumford lupanar. He stared at me, and for a second I had a confused sense that something dreadful had happened and that as a consequence Tony had suddenly immensely aged. I had scarcely taken in the fact that this was *not* Tony when the man before me spoke.

'Who the devil are you?' he said. 'And where, in God's name, is my son?'

It was a *coup de théâtre* which it would have pleased me to hit upon by way of livening up a third act. I explained myself to Lord Marchpayne's father, and he silently shook hands. It seemed to be his way of indicating that he had heard of me. I didn't think I could ever have met him, for it had been an oddity of my close friendship with his son that we had never done any vacation visiting in one another's homes.

'Will you have a drink?' Mr Mumford asked. 'There's bound to be plenty of the damned stuff in Ivo's cupboards.'

'Yes, there is. But, thank you, no. A Gaudy's a Gaudy, and mine's over. But Tony must still be keeping it up somewhere. He's bound to be back soon now. Only, I'm afraid I haven't a notion of where to go and look for him.'

'Do you happen to know if he's sober?'

'Tony?' For a second I had to play for time before this bald and sudden question. 'He says he can be, at the drop of a hat. And I believe him.'

'It's just as well.' Mr Mumford glowered at me darkly. He had been a heavy and fleshy man—which was what Tony in a few years was going to be—but had begun to shrink or shrivel. His skin hung on him loosely—rather as if he had been deprived of it in some lurid martyrdom and then perfunctorily reinserted in it on the discovery that a mistake had been made. I looked at him curiously, conscious that this macabre fancy didn't exactly make me comfortable in his presence. His turning up in college at this unaccountable hour called for an explanation which he appeared for the present disinclined to advance. Some family bereavement, or accident, or sudden and critical illness was one possibility. Had anything happened to Ivo? At least the heir of the Mumfords couldn't, like Paul Lusby, have perished with his head in a gas cooker; if he had, it could scarcely have occurred even to this rather savage old man to snap out that remark about the damned stuff in his cupboards. Ivo might still be the occasion of this irruption, all the same.

'Has anything happened to Ivo?' I asked.

Mr Mumford glowered at me even more darkly than before. I concluded that he regarded the question as entirely impertinent. I was a total stranger to him, after all, even though I was far from being that to his son. And his next remark gave every appearance of supporting this view.

'Aren't you the fellow who writes plays?' he demanded. 'I thought all scribblers had dirty finger-nails and long hair.'

I replied to these scarcely obliging words by sitting down—which would have been an odd response had I not suddenly realized that this vein of phrenetic insult was a consequence of the old man's being, for some reason, beside himself.

'My finger-nails were quite awful when I was a boy,' I said. 'And as for a hair-cut, the shilling for it didn't always come my way. Later on, your son successfully spruced me up. But I do write plays.'

'At least your head seems to be screwed on the right way.'

Mr Mumford betrayed no sense that this was an extraordinary conversation. 'And, talking of heads, you've hit the nail on one smartly enough. Am I right in thinking you're a reliable man?'

'Yes.'

'Then I'll tell you. My precious grandson looks like being put inside. A pretty pickle, eh? Within a dozen hours of Tony's making that confounded Cabinet.'

'I see.' In fact, I didn't quite see, since the information just conveyed to me was ambiguous. 'Inside' might mean what we had been accustomed to call the bin. But it seemed more probable that it meant gaol. 'You must all make what you can of it,' I said. 'At least it's not all that uncommon. I've noticed that the children of successful politicians are a good deal at risk. More so than the children of scribblers for example. It's because their fathers don't find much time to attend to them.'

'Perfectly true.'

This was a notable reply. It told me both that hostilities were at an end and that old Mr Mumford—if in a slightly senile way—was quite as acute as his son. He had been able suddenly to reflect that it was allies that were required.

'I don't go to the theatres,' he said, 'so I know nothing about your plays. But I imagine a certain realism attends them.'

'That's their ambition, but it commonly goes unrealized. Too much sparkle, as a matter of fact.' I paused, and then amplified. 'Too much damned and confounded sparkle.'

'Sparkle isn't going to help us tonight.'

'I can see that. And neither is dramatic criticism. If I *have* anything that helps, I lay it on.'

'Thank you, my dear sir. It's something, I suppose, that we all belong to this place.'

'No doubt.' The flash of sentiment had disconcerted me—and not the less because there was at least a wisp of substance to it.

'Not that the college hasn't gone to the dogs. Do you know? Ivo has just been elected to the Uffington. It's a thing the lad has been looking forward to immensely—and now the dons are talking about sending him down. What colossal cheek!'

'I'm afraid it may be an aspect of the matter that hasn't occurred to them.' For a moment the Uffington had eluded me, but now I remembered about it. It was an undergraduate dining-club of the most exclusive sort. Its members had a resplendent evening dress all of their own, and were celebrated for uproarious and destructive behaviour. Tony had been a member of it, but had always been careful to speak of it with a whimsical tolerance. His father, clearly, belonged to an age in which it had been unnecessary to dissimulate one's satisfaction in enjoying such superiorities, and it seemed probable that Ivo himself was a throw-back in this regard. But although the social assumptions hovering behind old Mr Mumford's remarks didn't greatly appeal to me I felt it would be indecent to appear other than sympathetic while still in the dark about the nature and gravity of the scrape the young man had landed in. 'I'm afraid,' I therefore went on, 'that what I said about politicians and their children wasn't particularly called for in the present case. Tony is, in fact, extremely concerned about Ivo. I believe that all through this Gaudy his chief determination has been to see what can be done to influence any decision about the boy's immediate academic future. I'm not confident that the effort is all that well-judged, but there's no question of the will he's putting into it.'

'Into smashing this nonsense of turning Ivo out? We can certainly settle *that* hash.' The senior Mumford produced this with what an unfriendly critic would have called a contemptuous snarl. 'I'm quite prepared to speak to the Provost myself. In which case he'll damn well learn something.' The outraged grandfather glowered at me anew—out of heaven knew what cloud-cuckoo-land of social self-importance. 'Haven't we,' he demanded, as if sensing my thought, 'subscribed to every tomfool appeal the place has put out for generations? And now they think to treat Ivo as if he were a charity-brat.'

'I doubt whether they'd treat anybody as if he were exactly that.' 'Charity brat', it occurred to me, would be Mr Mumford's term for Nicolas Junkin of Cokeville, and this thought a little antagonized me again. 'But I gather it's not the mere question whether Ivo remains in residence or goes down that's on the carpet now. It's whether he goes inside. Tony's the man you've come to discuss that with.' I turned at the sound of an opening door. 'And here he is at last.'

Tony was standing in the doorway, eyeing us steadily. He had no time to waste in astonishment, but for an arrested moment he was unnaturally still.

'Well,' he said, 'speak up! What is it?'

'It's that confounded boy.' For the first time, old Mr Mumford's voice was gentle. 'It seems he's been a bit rough with a girl.'

We had presumably been treated to an under-statement—an instance of what the school-books call meiosis. It silenced Tony for a second, and I myself had no impulse to speak. Old Mr Mumford hadn't turned up at the tail-end of a Gaudy—almost in the small-hours, indeed—to announce that his grandson had been guilty of a breach of manners. Our failure to produce an articulate response had the effect of throwing him back upon his own more settled mode of utterance.

'And it doesn't even seem,' he snarled, 'that the incompetent young fool was the one who had her in the end.'

'In heaven's name, think what you're saying!' Tony had gone pale, and I could see—with surprise, although surprise wasn't in the least reasonable—that he was trembling. 'Just what are you talking about?'

'I'm talking about all hell let loose. The trollop seems to have been fooling around with them for hours. But as soon as——'

'*Them?*' Tony said.

'A gang of young louts from the village. But she put on a turn as soon as she got home. She ran into the house, screaming out that she'd been raped.'

149

The ugly word reverberated in the room. I had the grotesque thought that the ladies in the picture over the mantlepiece were shocked by it. But it was no moment for nonsense.

'Are you sure,' I asked, 'that the girl is really what you call a trollop?'

'Of course she is. The village harlot, I suppose. Not that I know anything about her.'

'It's an odd way for a village harlot to end an evening.' Tony had swallowed before making this ominous point, and his face was twitching. I felt a sudden certainty that, Cabinet rank or not, he was going to prove unequal to the catastrophe. His head had been full of a situation he was confident he could manage—and it had suddenly announced itself, as with a thunder-clap, to be of no significance whatever. And his father, I saw, had shot his bolt. The effort of merely tumbling the thing out at us had—at least for the moment—finished him. I was left with a sense of being myself—in Jimmy Gender's phrase—on the bridge.

I felt, however, some way from being adequately clear-headed. I was trying to remember what had brought me in on this; what, at this outlandish hour, had persuaded me to enter Ivo Mumford's room. I failed to do so—which was unimportant, since the point had no relevance to the crisis on hand. But I was somehow convinced that there *was* a crisis in the sense that, if the thing could be got clear, there might be something that needed doing at once. And now Paul Lusby's story came back to me. Something of the sort had held about that dead boy. Somewhere, as the short fatal chain of his misfortunes was fabricating itself, there had been a slip-up which a number of men were now feeling unhappy about. It hadn't in the least been a matter of passing the buck between them. But there had been some division of responsibilities from which a certain inattention had flowed; and there had been that brief but fatal hesitancy while Cyril Bedworth (self-evidently the most conscientious of men) had weighed up this against that. If a few hours had been saved, Lusby might be sleeping soundly in his bed now.

I brought my mind away from this with a wrench, but not before glimpsing that I had gone after a false analogy. The college fellows had been confronted with a lad put at hazard through a wholly blameless folly and his own socially-engendered misestimation of the disastrousness of failing a trivial examination. The Mumfords and myself had on our hands the problem of extricating Ivo from something dreadfully different. Supposing it could be done, there was still what might conceivably be a daunting moral problem interposed between ourselves and the doing of it. The degree of the dauntingness depended very much on the exact nature of the facts. As far as Tony and I were concerned, we were still unprovided with them.

But even in mulling over the business like this—I asked myself—wasn't I behaving as Bedworth had behaved over Lusby—or like Hamlet, thinking too precisely on the event? I was sitting on a window-seat, uncurtained against the darkness of Surrey, that citadel of a secure and ordered life. Beyond it, all of a sudden, was this nebulous and perhaps horrible thing. I jumped to my feet—nervously, as if there could be any help in that. I had taken a couple of paces forward when there came a tap on the door. Tony and his father called out—irritably but simultaneously—to come in. It was a small point of curiosity; each of them had commanded the place in his time. The door opened, and framed the figure of Mogridge.

'Oh, Tony,' Mogridge said mildly. 'I'd gone out to the loo on the next staircase—it's a better one, you remember—and I saw the light in your room. So I thought I'd look in and say good-night.'

'Hullo, Gavin.' Tony managed the effort of being a host. 'I don't think you ever met my father? Father, this is Gavin Mogridge. We were up together.'

'How do you do.' Mr Mumford's concern for the intruder's welfare was curtly minimal. 'As it happens, Mr Mugbridge, we're in the middle of a private conversation.'

'Mogridge,' Mogridge said.

'Very well—Mogridge.' Mr Mumford checked himself and

stared. 'You wouldn't be the fellow who wrote that book the devil of a time ago?'

'Yes, I am.' Mogridge was presumably habituated to making this acknowledgement. What had been demanded of him was more or less the equivalent of that 'Do you still write plays?' with which I was myself so familiar. I now expected Mr Mumford's rejoinder to concern itself with hair and finger-nails. But this proved to be an error.

'A close-run thing, that,' Mr Mumford said. 'And you must have been not long out of your baby-carriage. You didn't do too badly.'

'Thank you very much.' Reasonably in view of what had been intimated to him, Mogridge made to withdraw. It was with an air, which was not the least self-conscious, of composed dignity. He might have been a white man of unquestioned standing on the frontiers of empire, retreating in good order after blundering in upon some native pow-wow or palaver that was no business of his. It was only another instance of the Mogridge imperturbability, but it somehow triggered off my one effective act that night.

'Tony,' I said, 'I think we ought to have Gavin in on our problem.'

It was perhaps because he was baffled and exhausted that Tony agreed with this strange-seeming suggestion. His father, surprisingly, made no protest; he may vaguely have supposed that the celebrated author of *Mochica* was now an equally celebrated silk at the criminal bar. As for Mogridge, he simply listened seriously to a recapitulation of what Tony and I had already heard. And then there was an expectant pause.

'Yes—rape,' Mogridge said. He uttered the word so vaguely that he might have been wondering whether we were discussing one of the administrative districts of Sussex or the kind of turnip which one feeds to sheep. But his next remark negatived this. 'It's regarded almost everywhere,' he said, 'as a very serious thing. The river-dwelling Mundugumor come to mind. And the Kikuyu and the Masai. There's a sharp distinction from marriage by capture.' He thought for a moment. 'I don't suppose Ivo would have any notion of marrying the girl?' Slantwise as usual, he glanced at us each in turn, and seemed conscious that the question struck old Mr Mumford as an idle one. 'One has to review the possibilities,' he said. 'One isn't being orderly if one goes about something in a random manner. It's a point that's missed by people who don't see it. Don't you agree?' Securing a savage mutter from the old gentleman by way of response to his striking tautology seemed to encourage him. 'Yes,' he went on. 'Rape, fortunately, is regarded very seriously indeed.'

'Very probably,' Tony said. 'But as we're not gathered here as guardians of public morals, I can't see that the fact's an encouraging one.'

'Oh, but Tony, you don't understand me. The point is that a judge won't let you be slapped down for rape at the drop of a handkerchief, as he will for assault or drunk and disorderly or even passing a dud cheque. And that's because it *is* so serious. It isn't at all easy, as a matter of fact, to get convicted of rape. I've noticed that in Moa and Marundung. And you'd find that what goes for places like those commonly goes for England too. Of course, we don't know nearly enough about this business yet. But I'd be very surprised, Tony, if your son were actually convicted of rape before a judge of the High Court. On this occasion, that's to say.' Mogridge turned back to Tony's father. 'Where is Ivo now?'

'I told him to clear out and lie low.'

'I see.' Mogridge didn't look as if he thought well of this. 'Do you mean abroad? I doubt whether there are many countries that would be much good. Tibet would have been not too bad at one time. I had one or two friends in Lhasa who would have arranged it. But things have changed for the worse there in recent years, as you know.'

'No doubt.' Mr Mumford was patently feeling that my recruitment of this owlish character had been either an absurdity or a disaster. 'But Ivo isn't abroad. I packed him off to the gardener's cottage on the other side of the park. The gardener and his family are away on their holiday. And I simply told this fellow that Ivo couldn't have been involved, for the good reason that he wasn't staying with me.'

'But he *was* staying with you?'

'Of course he was. Or, at least, it appeared that he was intending to. He'd just arrived.'

'In fact, you promptly lied to somebody?'

'Damn it, man, I wasn't in a witness box. When an impertinent fellow——'

'It wasn't perjury, of course. And you had a natural impulse to protect your grandson. It mayn't have been judicious, all the same. The inference would be—once the prevarication was discovered, I mean—that you admitted to yourself that Ivo had got on the wrong side of the law. Perhaps he had. Perhaps he'd confessed it to you.' Mogridge looked at his watch. 'Anyway, I don't like the sound of that gardener's cottage, and we'd better be on the move about it within the next half hour. So we must have the full facts, and in proper order, as succinctly as may be.'

'Very well.' The firmness of this demand made old Mr Mumford brace himself perceptibly. 'Ivo turned up on me late yesterday evening. He had some supper——'

'How did he arrive? Where had he come from?'

'He drove up in his own car—I don't know from where. He'd stayed a night or two with a friend, I think, after the end of term. I like him to turn up on me unannounced from time to time. I'm a widower, you know, living alone at Otby.'

'Alone? Haven't you any servants?'

'Of course I have servants. But there was only my housekeeper around. It was she who got Ivo some supper.'

'Just a moment. Where's that car now?'

'Ivo's car? He's taken it down to the cottage, I suppose. There's a shed.'

This kind of thing went on for some time. Except for the Mogridge slow-motion effect, which it would be tedious to reproduce, it was rather like one of those popular plays featuring a brilliant barrister or great detective disporting himself among the family skeletons. I kept a grip on the facts as they came together, since it would have been irresponsible to do anything else, but what I found myself wanting to get out of them was some clearer impression of the character of Ivo Mumford. Why had this newly elected member of the Uffington, this precocious connoisseur of brandy and champagne, engaged in what had proved so disastrous an escapade with a group of village lads? Part of the answer seemed to be that he had done it before. His visits to his more or less solitary grandfather were of their nature rather dull, and the neighbourhood was short of young people of his own sort. So as a schoolboy it had amused him occasionally to play around with whatever contemporaries he could get together. It was a picture, so far, of something as innocent, and indeed amiable, as could be. I didn't find this conclusion much vitiated by its appearing that on these occasions Ivo had insisted on enjoying the prerogatives of the squire's grandson in the way of bossing the other boys around. He had even at times—Mr Mumford interpolated with a momentary satisfaction which could scarcely have been called sagacious—imposed a pretty stiff discipline on some of them.

It was Tony who pounced on the significance of this last point—although I didn't, indeed, think it had for a moment eluded Mogridge. The lads of Otby village—Tony was very clear about this—would admire Ivo the more, the more commanding Ivo chose to be. They would also—and Tony was quite intelligent enough to be equally clear about this—hate his classy little guts. In fact, a thoroughly ambivalent attitude would build up in them, and at a pinch skilled advocacy could elicit this in a court and then exploit it. Here were young men, it could be said, who had it in for another young man, not of their own sort. It would be rash to accept a word they said about him, or about the degree of his participation in whatever had taken place. Didn't Mogridge—Tony demanded —agree?

'But, Tony, we're not facing that yet,' Mogridge said. 'It's a last resort. One should always leave a last resort to the end. Otherwise, one gets it in the wrong place.'

'If you can see any first resort, Gavin, for heaven's sake let us hear it.'

'We don't know yet that this thing is ever going to come before a court. Affairs of the sort often don't. They're a muddle and a mess, with potential witnesses saying first one thing and then its opposite, and so on. The police—and we don't even know as yet that the present trouble has got to them—therefore often think better of telling themselves they have reason to suppose a crime was committed. And that's the end of the matter. But the real point is this: supposing the thing does go into court, we don't want Ivo to go with it. We don't want him mentioned at all. If he were shoved into the dock along with the whole bunch of them, and then acquitted as having been so much on the mere fringe of the affair as hardly to be aware of what was going on, it still wouldn't be at all healthy for him, either in college or anywhere else.'

'It certainly would not,' Tony said grimly.

'But that's looking farther ahead than we need at the moment. We mustn't go too fast. You know, I've sometimes noticed that being in too much of a hurry can result in one's not getting along as rapidly as one otherwise might do.' Mogridge paused on this, so that I thought he was going to repeat it just in case the thread had eluded us. 'We left Ivo at supper,' he said with a surprising briskness. 'Please go on from there.'

Mr Mumford went on. Ivo had drunk several glasses of wine with his meal, and had then announced that he was going to stretch his legs. It was getting on for dark but a splendid summer night. He might go as far as the river, so his grandfather had better not wait up for him. There was apparently nothing in this that Mr Mumford found particularly casual or out of the way. He seemed resigned, indeed, to the view that Ivo always found these duty visits boring, and that the occasion of them was simply the expectation of a large tip. On this particular evening Ivo had been restless from the start. Thinking about it afterwards, his grandfather concluded that he had glimpsed some of his plebeian friends as he drove through the village on his arrival. They would have been hanging around the telephone kiosk, Mr Mumford added on a note of sombre rural realism, talking smut and abundantly prepared to be up to no particular good. It was a state of affairs which Ivo must have found perversely attractive.

That was the last to be seen of the boy until the murky incident was over. He had appeared in his grandfather's bedroom at six o'clock in the morning. Mr Mumford, awakened abruptly, had supposed his grandson to have heard burglars or to have been taken ill. In fact, a night of appalled realization had broken Ivo down. He was in a tearful panic, and it had been hard to extract much sense from him. He said he hadn't known this girl wasn't another girl, whom he was sure lots of the louts had had before. So he hadn't at all seen why he shouldn't join in the mucking around. Not that in the end he actively had, since he had become aware that there was some nasty sort of hitch. The girl had *really* struggled. And quite as much with the second chap as with the first.

This last particular, which made me feel that I didn't want to catch Ivo's father's eye, Ivo's grandfather relayed with no particular emotion. But it had at least been at this point in Ivo's confession that Mr Mumford realized he had quite something on his hands. He roused his housekeeper, a notably faithful family retainer who adored Master Ivo, and very sensibly had her prepare a quick but substantial breakfast. When this had been partaken of (and between blubbering fits Ivo managed to eat a great deal) he had banished the indecisive rapist to the untenanted cottage and sat back to think.

He was still thinking, it seemed, when Fairlamb came in. Fairlamb was the local pub-keeper. Although not a tenant of Mr Mumford's he was to a certain extent an underling, since Mr Mumford was a director of the brewery company which maintained him in his hostelry. Fairlamb was also the father of the outraged, or reputedly outraged, girl. His attitude, as it appeared through Mr Mumford's account, had been one of wary malevolence and furtive venality. It was clearly in his head that there was money in the thing.

Fairlamb, then, presented a narrative of his daughter's wrong, together with the information that Mr Ivo unfortunately had a hand in it—if hand, indeed, was the word. It was at this point that Mr Mumford advanced his rash assertion that Ivo could not have been involved since Ivo was not visiting Otby Park. Had he waited a little longer he might have taken another line. Fairlamb, while stoutly asserting his daughter's hitherto virginal state, did not deny that she had gone off freely with the group of lads, and that on previous occasions she had made similar but uncatastrophic nocturnal excursions with them. This particular jaunt had begun in the darkness of a moonless night and ended in repair to the deeper darkness of a barn. Miss Fairlamb wasn't confident that Mr Ivo had been with the group 'all the time'. Perhaps he had joined the others in the barn. But it was Mr Ivo who had begun doing things to her. Everybody knew—Miss Fairlamb declared and her father regretfully reported—that Mr Ivo was like that. Even when quite young, he had taught some of the other boys tricks so nasty that he, Fairlamb, quite declined to dirty Mr Mumford's ears with them.

This had almost been too much for Ivo's grandfather, and he had indulged the thought of continuing his colloquy with Fairlamb through the instrumentality of a hunting-crop. Alternatively, he had thought of getting out his cheque-book, which was the issue of the affair which the unspeakable publican pretty evidently had in mind. But, although aged and shaken, he had the wits to see that either of these courses would be injudicious. So he turned Fairlamb out of the house with the advice to take his slanderous rubbish to the police.

And Fairlamb—although later in the day—*had* gone to the police. He had perhaps done so only because others had gone before him. In thinking to see the matter resolve itself satisfactorily on a simple economic basis he had reckoned without something he was in a professional position very accurately to assess: the normal operation of village gossip. Miss Fairlamb had presented herself to her aunt (who kept the village shop and post-office) in the character of a ravished heroine; her aunt had told the story to the district nurse; the district nurse (as a lowly but unchallengeable auxiliary of the gentry) had told the vicar; and a conference with the local constable had been the result.

The constable spent an hour weighing things up, and then saw no help for it: he must march up the avenue and ring the front-door bell of the Park. Shown into the presence of its owner, he came out with the thing roundly enough. He had interviewed two of the lads; they had admitted there had been 'a bit of skylarking and mucking-around-like'; but nothing had happened that could be any business of the police until the young gent from the big house got silly and 'did what he oughtn't to have'. So could the constable see the young gent? Mr Mumford, keeping his nerve if not his judgement, declared that here was a pack of lies by a gang of revolting little brutes who ought to be in Borstal—and that his grandson, being a hundred miles away, could demonstrably have had no part in the matter. The constable agreed that this must certainly be the state of the case; he then got himself hastily out of the house, plainly believing nothing of the sort; and Mr Mumford was left to digest what looked like a rapidly deteriorating situation.

'Was anything said,' Mogridge asked, 'about how anybody in that barn saw anything that was going on? There has to be *some* light, or one sees nothing at all.' He looked earnestly from one to another of us. 'Wouldn't you agree?'

'A two-year-old would have to agree,' Mr Mumford snapped. 'One of the louts seems to have said that somebody had a candle.'

'A candle?' Tony said. 'What utter nonsense! A torch or a bicycle lamp might make sense. But nobody wanders about the countryside proposing to light candles in barns.'

As a generalization this struck me as valid. At the same

time there was a gruesome picturesqueness about the image of that single flickering flame; one glimpsed a composition like a sort of unholy La Tour: a point of light glinting on so bestial a floor. Mogridge's mind, fortunately, was undistracted by this sort of thing.

'Darkness,' he said. 'Do you know? It can be rather terrifying. It often terrifies children.' He paused. 'As a matter of fact, it terrified some of those people who found themselves tumbled into the middle of Peru. They had to be dealt with.'

'Most interesting,' Tony said.

'But the point is, of course, that this whole Otby affair was played out in darkness or near-darkness, from start to finish. It makes me increasingly believe that the notion of any sort of successful prosecution is nonsense. For all we know, or a jury could know, one of those village boys was working away quietly on that girl for an hour before anybody penetrated her. I believe that's the term.'

'It's certainly the one they use in court,' Tony agreed. 'What we say is fucked her.'

'Yes, of course. But you see what I mean. Plenty of young women who have been far from virtuous are capable of putting on a hysterical turn and screaming about rape. Every judge knows that. They're even capable, sometimes, of persevering in calumny in what appears the most malignant way—one seemingly quite alien to their normal commonplace character. Known facts like that, added to the other fact of the whole thing's having been a mess and huddle in the dark, are all in our favour for a start. It's most improbable, I repeat, that anything absolutely dire is going to come out of the thing. Still, we don't want even the disagreeable—not if we can help it. So it's just a question which of two lines we adopt.' Mogridge glanced at his watch. It was apparent that he judged there was just so much time for talk, and that then action must begin. 'By the way,' he said to Mr Mumford, 'where did you eventually get Ivo off to?'

'Get him off to? He's still in the gardener's cottage, of

course.' Mr Mumford spoke as if this ought to have been self-evident. I could see that some obscure territorial sense had been at work in him; he had felt that nothing could really happen to his grandson as long as the boy was within the shelter of the family estate.

'If nobody has come on him there,' Tony said, 'then so far, so good. But what's this about two lines we can adopt?'

'We can opt for the truth. That's to say we can somehow ease your father out of his story, admit that Ivo came to Otby and went fooling around with his village acquaintances, and deny that he had the faintest notion that anything like a sexual assault was going on in that barn. Alternatively, we can maintain the whole thing to be a malicious village slander. We can have your father stick to his story, his housekeeper support it, and Ivo adopt it too, supposing they really chase him up. In fact, lies all round.' Mogridge turned his oblique and mild regard from Tony to myself, and for the first time in my experience I thought I detected in it what might almost be a remote glint of humour. 'I'm for lies all round.'

'And gaol all round too?' Tony asked. He spoke ironically but on a note of sharpened interest. 'My dear Gavin, you're daft. The boy would require something out of a story-book. An alibi, or whatever they call it.'

'Oh, certainly.' Mogridge was at his most deliberate. 'It won't be difficult. Always provided nothing has happened at this cottage. Has Ivo, by the way, had any definite plans for the vac? Knowing about that might help.'

'He ought to be in New York by now.' Tony, although I believe he was in a state of simple misery, said this with some exasperation. 'He'd been very keen to go there, and he was booked for a night flight on Monday. He probably thought he'd touch his grandfather for a big tip first, and just roll up at Heathrow a night or two later. He has no sense about such things.'

'Splendid!' Mogridge was standing up. He clearly regarded our conference as over. 'He'll pretty well be there for break-fast—just as they say in the advertisements. Mr Mumford, you'd better drive straight back to Otby. But don't try to contact Ivo. I'll have done that before you arrive. Go straight to bed. Tony, do the same—here in college. And forget you know anything whatever. Talk to Duncan, but not to anybody else. It's only with Duncan I'll communicate at present. Duncan, how long shall you be staying here?'

'Until tomorrow evening. Longer, if you want me to.'

'No, no—that will do. If you get a message including the word "satisfactory" you'll know all's well.'

'Gavin, this is nonsense.' There was something like desperation in Tony's voice now. 'It's not like going over to the continent, where they no longer bother to stamp your passport. Nobody gets past immigration control at Kennedy without being absolutely clocked through.'

'It's the usual thing, I agree. However, don't worry. And oh, by the way, there will be a number of respectable people who saw Ivo in New York yesterday. And now I must be off.'

'Would you mind telling us just how you imagine you can manage this?'

'Well, no. I mean we'd better not waste any time on mere details. Come along, Mr Mumford. I'll see you to your car.' As he said this, Mogridge was looking steadily at Tony— and Tony steadily at him. 'Good night,' Mogridge said casually, and swept Ivo's grandfather out of Ivo's room.

Tony hadn't got to his feet, and now for some seconds he buried his head in his hands. A far-away bell chimed some hour or other. Tony looked up again.

'Duncan, is he mad?'

'You know he isn't mad.'

'You brought him in on this. Did you know something about him—something that had never come into my head?'

'Short of clairvoyance or telepathy—definitely not.'

'It's nonsense at this end too. Nobody can get on to any kind of transatlantic flight without the day and hour—'

'But this one won't be just any kind of flight. It will be a rather particular one.'

'Yes.' Tony was staring at me rather as he had stared at Mogridge in the moment of their parting. 'He must be damned high up.'

'I wouldn't know.'

'More or less at the top. I'd like to find out.'

'Perhaps you could ask the Prime Minister.'

'Oh, no!' Tony was really shocked. 'That wouldn't do at all. Not the drill.'

IX

It would have been indecent to say good-night to Tony without managing some kind of murmur, however awkward, indicative of sympathetic feeling before his suddenly untoward family situation. But when I had managed this I came away at once. He may or may not have wanted to go to bed or had any thought that he was likely to get to sleep. He must have had a strong impulse, I supposed, to go to the support of his son himself, and that he had acquiesced in a waiting and passive role was an index of the astonishing grip that Mogridge had taken of the whole affair. I didn't imagine that I'd myself be sleepless, although I was far from any state of post-prandial contentment. On top of the Gaudy dinner and the Gaudy speeches—at the end of which any reasonable man would have been disposed to call it a day—had come (from off-stage and messengered, as in some orthodox neo-classical drama) the successive reports of the unknown Paul Lusby's death and the unknown Ivo Mumford's disgrace. A disgrace it certainly was—this even although the boy had been singularly luckless in his ugly escapade, so that I found myself all on the side of cheating the law if the law was after him. I saw these two catastrophes as belonging to different orders: Lusby's, I imagined, had a certain representative character as being the sort of thing that happens, whereas Ivo's was grotesque and alarming as something that doesn't. A young man is not on his way to the dock on a charge of rape or conspiring to rape simply because he mixes brandy with his champagne. Something abrupt and utterly senseless had happened in the life of Ivo Mumford.

Out on the landing, I found that, attractive as was the thought of bed, a vestigial restiveness prompted me to prowl. I groped my way downstairs and into Surrey, much as if I were Mogridge remembering about a more attractive loo. The storm hadn't greatly cleared the air, and the darkness was warm and muggy again. It was also entire; one couldn't have guessed that one was surrounded by the slumbers of two or three hundred heavily-dieted middle-aged men. Or was there a glint of light from the room briefly restored to the occupancy of P. P. Killiecrankie? It probably wasn't so, and in any case I had no inclination to call on him—although he might, I reflected, have an informed view on just how far you could go without inviting opprobrium as a ravisher. Perhaps Ivo Mumford would end his days as a bishop since careers did seem so uncommonly unpredictable. Not all of them, of course; what could Ranald McKechnie have become other than Professor Ranald McKechnie? But nobody would have thought of Cyril Bedworth bedding with Proust. And it hadn't been Duncan Pattullo the Secret Service Boy who had become the Secret Service Man; it had been Gavin Mogridge the failed 'cellist.

My mind, wandering round like this in a drowsy fashion, came to rest on Mogridge. The secret life isn't the writer's sole concern. But it is a constant one; and here in Mogridge was the crude and archetypal thing, the kind of enigma to which there exists, awaiting discovery, the single all-sufficing clue. For a moment Mogridge seemed to stand before me, an apparition against the dark, in complete clarity. The vocational misfit who couldn't play that big fiddle; the active temper, the grip on perceived detail amid crisis and extremity; the inflexible will behind the achievement chronicled in *Mochica*; some unrecorded years; the emergence of the traveller and amateur anthropologist, blamelessly wandering the globe, disappearing and turning up again, publishing occasional stodgy books which breathed concerns about as contemporary as those, say, of some nineteenth-century country gentleman anxious to determine whether Victoria Nyanza or Albert Nyanza was of the greater significance in perpending the problem of the Nile: all this came together. Rather pleasingly, I thought. But more pleasing, even if also alarming, was the spontaneous and unquestioning old-boy solidarity under the impulsion of which Mogridge was acting at this moment. He might be high up, but that would scarcely help him if he were exposed as lavishing public money on clandestine Atlantic flights, foxing the immigration officials of the USA, persuading or obliging numerous persons to tell lies about the whereabouts of a young man who might reasonably be represented as a fugitive from justice.

I was surprised by the completeness of my approval of this. There were relevant facts I didn't ignore: for example, that the Paul Lusbys and Nicolas Junkins are commonly unfurnished with the sort of good fairy or *deus ex machina* which I had so casually, if intuitively, called into counsel on the peccant Ivo Mumford's behalf. This didn't disturb me now, but something else did. I hadn't seen Gavin Mogridge for a very long time, yet he had greeted me as if our last meeting had been yesterday, so that I had felt (not that there had been any fuss of feeling in the matter at all) I had simply recovered a friend. But in what did his personality consist? Looking back over the past hour, I realized that there had been two Mogridges in Ivo's room. There had been the more familiar Mogridge of heavy pace and slow if reliable mind, given to massive tautology and to proverbial remarks offered more or less as contributions to the general march of intellect. And there had been a Mogridge who was incisive, rapid, economical, unscrupulous, and in command. The first of these was surely the native Mogridge of long ago. But wasn't the second the real one now, so that the first had to be regarded as a blind, and as a blind cunningly preserved amid conditions in which entire candour ought to obtain? There seemed no doubt of Mogridge's integrity as a friend. He had unmasked himself in a manner which, professionally, he was quite certainly forbidden to do, and he had done so at the call of loyalty to Tony Mumford. I thought of those double agents— upper-class and therefore apt for the headlines of the popular press—who have been willing to present wholly artificial personalities to their intimates for years, and who will yet suddenly take some fantastic risk in the interest of just such a loyalty within the sphere of private relationships. It was unnecessary to suppose that Mogridge worked for the Kremlin in his off-time. But he belonged to a world if not of double agents, at least of deliberately double-faced men.

At this point I must have concluded that I had discharged my duty as a reflective person, since I found myself groping my way up the staircase again. I opened Junkin's door and switched on the light. As I did so I became aware that in my other hand I was holding a sheet of paper. It was a letter about a proposed Readership in Modern European Drama. So this was why I had entered Ivo's room, and I had been clutching the thing all through what had then transpired. I made to shove it in a trouser-pocket now and failed to do so, the action being impeded by the black stuff of my M.A. gown. Unaccustomed to don such a garment, I had also forgotten to doff it; so I had stood or sat through that whole grim conference dressed like a schoolmaster in a comic strip. I removed this garment now, and tossed it impatiently, and therefore a little too vigorously, over the back of Junkin's sofa. It went over the top, and with a surprising result. There was a cry or squeal of indignation and alarm. I wasn't alone in the room. In fact I was confronting a young woman, Oriental in origin although not at all Oriental in impassivity, who seemed to be dressed in nothing but a shift.

'Nick, Nick,' the girl shouted in an American English, 'come here—there's a strange guy in your room!'

If, as I suspect, I said something like 'Madam, please compose yourself,' it must have been because I was indignant as well as surprised. It was true that I had snared the lady rather as a fowler might snare a roosting bird. But if this room wasn't in any full sense mine it was certainly more mine than this young person's. There wasn't, however, an opportunity to argue this, for the bedroom door was flung open and a youth stood revealed in it. I hadn't, of course, a doubt that this was Nicolas Junkin, although his appearance didn't at all answer to what I had been imagining of the lad from Cokeville. My notion had been, for some reason, of a heavy, dark, and abundantly bearded junior citizen. Junkin was slim and fair; and his hair, although there was a lot of it, all flowed down the back of his neck. It was the slimness that was the most striking of these appearances. Perhaps because the night was sultry, or perhaps because he had been unable to find any pyjamas, he was wearing nothing except a pair of orange and green striped under-pants. It didn't seem to me that the Chinese— or was she Japanese?—lady could be indicted of poor taste. (But this was an opinion which, in the ensuing few minutes, was to prove itself based upon a false premise.)

The Oriental lady continued protesting exclamations, but these were not well received by Junkin. He told her to stuff it—quite inoffensively, although the expression is not one which should be addressed to a lady, whether Oriental or not. He then turned to me, and I could see that our situation didn't particularly bewilder him.

'Well,' Junkin said, 'here's a bloody mess! And all my own fault.'

'Not at all,' I said—for I found the admission disarming. 'They're your rooms—although they were mine a long time ago. They've made a muddle, I suppose, in shoving me in here.'

'Oh, no. Of course they do a lot of ruthless logistics when they have those awful banquets and balls and things. It's rather funny that balls should be called balls. Rightly be they called pigs.' Junkin paused on this irrelevance, and I remembered that Aldous Huxley's *Chrome Yellow* was among the more antiquarian books on his shelves. 'I'm definitely supposed to have gone down for the vac, so I ought to have guessed there might be a lodger. Come to think of it, there do seem to be some foreign objects around. Particularly in the bedroom. I ought to have thought. I suppose I was distracted by the girl. She says she's called Tin Pin. At least it sounds like that.'

'How do you do?' I said to Tin Pin. I had decided that to take Junkin's last remark as a formal introduction might conduce to giving some semblance of urbanity to the proceedings. Tin Pin, however, did not respond. She had retired to Junkin's best chair, and was now in the proprietorship not only of her single diaphanous garment but also of a smouldering cigarette. She just surveyed us sombrely through the fume. Her appearance was little more congenial than that of Ishii Genzō. And Junkin appeared to be aware of my impression as unfavourable, since his next speech was apologetic in tone.

'You see,' he said, 'I had to bring her here. There wasn't anywhere else.'

'Oh, quite.' It struck me that Junkin's lack of a full confidence as to the lady's name suggested that what I had tumbled into was an amour of the most casual sort. Yet the situation had features which it was difficult to reconcile with this. I hadn't been out of Junkin's room all that long, but what I had come upon was Tin Pin asleep on the sofa and Junkin himself snug in his bed. It seemed too expeditious and business-like to be true. 'The question,' I added, 'is where we go from here.'

'It's not exactly *we*,' Junkin said reasonably. 'I mean that it's rather a matter of how to split up, isn't it? *Exeunt* severally. Something like that.' Junkin was subjecting me to severe but not particularly hostile scrutiny. 'Did you say these had been your rooms years ago?'

'Yes. But it's not a point that much helps us now.'

'Aren't you Duncan Pattullo?'

'Yes.'

'My name's Nicolas Junkin. One of the dons——'

'Nick,' Tin Pin said, 'this is no damn good. Take me some place else.'

'Belt up, Tin. As I was saying, one of the dons told me you'd been on this staircase.' Junkin took a further appraising look. 'It's marvellous that you still write plays.'

'Yes, isn't it?' I hope I said this with spirit. Junkin's, I felt, was a remark which might have been offered appositely, if not with much tact, to the nonagenarian Bernard Shaw. 'One just soldiers on.'

'Sorry—I suppose that was rude. But you know what I mean. Suddenly confronted with a past age, and so on. It's like meeting Noel Coward.' Junkin thought for a moment. 'Or Sir Arthur Wing Pinero.'

I found myself laughing—much to Tin Pin's displeasure. Junkin wasn't being funny, and much less was he being impudent. He was just chronologically hazy. It was no doubt one of the intellectual insufficiencies which had got him into disfavour with his tutors and examiners.

'Look here,' Junkin said, 'you want to go to bed. Sorry about the sheets—and it's quite probable I used your tooth-brush. But there it is. Tin and I will go as we came.'

'Just walk out?'

'Well, no. The porter on the gate would probably have objected to my bringing in a girl. And if we go out that way now, he'll book my name and I'll be fined. They'll call it a room-fee, and produce a bit of talk about the necessity of putting up guests in a civilized manner. But it will be a fine, all the same. Tin and I will just scout round the college and find somewhere. She seems pretty tiresome to me.' Junkin offered the young woman a glance as candid as his speech. 'But I've taken her on, and I suppose I must see her through.'

'Do you mean she's not exactly your girl?'

'Of course she's not my girl. She's just a wandering sample. I don't have any exotic tastes. And as she's not my girl, I didn't see why she should have my bed. But the sofa was another matter.'

'I see.' I did in fact see that I was in contact with some chivalric code unknown to me. 'Then whose girl is she?'

'Whose girl are you, Tin? Did you say Julian?'

'Sure. Julian. The swine.'

'She says that swine Julian,' Junkin said, rather as if he were translating from whatever may have been Tin Pin's native tongue. 'He's a friend of mine, and it seems they had a date. Julian was going to take Tin somewhere for the night. Or probably for as many nights as his powers held out. And his money, of course. But Julian's quite in the money just now, because of somebody being dead and his father being mad and not allowed to spend any himself. I say, is this frightfully complicated?'

'Not really. But it doesn't just advance matters.'

'No, of course not. I'm afraid I'm not managing what you'd call a rapid protasis.'

'But I wouldn't. I'm not a Professor of Drama. Not even a Reader.'

'Aren't you really? I read plays a great deal. It's one of my troubles—just like Tin is now, and as I'm explaining.'

'I can certainly see she's rather a blight.' Junkin's discursive manner, I was thinking, might not be to his advantage in the scurry of the Examination Schools. 'You got landed with her. Go on.'

'Just that. Well, I don't think Julian was ditching her. I think he just forgot. You'd say that was a bit unusual, wouldn't you, when you'd got it all fixed to lay a girl? Particularly one with advanced techniques and all that—what the models in the shop-windows call special poses. I'd think the idea of Tin was that, wouldn't you, sir? At least I just can't see any other possibilities in her at all. Can you?'

'Well, frankly, Mr Junkin—no. But we mustn't speak unkindly of her. Here she is, after all.'

'Just that. In our room.' It was handsomely, I felt, that Junkin thus described the chamber in which this curious colloquy was taking place. 'Of course we could tie the sheets together, and lower her through the window into Long Field. I expect you remember it's quite often done. Then you could have the bed and I'd have the sofa and we'd be quite all right for the rest of the night. There isn't much of it left as a matter of fact.'

'But that would be rather hard on her,' I said. 'You'd be going back on the very charitable attitude you've taken up in the matter so far.' It occurred to me that I could simply return to Ivo's room and settle myself on the sofa there. But that might disturb Tony, whose circumstances made it improbable that he had got straight to sleep. And these same circumstances made me reluctant to involve him in this absurd travesty of sexual misconduct. 'Look,' I said. 'I've got an acquaintance called Killiecrankie who's got a set on the next staircase for the night. I could——'

'Killiecrankie?' My involuntary host seemed struck by the name. 'Do you know? I mixed up Killiecrankie and Malplaquet in a bloody exam, and they took it very badly. Unreasonable of them, it seemed to me. Actually, they were battles—or was it treaties?—that took place exactly within twenty years of each other, so it was an easy mistake to make. But then examiners are unreasonable, aren't they? Just as dons, they're as decent to you as could be from one end of the year to the other. Then they turn themselves into examiners, and behave like that.' Junkin spoke less in anger than in sorrow. 'It's one reason why I'm in a bit of a balls-up.'

'I'm very sorry. But I was saying that I can go over to this man Killiecrankie's rooms and fix it to sleep there.' I was discovering that this plan quite pleased me. The reactions of the Prebendary to the story promised interest.

'I go too,' Tin Pin said suddenly. I turned and stared at the girl, and saw her to be looking at me in a way that made my blood run cold. 'There's a sofa there, too—sure?'

'There certainly is,' I said grimly. 'And it's been a battle-field in its time. All the same, Malplaquet's out.'

'You see the sort of slut Tin is?' Junkin demanded. For the first time, he spoke with a touch of despair. 'I had the hell of it to persuade her I was bloody well no soap myself. I *have* a girl. But Tin just has no sense.'

'I see that. Look, Nick—may I call you Nick?—I'm coming round to those sheets.'

'Right! We'll get cracking.' Nick Junkin was immensely relieved. 'If you can find her a quid, that is. We neither of us had a bean, you see, and I was just going to sleep rough. So that was how this started.'

'We'll wind it up. I'll run to a fiver. It may persuade her to get on a train.'

'You're a gentleman,' Junkin said with conviction. 'And—I say—I do admire your plays. They're better than Congreve. Right in the Wycherley class, I'd say.'

'Thank you, Nick. And here goes.' Junkin's appraisal, although unlikely ever to be endorsed in any history of English drama, made me for the moment (for of course I was very tired) positively love the boy. 'Tin doesn't look very heavy, fortunately.'

'No. She's obviously the vest-pocket contortionist sort, isn't she?' He turned to Tin Pin. 'You hear that?' he said. 'You're financial again, and it's where you flake off.' Junkin was making decisively for his bedroom. 'The important thing,' he paused to say to me, 'is reef-knots.'

'Yes,' I said. 'I do remember that.'

Ten minutes after this, Nicolas Junkin and I were freely breathing a celibate air.

'It's a funny thing,' Junkin said, 'how quite sure I was she wasn't going to turn me on. I suppose I might have felt different after sleeping on it.'

'After sleeping on sleeping with her?' I liked this remark of Junkin's. A public-school boy, it struck me, however friendly he might be feeling, would have shied away from such candour; an inbred sense of propriety, also attractive in itself, would have inhibited his speaking in this way to a much older man. 'I can't think it could be much good after having had to be deliberated on.'

'I suppose not.' Junkin was now detectably a shade wistful, after all. 'But I admit Julian is on to something, in a way. There are things you wouldn't do with your own girl that perhaps you shouldn't miss out on altogether. There's some of it in Lawrence.'

'I don't believe for a moment that Lawrence was any good in bed.'

'Oh, don't you think so?' For a moment Junkin was round-eyed with astonishment. 'I see what you mean,' he then said surprisingly. 'All that about loins of darkness and Loerke and the subtle lust of the Egyptians and barely comprehensible suggestivity.'

'Quite so. I doubt if it really takes one very far. There's a bishop asleep in this college now who's upset because he's found what he calls an erotic manual in his room. He needn't worry, if you ask me.'

'Kind of Perfumed Garden stuff?' Junkin asked, and stretched himself luxuriously.

'I suppose so. The bishop ought just to realize that not many people continue sold on that view of sexual experience for very long.'

'It's the young being crude and ignorant and all that?'

'You can put it that way.' I saw that Junkin, unlike my dream children, would be quick to counter any instructive note with effective irony. 'By the way, what is Plot going to make of us in the morning?'

'Oh, Plot's all right. I like Plot. Of course he couldn't wink at a girl. His job's tied up with that. There are chaps who say the scouts are simply kept around the place as a bloody corps of spies. Not quite fair, I think. But it doesn't seem to me a man's job, all the same, running about with trays and emptying teapots. It's women's work. I've a couple of aunts who'd just love it—waiting on apple-cheeked young gents and getting a civil thank-you every now and then. But Plot won't mind my sleeping here on the quiet. Not if you O.K. it.'

'Then that's fine.'

'Thank you very much. I say, can I make you some nescaf?'

'I'd be most grateful.' Coffee at 2 a.m. was scarcely my cup of tea, but I wasn't going to turn down an offer as polite as this. 'We're making a night of it, after all.'

'I've a queer sort of powdered milk,' Junkin said, and busied himself in this new interest. 'I say, who *are* all those people?'

'Those people?'

'All dressed up like you. Are they the governors?'

'The governors?' I was puzzled by this.

'Grand schools and colleges and places all have governors, don't they?'

'Oh, I see. No, they're just old boys. Up for a spree.'

'I suppose that's what a Gaudy is. I didn't know. This place puzzles me a lot. Nobody ever explains it. They take it for granted you must know. I'm not even certain who bosses it. Perhaps it's the Senior Tutor.'

'I'm sure the Senior Tutor is a very important man. But if any one person bosses it, it's the Provost.'

'The Provost?' Junkin was surprised. 'I thought he was just some kind of clergyman. He dresses like that.'

'So he is. But he wears two hats.'

'Two hats?' Junkin, perhaps not conversant with the metaphorical use of this expression, looked as if the information only added to the general mysteriousness of the college. 'I told one of my tutors once that I didn't really understand the set-up. He said it was the same with him; he was a Balliol man, and had been here only twenty-five years, so he still couldn't make head or tail of it. He must have been making fun of me.'

'I don't think so. He probably feels just as he said. And you're likely, Nick, to end up knowing more about the place than he does, just because you've been here from the start. Institutions like this *are* mysterious. They have a sort of secret life of their own. And it's always in charge, too. The dons go huffing and puffing in this direction and that, and the college just holds on its own course. Or that's my guess about it. I'm an outsider. I don't really know.'

'I suppose that's how plays get written.' Junkin offered this mordant conjecture without irony; rather admiringly, indeed. I admitted that playwrights grope around amid vast ignorances —this while secretly telling myself that Junkin's character, at least, was something I was coming to know about. His realism and total incomprehension of social structures could be read as characteristic of his class; so, perhaps, could his crude but not unwholesome sexual precocity—although in this his attitudes must be diffused pretty well through his entire age-group. And I rather saw as the *clou* here the rationally measured-out hospitality which had put Tin Pin on the sofa and Junkin in his bed. Junkin was a sensible young man, and if he wasn't intellectual he was far from stupid. If one had to endow him with an idiosyncrasy—by which I mean thought to tip him into a play—it would be done by exaggerating his liability to mental inconsecutiveness and confusion and playing this off against a contrastingly stressed native sagacity. These simplicities of personality-structure belong, I suppose, to the theatre rather than to the novel. And if Junkin *was*, in fact, put together on simple lines, this was perhaps why the theatre attracted him.

These vague notions went through my head as I drank my coffee, but I don't think it occurred to Junkin that I was speculating about him; indeed, my manners would have been falling far short of his had I given him occasion for any thought of the sort. We talked in a relaxed and rambling way for some time. In fact the library was beginning to show in faint silhouette against a first flush of midsummer dawn before the hospitable youth—figuratively speaking—tucked me up in bed. I went to sleep at once, without taking time to reflect on the fact—not perhaps much to my credit—that the light comedy of Tin Pin and her unkindled rescuer had entirely driven the far from amusing, although indeed bizarre, history of Ivo Mumford from my head. It was, I had to suppose, rather more my sort of thing.

X

I woke up to what I supposed was the memory of a dream
—and one constructed on fairly orthodox Freudian lines. Its
sexual purport would need digging for, but it was com-
pounded, as it ought to be, of experiences of the past twenty-
four hours mingled with concerns drawn from remote childhood: all this to the effecting of a disturbing and fantastic
whole. I had returned to college, where I had encountered my
old friend Tony Mumford. And Tony had proved to have an
undergraduate son called Ivo, who had suddenly got himself
into deep disgrace (sex *did* come in here) and had then been
secretly flown out of the country at an hour's notice by
Gavin Mogridge, who no longer tried to play the 'cello and
had become instead something very high up in what the
Chancellor of the Exchequer still calls the Secret Service. I
was just satisfactorily linking this last dream-element with
that fantasy-life upon which I had retreated upon discovering
myself not to be the cleverest boy in Miss Frazer's form when I
came to my senses and realized that Ivo Mumford's abrupt
expatriation (if, in fact, it had successfully taken place) be
longed to the waking world. So did the prospect of becoming
a reader—a kind of mini-professor, it seemed—in the university. And so did the episode of Nicolas Junkin and Tin
Pin. The lady had, I hoped, departed for good. But her none-
too-willing host was presumably still on his sofa in the next
room.

Even on that uncommodious perch, he would with luck be
sleeping the untroubled sleep of youth. But I didn't care to
think of him as possibly tossing about, so I got out of bed and
quietly opened the communicating door. There was no Junkin
in the room. Was it perhaps Junkin who had been a dream?
More probably he had gone out to the loo. Then I glanced at

the mantelpiece, and saw an envelope perched just where the Provost's had been perched the night before. I crossed the room and picked it up. It said simply 'Mr Pattullo' in a bold, unformed hand. I opened it.

Dear Mr Pattullo,

7 a.m. and I think I'd better be off. I hope it isn't rude and I hope Plot will bring you tea. He does even me sometimes when he thinks I'm a bit down. It will be less akward— although Plot is really quite good when akward things happen as or course they sometimes must. And as a matter of fact I am meeting a man and we are going to Turky. I've always rather wanted to go to Turky and it is very much on now. We shall hike of course, although the college has given me a travel grant which is hansome of them considering how I stand with those rotten examiners. We wonder if we'll have to have our haircut at the frontier. I asked my tutor and he said it wasn't a thing English gentlemen stood for from wogs and wops in his time but that times change. He says 'English gentlemen' as a joke but not ofensively. He is called Lempriere, I wonder if you know him. I am so sorry about last night. It must have been very tiring for you after a Gaudy (which I now know about) and which must be particularly tiring when one is getting on. I hope to see more of your plays. If you don't get a ppc from me from Turky it will be because the college hasn't sent it on. They are often rather bad about male.

Yours truly,
NICK (JUNKIN)

I went back to bed—partly because I wanted Plot to have the satisfaction of waking me up, drawing back the curtains, and, no doubt, reporting on the state of the weather. A second reading of Junkin's letter confirmed me in the view that his examiners had at least certain superficial problems on their hands. It seemed improbable that Junkin's spelling and epistolarly style were in the least a characteristic product of Cokeville G.S. They were native to the man. I was pleased by his manner of signing his name. It seemed to signal that I hadn't been presuming in addressing him as Nick.

I considered the shape of the advancing day. It had a train to Paddington at the end of it, but was going to run to several social occasions before that. They would be overshadowed, I saw, by the still-undetermined state of Ivo Mumford's fortunes. One couldn't ride away from an affair like that, or be other than oppressed by Tony's anxieties, simply because its untoward nature draped it with a curious unreality. In any case, I was myself involved, if in a peripheral way, since Mogridge— following, it was to be supposed, some professional rule- book—had announced that he would use me as a first channel of communication with Ivo's family.

I was distracted from these thoughts by voices floating up from the Elm Walk in Long Field. They came to me, I believe, with a more immediate sense of familiarity renewed than anything else had occasioned since my arriving for the Gaudy. There is no such thing as an Oxford accent, since what phoneticians call Received Standard English came into exist- ence without the university's playing any very identifiable part in the process. But there is undoubtedly an Oxfordshire accent, and I had first become aware of it through the open window under which I was now lying. (The bed hadn't moved between my time and Junkin's, and the two of us had shoved it back into place after disposing of Tin Pin.) College servants arriving, perhaps at a rather later hour than long ago, to begin their daily round and common task were calling out to one another as cheerfully as if under the immediate inspiration of Bishop Ken's morning hymn.

It was going to be another hot day, and already the veil of mist over Long Field would be stirring, would here and there be catching gleams of golden light. Remembering this, I forgot my benevolent plan of being found comfortably asleep by Plot. Tossing aside a sheet and single blanket (although not to a far corner of the room), I scrambled to my knees on the mattress, pushed aside the curtain, and threw up the lower window-sash so that I could lean out. When I had got both arms flat on the stone sill, and my chin contemplatively lodged on them, I experienced one of those sensations of entire well-being and unflawed happiness which are never more than momentary, nor by any means always associated with nostalgic feeling, as this one appeared to be.

It had been, of course, early October when I had arrived in Surrey to begin my first Michaelmas Term. I thought I remembered golden mornings in its opening weeks, and myself greeting them just as I was greeting this June morning now. My feelings I didn't remember at all, but it was perhaps reasonable to assume that they had been buoyant, and that most of the sunshine I seemed to recall was supplied by my later imagination as a kind of climatic correlative to an inner weather. I had ended that term in love with the place to an extent which might have been said to constitute a disease, and it was fair to suppose that leading up to this there had been a substantial prodromal period when the bug was hatching.

The mist hanging over Long Field was still thick and almost motionless; it was with only a suggestion of the faintest sprinkling of gold dust that sunlight as yet flecked it. Suddenly a number of creatures like performing brown bears emerged from the haze, baggy and upright. There were eight bears and a hedgehog—the eight being oarsmen and the ninth their cox. All were in enveloping track-suits except for one tall youth who walked in front carrying his blade and wearing, for some reason, no more than Junkin had been slumbering in when summoned to the rescue by Tin Pin. All vanished into vapour as they had come, making for the river. They were a crew that had recently done well in Eights, I uncertainly supposed, and whose training was unbroken because they were ambitious of equal distinction at Henley. Rowing had always been mysterious; indeed, the entire life of athletes had remained largely closed to me. Some of us, intellectuals or aesthetes (although this was an outmoded word) had professed a kind of connoisseurship in that species of our fellows, lithe or lumbering, flannelled or muddy. It had been a taste, this indulgent spectatorship, either genuinely or ironically homosexual in its prompting, and I had to be taught by Tony and others that it was 'inhibited' to disapprove of it. Now I should have liked to know what went on inside the supposedly thick skulls of these hearties. And under—for that matter—those great mops of hair. For I had several times noticed on television-screens what I had glimpsed again now: that the devotedly athletic youth of England would be just as much at hazard on the frontier of Turkey as Nicolas Junkin could possibly be. The tall lad bearing his oar had been all raven locks brushing bronzed shoulders.

At this point another college servant, arriving belatedly on a bicycle, glanced up at me with what I thought of as amusement. I reacted to this as promptly as I should have done in my earliest tenure of the window, ducking away from it as if detected in some eccentricity. I banged my head on the sash as a result, and as a result of that again gave the window a further and indignant upward shove. It moved a couple of inches, and I found myself looking at a faint but curious appearance thus disclosed. It was another bear. Only this time it was a Rupert Bear, tenuously scratched and then inked into the woodwork. I was sure that Rupert Bear had his first home in children's comics when I was myself a child, but I had a notion that he had lived on to be adopted as some sort of mascot, or emblem of niceness and innocence, by young people believing that niceness and innocence are politically as well as morally feasible. So Rupert's present appearance was perhaps the handiwork of Junkin. But it now struck me that the figure was designed not as Rupert but as Rupert's sister—although I couldn't recall whether such a character was, or was not, canonical. My reason for this conjecture was that the figure appeared to wear what might have been a ballet-dancer's *tutu*. This was balanced, and with a certain sense of composition or equipoise, by a balloon issuing from the figure's mouth. The balloon had once said something, but no single scratch of the message remained. I looked again, and saw that here was Rupert himself, after all. What he was wearing was not a ballet-skirt but a kilt. And I could supply the vanished words. They had been, *Ye maun thole it, Dunkie*.

So in fact my first Surrey days had not been so blissful after all. I had been obliged to remind myself of what I had elsewhere been taught: that he who endureth to the end shall be saved. And now my memory held the whole picture. Waking up in this strange place on those mild October mornings, I had only to push up the window-sash to its fullest extent to have Rupert emerge from his den and deliver his wholesome admonishment.

I didn't find this suddenly recollected behaviour at all astonishing. Perhaps it was surprising that I had so effectively screened it away, and my fellow freshmen would certainly have been puzzled had one of them come upon Rupert in his mint condition. I was an unsophisticated lad—but then so, in one direction or another, were most of them; and I doubt whether I had to put much effort into appearing as self-possessed, as inclined to amusement rather than alarm in these new surroundings, as anybody else. Geographically I had made a longer hop than most, but my schooling had been of the semi-Sassenach cast I have described; and this, together with being my mother's son and certain other family associations, made me distinguishably the same sort of boy—if slightly exoticized—as those who, with a varying degree of the mysterious, referred to one another as Salopians, Wyke-hamists, or Carthusians. I don't think I ever felt myself as floundering. It had been something deeper that obliged me to call Rupert Bear to my aid—frustrated first love, in fact, with which Oxford had nothing to do.

'Dunkie' was my father's name for me. (He called my brother 'Nennie', believing Ninian to be the same name as that of the British historian Nennius.) His use of the vernacular to which he had been brought up—which Scottish journalists liked to refer to as the Doric—was on the whole confined to occasions upon which his habitual mild intemperance happened to take him in a cross-grained way; when its effect, as commonly, was merely mellowing it amused him to talk in fluent although grammatically imperfect French. 'A guid crop maun thole the thistle', he might say, contemplating some vexatious commission in a bunch of those lying ahead of him. My mother, too, had some command of this speech, although mainly confined within the bounds of family anecdote. My Rupert Bear, indeed, was probably indebted to her. Her grandfather's coachman, she would recount, being reproved for doffing his livery-coat on a hot day, had replied, 'Sir, I can barely thole my breeks'. My mother, simple-minded and fond of gaiety, found a story like this very amusing. And I recalled now that at Oxford I had myself been inclined to show off my command of peasant speech—something which would have been held wholly pointless at school. I would tell Tony that he was a flea-luggit dafty, or pronounce P. P. Killiecrankie a fair scunner.

During what I could now think of as three Mumford generations, the colleges of Oxford, as of Cambridge, must have been receiving a steadily increasing proportion of young men who had never been away from home before. There had been more Nicolas Junkins in Tony's time than in his father's, and there were now more in Ivo's time than there had been in Tony's. My own Oxford acquaintance with home-keeping boys had been in the main—and again those mysterious terms—with Paulines and Westminsters, who seemed to be encountering nothing out of the way. They may well have had their own Rupert Bears, all the same. Like Ninian and myself they had lived on the alarming fringe of boarding-school life. For boys like Junkin that life was a fiction: exciting, enticing, romantic, horrifying—but securely confined within the covers of school-stories. For boys in half-and-half places, whether English or Scottish, it was a presence, unnerving at least in some degree, just beyond a baize door. I seem to recall Graham Greene as describing this situation very well. Perhaps I myself had found more alarming than I consciously realized being pitched through the equivalent of such a door when I found myself on the staircase.

Ninian and I, again, had spent a good many years under the intermittent threat of being turned into boarders. This was because my father—at least during periodic dangerous moments of attention to the matter—had been aware that our domestic discipline was ramshackle and disorganized, and had concluded, rationally enough, that punctual meals, baths, prep and bed-time, together with an occasional thwack with a gym-shoe (which last was something he himself lived a universe apart from any possibility of administering) would have exercised a bracing effect on our young lives as a whole. Fortunately he never had, when it came to the pinch, the money or perhaps the heart to do anything about it. I say 'fortunately' because our boarders, of whom there must have been something under a couple of hundred, were a displeasingly tough lot, to whom we gave as wide a berth as we could. Many were the sons of prosperous Lowland farmers. Others, coming from impecunious Service families without much intellectual pretension, would have been comfortably accommodated at Kipling's Westward Ho! The day-boys—the sons of all those professors and advocates and doctors (to say nothing of such writers and artists as that part of the world managed to support)—viewed these young savages with fascinated horror. Every second one of them we regarded—exaggeratedly, no doubt—as a revolting bully with nasty (and by us only dimly apprehended) private habits. To be cast among them would be to suffer something like what we were hearing of as currently happening in concentration camps. This nightmare, if largely baseless, owned a considerable power of lingering on. Conceivably I sometimes imagined myself to catch a murmur of it from among the young bloods of the college to which my father's eventual dramatic action and my own facility in English prose composition had transported me.

My actual experience of being away from home, although of a different sort, had been almost equally daunting in its way. This was because of the broad facts of my family history.

My parents had met in Rome when my father was an art-student living there on some exiguous bursary and my mother was being 'finished' in an expensive school. They were thus both very young. Their first encounter was in the Sistine Chapel. There is something undeniably impressive in the thought of a life-relationship having its inception in front of Michelangelo's *Last Judgement*; and my mother, although I doubt whether she ever read *A Room with a View*, would declare that always thereafter she was to associate my father with that one among the twenty nude youths on the Chapel's ceiling who carries a burden of acorns. The meeting is conceivable. How they contrived to continue to meet, and much more how they contrived to be married within the precincts of the British Embassy, I don't profess to know—except, indeed, that my father was a hard man to beat.

My mother's people were deeply displeased—the more so because the marriage proved to have taken place, most unfortunately, on the day of her father's death. Her eldest surviving brother, Rory (who thus became Roderick Glencorry of that Ilk and twenty-second Laird of Glencorry), regarded his sister as a feather-headed child who had been practised upon by some obscure crofter's son, and for several years he treated the couple as non-existent. But he was a conscientious man, with an honest if perhaps provincial sense of the consequence of the Glencorrys and the decorum that ought to obtain in the family of the Chief. So eventually he swallowed his resentment, and relations of a sort were established.

Even so, I can recall only one occasion upon which we visited Corry Hall in force. I had myself made the acquaintance of my Uncle Rory by then, and I was terrified lest he should treat my father with outrageous frigidity or condescension. Of course nothing of the kind happened. The Glencorry was cool, but very much the courteous host. He made a polite show of interest in my father's profession, inquiring about it with a correct diffidence which he certainly showed himself as having no title to shed. It was about my father that I was then anxious; failing to be met with outrage, he was perfectly capable of turning outrageous himself. But this failed to happen either. The Glencorrys didn't run to a Raeburn, but there were several Allan Ramsays—the family having been more prosperous in the mid-eighteenth century, I imagine, than later on. My father found it impossible to think ill of anybody who treated heirlooms of that sort with respect. The visit ended in good order.

But it had taken place perhaps ten years after my mother's marriage, and that settled a good deal. My mother was volatile and, I suppose, rather silly; she was also of those who were beginning to be called neurotics. But she was very well aware of what was due from the head of her family to the husband of her choice; and so stiff a quarantine could not be atoned for by a few amiabilities in front of canvases depicting deceased Glencorrys. The reconciliation remained formal, and things went on as before. Uncle Rory had already judged it right 'to take an interest', as he expressed it, in Ninian and myself, and we were regularly invited to spend two or three weeks of the summer holidays at Corry. We didn't, however, go together. Ninian, as elder brother, had first innings; and I, as younger, had second. I never understood why this had to be so. Corry Hall would have held (and subdued) half-a-dozen boys much rowdier than the Pattullos. Possibly my uncle felt that the purpose of these visits was the improvement of our behaviour, and that it was best to concentrate upon us one at a time. As for my parents, I think my mother was always in two minds about our highland holidays. She disliked parting with her sons to a brother who was receiving them on a kind of sufferance, but at the same time she wanted us to be Glencorrys—to be, in fact, a laird's nephews as well as an artist's sons. This divided feeling became a factor in forming what was to be my own ambivalent attitude to my grand relations. My father was wiser, thinking not in terms of one side of our family and the other, and still less of painters and landed gentry. He simply judged it a good thing that we should get away from Edinburgh and run wild about the glens without any inconvenient cost to himself. Uncle Rory seemed not much to impress him one way or the other. My father had executed portraits of several men of that sort. They weren't quite *his* sort, but they belonged to an order he understood and after a fashion respected. They were certainly an improvement on people like the Dreich. Had he been invited (but he wasn't) to paint his brother-in-law he would have got on the canvas all the inner man there was. It might not have been a generous portrait, but it would have been alive.

Uncle Rory had an English wife, and two daughters who struck me as very English also. Indeed, my first fully formed, if not clearly formulated, impression of Corry Hall was that there seemed perplexingly little that could be called Scottish about it. I was grown-up before I realized that this was a superficial view. My expectation had been of kilts and bagpipes and even tartan carpets. (A school-friend with aristocratic pretensions had confided to me that the Duke of Argyll wore tartan bedroom-slippers, at least at Inveraray.) I never saw Uncle Rory in a kilt, and he once astonished me by advancing the view that it was a garment which had been more or less invented by the Prince Consort. The only kilt in evidence about the place was worn by an elderly man who was provided with bagpipes as well, and whose duty it was to walk up and down in front of the house before breakfast, producing from the instrument all those disastrously emotive strains of which it is so capable. Ninian—for some years more knowledgeable than myself, although I was to overtake him—declared that this was a practice no longer current except in tourist hotels in the Trossachs. He may have exaggerated.

I found it unnatural that my uncle, who didn't hale from England, should talk like my masters at school, who did. At the same time, I found the fact fascinating, since it revealed to me the existence of a caste or class unconfined by what I had accustomed myself to think of as unbreachable national boundaries. We had been taught that something of the sort obtained throughout Europe in the mediaeval period.

But there was a good deal else that was strange to me at

Corry. By the time our visits there were an established routine, both my brother and I had made ourselves confidently free of two distinct worlds at home. We understood what I have called the Bohemian character of our domestic situation: its untidiness and disorder; its indecorous rows and rumpuses; the fashion in which, ignored as irrelevant brats one day, we would on the next be whirled as companions and equals into bewildering and exhilarating jollifications improvised by my father and his cronies—this only to find ourselves, two or three days later still, groping through pervasive gloom or dodging nervous explosion because of some disaster in the studio or, it might be, merely in the kitchen. We were getting the measure of all this, and at the same time we were learning (as by rumour from afar) of the uses of tooth-brushes and combs, of the polishing of shoes, and of the comfortableness of clean socks. By means of such initial steps as 'staying to tea' in the houses of our school-fellows we were coming to inspect and in many ways to approve the orderly lives of the professional classes in what was still so unmistakably the capital city of an ancient kingdom. It was a society with strong intellectual traditions; if its assumptions and manners contrasted sharply with those which we knew at home, it yet presented to our fairly concentrated regard one facet, as that home presented another facet, of a more or less integrated urban life. We didn't of course—Ninian and I—put it to ourselves like this. It was simply a matter of our being intuitively aware that the Pattullos and the McKechnies in a last analysis hung together.

This conception gave us no yard-stick for Corry, and three or four years must have passed before I felt myself in a position to theorize to Ninian about this ancestral or demi-ancestral territory of ours. It just wasn't, I said, part of civilization—which meant the culture of cities—at all. It didn't belong to any *Bürgerzeit*, as Edinburgh did. It was a feudal set-up fossilized, and that was why it was so comically *thin*. Our uncle was the archetypal Thin Man. I admitted he was tough. But—intellectually, aesthetically, spiritually (if one presumed to know anything about that), he was as thin as he was also undeniably thick. You could unwind him a little. But the result would be just a short length of string.

The animus in this suggests a divided mind, or at least reflects bewilderment in a strange situation. What had holiday life at Corry Hall been like when we were too small to defend ourselves? It had certainly been possible to run wild about the glens—if a solitary boy can run wild about glens. But it hadn't been possible to do so without a cap. Without a cap (and it was a school cap, which was all I had, and a token of subjection which for years I'd have written any number of lines rather than been seen wearing in the street)—without a cap one mustn't go beyond the front door. This wasn't because of any archaic persuasion that wandering bare-headed constituted a menace to health; I had to wear a cap in order to be able to doff it to any female, old or young, I met around the estate. The laird had the habit, and it was proper his young kinsmen should acquire it too. I also had to know these people's names, saying 'Good morning, Janet' to the girls and 'Good morning, Mrs Glencorry' (since most of them really were Glencorrys) to those who had attained to the dignity of being married women. Before setting out, moreover, I was under orders to visit the stable yard and consult a young man called Mountjoy, who acted as my uncle's general factotum. Mountjoy would determine whether there was a dog to be walked, and with the aid of a map would delimit as out of bounds any area in which a shoot was likely to be going on. He was an efficient person, who had attained a position of some responsibility early, but he was also benevolent, or at least he was benevolently disposed towards me. He would often keep me talking for some time, and would then add to the packet of sandwiches I had received from the cook a somewhat burdensome bottle of a fizzy red drink called Kola. He kept a stock of it from year to year simply for the refreshment of Ninian and myself—Ninian being also a favourite of his. Neither of us could drink it, our palates having been vitiated by our father's insistence that we should be reared from an early age on

189

claret and water. Ninian claimed that he seldom failed to find, paddling in a burn, some contemporary of simpler tastes into whom the stuff could be tipped. I was too shy for this, and also fearful that word might get round to Mountjoy of so illegitimate a largesse, to an effect of wounding his feelings. My own Kola, therefore, was apt to go into the burn itself, where it would fine away in crimson streaks and whorls, like the blood of a wounded grouse.

It will be seen that life at Corry was much a matter of traditionally determined modes of conduct. It was also pervasively low-keyed. The family's conversation was like that. At home I was accustomed to bouts of passionate and sometimes hectoring and furious talk; to fierce arguments or absorbed discussions among all four of us on topics we often knew very little about. These exhausted, there would be silence for days on end—mitigated only by the too-noisy eating habits of Ninian and myself or our mother's bursts of full-lunged bravura singing around the house when her nervous agitations took her that way. At meal-times at Corry (and they were more prolonged than was necessitated by any abundance in the fare) conversation seldom stopped and never, never hotted up. It was a polite—just as slow mastication was a dietic—duty, and it certainly didn't much trespass on any realm of general ideas. Much was said about the dogs, their health and training; much about details in the not very complicated economy of the estate; a good deal about the tenantry (although they were few) and the moral hazards to which they were exposed through the encroachments of one or another modernization. The affairs of the neighbouring gentry were also sometimes discussed, but invariably with an inflexible circumspection, so that nothing scandalous or otherwise interesting ever emerged. (Our father's policy—if it was a policy—was to examine in our presence absolutely any of the vagaries of human behaviour to have come to the notice of his inquiring mind—although always against a background of stiff presbyterian probity which he had brought with him from his childhood to a much greater extent than he knew.) What worried me about the code of the Glencorrys was that its exactions were not in aid of anything I could distinguish. There didn't seem to be much around in the way of aims and targets; it all appeared depressingly a matter of the maintenance of a style. I thought I came to understand why my mother, in her readings to Ninian and myself from Scott's novels, kindled whenever she got away from the stodgy stretches to wild and romantic doings. There had been too much decorum in her childhood, and it looked as if there was going to be too much in that of my girl cousins as well, so that Uncle Rory might have rebels on his hands in the end.

Yet Uncle Rory remained formidable. On one occasion of Ninian's returning home and my own setting out I learnt with awe that my brother had actually been caned—and this at a date later than his sixteenth birthday—on the score of some gross and uncharacteristic discourtesy offered to a fishwife. That Ninian should have submitted to so humiliating and (as he assured me) fiendishly painful an experience, thus inflicted by one firmly declaring himself *in loco parentis*, showed that he at least, thought rather well of our kinsman. Had news of this sensational event reached my father it would certainly have been the end of our Glencorry holidays. That we kept it a deathly secret proves that, on balance, we prized and enjoyed them.

And it would be a good guess that during that summer at Corry Hall I behaved unnaturally well.

These pages—which might be called *Leaves from the Journal of our Life in the Highlands*—go a little way to suggesting that when I first went up to Oxford I was re-enacting, at least to some extent, my experience at a yet more vulnerable age of meeting a strange environment and almost a different culture. Later on, the Glencorry connection was to have a more considerable consequence. I have sketched in these people here very lightly—but, as it were, 'straight' and without thinking to amuse. On future occasions, however, I was to treat them (and people more or less similarly stationed in life, of whom I was to meet plenty) much as I was to treat, say, the Talberts, expending a great deal of perhaps misdirected energy in the endeavour to elevate them within the sphere of comedy. I do not believe that comedy possesses, as the classical theory of it would maintain, any particularly corrective or regulative function in society. But we do perhaps learn a little about ourselves by laughing at other people.

Plot might have been laughing at me now, had he owned the slightest inclination to such an impropriety. Having fallen upon the recollections I have here sketched, I was in fact still kneeling on my bed—Nick Junkin's bed—in a markedly juvenile fashion. Plot was standing patiently in the doorway, a large cup of darkish-looking tea in his hand, and an expression of solemnity rather than of amusement on his face. Perhaps he supposed himself to have disturbed me at my private devotions.

'A very agreeable morning, sir,' Plot said, handing over the tea. 'I hope you slept well. And most successful, the Gaudy appeared to me to be. Only one gentleman took bad.' Plot announced this with a satisfaction which might have been attributable either to the paucity of the casualties or to having something dramatic to intimate. 'Four of us it took, though, to get him back to his room. Right at the top of Harbage Six, it was, with a very awkward twist to the stair. A heart-attack, they say, and Dr Damian with him still. Full-fleshed gentlemen ought always to be put in ground-floor sets, if you ask me. It would be only a reasonable precaution—a Gaudy always having its chancy side for such types. Not that it isn't the emotion quite as much as the liquor, which is a creditable thing. I'm sorry those sheets look a bit crumpled, sir. How that could happen, I can't say.'

This was alarming. The sheets were crumpled for the good reason that they had been knotted together for the purpose of parting with Tin Pin. I hadn't made up my mind what, if anything, of the night's concluding adventure to communicate to Plot. Now, imprudently perhaps, I decided it should be nothing at all.

'I had a very comfortable night, thank you,' I said firmly. 'And I thought the Gaudy dinner was splendidly served. It must have been very hard work for you all. By the way, I found myself sitting next to Mr Killiecrankie. Prebendary Killiecrankie, I ought to say. I hadn't realized he'd become a clergyman.' I felt rather pleased with myself for thus introducing the name of my formerly scandalous contemporary. It might divert Plot from what could prove an awkward turn in our conversation. In an extremity, and supposing Plot to find (though it seemed improbable) any further inconvenient evidences in Junkin's rooms, Killiecrankie's history might even be exploited in a kind of counter-attack, since Plot had been so admittedly his henchman in that past time. 'He seems a changed man,' I added.

'It's only fitting, sir.' Plot paused on this in a fashion I didn't altogether like. 'Would the tea be to your satisfaction?'

'Oh, very much so. But now I suppose I'd better get shaved and dressed.'

'Breakfast is from eight-thirty, sir, so there's no call to hurry yourself. And I'll just be tidying round.' To my relief, Plot moved towards the door. There, however, he paused again. 'Adverting to what we were touching upon,' he said surprisingly, 'all in due season would be my motto. Mr Junkin, now, has a book on his shelf—one of the bookstall sort, I'd think, that's done up in paperback—called *The Heyday in the Blood*. I haven't looked into it, of course. It wouldn't be my place. But the title explains itself, you might say. When I was a lad myself I used to get so that I just couldn't stop myself. But the vale of years isn't for such goings on. Change must come. Responsibilities.'

'Yes, indeed.' I had a moment's bemused sense of Plot as being in on the Yeats joke. 'And we are none of us getting any younger,' I added with desperate sententiousness. 'Still, we retain our sympathies with the young.'

'It wouldn't be proper not to.' With this judicial observation, Plot withdrew, closing the bedroom door behind him. As I shaved I could hear him moving around, and producing those exaggerated flappings and rattlings with which scouts habitually signal that they are hard at work. The demonstration continued while I dressed. Then there was a knock on the door, and Plot was confronting me again. He was holding an ash-tray.

'It looks,' Plot said, 'as if somebody has been taking a liberty, sir. While you were dining, it might be. They get very slack on the gate, those porters do, when there's a Gaudy or the like.'

'I suppose it's inevitable.' I found myself thinking about Tony's father, and hoping that he had profited by this laxity. It might just conceivably become important that his coming and going had passed unremarked. 'But what kind of liberty are you thinking of, Plot?'

Plot silently held out the ash-tray for my inspection. It contained a single cigarette-end. This, most unfortunately, was heavily stained with lip-stick. I remembered the behaviour of Tin Pin. Here, in fact, was what might be called a fair cop.

'Dear me!' I said weakly. What Plot was imagining, it would have been hard to determine. I almost expected him to conduct a further rummage in the bedroom there and then. *Who goes with who*—an excellent poet has recorded—*the bedclothes say*. Plot might well be concluding that I had rounded off a jolly evening by brazenly importing a mistress into Nicolas Junkin's blameless rooms. It would have been a bold stroke. Not P. P. Killiecrankie himself—and in his own heyday—could have conceived of it. I found myself—weakly still—trying to remember how many five-pound notes I had in my wallet. But the situation was not one in which Plot would consent to be bribed. Nor, for that matter, was the attempt of a kind which a moment's decent consideration would permit me to pursue. 'It was a Chinese girl,' I heard myself say with staggering boldness. 'Probably from Hong Kong.'

Plot's reply to this—admirable in itself—was a stiff bow. He had the appearance of regarding the matter as closed. I was not an undergraduate, after all, and no charge of his. I found, however, that this conclusion to the affair was not supportable. It must all come out. If he didn't believe me, then he could lump it.

'We got her out,' I said. 'In the usual way. Mr Junkin and myself.'

'Mr Junkin, sir?' It was evident that, for the moment at least, I had been unpersuasive. It was also evident that Plot was angry. He was eyeing me in a very man-to-man fashion. I remembered my impression that Nicolas Junkin of Cokeville was a favourite of his. He didn't intend to accept any made-up story about him.

'He was in Oxford for the night, Plot, and not intending to come into college. But, somehow or other, he had this girl landed on him. So he brought her in here, not knowing his rooms would be occupied, and shoved her on the sofa. He wasn't interested in sleeping with her. When I came back it all seemed a bit crowded. So we gave her the price of a railway-ticket and dumped her.'

'I've heard that tale before.' Plot made this offensive-seeming remark in a perplexingly relaxed manner. 'On the very next staircase, it was, and not two years ago. Mr Withycombe, the gentleman's name was. One of those that call themselves Christians in College.'

'Christians in College?'

'A group organized by the Chaplain, that is, of them that take religious matters seriously. Very serious, Mr Withycombe was, and a nice gentleman by all accounts. But slow. Slower than Mr Junkin, by a long way.'

'What happened?' I asked. For I somehow knew that Mr Withycombe was going to see Junkin and myself through the wood.

'He'd been with friends in Rattenbury, it seemed, discussing the Virgin Birth and deep matters of that sort. A very sober coffee-and-biscuits affair. Absorbing it must have been, though, since he didn't get back to Surrey till two in the morning. Much your own case, it might be said.'

'My dear Plot—don't tell me he found a girl asleep on his sofa!'

'Just that, sir. Fancied she was in somebody else's rooms, she did, and had entered them at a lawful and respectable hour. So she sat down to wait for a gentleman who hadn't come and didn't intend to, and there she'd fallen fast asleep. It was a difficult situation for Mr Withycombe, particularly with him being slow, and his head full of the Immaculate Conception and other holy thoughts. Howsoever, he fetched a friend with better wits from across the landing, and they lowered her into Long Field and told her to make herself scarce.'

'So it all ended happily?'

'Well, not just at that moment. The night-watchman happened to be going by, and all they managed was to lower the young lady into his arms. So Mr Withycombe was up before the Dean next morning, with nothing to say for himself except this cock-and-bull story.'

'And what did the Dean do?'

'Why, believed him at once, of course. A very experienced man is Mr Gender.'

'And you're a very experienced man yourself.'

'Well, sir, I can advise you about breakfast.' Plot was actually smiling broadly, an abundant sign that I had been restored to grace. 'The porridge is something horrid and there's no disguising it—particularly from a Scottish gentleman like yourself. But where it says kippers it means kippers, and not a kipper. And very tasty they commonly are.'

I promised to profit from this inside knowledge, and Plot withdrew. But ten minutes later he returned, and for a moment I feared that he might have had second thoughts about his responsibilities in the grave matter of Junkin and Tin Pin. But he was merely handing me a note.

'From Lord Marchpayne with his compliments, sir,' he said. 'His lordship having had to leave first thing. On account of parliament and the like, no doubt. Not their own masters, such gentlemen are not. But the beck and call of duty hangs over us all.'

I accepted this improving thought, and tore open the envelope as soon as Plot had gone away again.

Dear Duncan,

I'm clearing out. Breakfast after the Gaudy isn't all that enticing in itself, and I don't like kippers—about which Plot has been chattering to me. I won't pretend that I'm not frantically worried about this thunderbolt, and I'm thankful you were standing by. Gavin too. If he has really brought off what he proposed then we do have a chance, at least, of getting in the clear. But the unknown factors are appallingly numerous. Think of my father's housekeeper. Think of Ivo's car. Think of village kids perhaps fooling around that gardener's cottage and coming on the boy. There are a dozen such hair-raising possibilities. It's a dreadful gamble, and that first fib of my father's started it. I've no illusions. People's children do get into trouble—people in my position, I mean—and there's a convention that it isn't let reflect upon one's public life or political career. But conspiracy, God help us, is another matter. If Gavin makes a muck of it and is boarded or something, of course I shan't be able to leave him in the ditch. I'll have to say I shoved it at him. And that will finish me as well as him—and without doing Ivo any good either. Oh, hell!

But I'm sure—the die being cast—that Gavin is right to stick to his drill. (Who would have thought the chap was *that*?) Please get through to me as soon as he gets through to you. Telephone numbers on the enclosed slip. On each of them ask first for my PPS. He's called Arbuthnot and is a very discreet chap. Destroy this *now*.

Yours ever,
Tony

XI

I PUT A MATCH to Tony's letter, and held it over Tin Pin's ash-tray (now emptied and wiped clean) until I had to drop it as the flame licked my fingers. Then—as if I were somebody in a spy-story or a romance of crime—I stubbed the ashes to powder with the match-stick. It made quite a mess for Plot to deal with later. I had a vision of him in a witness-box, offering a judge an unhurried account of this small unaccountable appearance. Under the influence of this fantasy, I almost took the remains downstairs to flush them away under the staircase's (inferior) loo. But I drew the line at that, telling myself one oughtn't to let funk be catching.

Tony was admitting funk—but perhaps not as much as he had actually been feeling. I took his point about conspiracy. If some unknown development in Ivo Mumford's situation defeated Mogridge and led to a more or less spectacular show-down, the plot hatched in Ivo's rooms at midnight could turn out uncommonly uncomfortable for us all. Its context in a high academic bean-feast graced by sundry persons of eminence would make it a spot-lit affair. But all this was no reason for being too late to join in the Gaudy Breakfast. I went downstairs and walked across Surrey.

Other men were doing the same thing. Some of them were hurrying—having succumbed to the persuasion that they were undergraduates again, and that at the stroke of some hour the doors of hall would be inexorably closed against them. Although this obviously baseless apprehension amused me, I found myself hurrying too. As a result, I failed to take the evasive action which my preoccupation and the generally unsociable character of the hour might otherwise have persuaded me to, and found myself walking towards the Great

Quadrangle side by side with P. P. Killiecrankie. We exchanged greetings.

'Do you remember Plot?' I asked.

'Plot?' The Prebendary had given me a sharp glance, but he repeated the name consideringly. 'Let me see. Would he have been a Rhodes Scholar reading Law?'

'He was a bicycle-boy, and he's now the scout on my old staircase. I ask because he mentioned you. He seems to remember you very well.'

'Ah! Well, I did have a bicycle. No doubt he cleaned it up from time to time. Not a service that one could expect nowadays, I imagine. But they tell me that the undergraduates still have their shoes polished for them. It seems to me unnecessary, and against the spirit of the time. It doesn't happen at a theological college with which I am connected.'

The Prebendary had changed the subject without haste. Unless he had really forgotten about Plot, he must have guessed that his former henchman had been indiscreet, and that my question was maliciously motivated. Undeniably it had been. So I thought better of going on to tell Killiecrankie that his exemplification of all the undergraduate virtues and graces had been such that the college servants still spoke with deep respect of Mr Killiecrankie's year. Instead, I said I hoped he had continued to enjoy the Gaudy after we had risen from the dinner-table.

'Yes, indeed—extremely pleasant. Such convivial occasions seldom come my way, and are all the more appreciated when they do. My duties in the vineyard have become more onerous of late.' Killiecrankie imparted to these last words that humorous inflection which the higher clergy are adept at lending to scriptural references without any unseemly effect of irreverence. 'Of course, one sometimes finds good company in Irish vicarages. But I have to confess that it is the exception rather than the rule. As for last night, I met and talked with a number of old friends. The Provost, in particular. It is heartening that he continues so much a man in his prime. When a mere lad, I was deeply attached to him—as I have no doubt you were, my dear Pattullo. His conduct of College Prayers was an inspiration to us all. One or two of his sermons influenced me deeply, even in my freshman year.'

'He might be astonished to hear it,' I said—and added hastily, 'being so modest a man.'

'I was anxious to have a few words with Marchpayne—whom I remember to have been, as Antony Mumford, a close friend of yours. I myself barely knew him in those days—considering him, to tell the truth, to be rather a frivolous fellow. I wanted, of course, to congratulate him on his Cabinet post. As it happened, I just missed him. And in rather odd circumstances.'

'Odd circumstances?' I must have been more nervous than I realized, since these unremarkable words of Killiecrankie's alarmed me.

'It was very late—really very late, indeed—and I was returning to my rooms in Surrey when I became aware of two men crossing the Great Quad. They might have been making their way to the car park. One of them was faintly familiar to me, although I couldn't put a name to him. The other appeared to be Marchpayne. But as I glanced at him I said to myself, "That's *not* Antony Mumford. It's his father, Cedric." A curious aberration, wouldn't you say? But it held me up for a moment, and the opportunity to have a word with Marchpayne was gone.'

'Very curious. You know Tony's father?'

'We have met from time to time. Cedric Mumford is a keen supporter of a Catholic missionary society with which I have a certain amount of contact. It is a difficult, and therefore rewarding, field for oecumenical effort.'

'I see.' I reflected—irrelevantly—that if I had been inventing old Mr Mumford, and obliged to provide him with some interest or other on the side, missionary enthusiasm was about the last thing I could have reckoned to render plausible. 'As a matter of fact,' I said rashly, 'Tony and his father *are* very alike.'

'Ah! Then you too know Cedric Mumford?'

'No, no—Tony has simply mentioned the fact—of the strong family resemblance, I mean.'

It was with astonishment that I heard myself tell this blank lie. When one is acting a lie one has an impulse, I suppose, to tell lies as well. That he really had seen old Mr Mumford in college after the Gaudy was something which it was certainly desirable to keep out of P. P. Killiecrankie's head. I was sure Mogridge very much hoped that his getting Ivo's grandfather off the premises had been unobserved. But I needn't have gone out of my way to assert that the pillar of missionary endeavour was unknown to me.

We had reached the entrance to hall, and I adopted the resource of making some comment on its oddity. Wyatt's solid, indeed chunky, staircase pushes incongruously upward beneath a late and elaborately traceried fan vaulting supported by a slender central shaft and dropping at regular intervals to pendentives like the ribs of an umbrella. A fantasticated and Brobdingnagian umbrella, indeed, is just what one feels oneself to be climbing beneath. But the Prebendary was inattentive to these appearances, or at least to my remarks on them, having fortunately espied a high dignitary of the church proceeding to breakfast just ahead of us. In the interest of making this contact he produced a graciously dismissive inclination of the head, much as if he were a very high dignitary himself. Thus happily released, I lingered behind for a moment and then went into hall.

The scene—or at least its atmosphere—was altered. There was a faint smell of expensive tobacco-smoke gone stale. The ranked portraits looked pale and jaded, as if they hadn't slept well. The shrunken body of breakfasting old members presented, many of them, the same appearance. Some had unsociably possessed themselves of newspapers, and one could guess that they were not all being sufficiently attentive to each other in the matter of passing the marmalade. Only the undergraduates looked cheerful—perhaps because they were getting a better breakfast than usual. There were a score of them at a table apart; and I noticed among them, looking extremely good-tempered and at ease, the youth who, the night before, had offered his companions the remark about self-exaggerating crap. The majority must be those still involved with examinations. I realized with a shock that the dead Paul Lusby ought to have been among them. The news about him had probably not yet got around.

I sat down at random, rather wishing that I had a newspaper myself. One couldn't exactly opt for a station apart, so I found myself at the end of a short row of my contemporaries. My neighbour turned out to be Robert Damian.

'Hullo, Robert,' I said. 'Has your patient kept you at it all night?'

'Oh, that.' Damian gave me an abstracted nod. 'Well, yes. The silly ass had convinced himself he was dying. How do you know about it?'

'My scout. He was a gratified member of the stretcher party. He believes that what overcomes people isn't the flesh-pots and the flagons, but the intense emotion stirred by our reunion. It's a romantic thought.'

'It's a bloody silly one. The college has had a real fatality, as a matter of fact.'

'You mean a lad called Lusby? I've heard of that too.'

For a moment Damian made no reply, but stirred his coffee.

'Those unpredictable things are never *quite* unpredictable,' he said presently. 'But with so many pins in the haystack it isn't easy to spot the needle. Have you ever lived on an American campus, Duncan?'

'Yes, for a time.'

'They have counselling services going like mad, but it doesn't improve the statistics. Ours aren't too bad, as a matter of fact. The university's as a whole, I mean. But this place, too. Unfortunately there's no comfort in statistics when the individual shock comes along. I had young Lusby talking several times. At risk a bit beyond the average, without a doubt. But nothing to panic about. Ordinary stress through over-anxiety to excel.'

'In the Schools? Then why did he let himself be drawn into that idiotic wager?'

'So you've heard of that too. An itch, it must have been, to establish some alternative image of himself, I suppose. The wager was with somebody not the least his sort. And who didn't even go to their blasted Commem Ball.' Damian hesitated. 'Somebody we were mentioning last night, as a matter of fact. Cyril Bedworth got the story out of a third chap not half an hour ago.'

I had a curious feeling that the hall had gone cold.

'Not Tony's boy?' I said.

'That's right. Ivo Mumford. Rough on him. But, of course, rough on Lusby as well.'

I found that I was looking at two kippers. It wasn't Plot's fault if I judged them unattractive. The lucklessness of Ivo was undeniably not to be divorced from certain displeasing facets of his personality. But for the moment I somehow felt myself to be, along with Tony and Mogridge, Ivo's man. In imagination I had been unkind to him—just as, in imagination, I had been kind to Nicolas Junkin. Junkin had turned up— in circumstances which were extremely absurd—and I had been able to tell myself I hadn't been wrong about him. He was an appealing lad. Ivo was yet to meet, and it was possible I should never set eyes on him. If I did, my facile build-up of an over-privileged young baddie might be vindicated too. But now I was hoping that it might at least have to be modified. And there was a good chance that it would be so. People commonly prove, when one makes their acquaintance, more mixed up and patchy than from hearsay one has concluded them to be.

'Whining schoolboys and lovers sighing like furnaces,' Damian said. 'Shakespeare missed out on undergraduates, who obviously come in between. An eighth and awkward age. But now I'm off to mere oblivion in North Oxford.'

'Your nonagenarians?'

'Yes. I get through two or three of them before morning surgery.' Damian had looked at his watch and stood up. 'Sans teeth, sans eyes, sans taste, sans everything except the remorseless application of scientific gerontology. One sometimes forgets that while there is death there is hope.'

Left alone, I glanced round the hall. At this meal it seemed the guests were expected to fish for themselves. The only one of our hosts in evidence was Arnold Lempriere, and I took this to indicate that he was a bachelor and lived in college. Even so, and particularly since he was so senior a fellow, he must have owned abundant facilities for breakfasting in private. I concluded that, alone among his resident colleagues, he regarded turning up in hall as a proper civility. He wasn't, indeed, going at all out of his way to make conversation: a spare remark, offered now on his one hand and now on the other, appeared to be what he regarded as the requisite thing. He was untidily dressed in ancient tweeds which might with advantage have gone to the cleaner's. I had a sense that this was less a matter of standards slipping in senescence than a deliberately contrived manner of setting an accent on something he would have retained if dressed in sackcloth or cap and bells. I wondered whether Plot would have credited him with belonging to the old gentry. He certainly didn't suggest any sort of gentry recently unpacked from the straw. He was indicating this now (much as if I had invented him in a light comedy of Edwardian flavour) by the nonchalant employment of a toothpick.

It was over this implement that Lempriere presently glanced at me across the hall. His eyebrows, which were grey like the rest of him, immediately elevated themselves; he might have been registering an injurious astonishment, if not before my actual existence (which would have been unreasonable), then at the fact of my having been detected as still hanging around the place. But this vertical movement was immediately succeeded by a horizontal one, the eyebrow switching across Lempriere's otherwise immobile features rapidly from left to right. The main door of hall lay that way. I realized that I had received, with an extreme economy, instructions to join Lempriere there at the conclusion of our meal.

Following him out a few minutes later, I noticed that his clothes were not only old, but baggy as well. I was reminded of Cyril Bedworth in his tails the night before. But if Lempriere's garments were too big for him it wasn't as a consequence of ill-considered purchase off the peg; it was because they had been tailored when he was a bulkier man than now. My first impression of a stout figure, gained in the dark, had been an error similarly induced. Physically, Lempriere was of much the same type as old Mr Mumford. It occurred to me that these two must be close contemporaries.

'We'll do a Long Field,' Lempriere said. He spoke as peremptorily as if I had been a pupil he judged badly in need of exercising.

'I'll be delighted to.' This seemed to me a suitable reply, although it wasn't exactly an invitation that I had received. 'It's very much a morning for it.'

Lempriere gave a sombre grunt. I clearly hadn't done too well in introducing climatic considerations after this fashion. There were those who 'did' a Long Field at some period of the day, wet or shine, throughout the year, and Lempriere was probably one of them. Perhaps I was fortunate in not being required to do the mile-and-a-bit involved at the double. It wasn't only athletically inclined undergraduates who kept in form that way. Elderly men did it—often modestly after dusk. And possibly some old members did it too, as part of the general nostalgic exercise upon which they were engaged.

'At least you're not going to be a tutor,' Lempriere said as we set out. He advanced this surprising remark in what he seemed to design as a comforting tone. 'Unless, I suppose, you positively ask for it.'

'I'm not positively asking for anything.' I made this reply with a slight asperity, having grown tired of these odd obliquities. 'And I have nothing but hints and nudges to tell me what you're talking about.'

'But hasn't Talbert put it to you?'

'Talbert hasn't put anything to me. I'm going to tea with the Talberts this afternoon.'

'Then he's deferred it till then. Or perhaps it has just gone out of his head. For years he has put on a turn as the absent-minded scholar, and now the real thing is catching up on the old chap. It's a professional risk with *poseurs*, I know.'

'I suppose he must be getting on.' The 'old chap' couldn't, I thought, be as old as Lempriere himself. 'After all, he was my tutor ages ago.'

'Of course he was. That's why he was the appropriate man to broach the thing. He was absolutely instructed to do that.'

'But I think the Provost has the job in hand at lunch-time.'

'No doubt. But you were to be softened up first.' Lempriere chuckled softly. (I have always regarded this verb as one to be avoided as a tired word for a not particularly pleasing activity. But Lempriere certainly chuckled: it was the faintest of noises in his throat, and I rather liked it.)

'You think I'd be no good as a tutorial fellow?' I asked.

'You'd be the wrong age, Pattullo. You'd be the wrong age even to hold down the job, let alone start in on it. It's a young man's job—as it was until the university turned silly in the middle of the nineteenth century. Of course an old man can do it, after a fashion. I can do it myself, although I no longer know anything about my subject worth speaking of. On the whole, the young men don't care for father-figures. They make what that college doctor of ours calls a negative transference, as often as not. But they'll accept a grandfather-figure. In addition to which, as one turns senile, one comes very much to like the young. And they like being liked—much more than they like being understood. Any intelligent middle-aged man can understand them like mad. But they find that unnerving. They much prefer mute communion and a decent glass of madeira.'

'I'm not sure that you aren't busying around proposing to understand me.'

'Understanding people is one of the minor satisfactions of life.' Lempriere chuckled again over this indirect reply. 'But it's best to go about it without letting on. And I don't expect other than a negative transference from you. What do your intimates call you?'

'Duncan. Or Dunkie.'

'So you can go away if you want to, Duncan.' Lempriere's choice between the alternatives offered him seemed to indicate his estimate of the degree of intimacy proper at the moment. It was surprising in itself, and I dimly felt there must be some reason for it. 'You and I, come to think of it, are at that disabling father-and-son remove.'

'I'm having a very enjoyable walk, thank you. And similarly, coming to think of it, you might have been a grandfather-figure to me if you'd been around when I came up. And surely you ought to have been. Why weren't you?'

'You're muddled. You probably drank too much last night. I warn you that it's another professional risk. You're thinking of me as being then the amiable dotard I am now.'

'So I am. But you're not a dotard, and I still require evidence of your being amiable. But I repeat: why weren't you around?'

'Because they kept me on in Washington for three years after the war was over. I'd proved a superb liar in high places, and they had a conviction that more lies were essential if the Empire was to survive. They were quite right. So I went on telling lies for all I was worth. It turned me most damnably truthful for the rest of my days. That's my liability in this place now.'

I laughed at this, not very sure that it was a justifiable claim. I had meant what I said in asserting that I still required evidence of this formidable old gentleman's amiability. And he seemed to me not quite impartial as between one sort of truth and another. The impression I had gained at our midnight conference was of his liking the uncomfortable kind best, and I suspected that a proposition sometimes appealed to him less because he thought it valid and consistent with whatever were his genuine convictions than because he spotted it as a useful peg on which to hang a pungent rhetoric.

'Were you an ambassador?' I asked. 'They've been said to be honest men sent to lie abroad for the good of their country.'

'That was certainly the object of the exercise. But my position was a modest one among the indispensable obscure. It remains just that—barring the indispensability.'

Silence was the only civil response to this. I had never heard of Arnold Lempriere as a scholar—which didn't, of course, mean that he mightn't be a most distinguished one in a recondite way. I wondered about the effect of Hitler's war on dons of his generation. They had been young enough to fight, and many of them had fought. But many more had become back-room boys whose abilities had eventually brought them close to the great centres of power and responsibility. And this sounded like Lempriere's story. I was curious to know whether his ambitions had been touched by that vaster theatre, and whether he regretted his return to quiet academic courses.

'But apart from that break,' I said, 'you've been here all your days?' If a man asks what you are called by your intimates, you are presumably entitled to fire direct questions at him.

'Yes, indeed. Another of those early points of no return. The fatal day came when I failed to go out of residence.'

'You mean you accepted a fellowship?'

'My dear Duncan, it is customary to speak of gaining one. But the terminology is unimportant. That was it, and here I am. They haven't even made me a thingummy.'

'Can you tell me about being a thingummy?' I understood very well what I was being teased about.

'You want the mortifying truth of the matter? A reader is somebody who won't quite do as a professor—I imagine because he is too learned, and at the same time possessed of too little guile. Yes, that is it. Harmlessness has to be his hallmark.'

'I suppose he has definite duties?' The speech just offered me was quite inoffensive in its effect; its tenor was disobliging, but not its tone. 'The chap must do something for his pay. I suppose there *is* pay.'

'Readers are paid enormous sums, and in return they engage in advanced study and research. You will get a letter instructing you to do that, but permitting you to scratch your own head as to just how? Without particular effort, Lempriere contrived to make all this sound highly ridiculous. 'Come to think of it, you will also have to give a great many lectures. I believe it's thirty-six in a year. As you will deliver them triennially for the rest of your days, it's advisable to have them typed out on durable paper.'

'It sounds as if it might be formidable at first—preparing all that eloquence. May I come to you for hints about it?'

'My dear chap, I've never delivered a lecture in my life. Lectures have always appeared to me completely pointless exercises. If I had to choose between lectures and examinations, I believe it would be examinations I'd plump for.'

It was obvious that Lempriere wasn't idly prevaricating, and I concluded that his freedom from what he regarded as a pointless obligation must be a matter of his possessing adequate private means. Such freedoms commonly are. This meant that further inquiry might sound impertinent—nor, for that matter, was I as interested in the hierarchy of Oxford learning as, no doubt, I ought to have been. But having been made fun of over the readership, I decided to try a shaft of my own.

'Not having to lecture,' I said, 'must give you a lot of time for research and writing books.'

What this drew from Lempriere was a swift glance of appreciation or amusement. He put a hand lightly on my elbow, and I had a sudden odd knowledge that he seldom touched anybody. It had been to draw me to a halt.

'And here is the river,' he said.

Nothing stays put—not even the Isis. The iron railings over which we were peering, indeed, were no more rusty and untidy now than when I had first become acquainted with them. The river steamers moored near-by seemed to speak of aquatic pleasures of the most outmoded sort, but precisely so had they done long ago. Down stream, however, much was changed. The row of college barges along this bank had, with one or two exceptions, vanished, to be replaced in the middle distance by a huddle of boat-houses which doubtless gained for commodiousness what they lost for the picturesque. Along the tow-path opposite there stretched a long line of cabin-cruisers and motor-launches hired, it was to be supposed, by the week for the recreation of urban populations far away; women were hanging out nappies on them, and men were contentedly peeling potatoes into the sacred stream.

'It used to be the young barbarians all at play,' Lempriere murmured. 'But it's the middle-aged philistines now. Cam and Isis, ancient bays have withered round your brows.'

'Yes,' I said—not troubling to sort out this mix-up of the poets. 'But there are nine young barbarians coming upstream at this moment.'

'Our own boat,' Lempriere said at a glance, but without much appearance of interest. 'I believe they go to some regatta or other tomorrow.'

We walked on in silence, listening to the plash of the oars, and to the voice of the cox, obedient to a bellow from a coach on a bicycle, beginning to give his crew ten.

'Awful sport,' Lempriere said. 'I used to do it as a boy—a good way further down this river. It's like living. People don't consider it at all the thing to stop off when you want to.' There was another silence, in which I guessed he was thinking of Paul Lusby. 'You probably did it yourself,' he added presently, 'on the Water of Leith.'

'No, I didn't,' I said. 'I played rugger. But the same consideration applied.' It struck me as curious that Lempriere should have acquainted himself with my provenance to this extent. 'You were grabbed by the ankles and pitched violently into the mud. But you had to jump up and chase after the damned ball again. My brother liked it. I didn't.'

'Ninian?' Lempriere asked.

'Yes—Ninian.' This really did pull me up. Lempriere seemed to have been doing research on the Pattullos. And now he had produced his chuckle again. It was like no more than a faint clearing of the throat. I saw that he was nursing some joke.

'Sit down,' he said, on his peremptory note, and pointed to a long wooden seat of the kind provided in public parks. It faced the river and was firmly bedded in concrete—no doubt to prevent its being carried off to a bonfire on the last night of Eights. Cut into its back was an inscription: *Presented by the Oxford College Servants' Rowing Club to Commemorate the Coronation of Queen Elizabeth the Second.* 'Very nice,' Lempriere said, looking at this. It was almost his first remark uncoloured by some hovering irony. He sat down—rather carefully, so that one felt his joints to be no longer in the best working order. 'It's at least decently warm. Not that you'll think much of it after Ravello. I like that bit of coast—and it's only a short run to Paestum. I'll come and stay with you there one day.'

The college address list, I thought, would give him Ravello. But I was becoming restive. The joke appeared to be that my companion had up his sleeve something that would legitimate his employing my Christian name at a second meeting and announcing that he proposed to be my house-guest in Italy. But I wasn't going fishing. I'd leave him to play the thing out.

'Paestum is invaluable,' I said, taking my place beside him. 'Greece without the Colonels. One couldn't ask for more.' At that time the misdeeds of those persons weighed heavily on all liberal minds.

> 'The Niobe of nations! there she stands,
> Childless and crownless, in her voiceless woe.'

This came from Lempriere with an effect rather different, I thought, from Ranald McKechnie's 'nothing so ill-bred as audible laughter'. He paused on it darkly. 'Or was that Rome?' he asked. 'You read English Literature, and ought to know.'

'Rome, I think. The bits about Greece come earlier on. Not that it wouldn't fit.' I didn't feel I wanted to be shunted off to *Childe Harold's Pilgrimage.* 'I really ought to say I'd be in two minds about the thingummy proposal, even if anything comes of it. That it should even be thought of pleases me enormously, and I have spasms of feeling there's nothing I'd like more. But you know—seriously and apart from all that of fabricating lectures—it strikes me as a stiff assignment to come at one out of the blue. It's clearly not what can be called a visiting job.'

'You could make it the next thing to that, if you wanted to. Nobody would object to your treating the place like a hotel, and dropping in on us for a couple of nights a week. But you mightn't find that particularly satisfactory yourself. We do have a certain corporate life of an amoebic sort. You might be drawn to study it. You were studying it last night, weren't you, when we were discussing that luckless affair in the dark?' Lempriere paused. 'And very much in the dark. Grandfather-figures or not, we have to admit the young as turning more and more baffling on us.'

'I was interested,' I said. 'I wouldn't like to be thought to have been studying anything. I suppose it would be a matter of pulling my weight in a general way. I doubt whether I could turn to at any sort of administration.'

'You wouldn't be asked to do anything of the kind—although, of course, you'd be on the Governing Body of the college.'

'Good Lord! What's the Governing Body's line?'

'Governing, one supposes. I'd describe its meetings as festivals of pusillanimity relieved by sporadic dog-fights.'

'I'd be interested in that too.'

'It's most kind of you to say so.'

I was startled by the tone in which Lempriere had murmured these words. It was such as to make them almost as outrageous as old Mr Mumford's incredible remark on long hair and finger-nails. I was being rebuked, in fact, without ever—so far as I could see—having put a foot wrong. I hadn't been indignant with Tony's father, because I had been instantly aware of his being in some overwrought state. But I was thoroughly indignant with Arnold Lempriere. He had tipped over my head a sudden small bucket of ironic urbanity as unlicensed by anything I'd said as it was incompatible with the whole character of our talk hitherto.

I had indicated my feeling by taking the initiative in standing up before I recalled the abrupt acrimony with which this very senior man had more than once turned upon his colleagues during their nocturnal discussion. There had been differences of view, but at the same time a perfectly evident admission of common concern. And then Lempriere had suddenly flung out this or that. It had been something more, I now saw, than succumbing to the temptation of quick wit or a tart phrase. It was rather that—in some obscure way—he wanted the college to himself. He had an impulse to savage not only anybody who infringed his monopoly of criticizing it but also (by way of a kind of warning off) anybody who might do so in the future. In fact there was a respectable passion for the place at the root of his bad behaviour—when he did sporadically behave badly. It was something his colleagues were certainly intelligent enough to understand. There was a high probability that most of them were fond of him.

This was a lot of considering to give to a tiny thing, and within moments we were continuing our walk as amicably as before. My sense of this was strong enough to prompt my next remark.

'You lose no time,' I said, 'in putting the new boys through their notions.'

'That's Winchester.' Lempriere now spoke humorously—but I thought he had to conceal a sense that mixing up one school's slang with another's was a serious matter. And I felt I knew something more about him. He was one of those men—and long ago I had discovered them to be quite thick on the ground—in whom the schoolboy is irruptive still. Tony, I remembered, had been aware of them too. They kept caps and colours and house photographs, he used to say, like french letters under their clean shirts and handkerchiefs, and sometimes they tumbled embarrassingly out of the drawer. The more weighted with tradition the school, the higher was the incidence of such retarded characters turned out. And Lempriere's role as champion of the Lusbys over against the Mumfords was a topsyturvy, and perhaps unstable, reflex from this. Believing there was only one real school (as he most certainly believed there was only one real college), he took a poor view (when this perhaps provincial view of things was bobbing up in him) of public schools at large as constituting any sort of club.

'Would you have been the same year as young Mumford?' Lempriere asked. 'Calls himself Marshmallow, or some such.'

'Marchpayne. Yes, Tony Mumford and I came up together.'

'Ah! That's why he wasn't a pupil of mine. But his father was.'

'Cedric Mumford?' For a moment this entirely astonished me. I had been reflecting, the day before, that Albert Talbert might now be teaching some old pupil's son. If Lempriere was not talking nonsense he was claiming to be at least in a position to teach an old pupil's grandson. But this, in fact, was perfectly possible. It merely meant that I had got the relative ages of these two old gentlemen slightly wrong. In an Oxford college an undergraduate of twenty may find himself with a tutor only two or three years older than himself. 'I think of him as old Mr Mumford,' I said with a shade of malice. 'What sort of a pupil was he?'

'Cedric Mumford? You know him?'

'We've met.' I said this before realizing that it blankly contradicted the assertion I'd made to Killiecrankie. It was inconceivable that the discrepant statements could become of the slightest importance, but I detected myself wondering whether Lempriere's native or acquired skill in telling lies made him a hypersensitive detector of lying in others. I even wondered whether, had he been at my own school long ago, he would have joined McKechnie in holding out against the romancing of the Secret Service Boy. 'I believe Cedric isn't very pleased'—I added with incredible rashness—'with the way the college is threatening to treat his grandson Ivo.'

'He wouldn't be. I've never had a pupil who gave himself such airs as Cedric Mumford. Positively intimated that he intended to put you at your ease.' Lempriere's chuckle followed upon this. 'And then, when you told him his essay was bloody pitiful, and that in fact you'd heard it from one of his chums the week before, he'd pretty well turn and snarl at you.'

'Yes—Cedric still snarls.'

'And who are they, in God's name, those Mumfords? Catholics, of course—but not old Catholics.'

'I suppose there's a big difference—but as a Scottish presbyterian, I just wouldn't know.' I managed a little irony of my own this time. The distinction propounded again pleasingly echoed Plot on gentry and old gentry—although, indeed, the *ambiance* wasn't the same. 'Tony Mumford'—I added this firmly, and by way of standing up to be counted—'was my closest college friend.'

'Was he, indeed? Well, friendliness seems much his thing. He was scattering it all over the place last night.'

'I suppose he was.' I felt it would be disingenuous to deny this charge. Tony had a little overdone kissing the babies. In some minds, at least, he had as a consequence created the impression against which the sagacious Mogridge had warned him. 'But Tony's a politician,' I went on, 'and seemingly becoming a distinguished one. A slightly too lavish agreeableness has to be excused as part of the tool-kit.'

'Humph!' (Lempriere really produced this noise—one more frequently printed than articulated.) 'Public means that public manners breed—eh? He needn't bring them into private places.'

'You evidently take a strong line on the Mumfords. Does it extend to Ivo in the present generation? And is Ivo your pupil now?'

'No, he's not. But he's a young man with a high nuisance-value. I'm aware of that.'

'Impertinently putting his elders at their ease?'

'That I don't know. Quite probably not.'

'I'm afraid you're going to hear a bit more about his nuisance-value.' There had been an instant fair-mindedness in Lempriere's last remark which encouraged me to take a chance in this way. 'It seems he was the man who made that wretched bet with Lusby.'

'Lusby! What the devil should young Mumford have to do with Lusby? They'd be poles apart.'

'Well, yes—I'm afraid that that's the rub. You'd expect it to be an intimate'—I thought it quite cunningly that I brought in this term of Lempriere's—'who'd make an idiotic wager like that with a man. Ivo must have gone out of his way to it, and I suspect that some of your colleagues may spy a certain malice in it as a result.' I rather held my breath as I thus, mere outsider that I was, ventured on this criticism of fellows of the college.

'Absolute rubbish!' It was to my great relief that Lempriere snapped this out. 'Mere callow thoughtlessness in the brat Ivo. Nothing more.'

'That's what I'd rather suppose myself.' I felt things were now going well. 'And, of course, the boy's in trouble already. Something about some examination or other. And that's why Tony was busying round a bit too much last night—making friends and influencing people. He's very concerned.'

'And why in heaven's name shouldn't he be?' Lempriere looked at me sternly, much as if I were setting up as *advocatus diaboli* in this affair. 'He is the lad's father, isn't he?'

'It's certainly very understandable,' I said. Lempriere—as I rather suspected was his vulnerability—had jumped at an attitude, and I calculated it would be useful to leave him in it. All this was happening, so far as my own feeling went, against the background of the wretched events at Otby a couple of nights before. Ivo Mumford might be an undesirable youth. But on the small academic front I wanted Lempriere on his side. If I'd managed this it would be a contribution of sorts (staircase-wise, it might sentimentally be said) to the much more sensational turn being mounted by Mogridge.

We were now back within the bounds of the college. Lempriere, a good deal to my relief at this ticklish juncture, had halted and was proposing to take his leave of me. But he had something more to say.

'Do you see much nowadays,' he asked with a fine casualness, 'of those folk at Corry?'

This stroke had all the effect at which it rather childishly aimed. I stared at Lempriere for a full second before managing a reply.

'No,' I said, 'I don't.'

'A pity. A man should keep up with his family connections. I do, and tuck away scraps of information that come to me as a result—for ages and ages, it sometimes is.' Lempriere's chuckle was even fainter and more internal this time. 'Ninian's licking, for example,' he said.

'How on earth——'

'You don't even register—or, at least, remember—the names of your kinsfolk. Too busy inventing Lovelesses and Backbites and Wishforts for all those stage puppets, I take it. Your Uncle Rory's wife—whom I hope you have the decency to think of as your aunt—was a Lempriere.' This revelation, by which it was evidently intended that I should be a good deal struck, put Lempriere in excellent humour. 'Nice day,' he said, looking up approvingly at the sky. 'Ever swim at Parson's Pleasure? If so, come and renew your acquaintance with it this afternoon.'

'I'm afraid I can't.' Lempriere, I supposed, was just the sort of old gentleman who nostalgically frequented that bathing-place of the young—the male young. 'I have to go to tea with the Talberts, and that won't be long after I get away from the Lodging.'

'Ah, yes—another time.' Lempriere spoke vaguely, as if already forgetting what he had proposed. 'Good day to you, Dunkie.' Once more he touched me on the elbow, and then he turned and walked away.

XII

Nɪɴᴇ ᴏʀ ᴛᴇɴ hours had now elapsed since the departure of Mogridge in quest of the lurking Ivo. I had said I should remain in Oxford until the evening, but I was already beginning to wonder when and how a message would come through to me. It was impossible to form any notion of what to expect, since we had been left—both Tony and myself—with only the vaguest intimation of what would be going on. I pictured Mogridge arriving at that gardener's cottage in some high-powered but unobtrusive car—one equipped, no doubt, with telephonic devices enabling him to hold scrambled conversations with various quarters of the globe as he went along. Ivo would then be extricated from what must be his nerve-racking seclusion, rapidly disguised as an exiled Tashi lama (or perhaps as a giant panda, comfortably accommodated in an air-conditioned crate), and thus despatched across the Atlantic to the care of persons alerted to receive him and expeditiously retransmogrify him into Lord Marchpayne's son, who had been moving—certifiably at need—in impeccably respectable New York society during at least the past forty-eight hours.

This might not be accurate in detail, but it scarcely managed to fantasticate what in essence was happening. I wondered whether the crazy plan—supposing it to succeed—would exert an elevating influence on Ivo's future character and conduct. It seemed improbable. But then nothing of the sort was the object of the exercise. If matters were now going badly at Otby (only I had a dim faith that they were not) it was pretty well the unfortunate youth's bare survival that was in question.

The weight of this last, and quite realistic, thought gave me a restless half-hour in Junkin's room and even in the inferior loo, and at the end of it I made my way back to the Great

Quadrangle. The vast enclosure, bleak in the staring sun-shine, was alive with tourists. Here Jamshyd—meaning the old members in their tails and gongs and gowns—had lately gloried and drunk deep; now the Lion and the Lizard—represented by the rest of the world and its cine-cameras—were on the prowl. They poured in in clots and clumps, each with its voluble and gesticulating cicerone, from long lines of motor-coaches parked outside. Here and there were small superior groups who had arrived in hired Daimlers or in private Cadillacs brought across the Atlantic with the baggage. Within a couple of hours they would be in Stratford-upon-Avon. But they were doing Oxford at the moment.

There is nothing offensive to academic piety in these invasions, which testify to the haunting American suspicion that somewhere or other there has been a past. But it was evident that a certain physical inconvenience resulted from them. Oxford colleges are full of bottle-necks: one spacious quad may be connected with another only by a tunnel of such modest dimensions that it is hard to spot. The builders appear to have lacked the conception even of persons walking conversably two abreast. When thronged with compacted gapers these incapacious channels almost cease to be negotiable.

I thrust my way through the scrum, and in the lodge passed the time of day with a porter. College porters, and not aged dons reminiscing over their wine, are the men with the best memories in Oxford, and this one greeted me by name as casually as Mogridge had done the day before. Properly gratified, I went out into the street. It was as crowded as the Great Quad, yet as little frequented, so far as I could see or hear, by the indigenous inhabitants of the city. In addition to more Americans, black and brown and yellow people thronged St Aldates, Carfax, the Cornmarket, their close juxtaposition reminding me of an improving if implausible picture in a devotional work given to me in childhood: it had represented nicely dressed and well-nourished children of every clime congregated smilingly round the Good Shepherd. And the clothing of these tourists, wanderers, or pilgrims was not so westernized as to preclude here and there a jostling of brilliant colours tumbling on one another as closely as pigments on my father's palette at the end of a long day's painting. There were people who appeared to have come straight from the desert, or the arctic circle, or improbable tropical isles. There were even (as in Wordsworth's London) Negro ladies in white muslin gowns. I remembered spending a fortnight of my first long vacation in Oxford, when there had certainly been no such kaleidoscopic cosmopolitanism as this in evidence. But at that time the nations were still largely immobilized within their own territories, having been ravaged or exhausted by war.

Even in the mid-nineteenth century topographical painters and engravers could confidently represent the main thorough-fares of Oxford as almost free of wheeled vehicles: dons and undergraduates, alike voluminously gowned, stroll in a medita-tive calm those cobbled streets, impeded by nothing more formidable than an occasional flock of sheep. The city had become what was thought of as horribly noisy in my time; now it could be described journalistically as submerged beneath the roar of traffic. It is an inaccurate phrase. If some distance off, even heavy traffic mutters; near at hand, its chief char-acteristic is a restless miscellaneousness not easy to repel from one's attention. I had enough on my mind, however, to induce a state of the most old-fashioned abstraction, and if I was presently hearing anything as I walked it was the Corry burn.

This came to me by way of my recalling my Aunt Charlotte, and that in turn from remembering my first glimpse of Arnold Lempriere the night before. What had struck me then—I realized it now—had been the obscure sense of some family likeness as revealed to me. Yet his connection with my aunt could scarcely be closer than a cousinship. Had I ever known that her maiden name was Lempriere? There was a good reason for believing I had not. It is a name with an odd celebrity in English literary history. No inquiring boy who loves Keats remains ignorant of the existence of Lempriere's classical dictionary, and the information sticks, since there is a curious fascination in the idea of somebody almost as young and ignorant as oneself quarrying a whole imaginative region out of such a book. So had I ever heard the name of Uncle Rory's wife I should have made this association in due course and the recollection would have remained with me.

What I happened to remember of Aunt Charlotte at the moment was her interest in careers for Ninian and myself. When I went fishing—an unproductive sport—she would sometimes appear carrying a camp-stool or a shooting-stick and settle down to a discussion of this topic. The burn babbled and brawled; in its glinting waters there rarely flashed and vanished minute presences which I believed to be trout; my aunt spoke to me seriously about what she called 'adopting a profession'. She can scarcely have believed that Ninian and I could ever become a charge upon the Glencorrys, so her insistence must have been disinterested or—more precisely—animated by the persuasion that she had one of God's ordinances to propound. Boys who won't inherit acres must adopt some honest means to a livelihood. It was a perfectly sensible view. Offered to me in Edinburgh, and among companions nearly all of whose fathers were professional men, I would have accepted it at once. But with the heather round me, the burn murmuring messages I just couldn't catch, the peewits crying, and above me a pale blue sky as unflawed as a dunnock's egg: amid these presences I judged my aunt's conversation inept and boring. Whether I showed this I don't know, since I have little memory of the stages by which I became a tolerably polite and civilized boy. If I resented these exhortations, it was principally because of what they were saying, by implication, about my father. Aunt Charlotte, who so plainly came of barbarians, contrived, far more than her husband, to be a philistine as well. Uncle Rory, although he seldom thought a thought or opened a book, had something in his blood which admitted the place of a certain strangeness in the world; to him my father was a crofter's son who had gone a little dotty but who, like other naturals, conceivably had a glimpse of something. A generation on, he would have muttered that the fellow was entitled to do his thing. To Aunt Charlotte my father had simply come from nowhere and *was* nowhere; if by marriage he had acquired sons who had some title to be regarded as gentlemen, then it was essential that these sons should find an ordered place in society. As it was improbable that either of our parents were giving thought to the matter (and in this Aunt Charlotte was perfectly right) then it was incumbent upon their kinsfolk to direct Ninian and myself in the way we should go.

Aunt Charlotte possessed, although not as strongly as Uncle Rory, a sense of the duties of kinship; had this not been so, my brother and I would never have been received at Corry Hall. My mother, too, had this feeling—intermittently, because most things were intermittent with her. My father had it not at all. His affections and interest (the latter, again, intermittent in its character) lay entirely within the nuclear family which his own household constituted, and about nearly all blood-relationships beyond it he was entirely regardless and vague. Something of this attitude both Ninian and I picked up—which is why it would never have occurred to either of us to be curious about Aunt Charlotte's origins. I had been obliged to learn about them from Arnold Lempriere, and had so learnt because Lempriere himself took a significance in such ties for granted. Remote as our connection was, he thought of me as a kinsman, so that his relationship with me at once acquired a character distinguishable from that which he enjoyed even with colleagues of long standing. At present, at least, I could find nothing in myself that responded to this idea.

I certainly hadn't responded to Aunt Charlotte's ideas. For one thing, she was an astonishingly ignorant woman—a fact which my own ignorance somehow didn't obscure for a moment. She was interested in lawn tennis, a game at which she had herself excelled in youth—which must have been at about the time, I had imagined, when women were first allowed to hit out hard at the ball. The absence of first-class tennis in Scotland was a vexation to her (like the absence of first-class cricket to my schoolmasters), so that she sometimes went to stay with relations in Kent in order to enjoy the satisfaction of watching it. But on the whole she disliked travel, and never left Corry except for this occasional purpose. Correspondingly, and apart from a few friends of her own sort, she didn't much care for any traffic in the other direction either. In particular she distrusted the importation of periodicals or books, as well as the invention of wireless, all of which she saw as likely channels of what she still called Bolshevism. She also disliked Americans, whom she regarded as pervasively ill-bred, boastful, and given to chewing tobacco and in consequence to the use of spittoons.

Confined within this universe of speculation and discourse, my aunt had, not unnaturally, little to say of relevance to the prospects and problems of penniless boys (as we should be) like Ninian and myself. It was her opinion that if I took Orders something might be done for me, and that Ninian was clever enough to become a barrister. In Scotland one doesn't take Orders but enters the Ministry, and barristers—for sufficient historical reasons—are called not barristers but advocates. But the only Scots words Aunt Charlotte ever employed were those applicable to various grades of menials—notably grieve, gillie, and caddie. (A caddie is a cadet, and the term is thus one of the traces of French civilization and influence which so oddly linger in North Britain. And this one has come down in the world. My aunt used it only when—no decent tennis being available—she ventured as far as the nearest horrible holiday resort for the purpose of playing a round of golf.)

I myself wrote off Aunt Charlotte as a Careers Mistress at once. Ninian, being harder-headed, checked up on her, and was told by our headmaster that the Scottish bar was best left to those who had uncles on the bench. I imagine no particular imputation of nepotism was designed to be carried by this; our headmaster must simply have had plenty of opportunity to remark a certain closed quality about the society into which he had come. Ninian, he said, would do better to aim at chartered accountancy. A little later he was to tell me, with a good deal of gravity, that boys who couldn't make up their minds what to do commonly ended up as chartered accountants. These two speeches, when collated, implied a comparative judgement on Ninian's abilities and my own which was the more injurious to my brother for being based not at all on our school records. It was an intuitive judgement. Like many such, it was to prove entirely wrong. Ninian was to become an advocate, and his career was meteoric.

Walking down Oxford's Cornmarket, and preparing to turn into Broad Street with some thought of visiting Blackwell's, I had thus in fact transferred myself to Corry Hall and then to Edinburgh. But I preserved at least half an eye for my actual surroundings, and into that half eye my native city now less insubstantially swam in the person of McKechnie. Carrying a shopping-basket, he was coming towards me on a pavement a little less crowded than I had been traversing hitherto. Unlike Lempriere's, his attire wasn't shabby, baggy, or in need of a vigorous brush-up. It was, however, notably drab, as if he felt most at ease moving permanently beneath a protective carapace of what the universities call subfusc. This clerkly habit was emphasized by a little row of pens and pencils clipped into his breast-pocket.

I ought to have been reflecting, during those moments in which we bore down on one another, that on the previous evening we hadn't done too badly—even to the extent of feeling a certain solidarity vis-à-vis the brick-faced men and contriving a modicum of properly reminiscent talk. And I ought further to have remembered that, having then taken one initiative in addressing my schoolfellow by his Christian name, it was incumbent upon me to take a further initiative now. But McKechnie, amazingly, had fixed his gaze upon the pavement. Equally amazingly—and much more to an effect of revelation—my own gaze had been attracted to the exceedingly unoriginal exhibits in the window of a chemist's shop. Within a second we had passed one another by.

What was sobering about this weird re-enactment (apart from the acute embarrassment it was going to occasion in both McKechnie and myself when we did next inescapably meet) was the extent to which I had been falsifying the original occasion or occasions. My memory put it, so to speak, all on McKechnie: I was the normally extravert and sociable boy, taking the establishment at least of some sort of friendly relationship for granted, and it was McKechnie alone who did the scurrying past with a gaze in the gutter. I now knew, as certainly as if some miraculous hand had veritably rolled back the years, that our juvenile fiasco had been a totally mutual affair. And if it hadn't had roots rather deep in our temperaments it wouldn't have produced this alarming and indecent late-flowering now.

I was so demoralized by what had just happened that I scarcely expected to reach the security of Sir Basil Blackwell's shop without some further grotesque disaster. Naturally nothing of the sort occurred. In the Balliol lodge two black men in commoner's gowns and white ties gossiped with two white men similarly attired; all four were relaxed and lounging, as if from the *viva voce* examination ahead of them they expected singularly little either way. An American gentleman was recording them—but whether by their leave or not wasn't clear—for exhibition to neighbours in Minneapolis or St Louis in the Fall; the industrious little whirr of his camera was for a moment the only sound in the Broad. Oxford, I thought, is an extravagantly easy place in which to pick up local colour.

Narrow is the entrance (appropriately, where such a temple of learning is in question) to Blackwell's shop; I jostled in it with a bearded sage who was emerging with every appearance of having bought a fishing-rod; he was a professor of the university, I supposed, pursuing divided interests in this transitional week between term and vacation. Inside, I found just room to edge comfortably around. There were people browsing from table to table or shelf to shelf; there were others who looked as if their nose had been buried in a single book since immediately after breakfast. (A reader can often get a book more quickly in Blackwell's than in the Bodleian

Library opposite.) If one wanted to buy a book there was a means of doing so, although it wasn't one much obtruded on the casual visitor. I could put in an agreeable hour in the place, after which I'd have to be preparing myself for the Provost's luncheon party. Not that I knew it was going to be exactly that. Possibly Mrs Pococke (of whom my memory was vivid) would be presiding over a board at which her husband and I confabulated tête-à-tête over the mysteries of readerships.

I had a look at a table stacked with new novels; they presented, somehow, a suggestion of being less morally insalubrious than those one reads reviews of in newspapers and journals. But this may have been illusory, and a consequence of the highly respectable company they enjoyed in this enormous repository of the Word. The shelves of modern drama rendered a similar effect—but then, again, they were being kept an eye on from the opposite wall by works with titles like *A Short View of the Immorality and Profaneness of the English Stage* and *Caterpillars of the Commonwealth* and *Playes Confuted in Fiue Actions*. Undeterred by these minatory presences, I turned over a number of plays—literally turned them over, since my interest was for the moment so idle that I looked chiefly at their back covers. John Arden (Junkin's favourite) was a decidedly photogenic young man, and Harold Pinter was a very serious-looking young man. But if both these *were* young men then I was myself not more than a couple of years past being quite a young man too. Heartened by this delusive discovery, I glanced up and saw that standing beside me was a lady more responsibly involved with the drama. She was my new acquaintance—and the only female (not counting Tin Pin) with whom I had as yet exchanged a word during this Oxford episode—Cyril Bedworth's wife.

'Good morning,' I said. 'I hope you had a pleasant dinner-party? The Gaudy was everything I expected. It was even a little more.'

Mabel Bedworth's gaze went from her book to my shoes—which fortunately had been handsomely polished by Plot.

'Oh, good morning!' Mrs Bedworth uttered this response

226

as a nervous exclamation and in a very low voice; it was the identical voice, nevertheless, that had a little shaken me the evening before. She still didn't raise her eyes. She might have been said, I thought, to be doing a McKechnie on me. Two such evasive performances within fifteen minutes seemed a bit much. I had to conclude Mrs Bedworth to be feeling that, given the slightest opportunity, I would insult her with a lascivious leer. (Neither McKechnie nor I, in our disgraceful joint behaviour, could quite have feared that.)

'Do you go much to the theatre?' I asked. We had begun— or at least I had—a conversation rather than merely exchanged a greeting, and somehow or other it had to be carried on.

'Cyril and I really did see *The Accomplices*.' As she thus named my own current play, Mrs Bedworth at last swiftly glanced at me. The effect was to lend to her features as a whole that appearance of floating behind a curtain of gossamer which might have returned to me in my dreams of the previous night had not coarser intervening experiences got in the way. My head swims comparatively seldom in the presence of women, but it did a little swim now. One had to admit that Mabel Bedworth, as the chaste wife (as she certainly was) of a dim scholar, had a good deal to contend with.

But I wasn't sure that she coped with her liability by simply shunning the duel of sex. She had just packed a good deal of mischief into three words. The assurance in 'really did see' carried all the mockery of authorial vanity that might have been achieved by a Meredithian heroine. Having planted her shaft, moreover, she now turned aside gracefully enough.

'But Cyril and I,' she said, 'don't very often get to town together. It means baby-sitting for too long. So we miss things we'd like to see. That's why I'm in Blackwell's. I haven't seen *Hartley's House,* and I want to read it. But it doesn't seem to be here. What did you think, Mr Pattullo, of *Hartley's House*?'

'It probably isn't published yet—but, of course, you could have them order it for you.' I made this point first because I hadn't myself seen *Hartley's House*, and for the moment could remember nothing about it. In the theatres of London a great many plays come and go. 'I haven't seen it either,' I then said briefly. Mrs Bedworth didn't pursue the topic. It was almost as if she felt it to have been rashly embarked on, and I had to think of something else. 'Does the vacation,' I asked, 'make a great difference to you when it comes along?'

'Oh, yes—a lot!' Mrs Bedworth paused on this, and then added swiftly, 'For Cyril, I mean. He can get on with his own work. Term is terribly heavy, particularly since he has had to be Acting Senior Tutor. And I'm afraid they'll make him Senior Tutor permanently next year.'

'But you mustn't be afraid of it, Mrs Bedworth. Cyril will be a very good Senior Tutor indeed.' I said this with conviction, feeling it pleasant to return to Bedworth, as it were, a little of the admiration he had once so mistakenly harboured for Tony Mumford and myself. And my words certainly gave pleasure, since Mrs Bedworth had faintly flushed. She was unmistakably a devoted wife.

'I must go upstairs,' she said suddenly. 'To the Spanish. We're trying to pick up some Spanish before going to Spain.' And she hurried away.

I had crossed Broad Street and was walking down the Turl before I remembered what I had read about *Hartley's House*. It sounded not a particularly distinguished play. The setting was a public school, and Hartley was a house-master. Several of the senior boys—eighteen-year-olds—believed themselves to be in love with his wife. One of them, the house-captain, really was. I could imagine this play, with its big scene dangling like a carrot before the playwright from a long way back. It wasn't hard to see why Mabel Bedworth, surrounded as she must at least intermittently be by her husband's pupils, should take an interest in its theme.

XIII

THE PROVOST'S LODGING, like the Provost's occupation, was quasi-ecclesiastical in character. What one first became aware of was the pictures—this not because they were outstandingly good or oppressively numerous, but simply because of the uniform nature of the exhibition. With very few exceptions that I was ever able to discern, they were life-size portraits of bishops: bearded, for the most part, in the nineteenth century; clean-shaven and bewigged before it; clean-shaven and sleek-haired thereafter. The parade had nothing to do with any dream of episcopal preferment indulged in by the Provost. Everybody recognized that Edward Pococke was modestly content with being widely acknowledged as an eminent theologian.

Had he been an agricultural labourer, his dwelling would have been described as a tied cottage. It went with the job—and so, in his case, did almost everything it contained, the pictures included. Provosts came and Provosts went—moving in or out (as Arnold Lempriere was once to say to me) little more than a tooth-brush and a tobacco-jar. This probably bore less hard on the Provosts than on their ladies. Frieda Lawrence, wandering from one impermanent perch to another in the wake of genius, would unpack an Indian shawl and throw it over a sofa. It was not apparent that, over a quarter of a century, Mrs Pococke had done so much. But the reason didn't lie in any weakness of character or infirmity of purpose. She simply owned a strong historical sense. The Lodging was full of stuff that had silted up in it for centuries, but the process of slow accretion appeared to have ground to a halt something under a hundred years ago, presumably when nothing more could comfortably be got into the building. As the only taste reflected, period by period, was that of one or another committee of academic persons instructed by their colleagues to provide the reigning Provost with miscellaneous chattels expensive enough to reflect the consequence of the college, the general effect, if not gaudy, was rich in rather a heavy way. The only exception to this undistinguished solidity was an enormous chamber known for some reason as the Provost's Day-room. Upon this principal apartment—and presumably in the later 1860's—Messrs Morris, Marshall, Faulkner & Co. had operated with all the terrifying energy commanded by the founder of that firm. Wallpapers and hangings, carpets, chintzes, carvings, stained glass, tapestries, tiles, metal-work, settles and similar uncomfortable accommodations believed to be in a mediaeval taste: all were poured profusely in—and the result, perhaps surprisingly, turned out to be extremely harmonious. It was certainly approved by the professional artists of the company, since Rossetti, Burne Jones and Madox Brown crowned the venture by all contributing pictures. The money came from a Provost's wife whose father had made a fortune in sugar—but the *ensemble* became college property, all the same. What distinguished Mrs Pococke was her being no more proud of this celebrated museum piece than of the general curiosity of the Lodging as a whole. She had a curator's mind, and had in fact been professionally just that. The young Edward Pococke was averred to have picked her up not in the National Gallery (a notorious locale for low assignations at that remote time) but in the more austere setting of the Victoria and Albert Museum, where she had been in charge of a notable collection of pastoral staves. (There was a copy of her monograph on these in the college library.) At constrained tea-parties, and when the Pocockes were new to the Lodging their entertainments commonly bore that character, it was helpful to remark to Mrs Pococke that one understood her also to have developed a substantial subsidiary interest in flat ornament. None of us had much idea what flat ornament was (no monograph appeared to have been devoted to it), but this bare remark was always well received.

A visit to the Pocockes in the Lodging—I recalled as I rang

the bell at one o'clock—had been even less conducive to relaxed entertainment than had a visit to the Talberts in Old Road. I used quite to yearn for the excitements of Scrabble as, agonisingly balancing a tomato sandwich on the rim of a small saucer, I tried to think of something to say to the Provost's wife. She was by no means unqualified to lead a conversation, but believed that the proper way to 'bring forward' the undergraduates (a phrase she was alleged incautiously to have used on some public occasion) was to require of them a strictly equal exchange in matters of this sort. Tony Mumford, if among the invited, was a stay—positively a stave, indeed —at these tea-parties in the Lodging. He owned considerable resource in being frivolous without being indictably impudent. I suspected Mrs Pococke of having a weakness for Tony, and used to build this up with much scandalous invention in the course of our post-mortems on these social encounters.

I hadn't quite lost myself in such reminiscences when the door was opened, just as it had been long ago, by the Provost's butler. Now, as then, he was a man instantly revealing himself as of depressive temperament, so that at the sight of him my heart sank with a comical familiarity. I murmured Mrs Pococke's name on a muted interrogative note. It was received with an affirmative inclination of the head; I was conducted into the interior of the Lodging; at the threshold of the Day-room there was a pause while my own name was communicated; and then I advanced upon the company.

For there was a company, although not a large one, and I found myself relieved that the luncheon wasn't going to be of a sheerly working sort. Becoming a Reader in Modern European Drama was something on which I was developing second thoughts. I was half-way through one career, and I couldn't see the appointment as not involving pretty well a complete switch to another. And I might well make a muck of the new one. Suppose, for example, that a second Paul Lusby somehow came my way. I might make a muck of him. And that, obviously, I wouldn't like in the least.

Lusby's tutor, James Gender, was one of my fellow-guests. He had put on a black tie. His wife was with him; she had the crisp address and rapidly moving eye often to be remarked in those who frequent the society of horses and dogs. There was also an unaccompanied woman, plainly academic in her own right, whom I supposed to have been brought along to balance up with myself. The Provost came forward and performed introductions with a courtliness a little in excess of the needs of the occasion. The effect was dampening. We stood in a constrained circle and sipped sherry. Mrs Gender alone adopted a different stance.

'I always enjoy your plays,' she said to me decisively. 'But you oughtn't to bring a man on the stage brandishing a brace of pheasants in the middle of June.'

'Have I really done that? Perhaps he was a poacher.'

'Poachers don't brandish pheasants in the libraries of country houses.'

'I suppose not.' Mrs Gender's comprehensive statement was incontrovertible. 'But how do you know it was in the middle of June, anyway?'

'The programme told us so. *A Warm Midsummer Day*. It said just that.'

'I'm afraid it sounds a fair cop. Please do tell me of any other similar solecisms. Dramatic critics don't know about such things. But it's nice not to offend the better informed.'

'Nothing but grouse round about Corry, I suppose.' Mrs Gender had answered my attempt at humour with an agreeable if mannish laugh. 'You wouldn't have fellows brandishing grouse before the twelfth of August, would you?'

'Probably not.' To have a not very important aspect of my past chucked at me twice within a morning was, I thought, excessive. 'Has Arnold Lempriere been putting you in the picture about me?'

'Not quite lately. When they began this talk about grabbing you we had a gossip. Arnold enjoys family gossip. He and I are related in some way.'

'I see.' I wondered whether this unknown woman was going

to claim that I too was thereby a kinsman of hers. 'But I don't see why they should want to grab me, as you call it. The thing's mysterious to me.'

'Wives are not expected to admit any knowledge of such matters. But, of course, it was dear old Albert Talbert who found the answer when the problem turned up. He told them at once it must be you.'

'Talbert! He doesn't know me from Adam for more than ten minutes at a time. There's no reason he should, since I've been so culpably truant from the place. His more settled opinion, as a matter of fact, is that I'm somebody called Dalrymple.'

'It's at least a Scottish name. Albert—or should one call him Geoffrey?—I never know—must have had the idea of you laid up in heaven. And he brought it down in a big way.' Mrs Gender seemed to me basically the sort of woman who might have banged a tennis-ball across a net at my Aunt Charlotte, but perhaps she was clever as well. 'And on the university side,' she went on, 'Miss Minton is most enthusiastic.'

'Who the dickens is Miss Minton?'

'My dear man, the Provost introduced you to her five minutes ago. Jimmy's stuck with her, over there by the window. Jimmy's always getting stuck with people.'

There was now another couple in the Day-room, and the company had a little opened up. James Gender was certainly in the situation his wife had described. A polite but not resourceful man, he stood silently beside the academic lady, his head inclined a little to the side, rather as if offering prolonged consideration to some matter of moment. Miss Minton—whether in embarrassment or not, it was impossible to say—was gazing into her glass.

'I seem to have heard of Miss Minton,' I said. 'But I didn't catch her name.'

'You were too busy, Mr Pattullo, being amused by the Provost's manner. Marking it down for future use, no doubt.'

'Writers really don't work that way.' I wasn't too pleased by Mrs Gender's rather routine pleasantry, and decided to try signing off banter. 'I'm very sorry,' I said, 'that your husband has had such sad news about a pupil. Did you know the boy?'

'Certainly I knew Paul Lusby.' Mrs Gender showed neither surprise nor displeasure at this abrupt change of key. 'I had my eye on him, but I wasn't quick enough. As for Jimmy, he finds it hard to forgive himself when he thinks he has let anybody down.' Mrs Gender gave this the timbre of a disparaging remark, so that I concluded her to be in fact another devoted wife. 'For God's sake grab the decanter,' she now said. 'That butler—he goes by the absurd name of Honey—is a perfect fool.'

I picked up the sherry obediently, although feeling, much as a nervous undergraduate might, that it was a most improper liberty to take. My discomfort was increased when I became aware of Mrs Pococke bearing down on me. She had the new arrivals with her. I recognized Charles Atlas, the young man whom I had fleetingly registered the night before as disapproving, if not of myself *in toto*, at least of my premature admission to a college confabulation. He was entirely civil during Mrs Pococke's introducing us anew. His wife, who was very pretty, was even younger than he was, and had not outgrown semi-acute terror on occasions like the present. I hoped I should be set down beside her at lunch. I'd prefer her, even, to the fascinatingly shamefast Mabel Bedworth. Like other ageing men, I supposed, I was coming to like my women younger and younger, and had no eye for anything else. I'd end up blamelessly offering sweets to little girls in public parks.

It is seldom prudent to muse upon oneself in this manner. The propensity is self-indulgent, and the spirit of comedy is always on the pounce. That spirit was going to achieve (to my interior sense) a staggering leap in something under the next half-hour.

Meanwhile, Mrs Pococke made the running—Mrs Gender having moved away on one of those unobtrusive sideways glides which party-going perfects. Mrs Pococke struck me as having changed more than her husband. Since she hadn't grown a beard she would have been, indeed, the more readily identifiable of the two. But she had aged more. One's first judgement on Edward Pococke, here and now, would be that he was an extraordinarily handsome man. One's first judgement on his wife would be that here, surely, had been an extraordinarily handsome woman. I found that I quite vividly remembered her as that. One would suppose it to be a dry stick who would curate staves in the V. & A. The young Mrs Pococke, on the contrary, had been on the opulent side. When her husband stripped her (I could recall Tony libidinously saying) what he had on his hands was a wench ready to step into one of the later Renoir's bath-tubs. Of course 'young' in relation to our first recollections of her meant something like 'in early middle age'. Not quite so old as her academically precocious husband, she must have taken over at the Lodging more or less in her middle thirties. I am certain that we never really thought of her as with decency beddable; that vision of pink and pearly flesh under the squeezed sponge had been strictly innocent and fanciful: amusing because so distanced by the Oxford *grande dame* in the making. 'You wouldn't call *her* a flat ornament,' Tony used to say. '*Les fesses et les tétons* are very much in order, if you ask me.' And he would wave a familiar salute to the ladies over his mantelpiece, presumably by way of asserting himself as an authority on this matter. It was at least true that we had been aware of Mrs Pococke as a sexual presence, and not merely as another of the odd and rather alarming tribe of Oxford's learned ladies. She was an old woman now, her ash-blonde hair a perruquier's blue and her skin beginning to be all well-tended pouches and wrinkles. I wondered whether (as with the ageing poet) her meditations were of time that had transfigured her. More probably she had a wholesome sense of herself as in vigorous middle life still.

'Mr Pattullo,' Mrs Pococke said to the Atlases indifferently, 'was among the most satisfactory men of his year. He came to tea if I invited him, and went away afterwards without having to be turned out of the house. As much couldn't be said of some more socially pretending youths.'

This speech surprised me. It is said that husbands and wives tend to become increasingly like one another with the years, and I have observed instances in which something of the kind appeared to be true. But in three sentences Mrs Pococke had made evident a contrary development. Formerly, her style had been very much her husband's; although much too young to be stately, stately she had resolutely been. She had totally lacked anything one could think of as spontaneity, since her comportment had been designed to project an artificial personality which she judged appropriate to her position. Now, she had become a perfectly direct woman. Perhaps, I conjectured, she had begun her married life by dutifully approximating herself to her husband's style, and been intelligent enough to realize that it wouldn't do; that a double dose of Edward from, as it were, either end of a dinner-table must conduce to covert levity rather than a becoming awe. What Edward's interest required was a counterpoise, a contrasting accent, operating at least within the sphere of his social relations. And just that she had set herself to create.

None of these thoughts would have been going through my head had there not plainly been some hitch about Mrs Pococke's luncheon party. We ought by now to have been at the board. Honey had disappeared, so that I wondered whether his melancholic disposition had finally overcome him, with the result that he was hanging on a pair of braces from a convenient hook in his pantry. More probably he was replenishing the sherry-decanter, upon which my unauthorized incursion had made a visible effect.

It looked as if there must be guests still to turn up. Meantime, I was protractedly talking with Mrs Pococke and the Atlases—although not awkwardly stuck with them as Gender still was with Miss Minton. That impasse was now so pronounced as to have become our hostess's urgent business. She failed, I noticed, in a telegraphic attempt to direct her husband

236

across the room to the relief of the dumbfounded pair. The Provost, unheeding, discoursed with some particularity to Mrs Gender on an architectural drawing, presumably of a proposed addition to the college, which he had spread out on a table before her, and over which his hands hovered in restrained and graceful gestures. His sense, I thought, of the minutiae of an actual social occasion didn't quite match his diffused vision of the Lodging as a scene of augustly polite intercourse.

Mrs Gender, however, was evidently habituated to handling such situations with untaxed ease, and this one she resolved by summoning Miss Minton and her husband across the room in a voice which would have been wholly adequate on a parade ground. Mrs Pococke was thus relieved of her anxiety, and her attention was restored to the Atlases and myself. I made a sudden resolution—and it showed what, in the midst of all this small talk, was most on my mind—to tackle her on the subject of the Mumfords: on Ivo Mumford really, but using his father as a lead-in. Mrs Pococke didn't run the college. But it was conceivable that Mrs Pococke —the new Mrs Pococke, as I thought of her—did run its Provost.

'Do you remember Tony Mumford at those tea-parties?' I asked. 'He was always rather amusing.'

'He was, indeed. Lord Marchpayne, as we have to call him now, was more amusing than you were, Mr Pattullo. Not that I didn't think of you as the nicer young man. That Scottish seriousness was most attractive.'

'Dull, but meaning only improvingly and well.'

'Nothing of the kind. You were much too clever, and much too well-informed a boy, to be in the least dull. Mr Mumford's particular charm lay in his disposition to be amused by *me*. I found it extremely wholesome.'

I saw Mrs Atlas blink, and then glance at her husband in alarm—much as if our hostess had suddenly revealed a vein of reprehensible eccentricity in thus condoning the impropriety of Lord Marchpayne's conduct in his nonage.

'Have you seen Tony this time?' I asked.

'No, I have not. I made an effort to catch him when Edward suddenly arranged this lunch. But it seems that, having honoured us, he has hurried away.'

'People in Tony's walk of life don't command their own time.' I advanced this proposition (which came to me from Plot) with confidence. 'He left me a note saying he had been called away a little sooner than he intended. Otherwise, he was going to have called on you, of course.' I celebrated these last two unblushing words by finishing my sherry.

'I don't recall his doing so on any previous occasion. But now he is worried about his son.'

This time, it was Atlas who reacted. I observed him to compress his lips. He was so much a purist about college affairs that he disapproved even of the Provost's wife taking passing cognizance of them.

'Yes,' I said. 'Ivo's having difficulty with his examinations troubles Tony a good deal. I think myself that he attaches an exaggerated importance to such things.'

'A college is something more than its examination results,' Atlas said abruptly, and rather like a man getting to his feet at a meeting. 'I'd never dispute that. And, of course, this particular college is in a strong position not to care a damn if it hasn't a mind to. Our men have pretty well been running the country since before Honour Schools and so forth were invented. And even nowadays, as Arnold Lempriere is so fond of telling us, it's clear that nobody cares twopence for such things as soon as you get high enough up. But Oxford isn't, and this place isn't, a glorified public school—building character, and codifying manners, and raising hymns of praise for the gifts of all-roundedness and leadership. It's one of England's two traditional major centres of education and research and learning. And you must have at least some sense of intellectual standards running right through such a concern, or it simply begins to lose coherence and identity. Heaven forbid that we should have unremitting egg-head endeavour all round. But a limit has to be set on sheer bloody-minded idleness.'

I had an impression that this speech (it couldn't be called an outburst, since Atlas had very adequately invested in codified manners himself) was one which Mrs Pococke had heard before. So, more certainly, had Atlas's wife, but this didn't prevent her from now gazing at her husband with a becoming admiration. I didn't myself find it uninteresting, chiefly because it had bobbed up in connection with Ivo Mumford's name. I had a suspicion that Ivo's academic insufficiencies were shaping up as a test case, so that if he escaped being put in gaol for a crime, his follies were still going to land him with plenty of trouble ahead. I saw no reason to suppose that I'd much care for him, but I was nevertheless continuing to see myself in the role that had prompted my conversation with Arnold Lempriere. Under this impulsion, I continued to build on the tenuous hypothesis that Mrs Pococke had owned a greater fondness for Ivo's father than she realized.

'I expect you've made the acquaintance of Tony's boy,' I said to her. 'Does he venture to make fun of you too?'

'Certainly not. And it wouldn't be at all the same thing.'

This was a just rebuke. At the same time it perhaps acknowledged, if obscurely, the former existence of a mild flow of feeling between Tony and the Provost's then decidedly attractive wife which would be inappropriate and displeasing in the case of a second Tony now.

'I like the boy,' Mrs Pococke suddenly said—surprisingly and firmly. 'He is a graceless and idle youth, no doubt. But there are plenty of such around.'

'Not all that many.' Atlas took this up at once. 'A quite small, but nevertheless occasionally subversive, minority.'

'That may be, Charles. You must know more about the undergraduates than I do.' Mrs Pococke said this to the young man quite without sarcasm, but it wasn't a wholly uncoloured remark, all the same. She then turned back to me with what was clearly to be, for the moment, a valedictory word. 'Ivo Mumford reminds me of his father—and of his grandfather, for that matter, who turns up from time to time, and whom I can't say I greatly care for. But Ivo has the misfortune to be not nearly so clever as Lord Marchpayne.'

'Do you really think it a misfortune,' I asked, 'not to be clever?'

'Not in the least—provided one's father and brothers aren't clever either. What may be called drive is a different matter. Everybody is the better of that. And Ivo lacks it as well.'

'You would say Tony has notable drive?'

'When you enter the Cabinet, Mr Pattullo, I shall credit you with it too. Meanwhile, you do have your designs.'

I had asked for that, I told myself as Mrs Pococke turned away. She must have been fully aware of what I had been about—which didn't mean that she mightn't be an ally, all the same. I was now addressed by Mrs Atlas, who made a little conversation—nervously, and rather as if it was something her husband required of her. She was even prettier than I had at first concluded, so that I wondered at a restlessness which I was beginning to feel. Perhaps it was simply that a sense of something oppressively slow in the passage of time assails one when the production of a meal appears unreasonably delayed. This explanation received some support when James Gender moved across the room to us—no doubt under the direction of Mrs Pococke, who had now taken on Miss Minton.

'It's the McKechnies,' Gender murmured to us, after he had exchanged punctilious greetings with me. 'They haven't a high reputation for punctuality. It's because McKechnie has pretty well to be brought along on a lead.' Gender spoke with such an air of diffidence and whimsical charity that he couldn't possibly have been taken as advancing a serious social stricture. 'You positively see the little thong in the hand of his charming wife.'

'He's been out shopping,' I said. 'I came on him in the Cornmarket. And I can imagine his being difficult to coax into company.'

'He hasn't been with us long, and he doesn't come in often.

We are terribly pleased when he does. McKechnie is a great scholar, and an extremely nice man.'

'We were at school together,' I said—perhaps not very adequately in response to these courteous enthusiasms.

'Of course you were!' Gender said this as if delighted to have been reminded of a pleasing circumstance widely known among men. 'And you know Janet McKechnie?'

'His wife? No—I didn't even know he was married. I'd rather have supposed he wasn't.'

'Yes.' Gender's agreement was tentative, and he directed his gaze (rather like Miss Minton) into his empty glass. I supposed that my last remark hadn't been quite in order, and that civility therefore required that some token support should be accorded it. 'I believe there are no children. Not by the marriage.'

Ranald McKechnie's marriage didn't interest me very much; no more, say, than did his violin. Our encounter, or non-encounter, less than a couple of hours before must cast a slightly ludicrous character over the meeting now about to take place. Ought I to ignore—ought we both to ignore—our singular lapse from adulthood? I knew that he had been as aware of me as I had of him, and perhaps the most civilized thing would be a tacit acknowledgement of our infirmity conveyed in an exchanged glance.

It didn't look as if there was to be opportunity for further thought about this. Honey had appeared again at the door of the Day-room, and it was reasonable to suppose that the McKechnies were to be ushered in at last. He proved, however, to have nobody in convoy, and was carrying a needlessly large silver salver upon which a small buff envelope reposed. He went up to the Provost, appeared to give him a message, and then turned and with a deliberate pace came over to me.

'A telegram, Mr Pattullo. The porter has sent it over from the gate.'

I knew at once why time had been behaving irksomely. It was a fateful telegram—so fateful that I was reminded of a telegram that had arrived in Edinburgh long ago and opened

241

on the news that I was to be the John Ruskin Scholar of my year. This one had no bearing on my own affairs, but was far more fateful for another boy. The success or failure of Mogridge's mission was a grave matter, however fantastic that mission's trimmings. It was true that an obstinate rational doubt about the Otby episode remained with me. Nevertheless nothing throughout the morning had been more than a passing distraction from it. Mogridge's promise to communicate with me had scarcely been out of my head, and he was keeping that promise now. I said some word of apology to my companions, picked up the envelope, and tore it open. The message came from New York. It read *Satisfactory contract negotiated* and was signed—not very inventively— *J. Smith.*

'Thank you very much,' I said to the waiting Honey. 'There's no reply.'

A sense of immense relief overcame me—censurably, no doubt, since the news I had received was of the success of a criminal enterprise. I think I may even have given Gender and the Atlases cause to stare, and when I was again capable of attending to my surroundings it was to hear the Provost addressing Miss Minton with a largeness of effect which made his words available to the whole room.

'Gracious lady,' the Provost said, 'happily, I have to implore your patience for only ten minutes more. My butler has had a call from the McKechnies, who are held up by just that further span of time. Our pleasure in their company will be but enhanced when they do arrive.'

Miss Minton showed no sign of being disconcerted by this oratundity; she was presumably habituated to her host's liability a little to overplay his part. If there had been an inadvertent suggestion that she was ravening for food it was an implausible one, since she was of so ascetic an appearance as to suggest that she habitually lunched off a dry biscuit. As we had, in fact, been introduced at the start of the proceedings, it was time that I displayed some inclination to talk to her.

But I saw that I must employ this further pause in an effort to contact Tony and pass on Mogridge's message; Tony, I was fairly sure, would be in a great state of agitation until he received it. So I made the necessary appeal to Mrs Pococke, and Honey led me to a telephone in the seclusion of the Provost's library. It was the room in which my father had intimated his intention of entering me at the college.

Tony was instantly available at the first number I dialled —something that one had to suppose uncommon with Cabinet Ministers. He must have been sitting beside the instrument.

'It's Duncan,' I said—and added absurdly (for I had entered the Mogridge world again), 'Is this telephone all right?'

'Absolutely. I've seen to that.' (Tony was in the Mogridge world too.) 'For Christ's sake, Duncan! Is there any news?'

'A telegram from New York. It says *Satisfactory contract negotiated*. And it's signed *J. Smith*.'

'In God's name! Mogridge?'

'Yes, of course.'

'What the hell does he mean about a contract?'

'That's bosh. Don't you remember?' I wondered whether Tony's wits were deserting him. '"Satisfactory" is the key word.'

'I see. Repeat it, please.'

Patiently, I repeated the message.

'Nothing else?'

'No, nothing else. But it means he has brought it off. You can rest easy.'

'That's marvellous! Gavin's a true friend. A bloody hero.'

'Just that. Think of that *Mochica* thing. *C'est son métier*.'

'Don't drivel, for the lord's sake.' Tony snapped this out with no reason at all. 'But I'm eternally grateful to him. And to you too, Dunkie. You brought him in.'

'So I did.'

'But think of all those snags! They're still there. It's madness. We're right out on a limb.'

'Only if we've very bad luck.' I saw that Tony really was

distracted to the point of frenzy. 'And remember he's a top pro.'

'So he is. Good old Gavin! I could grovel to him. He's been a gift from heaven. I say! What about that cottage?'

'What cottage?'

'The gardener's cottage at Otby, you fool. And then that housekeeper of my father's. If she——'

'Listen. Gavin wouldn't have gone ahead without making sure of all that. It would be second nature to him. Your boy's alibi—if that's what it's to be called—is in the bag.'

'And we shan't be in the jug? Oh, glory! Dunkie—waiting has been sheer hell. I tried one throw myself, as soon as I got back to town. Not that it would have been any fucking good. You're sure Gavin says nothing more?'

'Of course I am. I can read, you know.' Fleetingly, I wondered what Tony had been up to. 'You'd better not do anything more. Just sit tight.'

'Yes. I must say he might have been a bit more communicative. Telegrams don't cost all that.'

'Don't be an ass, Tony.' I was astonished by the unreasonableness of this last remark. 'He trusts us to trust him—just on the strength of that one word. He was being cautious—that's all.'

'Of course, of course. Reliable man. Knows his onions. I say, Duncan! What happens next?'

'I've no idea. Perhaps, with the crisis past, he'll ring you up. Or perhaps you'll just get a quiet family letter from Ivo, full of the sights of New York. And now, unwind. I've got to ring off. I'm lunching with the Pocockes.'

'With who?'

'The Pocockes, you idiot. And a gaggle of dons and dons' wives. I'll look you up when I get back to town. Good-bye.'

'Dunkie—I'm fearfully anxious still.'

'That's inevitable. Go on the bottle a bit. *But do nothing.* Understood?'

'Yes, Dunkie. And bless you. Bless dear old Gavin. Good-bye.'

I rang off, got out my handkerchief, and dabbed my brow—a

piece of private theatre excusable in face of such demoralization. And then I returned to Mrs Pococke's little party.

The McKechnies had arrived and been given drinks, so that lunch was in immediate prospect at last. The awkwardness between Ranald (as I must remember to call him) and myself had entirely gone out of my head. Tony's condition—which the bare record of his words on the wire scarcely conveys—was affecting me in a curious way. For the time, at least, he was sagging beneath the burden of parenthood to a pitiful degree. It seemed an unenviable situation, and what came strangely to me was that, in a sense, I envied it. Apart from Ninian and perhaps his children, there was nobody in the world sudden disaster to whom would mean a great deal to me. I should feel decent distress and regret if misfortune struck here or there among my friends. But if acute misery or apprehensiveness was going to assail me, it could only be on behalf of my precious self. This insulated state it was not going to be salubrious to grow old in. I have mentioned those long-haired, long-legged boys who on sentimental mornings would sometimes lounge at my breakfast-table. I could have no anxieties about *them*. They were as immune against crass casualty as those good folk or elfin people whose voices and laughter had momentarily come to me while waiting for the Gaudy dinner—undergraduates in waking fact, fooling around in an adjacent quad. No doubt I had been prudent, obeying—or obeying all but once—the poet's injunction: *Never give all the heart*. But neither as artist, statesman, or anything else does the prudent man set any mark upon his time.

These sombre thoughts were occasioned perhaps as much by inanition as by the troubles of Lord Marchpayne; the Gaudy breakfast kippers now lay a long time back. Not to delay the remedy, I said a brisk and cheerful word to Ranald McKechnie, and glanced—by way of preparing for brief introduction—at his wife.

My heart turned over. I had known Janet McKechnie as a girl. I had expected to marry her.

XIV

My brother Ninian had been sexually precocious, and since he was so little older than myself this considerably affected my own condition. He had early successes as well as desires, and it is an odd reflection on the patchy way in which manhood arrives that he had slept with a girl some weeks before the celebrated occasion upon which Uncle Rory caned him. The sleeping had been a literal matter, since he had smuggled her out of her parents' house to spend a short summer night in his arms in a fold of the Pentland hills. This exploit was to be the only one he ever communicated to me other than in the most allusive way, despite the fact that we were much in one another's confidence. It had been an initiation too tremendous to bottle up. But he never boasted again. His reticence about succeeding love-affairs, none of which can actually have been much more than clandestine encounters with girls easily won, was a result of their taking colour from his imagination and appearing to involve a gravity of relationship which precluded kissing and telling. He was not by nature a casual amorist (such as the unredeemed P. P. Killiecrankie had been). He was really looking for something quite different.

Ninian's reserve here, a function of rapidly approaching maturity, made life difficult for me. I was tormented by a need to know just what was going on—unreasonably, since I knew I couldn't myself manage what Ninian was bringing off. Had it come, with me, to what Victorian novelists call the embrace, I could as soon have jumped off the Forth Bridge as achieved the thing at that time. I was inept with girls, and my romantic imaginings concerned a snub-nosed younger schoolfellow with the awkward name of Tommy Watt. I was faithful to Tommy Watt, clinging to his image for several years.

Ninian, I am sure, never felt such an attachment. Without being in the least the sort of small boy who always plays with the girls, he did naturally turn to them; when still in shorts and jersey he owned a kind of contained gentleness towards the other sex which was thoroughly masculine. Girls noticed that my clothes were sometimes ragged and always scruffy, but they never marked the same qualities in Ninian's. When quite small I naturally hadn't been troubled by this sort of thing. It became different as we grew older. I had grown a great deal older—in fact I was seventeen—when something traumatic occurred. Tommy Watt was a solicitor's son, but he had an uncle who was a farmer. Tommy used to spend holidays on the farm, and on one occasion sent me a picture-postcard depicting the dreary little lowland village near which it lay. It seemed to me at once to be a magical place—and I had, for that matter, to make the most of the card, since it was the only tangible token of regard that Tommy had ever accorded me. Then, helping with a harvest, Tommy (who was very stupid) contrived to feed himself into some mechanical monster and be chewed to bits.

I found myself unable to touch bread, since I believed there might be some of Tommy in it. This extravagant behaviour baffled and alarmed my parents, but like most hysterical performances didn't last long. For a time I groped around for another Tommy. This didn't last long either. My imagination, which had largely created him, simply refused to take on a further job of the kind. Tommy had died on me both in fact and in his representative character, and that sort of adolescent attachment wasn't to be available to me again. Faced up to, the change seemed encouraging, since for some time I had been feeling (very reasonably) that I ought to have advanced beyond picturing life on a desert island with a younger boy whom I would rescue from sharks, boa constrictors, marauding cannibals and similar hazards drawn from Ballantyne or *The Swiss Family Robinson*.

It is among the discomforts of growing up that mounting emotional muddles can be coincident with rapid intellectual development, and in my later years at school I had been making up for the uninteresting and depressing character of the institution's overt sexual *mores* by reading popular expositions of the discoveries or theories of Freud and Adler and Jung. Poking about in these regions in some alarm but optimistically on the whole, I concluded that I had passed through a crisis of development and was now going to be just like Ninian— which I desperately wanted to be. So unflawed was my faith in almost immediate transformation that I bought, in a furtive little shop behind Scotland's General Register Office, a packet of what Killiecrankie's friend the bishop would have called sexual engines. I remember thinking that the shop must be just like Mr Verloc's in *The Secret Agent*—a reflection proving my literary education to have run well ahead of that obtainable in the school of life. The fascinating and revolting objects remained unused. I was in fact quite like Ninian, but some marginal difference between us got in the way of my emulating those preliminary and tormenting skirmishes of his with the strength of lust and the enigma of love. When Tony Mumford and I were ending our first year together as cronies in Surrey Quad, and were rivalling most of our companions in outrageousness of bawdy invention, I was still a sexually untried youth—this despite episodes of a certain laxity between myself and the elder of my Glencorry cousins. So—almost, if not quite—was Tony. Belonging to a Catholic family, he was sent (as Ivo was not to be) to a Catholic school, and although I was never to detect in him the slightest vestige of religious faith I imagine that certain stiff teachings on the sinfulness of sexuality unsanctified by marriage took time to wear off.

Ninian and I were unaffected here by either parental attitudes or the doctrines of a church. My mother, like many people in Scotland with her background, was an episcopalian— which was why my father, to my perplexity as a child, would sometimes refer to her as the wee piskie. Three or four times a year she attended communion in St John's Church at the end of Princes Street—on which occasions my father would accompany her to the door, pay a visit to the tomb of Raeburn (who must also have been a piskie) in the adjoining mortuary chapel, and return home for what he called a quick peg before picking her up again. She was, in fact, innocent of any serious religious consideration, and her attitude to sexual conduct was entirely romantic. She had adored young Lachlan Pattullo from that first moment in the Sistine, and although incapable of cooking him a good meal or washing his children's ears she continued so to adore him all her life. He certainly adored her, and this she believed to be in the nature of things rather than some miracle of the heart.

My father was completely faithful to her. Neither Ninian nor I would have called this in question for a moment; indeed, any speculation on the point could never have entered our heads. Later, I was to consider this facet of my father's character in the context of that easy Bohemianism—conventionally predicated of the 'artistic' temperament, and in fact going with it often enough—which he constantly exhibited. There seemed to mingle in him a feeling for the broad continental culture of which he had seen a good deal and a yet deeper instinct, submerged but miscellaneously eruptive, for the severe rules of conduct to which he had been bred. Certain small Scottish conformities were dear to him. One of these brings me back, after a fashion, to religious matters. It brings me, too, to Janet.

My father had an elder brother, Norman, who like many another dogged Scottish peasant lad had attained to being a minister of the Kirk. His parish lay in a remote region of Aberdeenshire, so that we saw little of him or his family. (As children, Ninian and I had spent a week in the manse, behaving so badly that, to our satisfaction, we were never invited again.) Uncle Norman had a domed head with only a few wisps of hair, a drooping moustache, and some affliction of the eyes which required him to be constantly dabbing at them with a handkerchief. It was often difficult to understand what he said: partly because his accent was as remote from the genteel Edinburgh speech to which we were accustomed as, in a different fashion, was that of Uncle Rory and Aunt Charlotte; but partly, too, because his remarks tended to fade away into a discouraged murmur. A man more different from his brother it would have been hard to conceive. I cannot think that the Dreich himself was as dreich as the Reverend Norman Pattullo.

My father, however, although in general uninterested in his family connections, had a very high regard, as well as deep affection, for Uncle Norman. Years afterwards, I was to learn from family papers that, when himself still extremely poor, he had supported his brother during his theological studies with money earned by anonymous and demeaning labours as a commercial artist. He must have thought his efforts amply rewarded, since he judged it a great thing to become a minister. And although before his death he had pictures hanging in many of the great galleries of the world (and incidentally become, to his considerable amusement, Sir Lachlan Pattullo), he never had any doubt about who was the real credit to the family. My own pride in my father (which I hope appears) was to some extent a reflex of his pride in Norman.

It was this distinguished connection that made my father, somewhat surprisingly, a church-goer and one who insisted on church-going children. We weren't, indeed, haled off to worship every week, but our attendance in our parish church was sufficiently regular to have satisfied Uncle Norman himself that we were not 'sitten-up'—an expression applicable in Aberdeenshire, if not in Edinburgh, to those who are culpably neglectful of their religious duties. When we stayed away the fact was bound to be remarked, since we rented our own pew, with my father's name on a card set in a little metal frame by way of intimation that none but Pattullos might lawfully worship there. This curiosity of the devotional life lingered longer, I believe, in Scotland than in England.

My mother had no objection to the Established Church of Scotland, and a considerable fondness for showing off her handsome husband and, as she conceived them, handsome sons. So she always came with us, taking satisfaction in the hymns and metrical psalms (which she sang loudly and erratically), and spending the sermon-time, which could be inordinately long, in studying the hats of the well-dressed women who frequented our rather fashionable conventicle.

Whether Ninian ever believed a word that we were told in church I don't know. I certainly did not. It all seemed the greatest nonsense to me: for the most part merely boring, but occasionally—as in the lugubrious hymning of Gethsemane and Calvary and the Crucifixion which led up to the Lord's Supper—revolting as well. For a time, indeed, the star preachers of the Scottish Kirk did occasionally sweep me away with a torrential and essentially Gaelic eloquence which seemed endlessly at their command. Such a flow of words, and words on top of words, was exhilarating. But when I came to listen more analytically it was revealed to me that no one thing they said hitched intelligibly on to another. The preachers were in an advanced stage of what I was one day to think of as Junkin's Disease.

The girl whom I knew to be called Janet Finlay sat in the pew behind ours. It was, in fact, the Finlay pew, with a card saying *Professor Alasdair Finlay* at the end of it. Janet sat invariably in the place immediately behind what was equally invariably mine—so that Ninian, sitting next to me, was in a marginally better position to catch a glimpse of her than I was. But it wasn't easy for him either. Looking round in church was perfectly permissible. (As our pew was in a species of transept, my mother could thus rake the whole nave with unviolated propriety.) But turning round—attempting to rotate one's head through 180° in order to remedy the defect of not having eyes in the back of it—was bad manners.

Both Ninian and I must several times have been in the same room as Janet, but I doubt whether either of us had ever spoken to her. Already some way behind us was that phase of development in which children's parties give place to young people's dances, and to dances we didn't much go—nor were we much invited to them, since our social contacts, although variously enlarging themselves, were as a matter of family conditions and assumptions apart from such things. Janet must have been about sixteen before we were really aware of her, and it was Ninian who admitted being aware of her first.

'She's very beautiful,' he told me—gravely, dispassionately, and with what happened to be an unjustified sense that my attention had to be directed to the circumstance. 'Those Finlays come from Skye, but it's not a Highland beauty at all. Ancient Skyros would be nearer the mark. It was where Achilles hid among the women—and I expect he knew what he was about.'

'So you'll be going after her?' I asked—at once sarcastically and with a feeling less easily identifiable than the diffused jealousy Ninian could commonly rouse in me. But I knew that the question was an idle one. Ninian clearly felt that Janet was inadmissibly young for him. He had a strict sense of honour about his conquests. But there was something beyond this. He was now, while awaiting call-up, at the university studying law. It was already apparent, to the confounding of our headmaster's predictions, that he was going to sweep the board clear of every prize and honour available to him. Emotionally—sexually, rather—he had in consequence dropped into a curious period of belated latency; and this was to continue until, a few years later, he startled us by getting married. He was going to be the youngest Senator of the College of Justice that the records of the Scottish bench disclose—and that was that.

So it was now I who was alert to—who actually trembled at the sight of—Janet Finlay, the girl who merited a Homeric hero as her lover. This made it unfair that every Sunday (for I had begun to urge my parents to unremitting piety) it was Ninian who had that slightly superior opportunity to catch her in what was no more than a connoisseur's glance. I was myself pretty well confined to the few moments of arrival and departure. One didn't kneel in our church (it would have been

252

regarded as a papistical action) but at the end of the service one did bury one's nose and pray. One then stood up, and while the congregation was skailing (which would have been Uncle Norman's word) one was free to stare around as one chose. As there was a gallery at the back of our transept, I could always turn round as if to look up at it and identify acquaintances whom I might later join outside. But the timing of this was tricky; I couldn't prolong the stance, and if I embarked on it too soon Janet's prayers might still be continuing when it was necessary to abandon it, so that I'd glimpse nothing but the top of her hat.

All this must seem an absurd prelude to what was to be a serious matter. I was physically clumsy in these manœuvres in a fashion that must have represented an externalizing of interior confusion. I was in love. I was in love with a girl, not a snub-nosed boy—and, moreover, with a girl I had never spoken to. I didn't really know this then. But Ninian knew it. He never teased me about Janet Finlay; rather he preserved what might be called a holy silence in face of the whole phenomenon. For a long time I was to draw comfort from this, the severity of my brother's attitude somehow validating what was going on.

It will be evident that what was going on was as yet no sort of spiritual communion. I have had occasion to speak of Charles Atlas's young wife as so pretty that I hoped to be placed beside her at Mrs Pococke's luncheon-table; of Mrs Pococke herself as having been a notably handsome woman in her prime; of Mabel Bedworth as owning a soft motility of feature making for beauty. This does no more than distinguish me as a man who notices such things; and these several instances are of little consequence. Janet Finlay was beauty's self, and my love assuredly began as eye-love of the sheerest sort. It was a long time before it so much as occurred to me that she must have a voice. This may have been because of the circumstances of our first contiguity; we were two devout (or supposedly devout) young people, comporting ourselves properly at church. But Janet seemed to take this decorum to an extreme. I never detected her as murmuring a word either to her father on her left or to her mother on her right. Nor did she (and it might have struck me that this was odd) either sing the hymns and psalms or audibly repeat the Lord's Prayer.

She stopped coming to church. For a couple of Sundays I was disappointed but not alarmed. Then I began to wonder whether she was ill, or had suffered an accident. I lacked the courage—and, indeed, in that rather stiff society, the title—to make a bold inquiry of her mother. My father treated Professor Finlay as a stranger, and I had no idea whether they had ever met; it was quite probable that they had, but that my father took as poor a view of Janet's father as he did of that other professor of the university, Ranald McKechnie's.

Then a dreadful thought came to me. Totally overestimating any effect I could have made on Janet, and remembering all my clumsy goggling at her, all those gapings up at the gallery with the corner of my eye elsewhere, all those twists and turns so ineffectively dissimulating my fascination: suddenly remembering these things, I decided that I had offended her, and that this was why she was staying away. When our eyes had met, she had dropped hers—not before giving me a steady glance, and certainly with nothing of the suggestion which somewhat similar behaviour on Mrs Bedworth's part was to occasion so long afterwards. But at least the action had been quite definite enough to make it clear that she had no disposition to exchange meaningful looks with a strange young man. My agony upon thus imagining that I had driven her away was extreme. I even hinted the possibility to Ninian.

'Jesus, Dunkie! Why should she *go* to the place?' Ninian's reaction was robust and immediate. 'Why should *we*? I'm blessed if I know.'

I knew why I went. I also knew one reason, again not wholly edifying, why Ninian went: if he was going to make his way in our native city a good many wise conformities would be required of him. But it was, furthermore, a matter of being dutiful children, or at least of our having for our father an immense respect which made us decently amenable to those Sunday kilts (not that we hadn't by now exchanged them for honest grown-up trousers) and devastated hours. If my father, incidentally, had noticed my behaviour he made no reference to it; and he certainly couldn't have regarded as censurable any impulse to contemplate a beautiful woman— or beautiful landscape, which he would have thought of as much the same thing. My mother did notice, and was a little tiresome as a result. She was given to the spinning of facile romance, and would have dearly liked to see me standing up in a ballroom with such a girl as Janet Finlay and treading a measure like young Lochinvar. She was even not above regarding Janet's absence from the Finlay pew as a matter of a maiden's coy retreat from her swain.

And then I ran into Janet in the public library on George IV Bridge.

I literally ran into her, having dashed into the building for some urgent purpose which I now forget. A book she was carrying went to the ground, and I had picked it up and apologized before there dawned on me the apocalyptic thing that had happened. I also recognized the book. It was *The Plumed Serpent*. Janet appeared to be on her way to return it to the desk.

'Did you like it?' I asked.

This was an eternal moment, for I had done something I couldn't—until the words were spoken—have believed myself capable of. And it had never occurred to me that Janet Finlay might read books.

'No, I didn't!' Janet replied instantly, and with a vehemence apparently unconnected with any just sense of outrage she might have felt at being addressed by me. 'That woman Kate. She watches her husband murdering people, and their blood being sprinkled on a sacred fire. And it makes her "uneasy". Just that! Not mad with horror, or crazed with some daft religious ecstasy. "Uneasy"—and "gloomy" too. I'd be gloomy! But I suppose it's all deeply true.'

'I don't think it's anything of the sort.' Although my admiration for Lawrence at that time was fathomless, I felt it should be made known to Janet that a line has sometimes to be drawn in him. If she thought I was necessarily, because a man, at all like Don Cipriano or Don Ramón, I just didn't see how she could be made to put up with me.

'And all that idiotic inventing of a new religion——'

'It's meant to be the reviving of an old one.'

'I suppose so, but it comes to the same thing. One religion is quite enough, it seems to me, without thinking up other ones.'

'Is that why you don't come to church any longer?'

'Yes, it is. I've said I won't and I won't. Not if they beat me.'

'But they wouldn't do that!' I cried, horrified—although I knew perfectly well that university professors don't tan their daughters.

'No—but they can be beastly.' Janet suddenly looked at me round-eyed. It was only now that she recognized me. 'Sorry,' she said. 'I didn't mean to be rude about your belief in Jesus—that sort of thing.'

'I haven't any belief in Jesus.' I was now wildly excited, and I had said this so loudly that a couple of women near by turned and looked at me disapprovingly.

'Then why do *you* go to church, and listen to all that styte about rising again on the third day?'

'I say, have you tried *The Man Who Died*?' It seemed to me that this was a brilliant diversion. 'It's smashing Lawrence. Jesus gets up and feels very sick about everything, and can't stand the old crowd any more—so cuts out.' I was particularly pleased with myself for thus being able to quote verbatim from a letter. 'So he goes——'

'No, I haven't. And you're not answering my question.'

'But I'd like to. Only it will take a little time. Look—will you come and have tea somewhere?'

I had again uttered unbelievable words. Had I known Janet well, I might have said, with reasonable Edinburgh propriety,

'Can you come home with me to tea?' But the notion of a schoolboy entertaining a schoolgirl in a tea-shop was (or so I imagined) an extremely daring one. I was in my last term at school, but I was dressed, except for long trousers, exactly as I had been dressed when seven or eight: in a blazer and cap with bold identifying badges of a spuriously heraldic order— although the cap, indeed, I tended to keep in my pocket. Janet, who was of course younger, conformed to the same general pattern—except that hers was a straw boater with a hideously striped ribbon, impossible to conceal anywhere. I think I had a weird idea that we might be turned away from a tea-shop just as we should be from a pub.

'Are you the painter's son?'

'*You're* not answering *my* question, Janet Finlay. But, yes, I'm Lachlan Pattullo's son. My name's Duncan. I'm called Dunkie.'

'Dunkie?' It sounded as if Janet was amused. 'Yes, let's have tea.' She frowned, since this left a necessary point unsettled. 'Nobody has ever invited me out to tea before. What fun!'

She meant, I supposed, that no young man had done so. I felt panic—partly because I hadn't stopped to ask myself if I had more than a couple of shillings in the world. I slipped a hand cautiously into a trouser-pocket; there were half a dozen coins, and an exploring thumb nail revealed them as having milled edges; this meant that I was rich enough for anything. But we were not in very good tea-shop territory. Those near by were poky places, and might give, I felt, a clandestine flavour to the occasion. I wasn't going to have that—for hadn't I something to display with which I could have walked proudly into the Palace of Holyroodhouse itself? (Moreover, Oxford was ahead of me, where I was to be John Ruskin Scholar—and, no doubt, President of the Union, and everything else as well.)

'We'll take the bus down to Princes Street,' I said with decision.

So we sat on a balcony in mild summer sunshine, with the

Castle in front of us, and around us prosperous gossiping women eating oat-cakes and drop-scones. I recklessly hoped that my headmaster would turn up at the next table, or at least one of my schoolfellows in attendance on his mother. Not that this sort of self-consciousness lasted long. I became absorbed in the girl beside me.

It would have been a reasonable bet on a wise person's part that what we were in for was an hour's constraint and anticlimax. But nothing of the sort happened. The eternal-moment effect went on. I wasn't to know that, on rare visits to Edinburgh years ahead, I should be unable to look up at this balcony without a stab of pain; should be glad, even, when it disappeared as a result of some hideous developing of the site.

That we talked very coherently about religious faith and doubt is improbable. We were too much children of our time for such matters to have real import for us. We were also children suddenly launched upon a strange ocean. The surge and swell of it made me deliriously happy. I didn't only believe that I was in love with Janet Finlay. I also believed that she was going to be in love with me. I wasn't entirely wrong.

But lying awake that night, I gave myself all sorts of cautions, armoured myself in all sorts of second thoughts. For I wasn't only wary of happiness; I was afraid of it. This was not from any adult knowledge that it is the most vulnerable of human conditions, but rather from a feeling which could fitly have been examined by Janet and myself in the course of any theological discussion we did have. It must have been as an inheritance from my Calvinist forebears that what I had often felt, but now felt more strongly than ever before, came to me. That sexual pleasure pursued as an end in itself is sinful was something I was one day going to believe Tony Mumford had been taught at Downside. I think it may be not untrue, and that a wise humanism can say something very like it. But what lurked in me—almost as if I had been my uncle Norman's son and not my father's—was a sense that *all* pleasure, that happiness of any sort, speaks of danger, ought to be treated as a warning that one is approaching at least the antechamber of Auld Nick. I couldn't remotely have articulated this evil doctrine, and it would be misleading to suggest that it had more than a dim and ghostly existence in recesses of my mind. So it was much more another kind of magic that prompted some of my thinking before I went to sleep: the kind of magic that says things won't happen if one forces oneself to expect them to happen. I had embarked, I told myself, on a boy-and-girl affair of the kind that comes to nothing, that one lives to laugh at, that is followed by others of the same sort, that is just part of the ignominy of growing up. Ninian had gone through several such episodes. And although he had been without the temperament to treat them lightly or see them as ephemeral, ephemeral they had been in the end. Janet and I were just kids, and we hadn't a chance. And it seemed to me that this necessitated my being very pure of heart in my love for her.

I fell asleep at last, and it seemed almost at once that I had a dream. It was a very simple dream, but I think not one that a psychiatrist would have predicted so soon after such a radically new experience as that day's. I was in bed with Janet, and we were making love. We had made love; the wet dream was over; I woke up. And as I woke up I heard Ninian's voice say, 'That won't ever happen, Dunkie.'

Of course I had not really come awake—not till seconds after. Ninian and I didn't even share a room. But his voice often came as an admonishment or a challenge inside my head, and I rose to it now.

'Yes, it will,' I said aloud into the darkness. And I went to sleep again.

Whether it would or wouldn't had no more been a calculation of mine during our balcony tea than, presumably, it had been of Janet's. The unsensual character of early love (on which Plot was to prove an authority) made all the going. I wanted, above all things, to know about Janet—to *know* her, indeed, but not in the queer sense of the word that sometimes cropped up in the First Lesson during church on Sundays. I think she had an answering impulse, but got less chance to exercise it. All through our tea I held the initiative, being buoyed up by my astounding achievement in the public library. There was no information at all that I didn't want to have. I must have asked a score of absurd questions—whether, for example, she preferred cats or dogs—as well as others more pertinent. For I was in the grip of that desire to possess in totality which no doubt represents the predatory side of love. My father, absorbed in some vista of glens and lochs and mountains with a blank canvas or sketch-book before him, was the type of the lover his son was that afternoon.

I questioned Janet about her family. She seemed surprised—but pleased rather than offended—at my not knowing her father to be the university's professor of clinical neurology. She plunged—rapidly, vehemently, and even with a kind of passion which puzzled me—into family history. Both her parents came from Skye. Both came from humble crofting backgrounds. ('So does my father,' I said quickly, since establishing anything in common with Janet was precious to me.) They had been unable to marry young, since her father's struggle for a medical degree had been hard and long. Her mother had become a school-teacher on Raasay, and had sent him her pay secretly, since it would have been held an improper thing, if known. I noticed that Janet seemed to regard this as having been to her father's discredit, a point on which I should have thought it sensible to keep an open mind. We made common ground—although, indeed, most of my friends regularly announced such impatient feelings—about the stuffiness and snobbishness and conventionality of our native city; we had even got hold of the word 'provincial' for it, which was not really an accurate term. But Janet had her attitude to this bound up with her attitude to her family in a way I had not. Perhaps I had an advantage here. My ears and neck would have been cleaner sooner if either of my parents had been *bürgerlich* in the slightest degree, but for the same reason I had largely escaped the exhausting business of being a rebel in the home.

Janet was a rebel—but chiefly, it seemed, against her father rather than her mother. She criticized him as given over to foolish schemes of social aggrandizement. She was reluctant to disclose (even amid all this frankness, which I was certain wasn't her habit with new acquaintances) that she lived in the very grandest part of the New Town—which she scoffed at as 'all those draughty parallelograms'. This told me more than that she had read Stevenson as well as Lawrence. And although it seemed in a way to make allies of us, I had an obscure sense of being in the presence of something that might work against me.

'Well,' I demanded, 'what do you *like*?'

'A lot of things.' Justifiably, Janet resented thus being indicated, by implication, of too much discontent. 'But going home for the holidays, mostly.'

'Going home?' I repeated blankly.

'Home to Skye.'

'Oh,' I said 'You have a house there too.'

'We haven't. But my uncles have. They're crofters there. And fishermen.'

'I see.' Perhaps thinking of Uncle Rory and Uncle Norman, I judged the possession of relatives even of that degree of consanguinity an inadequate reason for claiming to have a home in distant places. 'Janet!' I said in sudden dismay. 'You're not going to Skye in these coming holidays?' We were already near the end of the summer term.

'But I *must*!' As she said this, Janet looked at me with a divinely uncalled-for remorse which more than made up for what seemed a senseless vehemence. It was as if China tea (a very sophisticated thought, this had been) and currant baps (more native fare) were being acknowledged as having established a bond between us. I was suddenly and most wholesomely overwhelmed by my consciousness of Janet's beauty. My head swam. 'Don't *you*,' she asked—and it was almost accusingly—'ever get away from home?'

'Yes, of course.' I was a little stiff at the suggestion of being childishly attached to apron-strings. 'My brother and I sometimes go to relations at a place called Corry.' I said this guardedly, having an instinct that it wouldn't do hastily to claim kinship with members of the Scottish aristocracy, if that was what Glencorry of that Ilk was to be thought of as belonging to. 'It's right in the Highlands,' I added hopefully— thereby no doubt revealing how lowland and urban I was. 'We're sent to run wild in the glens,' I amplified—this with a humorous intention which didn't seem quite to come off.

'Hasn't your father,' Janet asked at a tangent, 'got pictures in the National Gallery?'

'Yes, there are two there. And, of course, you can see him every year at the Academy.' This was the institution of which my father was so soon to become President. 'And I've got one at home myself, which I want to show you. It's a water-colour, with Ninian and me in it as young Picts. But we're lying in whins, so that all you can see is our heels, really, and our bottoms in anachronistic kilts.' I must simply have babbled this, for the great waters were now sweeping over me.

'I like the National Gallery,' Janet said. 'I like the Millet and the Israëls.'

'They're very fine,' I agreed stoutly—although these sombrely sentimental evocations of peasant life in fact held no great appeal for me. 'Let's go there now.' The severe Doric building which is the Scottish National Gallery, perched on the Mound, was on view from where we sat.

'We'll go another day. I must go home now. I've got a lot of rotten home-work. What else do you like, Duncan?'

'Dunkie.' I was determined to assert this ultimate intimacy.

'All right—I'll always call you Dunkie.' Janet had taken the point. 'But what else do you like?'

'I think I'm going to like going to Oxford. At least I hope so, because otherwise there won't be much point in it. I've won a Scholarship.'

'A kind of bursary?' Janet was obviously ignorant of the glory of an Open Scholarship—which got one's name put up in golden letters in our school hall. 'Isn't your father very wealthy?'

'Of course not.' I was almost as horrified as amused. 'We never seem to have a penny.' I felt that this was an awkward overstatement, since I was standing the tea. 'Or say a five-pound note. Painters don't make money, or not for ages and ages.'

'I didn't know.' Janet appeared mollified. 'Once you go to England, I suppose you'll stay there. And paint state portraits of the King and Queen.'

'What a daft idea!' It hadn't occurred to me that Janet might take it for granted that in the modern world painting was a hereditary affair. 'I can't draw a line.'

'Then what are you going to do?'

'I'm going to be a writer.'

I had never said this to anyone, not even Ninian, before. My father must have known it was in my head, but only because of the scribblings I sometimes showed him—although his awareness of my ambition had become more or less explicit, indeed, in his dark remarks about Galsworthy and Wells. But that I should myself utter such words, and give them the cast of a stated fact, was a new thing.

'You'll be a great writer, Dunkie,' Janet said with gravity.

I knew—for there was much that was clear-headed in me, at least when I was a boy—that I wasn't going to be that. Janet Finlay had completed her conquest of me, all the same.

After its whirlwind beginning (or what I thought of as that) our relationship became unexpectedly cautious and hesitant. We met several times in the National Gallery, simply because the place had turned up in our first conversation. We were naturally a good deal less aware of the pictures than of one another. But this consciousness was a self-consciousness as well. Our shyness—for we were shy in each other's company, after all—must have been in part socially determined: we couldn't pretend to be art-students and there didn't seem to be other schoolboy-and-schoolgirl couples around. We did better on Saturdays and Sundays, out of school clothes and going for walks together. But this attracted the awareness of our parents, and soon we had been to tea in each other's houses and were established as having formed a friendship entirely right and proper for our years. There was a certain depressant effect about this. It acted particularly upon Janet who, although so much younger, was more in need of a sense of enlarged independence than I was.

My mother was a little too enthusiastic about my new association. Ninian's affairs had sometimes bewildered her and taken her out of her depth, and she was determined to see Janet and myself in another light. Ninian had been a hunter abroad, and had never willingly brought a girl home in his life. My mother's notion of an ideal love-affair had generated itself out of her own history; it must be highly romantic while at the same time not disruptive of existing family ties. This led her to insist on making the acquaintance of Janet's mother. It required considerable address. Mrs Finlay was a maternal woman—simple, reserved, and domestically competent—who shared with her daughter a lack of enthusiasm for the social ambitions of the professor of clinical neurology. She must have been much more distrustful of the disorder of our household than impressed by my mother's being a sister of the Glencorry. Janet, when she discovered this kinship, wasn't impressed either—or at least not favourably. When she wanted to do battle with me (and that she sometimes did was perhaps a sign that our relationship, although adolescent, held the seeds of maturity) she would pretend that I was virtually the Glencorry myself, fatuously convinced of the devotion of feudal dependants who, in fact, hated me in their guts. I resented this joke—I thought justifiably, since my own views were of a thoroughly egalitarian sort. I wondered how Janet could have come by such stuff.

The holidays arrived, and Janet went off to Skye. We didn't write to each other. The initiative ought to have been mine. What seemed to deter me was a sense that anything I did write would be received by Janet in circumstances and amid surroundings unknown to me—and that these would somehow render shallow, callow, or otherwise unsympathetic anything that a schoolboy thought to scribble. It was an instinctive feeling of the kind that is seldom wholly astray. But now, looking back, I see in this abstention the first intimation of something in myself—an unready or unripe condition, it must be called—which ill fortune was to render definitive.

The holidays ended, and schoolchildren were back at school. Oxford, however, was still some weeks off, and during these weeks I managed to see a great deal of Janet. While she was away I had formed the superstitious conviction that if I didn't succeed in kissing her before my own imminent departure I should lose her for ever. But how was I to go about it? Did I ask her permission? Or did I firmly announce what I was about to do? Or did I just do it? I had no means of coming to a decision, but in fact I ended by kissing Janet with no more preparation than a swift glance. This action, which turned out triumphantly natural, took place, whether appropriately or not, in front of Vermeer's *Christ in the House of Mary and Martha*.

Our subsequent kisses, like the first one, were unembarrassed affairs, but unaccompanied by words. They took place, reasonable privacy permitting, on meeting and parting, and I think not much at other times. It was as if shaking hands had become infinitely precious and exciting, but could not without extravagance be indulged in at all hours as a result. I suppose we were happy rather than unhappy in those brief weeks, but at the same time we were both aware that something disturbing and paradoxical had entered our relationship. The paradox had to do with what in another context might have been called growth-rates. Superficially, I had taken a jump ahead of Janet. Emancipation had arrived. I should never again hurtle into a school yard on a bicycle at nine o'clock; never again call anybody 'sir' unless I chose to; never again be under the slightest compulsion to solve trigonometrical problems or memorize the principal exports of Chile. I had acquired a surprising array of new clothes from a good tailor—my father having perhaps taken it into his head that Wee Dreichie might be overgone (as he certainly might) in this department also. More significantly, my thoughts were beginning to project themselves with an increasing sense of contact and reality into an adult future.

If Janet thought very coherently about an adult future I didn't hear about it. But she was certainly concerned to get away from where she was, and out of that symbol of subjection which she called 'this bloody nunnery stuff'—meaning her school uniform and awful school hat. I was rather shocked at hearing Janet say 'bloody', although among my male contemporaries I enjoyed using as many improper words as they did. (There were some boys—Ranald McKechnie, for instance —who were chaste of speech. But we didn't admire them.) But if Janet was increasingly impatient with her schooling it wasn't because she was no good at her books. It was obvious, indeed, that she was much more generally successful at school subjects than I was. She liked languages, and particularly she liked French; my father had been astonished and delighted when he had one day thought to tease her with his own rapid command of it, and she had been suddenly fired to give him back quite as much as she got.

But I had grown older only on the surface and as a matter of changed status; whereas Janet, still in thrall to all the circumstances of childhood, had grown older deeper down. I had been aware of this almost in the first moments of seeing her on her return from Skye. It was an awareness difficult to get clear or express. There was more of her that was mysterious to me than before; she would sometimes look at me with a brooding reserve which reminded me of her mother; I had an uneasy sense of being left out of something that was going on.

This was the new paradox in our relationship, and she certainly understood it better than I did. The fact emerged in one of her sudden plunges into mockery. These didn't happen frequently. Although she was a prize girl on a much less narrow front than I was a prize boy, she seemed, indeed, to

266

set increasing store on possessing in me a kind of unofficial tutor. I was drawn, in consequence, into an instructive role which I wasn't stupid enough not to distrust. I explained books and pictures to her (matters about which I knew quite a lot)—and also music and politics (of which I was almost entirely ignorant). It was as if I represented something to which she had an impulse to cling. I was alert enough to dislike this impersonalizing of me, even although I was sure it constituted only one element in a complex state of feeling. She wasn't regarding me (I can recall specifically telling myself) merely as a walking and talking junior encyclopaedia, as she might regard, for instance, somebody like Ranald McKechnie. This was a random thought. It had never appeared that the Finlays and McKechnies, although both university people, knew each other.

'Off to boarding-school at your age!' she suddenly flashed out at me. 'When you might be growing a wee moustache, and even hoping for a wee beard, so that you'd be able to turn into a perfectly respectable gamekeeper and get a job with your grand uncle.' (She may have been reading *Lady Chatterley's Lover*—although this is improbable, that novel being not yet rampant in public libraries. Whether Mellors is bearded or not, I don't recall.)

'What do you mean, boarding-school?' Although Janet's words seemed absurd, I made this demand with a sinking heart, having an intuition that there was a sense in which she was saying something true.

'An Oxford college is like that, isn't it? A lot of young men behaving like children—kicking footballs, and rowing up and down a river in daft little boats, and ragging around, and being no end swells and mashers.'

'Certainly not mashers,' I said feebly—and indeed wondering where Janet could have raked up so outmoded a word. 'And I suppose I'm going to do quite a lot of work. They'll let me do what I like doing, more or less. Or so I'm told.'

'I'd like you to be a gamekeeper.'

'Don't be silly. You'd like nothing of the sort. And I'd be

a damned bad gamekeeper, anyway. I shouldn't even make a decent gillie.'

'I don't agree. You're clever enough to be anything, Dunkie.'

'But gillies don't need to be clever. In fact cleverness is regarded as a disadvantage in humble life.' I had been melted, as I always was, by Janet's using my pet name. 'But of course if you give an order, that's another matter.'

This was a not unamiable wrangle, and it went on for some time. But there was something I distrusted in it. And Janet was aware of this. We kissed with an unusual and incautious ardour at the end of that encounter.

It seems strange to me now that just this perplexed relationship with Janet should have continued unaltered for a considerable span of time. We wrote to each other sufficiently regularly for the mere fact of our so writing to be interpretable as reflecting a love-affair. But our letters were not in the common sense love-letters; they belonged to the same hovering world which we inhabited whenever I was spending in Edinburgh some part of a vacation during which Janet didn't happen to be on holiday in Skye. This simple chronological statement tells a lot. Janet had been right about Oxford—at least to the extent that I was absorbed in a new and (as it seemed to me) much larger world. There wasn't only Oxford. There was the continent—Hitler's continent during so much of my later boyhood—rapidly opening up as well. I had rather a lot of money: this because my father judged it natural to share with Ninian and myself a prosperity which—as can happen with artists, even good ones—had come tumbling in over-night. But there was something, too, more inward than all this. Janet had been right about the boarding-school as well. If intellectually I was looking ahead to adult concerns, socially and even emotionally (like an old gentleman advertising beer at that time) I was growing younger every day. Nearly all my companions, with the exception of a few older ones back from the war, were recent products of a system which retards sexual development in all but the crudest and most boisterous expression. They looked down on P. P. Killiecrankie's overtly behaving as he did—at least within the ring-fence of the college—but were to some extent P. P. Killiecrankies at heart. Sexual behaviour as something to be interwoven with the other facts of life was still some years ahead of them.

Of course it is silly to shunt on to a new environment in this way the burden of my own pusillanimity. And I'd have done better but for certain events at home. Janet at times seemed to be watching and waiting with amusement. She no longer much made fun of me. On the contrary she occasionally betrayed a kind of remorseful tenderness which at once troubled me and went deeply to my heart. And she wasn't puzzled about me. It was I myself who was that.

My mother—who had married when so young her lover of the Sistine Chapel—thought that Janet and I should at least be engaged. She tried to treat us as engaged, which was a great embarrassment. She tried to exploit in this interest a discovery she believed herself to have made about the health of Janet's mother. It would be a comfort to Mrs Finlay, she maintained, to know that all was going to turn out well.

This solicitude was in part vindicated, since Mrs Finlay did rather suddenly die. The event precipitated changes still so strange and poignant to me that I must simply hurry over them without analysis. Janet's mourning turned within months into a strange desperation not to be penetrated by anything I could write or say. Then she sent me, very briefly, news that went some way to explaining this. She had been—there had never been any doubt of it—very much her mother's child. And now her father—she wrote—had married again, and with what she called indecent haste, the daughter of somebody very much grander than Roderick Glencorry. The clinical neurologist's social ambition had fulfilled itself.

I am certain I didn't think about this information, or rather about the tone in which it was conveyed, as clearly as I ought to have done. It is sad to lose a mother, and commonly upsetting to acquire a step-mother; and when I heard of Professor Finlay's precipitancy I very much wished that I had been at home and in a position to support Janet as I might. I was at a maximum of obtuseness which in the event was to be shattered rapidly enough. The letter I wrote to Janet was long and far too full of wisdom. Since I did at least know this the moment I had posted it I wasn't surprised that it received no direct reply. When Janet did again write it was as briefly as before. But I took what she had to say as reassuring—to the extent that it seemed to mark a return to practical interests. As soon as I came home for the next vacation I must teach her to drive a car. It was going to be essential that she should be able to do that.

I had only recently passed my own driving test. It had been in a sports-car owned by Tony of the sort in which the bonnet purports to be held down by enormous leather straps; and as nobody employed by a Minister of Transport to test young drivers could possibly remain unprejudiced at the sight of so lethal-seeming an object I felt a reasonable confidence that I must be pretty good. So I looked forward to teaching Janet rapidly and well. I also decided that I wasn't returning to Oxford without having asked her to marry me.

The first part of this plan presented no difficulty. In the Finlays' car—the newness of which was more of a rarity than it would have been a year or two later—we drove round the environs of Edinburgh, and later through the city itself, for hours on end. On several occasions we did longer runs in the countryside—sometimes threading our way through those hills in which I couldn't but remember that Ninian had first made a girl his mistress. But Janet was so tense and withdrawn that I found it astonishing she never did anything wrong. Her concentration on the job she had set herself was absolute. I had a sense of this singleness of purpose as ominous, as somehow alien to our relationship as I believed it to be. But what did Janet believe it to be? I realized I simply didn't know. I had deferred, avoided indeed, for too long those explicit questions and avowals through which it is a grown man's part to further a love relationship. And now to Janet—almost, it might be said, to a Janet afforded no token that I really existed in an adult world—something had happened. I understood it not in the least, or only as something that took me quite out of my own range of feeling, power to action. In fact, these were the last days of my adolescence. I was soon, at least, to be clear of confusion.

I returned to Oxford with nothing achieved. I was bewildered and in some mysterious way humiliated. A letter came from Janet a few weeks later. It was addressed from Skye.

Dearest Dunkie,

I am married to Calum—and as I write his name I realize I have never spoken it to you. So I have treated you very badly. Dunkie, I *had* to get away. But it has been more than that. I have just been driven—with no more will than a leaf before a gale. It's hardly even me, or a personal thing in any way. *C'est Vénus toute entière à sa proie attachée.*

With much love and I am very sorry.

JANET GRANT

I stared at Racine's line stupidly, and told myself that this was what came of doing French. I remarked that Janet had got her accents right. I then tore the letter into very small pieces, being determined that it wouldn't live on in a drawer to be taken out and brooded over many years ahead. I wrote to Janet at once about her rightness and about the happiness I hoped she would enjoy. I did this strangely without effort, and before any grief or bitterness came to me. There was nothing else to do. I knew that I loved her very much.

We never wrote to each other again, and I was very far from wanting anybody to talk to me about Janet. At home, however, the subject couldn't be simply ignored. My mother expressed astonishment and indignation, and had to be stopped. My father spoke briefly and, I think wisely—taking what had happened as very much in the nature of things. Whether he thought I had behaved feebly I don't know; more probably he saw me as having escaped—but hurt rather more badly than might have been expected—from a commitment beyond my years. I found comfort in his indisposition in the least to censure Janet. That I was a meritorious and accredited lover lightly jilted by a faithless girl was the one vision of the thing I couldn't at all suffer, since nothing would have been less fair. I hadn't, for example, been without knowledge of Calum Grant's name and calling. They had appeared, once and enigmatically, on one of Janet's postcards, a signal which I neglected to read. The inhibited condition which Oxford had caused to linger with me, Oxford was just at this time breaking up. We were no more, perhaps, than liberated schoolboys still, but here and there among my companions what we called girl-trouble was declaring itself, and my own necessities were changing as if in mysterious sympathy with those of my friends. In this new context, narrow but commanding, I equally with Janet had been faithless. On me, too, Venus had been at work. I had been experiencing for another girl—a fatal one in the end—a sudden and dreadfully simple sexual infatuation.

Before the whole spectacle of his brother in those final growing-pains Ninian was wary and perceptive. He knew very well where my heart really lay. He knew too that the last thing I would want to hear about Janet was that she had landed herself in fiasco or misery, and he probably had a realistic sense that it was not altogether unlikely to turn out that way. His first discovery on my behalf—one not difficult to make—was of a neutral and unsurprising sort. Calum Grant was a crofter's son, and of a family related to Janet's own. He had himself become a fisherman. And he was likely to be something between poor and very poor. What Janet had taken lessons with me for wasn't the driving of a Rolls Royce. It was trucking in the peat from where it was footed on the moss.

Some years went by before Ninian had more to tell. He had been to Skye on legal affairs. He hadn't tried to glimpse Janet Grant—that, his delicacy would have forbidden—but he had seen her husband. Calum, he told me firmly, was what any woman would call a lovely man. And there were now two boys.

I formed a picture of these four people. My father, could he have seen inside my head, would have pronounced it an early David Wilkie, and I might myself have thought of it as an Israëls with most of the sombreness left out. The children were prominent at that fireside, for the thought of Janet's two stalwart sons pleased me. It is curious that the long-limbed, long-haired creatures whom I have reported as sometimes visiting my breakfast-table were so very unlike them: were so very English and public-school. I don't think that Janet Grant was the mother of those dream-children. There are limits to the sentimentality into which a more or less sophisticated mind is willing to deliquesce. And, of course, I had long since ceased to think very constantly about Janet Finlay, who had become Janet Grant.

But now I was sitting at the same table with her in the Provost's Lodging. And Janet McKechnie was her new name.

XV

Miss Minton—as I had remembered just in time—was the author of a book on *commedia a soggetto*, and when I wasn't being talked to by Mrs Pococke I conversed on topics prompted by this learned circumstance. Both ladies must have judged me distraught; since they knew about the readership they may have concluded me to be much preoccupied by it.

Janet being on the Provost's right, and myself on Mrs Pococke's, we were beyond speaking range, but had a clear view of one another diagonally across the table. I wondered whether Janet had expected to meet me. It seemed to depend on how Mrs Pococke had gathered her party. If it was an impromptu affair, it might have been natural for her to say on the telephone something like 'Edward hopes that Duncan Pattullo may be coming'. If it had been organized some time ago, my own possible presence was the less likely to have been mentioned. On the whole, it was probable that our meeting had been a surprise to Janet. In the few seconds of our confrontation before moving into the dining-room she had said nothing to prompt either one conclusion or the other.

I wondered, too, whether on his return home from the Gaudy dinner Ranald McKechnie had mentioned to his wife having sat beside a schoolfellow. And from this a more curious question sprang. What did McKechnie know about the romance of near-childhood between Janet and me? I had learnt as yet nothing of the circumstances under which Janet's second marriage had come about. But it must have been entered into in maturity, and it would seem natural that innocent relationships in an almost distant past would be among the confidences exchanged between a husband and wife. Could Ranald McKechnie, knowing about it, regard it as an occasion for constraint between us? Had it even been a factor in that morning's awkwardness in the Cornmarket? The idea seemed absurd, but I saw sufficient possibility of substance in it to be glad I hadn't obeyed an impulse to ask bluntly 'Are you married?' during our encounter the night before. McKechnie was now listening attentively to Mrs Gender, who had settled for gardening as the best table-topic between them. McKechnie still displayed pens and pencils in his breast-pocket, and I saw that he also maintained another old habit: that of seizing upon something uncommonly like a shoelace to serve as a tie. Catching myself noting this, I had to conclude that the new situation found me not incapable of jealousy. It was certainly producing early intimations of emotion of one sort or another.

Janet several times looked at me gravely, and once she smiled. She was a beautiful woman in her earliest forties. But the smile took me back a long way. I remembered her occasional air of amused yet tender expectation, so at variance with her habitual vehemence, and it now seemed to me that there had been something maternal in it; that the schoolgirl had once watched me as a woman watches and waits over a growing son.

We rose from table to take coffee in the Day-room. There was no time to lose, since at any moment the Provost might propose withdrawing to his library to discuss the readership. I got close to Janet, and when our cups had been handed us carried her off by a glance to the far end of the big chamber. Rossetti's contribution to its splendours—a portrait of Elizabeth Siddal, sultry, fated, magnificent, and as ill-painted as could be—thus presided over us as we talked.

'Janet, I just never had word of you. What happened?'
'To Calum and the boys? They were drowned. Twelve years ago.'
I had expected that mortality would be part of the story. It was unlikely that Janet had been divorced. But I had expected nothing like this. I felt my eyes fill with tears.
'He must have taken them out very young.'
'They were to follow him.'

'Yes, of course.' I was entirely off-balance, and judged my comment, since it implied censure of Calum, to be as luckless as anything I had ever said; nothing even in the emotion of the moment could excuse it. But Janet showed no displeasure. Could I now say, 'I wish I'd known'? The words would have been prompted by sympathy and sorrow, but they too might have sounded ill. 'And then?' I asked.

'Naturally, there was no money. I went back to Edinburgh and qualified as a nurse.'

'I see.' Now I was really stumped, for any further question must lead to McKechnie and suggest inquisition. Janet appeared to feel that her account of herself was, for the moment at least, concluded, and that my own history might be inquired into.

'Dunkie,' she asked, so that the name went to my heart like an arrow, 'were you married for long?'

'No, not at all long. Under three years. My wife and I weren't in the least right for each other.'

'I'm very sorry. I read about your marriage, and was glad. But I never heard anything more—not until quite recently. Ranald and I always try to see your plays.'

'Do you think they're any good? You had considerable hopes of me, Janet, a long time ago.'

'I don't think the plays you've written are as good as the plays you may still write.'

'That's rather my notion, too.' As I said this our eyes met, and I was conscious that we had both found a moment's amusement. I was conscious, too, of happiness, and that it sprang from a sense of how much we could trust one another. There was no possibility of my saying anything wrong again. This ecstatic conviction prompted my next words. 'Does Ranald,' I asked, 'know how much I was in love with you?'

'He certainly ought to. I quite went to town about it.' As Janet said this there was straight mischief in her glance. 'But there are things that don't make much of a mark on Ranald. He's a very learned and abstracted man.' Janet paused, and I told myself, apparently without dissatisfaction, that here was yet another of those loyal and devoted wives. 'But he produced, out of his head, a list of the prizes you'd won at school. He said you'd beaten him hollow for one of them.'

'Yes,' I said, 'so I did. I think it was for an essay on the advantages and disadvantages of civilization.'

'It's possible to feel both acutely, wouldn't you say? I'd have expected Ranald to produce the more balanced view.' Janet looked across the room. 'Dunkie, the Provost's coming to nobble you. Good-bye.'

Would I be willing to consider—the Provost was asking me ten minutes later—an appointment for five years in the first instance? The university had not come quite unprompted to the discovery that a Readership in Modern European Drama was one of its first priorities at the moment. But that caution—the Provost continued smoothly—was not at all to its credit, for wasn't the subject eminently one which ought to be brought more securely within the sphere of serious criticism? Moreover, one had to consider the young people, and anything they showed signs of being prepared to interest themselves in. Anything of the intellectual sort, that was. There were grave persons around into whose heads this consideration never entered. But the Provost himself gave it much thought. That was why—noticing, as he had, the disposition of undergraduates to absorb themselves in theatrical activities—he had concerned himself with the benefaction from the start. For—he must be candid with me—a benefaction there had been: from an American source, wholly unsolicited, and (to return to the point in hand) for an assured period of five years only. What did I think of that?

'Five years,' I repeated, and tried to give a considering tone to the words. But five fours are twenty, I was telling myself, and it was through nearly that span of years that it had not occurred to me to continue acquainting myself with Janet's fortunes. All I had done was to think of her from time to time. Or hardly even that. It had been a matter only of picturing her—with Calum the lovely man on the other side of the

277

hearth, and the boys playing around. And this reverie, as thick with sentiment as Burns's *The Cotter's Saturday Night*, I had continued to indulge during the brief period when my marriage seemed a happy one. Now I was shocked at myself. 'Yes,' I said, 'five years seems to me about right.'

'It represents the formal position only.' The noble features of the Provost signalled encouraging intelligence from some inner circle of the initiated in the university's mysteries. 'There could be no possibility of an actual termination. Indeed, I should imagine that at the end of that period the post would become fully professorial. A chair would be created.'

'So I'd become just like Ranald McKechnie.'

'Just so.' The Provost's voice hinted mild surprise. He was entitled to feel something of the sort at such a dotty remark. It was probably his conclusion that I had attempted some uncertain stroke of humour. 'But of course you were at school with him!' he exclaimed, as if this explained the matter. 'It's why my wife had the thought of asking the McKechnies to her luncheon party. Had you met Janet McKechnie before? She's a most charming woman.'

'I had. She is.'

'Yes, indeed.' This had been too brisk for the Provost, who had to recollect himself. 'But as we were saying, five years.'

'Five years.'

If this further inane repetition disconcerted Edward Pococke I didn't trouble myself with noticing the fact. For I was again doing sums in my head. It had been four or five years after Janet's first marriage that Ninian gave me his last news of her. Probably he never had occasion to return to Skye, and she and her family must have passed as completely out of his knowledge as out of mine. It was now twelve years, Janet had told me, since she had lost all her menfolk to the sea. And that had been the year—I worked it out—in which my marriage was dissolved. Janet had heard of the marriage, but not till long afterwards of the divorce.

I stared at these facts, and incidentally at the Provost, since the facts appeared to float like a tenuous but material substance somewhere in the region of his well-trimmed beard. I felt stupidly that some lesson, some precept, was to be learnt from them. They were facts that could be drawn upon, I concluded, for the material of one of those foolish advertisements with which the Post Office seeks to revive the declining practice of letter-writing. *Somewhere somebody is waiting for a letter from YOU.* This, of course, was idiotic. Had Janet Grant in her bereaved condition had a thought of the inhibited youth who had given her driving lessons she could have got news of him readily enough. Just when she had married McKechnie I didn't yet know, since to have put the question to her in the context of our talk might have carried the most impossible implication. But I did want to know. It was when I found myself on the verge of inquiring whether the Provost could enlighten me that I saw I must pull myself together. At least I saw clearly where the true lesson lay. It had been inadequate in me, and uncivilized, not to try to keep Janet Grant as a friend—a pen-friend at a safe remove, as it would have had to be. Making up that fireside Wilkie and telling myself I reverenced it had been a weak and unwholesome abnegation, a vagary of a writer's imagination soppier even than thinking up those long-limbed boys. And I couldn't plead that my own marriage had been responsible. The years, the brute chronology again, negatived that. I continued to stare at Edward Pococke—aware of the insufficiency of Duncan Pattullo as I had never been aware of it before.

'I can see the five-year term only as thoroughly advantageous, Provost.' I heard myself say this in the most level way. 'The notion of a trial run—of giving the thing a go—is implicit in it. And I think that entirely right.'

'Quite so, my dear Pattullo. It leaves you free. We will regard it like that.' The Provost smiled urbanely, which was the nearest his temperament and training permitted him to go in the way of triumph. For a moment I found myself speculating on the identity of the unacceptable candidate or candidates whom he was feeling his expert handling of the situation to have put to rout. It was a vain search. I could think of half a dozen men much better qualified than I was to put Modern European Drama on its feet within the University of Oxford. 'I am most happy about it,' I heard the Provost say. 'After all, you know our ways, my dear fellow.'

I accepted this encomium (as I supposed it to be) becomingly, although I had no reason to judge it particularly true. And the interview was concluded. When we returned to the Day-room it was to find that the party had broken up—with an informality which would have been impossible in the early days of the Pocockes' tenure of the Lodging. The style of the later Mrs Pococke was evident in the change. I was glad not to have to say a second good-bye to Janet—or even, for the moment, to look her husband in the eye. It would have been trying to have to hear an announcement of my probable accession to whatever faculty of the university traded in Modern European Drama. But that would have been unlikely. The appointment, presumably, had yet to be worked—although that was a crude expression, of a sort which in future I should doubtless have to eschew.

As I was taking my leave of Mrs Pococke her husband referred to me as Duncan. It was gracefully done, but there was something dreadfully definitive about it.

XVI

I LEFT THE Lodging, bowed out by the sombre Honey, and walked across the Great Quadrangle to the gate, where I consulted the porter about late-afternoon trains to London. Then I returned to Nick Junkin's rooms, packed my suitcase, put a tip on the mantelpiece for Plot, and told myself to relax. In front of me there was only the Talberts' tea-party. After that I was free to depart, and to begin thinking about the five years' assignment I had committed myself to.

It was a sun-soaked afternoon. I threw open the windows upon the spectacle of the library in apparent sinuous movement as warm rising air washed over it. Formerly, when the great façade with its massive columns was crumbling, flaked and tettered, the effect had been curiously submarine, as if one were peering through glass at the superannuations of sunk realms, and might at any moment spy finny monsters emerge with clammy quartos or folios in their jaws. But now the massive building, re-edified and gleaming, held the same suggestion of *mise en scène* as had Howard with its litter of rope and canvas the night before—rather as if somebody had painted on enormous flats a Veronese-like architectural fantasy which a strong draught from the wings kept faintly stirring.

It was with some satisfaction that I took refuge in this idle word-spinning; I'd had enough of the pressure of immediate life for a while. I sat down and tried—it was a similar exercise— to recall Nicolas Junkin of Cokeville clearly. By now he must be thumbing his way efficiently towards the corner of the globe known to him as Turky. He would manage it almost for free—which had proved, in an unexpected fashion, to be the manner in which his neighbour Ivo Mumford had reached New York. Paul Lusby, whom Ivo had so lucklessly challenged to harmless folly at the Commem Ball, had departed on a longer journey.

Others untimely dead—a lovely man and two Highland boys—were closer to me, although them Fate had overtaken twelve years ago. I found myself back with the sums, calculating Janet McKechnie's age. Conceivably it had been after a long widowhood, conceivably it had been no time ago, that she had married an Oxford professor. The Talberts might know. Perhaps Janet might have other children still.

I sat for some time, uselessly brooding. Then I looked at my watch. In half an hour I could have a porter summon me a taxi to take me out to Old Road. But that—I suddenly remembered—wouldn't do. Hadn't I promised Albert Talbert to walk? He was certain to question me closely on my afternoon's pedestrianism. Acknowledging an ancient compulsion to obey a tutor's behest—and being restless, too, under my own company—I got up and set out walking now.

The High was uncrowded. A few bicycles had been chucked, negligently and illegally, against the walls of the Examination Schools. Farther east, where the quiet vista closed, somebody had outrageously perched the peeping top of a structure like a silo or a grain-elevator. Punts waggled familiarly under Magdalen Bridge. Beyond that were several new buildings, chunky but towering, as if the children of the gods had been tumbling out their building-blocks on some supernal playground on the banks of the Cherwell. But beyond this again nothing much had changed. I was passing through an area not greatly favoured for residential development.

I became aware of the Bedworths—Cyril and Mabel—walking ahead of me. They might have been making for anywhere within a wide segment of outer Oxford—or, equally, open country beyond. Bedworth, now Talbert's junior colleague, must have been in some degree Talbert's pupil long ago—a circumstance of which I couldn't have been ignorant, although it had entirely faded from my memory. Talbert had no doubt marched him around the countryside quite as much as he had me; and with Bedworth the habit had stuck. So Bedworth and his Mabel were off on such a tramp now.

As I came to this conclusion I lost interest in it, and the detail of my excursions with Talbert (and, often, with Boanerges) flooded into my head instead. The walks always began with an air of purposeful research. We were to find the Scholar Gipsy's Elm, or visit the stripling Thames at Bablockhythe, or trace the line of the roadway constructed by undergraduates under the direction of Ruskin, or peer into that garden at Littlemore in which a spy sent out by Keble or Pusey or some such person had detected John Henry Newman fatally attired in flannel trousers—this apparently revealing beyond any possibility of error that the first intellect in Anglican Oxford had perverted to Rome. It had been impossible to tell how serious Talbert was in conducting these instructive peregrinations, since his fathomless gravity was always liable to yield place at crucial moments to equally fathomless mirth. And often the expeditions ended well short of their mark. We would come to a halt at a pub; Talbert would stick his head inside and call out loudly, 'Weak tea for two!' and confidently await the arrival of this beverage on a bench in the garden or by the door. I can recall no pot-house, however unpropitious in seeming, that ventured to refuse what was thus demanded.

I walked for a hundred yards or so in the luxury of these reminiscences, and then it occurred to me that the Bedworths were scarcely dressed as for a rural ramble. Bedworth was in a London suit—which again didn't quite fit. Mrs Bedworth's clothes, too, were distinguishably on the formal side. They fitted very well. So the couple were probably making for the same tea-party as myself. And like me they had undertaken to arrive on foot.

They were walking briskly, but nevertheless it seemed incumbent upon me to catch up with them, since it would be an unfriendly thing if I were detected with any appearance of lingering in their rear. There was something, moreover, I

283

wanted to get out of Bedworth if I could. So I quickened my pace, and presently gave a familiar hail. Bedworth turned round, and at once signalled his pleasure in recognizing me. His wife turned too, but seemingly with the intention of studying the pavement a yard or so in front of me. The effect was something to which I now felt habituated.

'Are you by any chance going to tea with the Talberts?' I asked.

'Yes, we are.' As he said this, Bedworth took a step away from his wife. The vacancy thus created was plainly designed for me, and we walked on three-abreast. 'Do you remember, Duncan, how we used to go to tea there as undergraduates?'

'Yes, indeed.' This, I am afraid, wasn't true. I couldn't remember ever having visited Old Road in Bedworth's company—although equally I couldn't have sworn that I had not. Nobody more than Bedworth had impressed on me during the past twenty-four hours some of the oddities of memory. When we say that a man has changed or not changed over a period of years we are likely to be making substantially a subjective statement. We may even, in a sense, be saying what it was determined we should say before the renewed encounter took place—this since our temperament, our disposition to confront or deny the flow of things, is a factor in what we believe to be a truth of observation. Again, some people and things return to us as from fifty years back, although we know perfectly well that our own fiftieth birthday is still far ahead. In extreme cases the effect can constitute a kind of ontological puzzle, and evoke notions of pre-existence to which I seem to recall that a learned name was given by Plato. I didn't at all suppose that I had known Bedworth or the Provost or P. P. Killiecrankie dimly in another life. But they did tend to flow to and fro in time, and with Bedworth in particular I was now conscious of harbouring patches of amnesia. I suspected that in some way my spirit had been rebuked by his. A serious and responsible youth, capable of a warmth of friendly feeling I had accepted without much bothering to reciprocate: these qualities had conceivably made of Cyril Bedworth a Gunga Din figure I had been ready virtually to forget. A totally different effect had accompanied my renewed acquaintance with Tony Mumford. In point of fact, Tony had obviously changed more than Cyril had; the political man he now was had been, prelusively, only glimpsed by me. Yet Tony had swum back to me at once as from no further away than the length of a bathing pool.

'I hope,' Bedworth was saying, abruptly but cautiously, 'you had a satisfactory talk with the Provost?'

'Yes, I think I had. At least I hope it was that.' Here was an introduction to the point I wanted to get at. 'I was very much flattered, Cyril. I can't think how the idea has come into anybody's head.'

'It gathered force very quickly. Almost everybody is dead set on it.'

'That's more flattering still.' I wondered vaguely what individuals were covered by that qualifying 'almost'. 'I met James Gender's wife, and she said a most unaccountable thing.'

'Anthea Gender goes in for saying unaccountable things.' Mrs Bedworth came out with this decisively.

'She's really a very good sort,' Bedworth said anxiously. 'Of course, her wave-length is a little remote at times. She comes of county people. Like Arnold Lempriere.'

This mild absurdity *was* familiar. Bedworth might have been saying 'She was born on the upper reaches of the Limpopo'. I marvelled again at the particular corner of literary history to which he had applied himself.

'English is really the most idiotic language,' Mabel Bedworth said, again with decision, '"Country people" means one thing, and "county people" means quite another. Don't you agree?'

I did agree, but before I could say so Bedworth came back to the point in hand.

'What did Anthea Gender say that was unaccountable, Duncan?'

'She said that the idea started with Talbert. As a matter of fact, the old boy barely remembers me.'

'Oh, but that can't be so! That he barely remembers you, I mean. Talbert has supported the proposal most strongly from the start.'

'Anthea got things muddled, all the same.' Mabel Bedworth glanced at me briefly and sideways, but with perfect frankness. 'It happens, you know, when the little women trespass on the mysteries.'

I remembered Mrs Bedworth saying something about the 'little women' the night before. It was a joke, obviously, reflecting her discipleship of Mrs Woolf on that talented writer's feminist side. I wondered whether Bedworth would rebuke his wife's levity. But nothing of the sort occurred, and I asked what Mrs Gender's muddle could have been.

'She just got her Eng. Lit. tutors mixed up, Mr Pattullo. Of course it was Cyril who had the idea first. Didn't you know?'

'Well, I've wanted to be sure. But it has certainly been my guess. And it pleases me very much.' It didn't seem to me possible to say anything less handsome than this. And the shamefast Mabel Bedworth—rather to my surprise—repaid it in kind.

'It seems a very good idea to me. One of Cyril's best.'

'Thank you very much.' I was quite touched that Mrs Bedworth seemed disposed to pick up something of her husband's too charitable attitude to me. But there seemed nothing more to say, and it was in a convenient traffic-imposed silence that we covered the next stretch of our walk. Then Bedworth spoke—with a return to his anxious manner, and as if there were still explanations to give.

'Of course Talbert is getting on,' he said. 'He'll be due for retirement quite soon, and any sort of college business doesn't much more than come and go in his head. I believe, too, that the Massinger is proving very heavy—very heavy, indeed. There are bibliographical puzzles that are extremely complex. So one has to forgive his occasional inattention even to quite important practical matters. Matters of policy, even.'

'I see. But is he unique in that?'

'Oh, no. Oh, no—not at all. There are always people who are so wrapped up in their research and so on that they tend largely to detach themselves from the life of the college. It can be quite disheartening at times. I mean, you can explain a problem to a man very clearly, showing him just what the best course would be. He'll agree with you, he'll see the whole thing as clearly as you do—or more clearly, for that matter. And then when it comes to a vote on the Governing Body he'll be staring absently out of the window, and won't raise a hand either on one side or the other.'

'Cyril always does *that*,' Mrs Bedworth said—and this time, it seemed to me, mingling mischief with her admiration. 'He says it's one's duty always to make up one's mind firmly pro or con.'

'But one has to agree that there are special cases.' Bedworth had a fair-minded thing to say. 'Professorial fellows, for example. They don't teach for their college, and quite a lot of them have a considerable pressure of administrative business elsewhere. So one can't expect them not to be rather vague about a good many domestic matters.'

'Ranald McKechnie, for instance?'

'He's a very good case in point. In fact, he hasn't the faintest notion of anything that's going on.'

'So professorial fellows are a kind of caterpillars of the commonwealth? I expect readers are, too.'

'Oh, but I wouldn't say that, at all.' Bedworth was dismayed before this misapprehension. 'The system by which these university people—which is what you're going to be—are attached to colleges and sit on their G.B.'s is of the utmost value. Socially, of course, it's a very pleasant thing. But it also helps to circulate ideas, and it means that, whenever an intricate or even recondite academic problem turns up, one is likely to have on tap a man who's a first-class authority on it.'

Bedworth proved to have a good deal more to say on this theme. He was still pursuing it, indeed, when we were half-way up Old Road. I listened quite without impatience. It was new territory to me, and I felt myself being conducted over it by a sensible if unexciting guide. Mrs Bedworth, although she dutifully made one or two relevant remarks, was perhaps not quite so absorbed—and, for that matter, I detected her glancing at her husband in faint amusement on one occasion. It must be a region of discourse that had become fairly familiar to her with the years.

My own thoughts did eventually a little wander. Individuals commonly interest me more than their institutions, and what came into my head was the fact of a certain similarity (which I am sure had never struck me as a young man) between Cyril Bedworth and Gavin Mogridge. It is usually easy to analyse how characters differ; consequently, a more beguiling exercise is sometimes to be found in rendering articulate an obscure sense of where they overlap. I couldn't imagine Bedworth writing *Mochica*—but then there had certainly been a time when I couldn't have conceived of the 'cello-bashing Mogridge doing such a thing either. Mogridge, if he addressed himself to the task, could possibly produce a book with a title like *Proust and Powell*, but it would be a distinctly plodding affair. Yet Bedworth's own book might be that. (I felt guilty at having been for so long unaware of its existence.) In fact, where these two men came together was in the common possession of slow to medium paced minds, and perhaps in certain consequent similarities of speech-rhythm as well. Mogridge, however, was certainly capable of changing into a different gear at will; unless Tony and I had been mistaken in identifying the position which enabled him to spirit Ivo across the Atlantic at the drop of a handkerchief, it was inconceivable that his mind couldn't, in a crisis, work very rapidly indeed. And I doubted whether Bedworth's could do that.

These speculations were checked by the sudden appearance of the tiled roof of the Talberts' house towering above our heads. This effect was occasioned by the fact that the building, itself of the most modest elevation, stood perched on a high bank or terrace which had to be scaled by a flight of steps resembling a ship's accommodation ladder. We went up in single file. I remembered how, on the previous day, I had quarrelled with Surrey Quad (the scene of my renewed acquaintance with Talbert) for not being as I had come to imagine it, and I wondered whether a similar experience was immediately in front of me now. It seemed not possible that I could find this suburban dwelling smaller than I had come to suppose; quite probably, indeed, it would prove larger. Oxford dons—who are all assumed to be much of a muchness, socially regarded—had housed themselves in my undergraduate time at a striking variety of economic levels. Some almost approximated to what is fancifully provided for them in popular films of academic life—being exhibited as receiving or harbouring their mistresses (since their morals are commonly represented as of a highly enlightened sort) in what would appear to be the remoter wings of large Cotswold manor-houses. Others lived very simply indeed, and the Talberts had been among these. Viewing the exterior of their villa, one felt surprise that so inconsiderable a structure could be so ugly. Once inside, one asked oneself how apartments traversable in three or four strides came so notably short of rendering any impression of the cosy or snug.

As our heads emerged above what here became ground-level, I saw that the locus of the Talbert's heroic services to scholarship had lived on perfectly faithfully inside my head. I thought now, as I had perhaps thought on my very first visit, that the house ought to have two little porches instead of one, so that Talbert might bob out to the left by way of presaging fine weather, or Mrs Talbert appear to the right, announcing rain. The front door was ajar, and I wondered whether, as is common at parties nowadays, we were expected simply to walk in. Bedworth, however, pressed a bell with polite brevity. The door was opened at once, and through an agency impossible to become aware of without surprise. A canine paw had appeared in the interstice and effected the operation with what was evidently practised skill. The creature thus revealed could not conceivably be Boanerges;

he must be, at the least, a grandson—if only a spiritual grand-son—of that vigorous third pedestrian. He regarded us for a moment mournfully, acknowledged our presence with what could only be called an unfriendly but respectful bow, turned, and led us into the house. It was unnervingly like being received by Honey at the Provost's Lodging.

'Cyril,' I asked cautiously, '*is* that brute called Boanerges?'

'It's called Thunderbox.'

'I don't believe you!'

'It's certainly no name to give a respectable dog.' Bedworth frowned, as if feeling there had been discourtesy or even disloyalty in thus aspersing the taste of his immediate col-league. 'Of course, one sees the joke,' he added anxiously. 'A kind of affectionate reference to poor old Boanerges. I remember him very well.'

'Quite so,' I said—and again thought of Mogridge, himself somewhat given to otiose explanations.

There was no party. So informal was any designed occasion, indeed, that the Talberts were absorbed in their common pursuit as Thunderbox ushered us into the sitting-room. They sat on hard chairs facing each other across a square table, each with the prescriptive brace of enormous volumes deployed—lost, it had to be supposed, in the textual quiddities of *The Great Duke of Florence* or *A New Way to Pay Old Debts*. It was possible, of course, that our arrival wasn't designed at all, Talbert having failed to inform his wife of any hospitable proposal he had made whether to the Bedworths or myself. Mrs Talbert was not, in any case, perturbed—or not perturbed by people turning up for tea. She was in some agitation, all the same, since she had just discovered in the text before her a lurking typographical nuance conceivably holding porten-tous implications which she at once fell to expounding to us. Like Mrs Pococke, she had changed more than her husband, so that it was now less evident that she was by a good way the younger of the two. The rise and fall of her voice, with its extraordinary ability to produce precise articulations on an indrawn breath, had become a little uncomfortable to listen to, since it seemed no longer merely a nervous eccentricity but rather a physical disability having to do with a troublesome chest. Mentally, however, she struck me as wearing the better of the two. Although I had no understanding whatever of the learned matters she was pitching at me (and could only be amused and gratified that I was being taken for learned too) I did receive an impression that she was dead on the ball herself. Talbert listened to her respectfully, but as if being carried over technical ground a little beyond him. The higher bibliographical mysteries with which they were involved no doubt grew more complicated and rarified with the years, and it was Mrs Talbert who was athletically keeping up with them. When at length there was a pause Talbert introduced another subject.

'I have been most sorry,' he said to Bedworth in his huskiest tone, 'to hear the sad news about poor Luxmoore.'

'Luxmoore?' Bedworth repeated. 'Has anything happened to him?'

But Talbert had turned to me at once—whether as Dalrymple or as Pattullo I had no means of knowing.

'Did you know poor Luxmoore?' he asked. 'The most brilliant of our junior research fellows. And now the unhappy man has made away with himself.'

'Made away with himself?' Bedworth was horrified.

'In Bethnal Green, it seems—which is a peculiar thing. He must have had relatives in humble circumstances there. His father is a substantial landowner in Yorkshire.'

'Good God, Albert! You've picked it up entirely wrong.' Bedworth spoke almost with irritation. 'It's an undergraduate called Lusby who has died in Bethnal Green—a pupil of Jimmy Gender's. Nothing whatever to do with Luxmoore, who is a most disgustingly cheerful man at all times and seasons.'

This speech of Bedworth's surprised me. I judged it out of character—or did so until I recalled that by his 'character' I must still largely mean how he had struck me more than twenty years before. I was also surprised by his wife. Mabel Bedworth didn't indeed, speak. But she raised her eyes from the carpet (a very threadbare carpet) for the astonishing purpose of giving me a faint but unmistakable wink. I am certain that she had very proper feelings about Paul Lusby. She was bidding me note, however, that it was not solely the little women who could get college affairs muddled.

'I am relieved to hear it.' Talbert said this only after a moment's deliberation. He had perhaps been tempted to dispute the matter, having—once more—a natural dislike of being corrected in a question of fact by a former pupil. 'Yes, it is a great relief to me. I think we ought now to have tea. Weak tea.'

'But, Geoffrey, there can be no question of a relieved mind.' Mrs Talbert said this to my complete perplexity for a moment, since I had forgotten her habit of addressing Albert Talbert in this way. 'The untimely death of one young man is no less sad than the untimely death of another.' Mrs Talbert wrung her hands as she said this, and her voice went up and down quite wildly. I realized that when her switchback of a nose was not effectively buried in Massinger and his kidney she was probably rather a tiresome person about the house.

'But, my dear, Luxmoore is a scholar of altogether exceptional promise.' Talbert, I imagine, felt himself on weak ground, since the effect of weight he gave to this assertion was something of a *tour de force*.

'I am aware of it. But Mr Lusby, Geoffrey, may have held the highest promise too—even should the fact not yet have manifested itself.' Mrs Talbert clutched her bosom and threw her head in air. 'Not, perhaps, as a scholar. But as an actor, or an artist, or an aviator——'

'But we should neither of us have known him had he passed us in the street.' Talbert rallied to cut short what had threatened to be an alarming enumeration. 'And it is idle, Emily, to encourage oneself in metaphysical distresses.' He paused on this crushing aphorism, which I had a dim sense of once having quoted to him myself in my essay on Samuel

Johnson. 'May I suggest that we make no reference to this in the presence of the children? They might be upset by it.'

I wondered whether Talbert's faculties were much more in decay than had hitherto appeared, so that his mind was slipping back over a long term of years. Alternatively—and it was a more cheerful thought—the Talberts were now grandparents, and we had arrived upon the occasion of a family reunion. These speculations, however, were short-lived. The door opened, and a large and bearded man came into the room, followed by a not quite young woman who, although somewhat plain, had an intelligent expression and, if on the abounding side, a good figure.

'I think you will remember Charles and Mary,' Mrs Talbert said to me.

There were greetings and—on my part and that of the children—proper assurances that we remembered each other very well. Thunderbox was active at this point; he gambolled with Charles and Mary in a manner suggesting that, although a dog of something more than mature years and temperamentally disposed to regard himself as of the graver sort, he nevertheless possessed (like his owner) a spring of submerged gaiety which sought issue from time to time. He now even offered quite amicable advances to the Bedworths and myself. So there followed for some moments one of those episodes of general attention to a family pet which are so useful upon rather flat social occasions.

Mrs Talbert then produced tea—which was not notably weak—together with a plate of those tea-time stand-bys which are well denominated rock buns. Talbert, who at one point on the previous day had been aware that I was to hold a weighty conversation with the Provost, now gave no hint that he had so much as heard of Modern European Drama. But he addressed me accurately by my Christian name, and embarked upon a long story about an encounter with an unknown American in the North Library of the British Museum. This unlucky scholar had, in some fashion that remained obscure, deeply offended Talbert. 'I gave him the rough side of my tongue,' Talbert concluded with extraordinary grimness—and suddenly his eyes sparkled with glee, while his subterranean laughter rumbled within him like something gone wrong with the plumbing. I remembered that he took the darkest view of American students. He was convinced that they pilfered books from the great libraries of England—not to sell them (as would be comprehensible, and even sensible, granted a certain ethical stance) but to display them as souvenirs to their folks back home. (Talbert would produce 'folks back home' with enormous malice, and also as exhibiting a recondite acquaintance with the American language.)

I concurred in the view that there was something peculiarly repellent in the notion of books as souvenirs, and then began cautiously to inquire into the present condition of Charles and Mary Talbert, whose continued domestication within the parental home I found vaguely disturbing. This—illogically enough—was a consequence of the mere spatial dimensions of the place, or of this in combination with their own general largeness of physical effect. Had the senior Talberts commanded one of those Cotswold manor-houses, the continued presence of their progeny would not so immediately have suggested a state of existence cabined, cribbed and confined. One could have thought of the robust Charles as more and more taking on the running of the estate (or at least of a market-garden), and of Mary as multifariously occupied with Brownies and good works. Recalling their father's apprehensiveness lest the news of a fatality in college might upset the children, I wondered whether Charles and Mary were afflicted to a disabling degree by nervous distresses. Their mother, after all, was a jumpy woman, and a married couple long in the grip of obsessional scholarship would doubtless be regarded in Harley Street as an ominous phenomenon.

This last, however, was a modish conjecture. As actual children, Charles and Mary (unlike the personages of literary history after whom I supposed them to have been named) had shown no signs of a neurotic constitution, although they were perhaps a little more docile and well-behaved than would accord with modern notions of the wholesome. Presumably they had simply elected, in a rational manner, to lead quiet lives. If any wish to startle the world had lurked in them it had conceivably been satisfied in such devious ways as giving a scandalous name to a dog. Albert Talbert's sense of humour was occult and unpredictable. But I doubted whether it would have run to Thunderbox.

Mary Talbert, it presently appeared, taught classics in a girls' school of a genteel order only a stone's throw away. Her brother was constrained to earning his living farther afield—across the length of Oxford, indeed, since he was a proof-reader of the more learned sort of books uttered by the Oxford University Press. But the bearded Charles had another distinction. He had invented something.

'I believe Cyril and Mabel have had a glimpse of it,' Talbert said huskily. (These were two names of which he appeared to be in unintermitted control.) 'But I am sure, Duncan, it will interest you a great deal. Charles, my dear boy, do fetch it down.'

Charles abandoned his rock bun at once, and left the room. He was either a submissive creature or an uncommonly good-natured one. I waited in some curiosity for what he should produce. Would it be a machine for contriving the perpetual motion? Or perhaps one for the rapid collating of texts merely by pressing a button or turning a handle? Talbert's next words, although interesting, failed to afford much of a clue.

'We are inclined to think,' he said, 'that there may be money in it.' His voice had taken on that note—as of confidential discussion between men of affairs—which distinguished it when the question of the economics of dramatic composition had been touched on between us on the previous afternoon. 'Charles,' he continued, 'has a strong business sense, which ought to take him far in publishing. And, of course, in Walton Street the opportunities are unlimited. He may well become Secretary to the Delegates one day.'

I was expressing my own confidence that Charles would

attain this elevation when the young man returned to the room. What was to be produced became, in its general nature, instantly apparent. He was carrying a large folded board and a shallow oblong cardboard box. Almost as if from the dawn of life, memories of one or another form of the Talbert family addiction returned to me.

'The really difficult thing,' Charles said, 'is to find a good name for it.' He set down his burden on the square table, from which his sister had removed the tea things. 'I've thought of *Babylon*. It would carry a play on *babble on,* and of course the Tower of Babel would come in too.'

'An alternative is *Liddell and Scott.*' Mrs Talbert had expanded her lungs as if about to embark upon an aria. 'We believe it might be catchy—particularly in schools, where the chief market is likely to lie. But we are a little disturbed by a lack of precedent. There appears to be no instance of proper names being used to distinguish a really successful game.'

'That's a pity,' I said. The cardboard box had now been opened, and its contents tumbled out. The appropriateness of calling the projected new *divertissement* after two eminent lexicographers was at least apparent. The little wooden oblongs had letters of the Greek alphabet in red on one side and of the Russian alphabet in black on the other. The effect of second-cousinship gave a most confusing appearance to the whole, but one had to suppose that the game, whatever it was, would be played in one language at a time. I poked a finger amid the litter of epsilons and sigmas. 'Do you include a digamma?' I asked.

This learned inquiry was well received, and a short discussion ensued. Too plainly, however, it only put off the moment when we should all settle down to playing word-grabbing in ancient Greek. (Only Charles, Talbert explained with innocent pride, was capable of any sort of expert performance in Russian, a tongue in which he largely traded at the O.U.P.) Mabel Bedworth, I was fairly sure, could know not a word of Greek, and would have the spirit and good sense to say so at once. About Bedworth himself the probability was that he had conscientiously addressed himself to the rudiments of the language round about the time that I was happily forgetting them.

Fortunately, Mary Talbert proved to take less for granted than the other members of her family, and tactfully ensured that what now succeeded should be not a contest but a demonstration. It was possible to enjoy this without fatiguing the intelligence. There was something very pleasing in the absorption of these four learned persons in their harmless pursuit—and even, indeed, in their preposterous persuasion that it would prove a money-spinner. When eventually I glanced at my watch (inevitably in a covert and undergraduate manner) it was to find the hour later than I had supposed. Just as had happened long before, I was feeling at home with the Talberts. It was even with a sense of recovered familiarity that I found Thunderbox to appreciate, as Boanerges had once appreciated, a respectful scratching between the ears.

Babylon (or *Liddell and Scott*) was eventually put away—not without being replaced (it was a hint I recalled as prescriptive) by the volumes currently being collated. The Bedworths and I accordingly made our farewells, and the Talbert household moved *en masse* with us into the garden. We admired some red roses, trained—I am afraid to an effect of mild discordance—round the brick-work of the porch. Then Talbert, attended by Thunderbox, led the way down the narrow flight of steps and into Old Road. There was a certain amount of traffic, occasioned in the main, perhaps, by Oxford citizens returning from a summer afternoon jaunt. We had to cross over, and Talbert cautiously toddled into the road to survey the scene. He stepped back, motioning to us to wait. Thunderbox, however, decided to have a look for himself, and lumbered into the fairway. Above our heads, Charles Talbert gave a warning shout. There was a sudden scream of brakes, and a single yelp.

Seconds later, we were all standing, stricken, round the body of a dead dog.

XVII

I WALKED BACK into Oxford alone. The Bedworths had remained with the Talberts, who were very upset. I supposed that I myself was taking an objective and dispassionate view of the death of Thunderbox. He was an elderly dog, and one could conjecture him to have led an honourable and useful life. His sudden end had spared him the distresses of a slow decline, and very possibly spared his owners from having one day to decide—in a horrible phrase—to 'put him down'. In fact, nothing was here for tears.

Half-way across Magdalen Bridge, I found that my feet were not in their accustomed unnoticing contact with the ground. They were behaving in a slightly uncontrolled fashion, and I had to be careful with them. Something of the sort was true, too, of my physiological make-up as a whole. I had to lean on the parapet of the bridge for a couple of minutes and stare down at the slowly moving stream.

Shock is, of course, infectious. And I did very much feel with the Talberts—particularly with Albert Talbert, who had clearly been as attached to Thunderbox as ever Launce had been to Crab his dog. (This is perhaps an undignified comparison, but I have confessed that for me my old tutor was inescapably a figure of comedy.) I believe that even if the dead creature had been an unknown stray this disturbance would have visited me. Years ahead, when I had forgotten the existence of Thunderbox, it was probable that I should remember with some sadness the fate of Paul Lusby. Impelled by what was in an adult regard almost no reason at all, the boy had taken his own life while his mother went from shop to shop collecting the supper he wasn't going to eat. It was a small authentic tragedy, vivid for the imagination, formidable to the intellect. But I hadn't witnessed Lusby die, whereas

Thunderbox I had seen alive one moment and mangled and dead the next. More notably, the same twenty-four hours had brought me an experience as deep as any that a man like myself is likely to meet with in years. But in point of sheer somatic response to stimulus it was this inconsiderable brute fatality that carried the day.

I walked on, recovering my equanimity as I followed the gentle curve of the High. I was now anxious to get out of Oxford, and it was just going to be possible to catch the later of two trains I had been told about. Whether I was really going to return in a semi-permanent way had become obscure again, or had become like one of those issues which, as one works towards the resolution of a play, one discovers to be no part of its story. Did I—to put a question cautiously— want to sit on a college council, or whatever it was called, with Charles Atlas, and Jimmy Gender, and my new-found kinsman Arnold Lempriere, and Ranald McKechnie? Perhaps I had been precipitate in my acquiescence. The thing needed distancing. I resolved to take the next day's plane to Naples, and to consider this and other questions amid the little tumble-down *poderi*, the dead chestnut trees, the interminable stony *scale* of Ravello. I could go anywhere in the world on impulse, I told myself. So why should I put my unhoused free condition into circumscription and confine? It was a question which Othello ought to have asked himself twice.

This grandiose comparison brought me—hurrying now— within the college gate. And there I bumped straight into Tony Mumford, Lord Marchpayne.

It was my first thought that something must have gone wrong with Ivo Mumford's rescue operation, after all—a confused notion, since it didn't marry with Tony's return to Oxford in any way.

'Good God!' I said. 'What are *you* doing here again?'

'Why shouldn't I be here again?' Tony appeared to regard my surprise as uncivil, as perhaps it was. But his tone, at the same time, was one of easy good humour. 'I'm on my way, as a matter of fact, to a couple of nights' conferring with a batch of American economists. They're hutched in some grand mansion or other near Warwick. But it occurred to me I ought to stop by—as they'd say—and offer a civil word to the old girl.'

'The old girl?'

'Mrs P., you idiot. Your saying you were lunching with her put it in my head. I rather hurried away, you know. And she expects a call.'

'I'm not at all sure she expects anything of the sort.' I found myself staring at Tony. He was a man transformed. 'You want to butter her up?'

'Coarsely put, Duncan. In fact, with your habitual Caledonian *gaucherie*.'

'I lost that before I lost my maidenhead, God help me. And at your hands, largely.' It was impossible to talk to Tony in what was plainly his present mood without falling into rubbish of this sort. 'Is she really going to be useful to you?'

'If you ask me, she runs that pompous old donkey. Don't you get the whiff of that?'

'Perhaps so. But perhaps you underestimate the Provost. You ought to go for him direct, as Mogridge advised. Talking of Mogridge, have you had anything further from New York?'

'From New York?' It would have been impossible to affirm that Tony's momentary blankness was an affectation. 'Oh, all that! It was a complete mare's-nest. All my father's doing. Between ourselves, Dunkie, the old boy's getting a bit past it. He panicked.'

'He panicked *you*. Stop fooling, Tony, and explain yourself.'

'Oh, all right.' Tony's euphoria would have been absurd, if it hadn't been rather touching. 'The moment I got back to town, I sent a chap down to Otby. A top silk on the criminal side. Incognito, more or less—or at least just as a family friend. I felt the time to act had come.'

'I see.' Tony's state of mind when on the telephone came back to me. He had spoken of trying one throw himself, and employed strong language about its probable uselessness. 'And what happened?'

'He rang up and reported, just before I came away. He interviewed this little whore in the presence of her precious father and a senior local copper. All perfectly regular.'

'No doubt. Q.C.'s don't go out on a limb. So what?'

'The bitch didn't stand up to it for five minutes. Half the lads of the village tumble her in that barn every week—with no more rape to it than a slap and tickle. It was nothing but a commonplace gang-bang. And when she put on her senseless turn later, she just threw in Ivo for good luck.'

'But Ivo *was* there.' I looked curiously at this eminent public figure whose son had assisted at a commonplace gang-bang. Tony was perhaps keeping some feelings to himself. He presented, as much to me as he would to the world, an appearance that was buoyant and assured.

'Doesn't matter a damn,' he said.

'And Ivo did think something not too pretty was going on.'

'Doesn't matter a damn, either. There's nothing the fuzz feel they need be concerned with.'

'The locals?'

'No more bark or bite to them than to a dead dog. They know their place at Otby still, thank God. So I tell you it's water under the bridge.' Tony laughed suddenly, and so loudly as to attract the attention of the porter in his little glass box. We moved into the Great Quadrangle, which was serenely empty. 'Dear old Mogridge!' Tony said. 'He didn't half over-react, wouldn't you say? Still, it has got Ivo to New York for free. He'll get his air-fare returned, if you ask me, and paint the place red with it. Well, that's that. Duncan, give me a ring some time. We must dine together. And now I'll just drop into the Lodging. This damned nonsense about exams. That's the next thing to deal with. Splendid Gaudy, didn't you think? Good-bye.'

I watched Lord Marchpayne stride confidently towards the Provost's Lodging. Then I asked for a taxi, and made my way back to Junkin's room. Bottles and all, it had entirely lost its strangeness. Over the mantelpiece Ishii Genzō seemed as familiar a sight as *Young Picts watching the arrival of Saint Columba* had been long ago. I picked up my bag and carried it down the staircase into Surrey.